The Glass Fountain

Jeffrey Rosoff

The Glass Fountain

First edition. April 4, 2025
Written by Jeffrey Rosoff

With support from Frani, encouraged by Cookie, and inspired by Julia.

In a puzzling contradiction, all living things are both programmed with a will to live, and yet simultaneously encoded to die.

Part 1: Promises

Chapter 1: Old Man

Wednesday

The door clicked shut, and silence settled over the room.

An old, frail man shifted, his mind clearing slowly from the fog of unconsciousness.

Thirst hit him first—his tongue scraping over cracked lips but offering no relief. His throat felt dry and tight, each swallow painful. He tried to speak, but the sound that came out was raspy, alien. The stench of his own breath made him gag—a grim realization of his circumstances.

What happened? Where am I?

The darkness around him felt absolute. He blinked, trying to make sense of it. Was he blind? Or was this just a deep, endless abyss, the kind the church had warned him about?

He tried to move, instinct awakening, but pain shot through every joint. His body, weak and emaciated, pressed against something hard. The cold seeped into him, his frame too frail to even shiver. His mind raced, trying to piece it all together, but everything remained unclear.

He lifted his arms, but they didn't go far. *Restraints.* His wrists were tied tight, the ropes cutting into his skin. His ankles were bound too. He tugged, trying to pull free, but it only made things worse. His wrists burned from the effort. He paused. This wasn't random. Someone had done this to him—purposefully.

The air was thick, stale. He inhaled. A cocktail of odors assaulted his senses—formaldehyde, sweat, bleach, burnt dust. Beneath it all lingered the unmistakable tang of plastic.

Panic gripped him. The air was too heavy, too suffocating. And then it hit him: the air wasn't just stale—it was finite. He was in an airtight enclosure.

A body bag?

The thought struck him like a fist to the gut. There was no way out. Any struggle was pointless. Death seemed inevitable— perhaps even easier than this impossible fight. He stopped struggling, resignation creeping in like a slow poison. It was time to join those who had already made their final journey—the ones he had failed.

Images began to flash in his mind—familiar faces, blurry memories. A man's face. Promises made. Each recollection cut through his mind sharply, but they didn't feel right. Had he been tricked? Was this mistaken identity, or something far worse?

Resentment built deep within him, sparking an unyielding force refusing to break. There were wrongs that demanded explanation. He wasn't done yet. Not now. Not like this. He couldn't just let it end here. He had to act.

Renewed in spirit, he clenched his teeth and tried to bite into the plastic, but it slipped away. Again. And again. His own nose kept the bag from his lips, sabotaging his effort. But then a thought came to him.

He sucked in, pulling a section of the enclosure to his open mouth, the plastic curling around his nose. He bit down hard and jerked his head, tearing a small hole. The plastic gave way just enough for a breath to slip through.

He gasped, filling his lungs with fresh air. It felt like life returning to him.

But the relief didn't last long. His mind was already racing again. Who had done this to him? Left him in a bag, like trash? Had he been used, deceived? If so, there would be a reckoning. He'd make sure of it.

The faint creak of a door broke the silence. His heart skipped. Someone was coming in.

Survive. Justice will come later.

He would not cry out for help.

A dim sliver of light crept through the tear, cutting into the suffocating dark. He blinked, vision adjusting. For the first time, hope stirred in his chest.

He could see.

Chapter 2: Jason

Jason Fabrikant sat alone in his Ford F-150, parked just out of view of his sister's house. The engine was off, but he kept the windows cracked, letting in the faint, earthy scent of spring. He stared at her neighbor's tidy suburban lawn, mesmerized by the blades of grass. What once appeared as blurry impressionist brushstrokes were now rendered in crystal-clear realism, as if the optometrist had finally selected the perfect lens for his glasses. It reminded him of how his friends had described cataract surgery—colors sharper, edges clearer.

For Jason, though, it was more than just clarity. After decades of no depth perception, he could now see out of his right eye—the one blinded in a shameful incident. He sat in the cab, gripping the steering wheel with hands that looked alien in their youth. No bruises, no age spots. Everything felt new, yet familiar—an odd déjà vu of what had been stolen and then restored. A lump formed in his throat. It was all so overwhelming. His journey had been a long one.

A flash of movement caught his attention. A pale brown cardinal landed on the lawn, hopping with an odd rhythm. The female bird pecked at the ground, searching for something Jason couldn't quite identify. Nearby, her bright red mate stood watch, chest puffed out like a miniature sentinel. She finally found what she was looking for—a strand of brown turf—and took off. Jason watched as her companion followed, a streak of crimson against the pale blue sky.

The scene stirred something inside him—a longing that had driven this journey. He envied their connection, the way they moved together with effortless purpose. The cardinals seemed to know exactly where to be, instinctively aware of their roles. Jason, in his re-sculpted body, felt adrift. This second chance at life wasn't just about youth—it was his shot at something more. He wanted something deeper this time, a relationship with real meaning, not the empty, disconnected ones of his past. He promised himself he would avoid making the same mistakes.

This was his first outing since the procedure, and anxiety clung to him like static. He hadn't seen Emma in months. His sister had always been his ally, the one person who accepted him without judgment. Even so, he hesitated. Things were different. He was different.

Jason's thoughts were interrupted by the creeping sensation of claustrophobia. It was a new affliction, a side effect of the transformation. He needed to move, to breathe. He opened the truck door and stepped out, forcing himself to approach her house. Each step felt heavier than the last, until he reached the door. He stared at the glowing yellow doorbell. To him, it looked like a flashing red button, a harbinger to irrevocable damage.

He pressed it.

The soft thud of approaching footsteps grew louder, and then the door swung open. Emma stood in the doorway, her figure as fit as ever, showing no hint of being in her early fifties. Her eyes widened in surprise, and she froze. Jason's stomach dropped. *She disapproves! I knew it—I shouldn't have come!*

"Jase?" she whispered, her voice a mix of awe and disbelief. "Is that you?"

"Hi, Em," he replied, his voice cracking.

Emma's hand shot to her mouth as tears filled her eyes. "Oh my God. It's a miracle! You can't—this can't be—" She laughed, though teary eyed, shaking her head as if trying to wake from a dream. "You look—Jase, you look incredible. You're—" She paused, trying to find the words. "Young...years younger."

"It's still me, forty-five years rolled back," he said softly, his chest tightening as she pulled him into a fierce hug. Her sobs were muffled against his shoulder, her body trembling with emotion. When she finally stepped back to look at him, her smile was radiant, but her eyes held a hint of sadness.

"I guess my older brother doesn't exist anymore," she said, half-joking.

Jason chuckled, the tension easing slightly. "Well, the grumpy old guy's still in here somewhere."

Emma smiled through her tears. "I don't know whether to cry or laugh."

"Go ahead and craugh, then," Jason said with a grin. "It's a thing, apparently."

Her laughter came freely now, and she stepped back to inspect him. "You're taller," she noted. "Six-two—maybe?"

Jason straightened. "Yep. No limp anymore either."

"Or stoop. Your hair—Jase, it's jet black again, not a single gray. And these clothes..." She gestured at his slim-fit jeans and white polo. "You look like a damn model, an Adonis. But it's your eyes that get me. They're still green, but now they're... vibrant."

Jason felt a warmth spread through him. Emma had always been effusive with her praise, but this felt different—unfiltered, even more genuine. He followed her inside, taking in the familiar French country decor of her home. It was spotless as always, with soft pastel tones that felt welcoming. Emma led him to the sofa and sat beside him, leaning in with her knees turned toward him.

"How are you?" she asked, her tone gentle but searching.

Jason hesitated, unsure how to put his feelings into words. "It's... a lot. Overwhelming, really. They warned me about this—how hard it would be to adjust. Everything's different. My body, my relationships... hell, even time feels out of sync."

Emma nodded, her expression empathetic. "You've always been older than me, Jase. Now? It's like someone hit a rewind button. That has to mess with your head."

"It does," he admitted. "But don't get me wrong—this is a gift. It's like I've been handed a new set of batteries. I have energy I didn't even know I'd lost." He hesitated, "I've got a new body. Hell, I'm technically a virgin again."

Emma snorted, rolling her eyes. "TMI, Jase."

He laughed, the tension between them breaking.

She reached out with her arm. "You mind?"

"No, go ahead."

Her fingers brushed the back of his head. "The scar's barely there. They did an amazing job. You're a damn miracle. The Neil Armstrong of anti-aging."

"Or the first guinea pig," Jason said dryly.

Emma tilted her head, curiosity flashing in her eyes. "There's one thing I don't get—why hasn't Gordon Formell gone through the transformation himself? He's the CEO of FOY, Fountain Of Youth, Incorporated. You'd think he'd be first in line."

Jason shrugged, leaning back against the sofa. "Maybe he wanted to see it successfully work first. Or, perhaps he's holding back intentionally, wanting to oversee the operation's early stages. A man like Gordon would want everything running like clockwork before being out of commission for a few months. Marketing and optics come first."

"That might explain it," Emma said, her face revealing that she wasn't satisfied with the answer.

He gave a half-smile. "Speaking of FOY, I need to be prepared once this goes public. Even the simplest questions are going to hit like curveballs. You know, things like, '*What's next?*'"

Emma arched an eyebrow, leaning forward with interest. "And what *is* next?"

Jason chuckled, scratching the scar on the back of his head. "I walked right into that one, didn't I? Honestly, I'm still taking baby steps. This afternoon, I'm headed to what Mr. Formell calls a Newlife party. He thinks mingling with potential clients will help me ease into the spotlight before Friday's press conference."

Emma's eyes widened. "I can't believe he's letting you see Mom and me beforehand, let alone attend a party. Isn't he worried about leaks?"

Jason nodded. "It's all part of a bigger strategy. He's taken precautions to make sure everything stays under wraps. The man uses the universal currency of all powerful people."

"What's that?"

Jason nodded. "Leverage. He offered me a nice salary—two years, fully paid. At first, I thought it was pure generosity. Then came the catch: If word of my transformation gets out before the unveiling, I lose it all. I'm sure he's established consequences to anyone attending that party."

Emma smiled warmly. "You can tell Gordon that Mom and I won't say a word until after Friday. Promise."

Jason shifted, his tension easing slightly, then rising again. "Thanks, Em. Speaking of Mom... I'm planning to see her just before the press conference."

Emma's expression softened, and she reached out, rubbing his arm. "Don't take anything personally, Jase. You know this doesn't fit with her faith." She hesitated before adding, "But Dad... Dad would have understood."

The mention of their father brought a bittersweet comfort to Jason. His gaze drifted to a small photo on Emma's coffee table.

"I love this one," he murmured, picking it up carefully. "It's so different from the others. It wasn't staged. No one was posing. You can almost feel the moment."

Emma smiled, her voice tinged with nostalgia. "You always loved our old family videos too."

"Yeah," Jason said, his voice soft. "But this particular picture... it captures time. Videos move by fast, leaving no chance to reflect. A photo lets you stop, lets you imagine what everyone was thinking at that exact moment." He paused, his eyes lingering on their father's face. "Especially Dad. Look at him. He's smiling, but there's this... quiet sadness. He knew."

Emma frowned slightly. "Knew what?"

Jason placed the photo back on the table, his movements deliberate. "About his health. Even then. He never said anything, not to Mom, not to us. But he knew."

Emma's lips parted in surprise. "You're sure?"

Jason bowed his head. "His doctor told me later."

Emma squinted at the picture as if seeing it for the first time.

Jason continued, "I believe he was thinking about his legacy, measuring his worth. And now... now I can't stop thinking about mine, and the pain I caused—to Anna—her family."

Emma leaned down and looked up, to make eye contact, "It wasn't your fault, Jason. She chose to come to your game; you didn't ask her."

For Jason, the painful memory was almost too hard to suppress. "Two lives were lost that night, hers…and mine. It's part of my legacy, flawed." Trying to change the topic, he diverted his eyes from the photo. "This second chance is my shot to make something of myself. It's not lost on me that my connection to Dad is through a timepiece, as if he's inviting a do-over."

Emma slid back his sleeve slightly, revealing a Rolex. She kissed her fingers and pressed them to the watch.

"Thanks for letting me have it, Em. It's a reminder to do better."

They sat in silence for a moment, the ticking of the Rolex almost audible in Jason's mind. Finally, he registered the actual time, and he stood. "I hate to cut this short, but I've got to get going. Formell's expecting me."

Emma stood with him, her expression turning mischievous. "Oh, before you go—Rufus. Are you sure you don't mind watching him?"

Jason chuckled, shaking his head. "I could use the company."

Emma disappeared into the other room and returned with a domed cage covered in cloth. The sound of frantic rustling and a faint squawk emerged from beneath the cover. Emma grinned as she handed it over.

"We'll be gone for a week, so your nephew, Adam, owes you one. But… fair warning. Rufus is obsessed with one phrase. You'll probably hate it by the time we're back."

Jason laughed as he took the cage. "Challenge accepted."

Emma pulled him into a tight hug. "Take care, Jase. And remember, although you're a spring chicken again, you still need to listen to your doctors."

Jason returned the hug with a playful "cluck," earning a laugh from his sister. As he walked back to his truck, he reflected on the conversation. Their bond had always been close, but something felt different now—like he was the missing piece in a familiar puzzle, reshaped, somehow not fitting the same.

Jason settled into the cab, staring at the cage beside him. Rufus was quiet, the stillness oddly comforting. With a sigh, Jason started the engine and eased onto the road, the hum of the tires filling the silence.

As the stretch of highway unfolded before him, his thoughts turned to the upcoming Newlife party. How would the Dumas family react as they took their first steps at their own transformation?

But Emma's earlier question lingered, a loose thread hanging in his mind. Why *hadn't* Gordon Formell undergone the procedure himself? Was something wrong? Then he thought about himself, proof of the transformation's success. *It obviously worked. Chillax.*

Chapter 3: Dr. Schickel

A fluorescent light hummed in the bright room on the seventh floor of FOY headquarters. Two men stood over a gurney, their attention fixed on the still figure before them.

Dr. Schickel, the older of the two, struggled to reach across the bed, his rounded belly obstructing the motion. In his mid-fifties, he seemed out of place in the sterile setting. His wrinkled white smock and thinning, uncombed brown hair gave him an air of disregard for the clinical environment. Beside him, Robert Gruber—fifteen years younger—stood tall and composed in a tailored business suit. His blond hair was neatly styled, and a deep scar on his chin only accentuated his striking appearance. In contrast to Schickel, Gruber seemed to fit the formality of the room perfectly.

On the gurney lay a pale, unconscious woman. Her breathing was steady but shallow, and her hairless body was draped with two small strips of cloth—one across her chest and the other covering her lower half. The room reeked of disinfectant and finality. At the foot of the bed, a stainless-steel tray gleamed under the harsh light, its medical instruments neatly arranged.

"She's beautiful," the doctor murmured—his voice tinged with detached curiosity. He adjusted his glasses and glanced at a clipboard. "Odd, though," the doctor continued, "her A1C is significantly elevated. I'll have to discuss this with the nutritionist."

Robert ignored the remark, his sharp blue eyes scanning the woman's motionless form. "All is not lost. I've got a few tests I'd like to run before…" He trailed off, noticing the doctor's reaction.

Dr. Schickel was shaking his head firmly. "No experiments. Gordon's orders."

Robert frowned, his jaw tightening. "What a waste. What's her number?"

The doctor hesitated, his gaze lingering on the woman as if she were a complex puzzle. After an awkward pause, Robert prompted again, a more forceful tone this time.

"Doctor?"

Snapping out of his reverie, the doctor adjusted his smock. "Oh, yes. She's shell 66. Check the markings on her left ear to confirm."

The younger man leaned in, squinting to inspect the small tattooed mark behind her left earlobe. He straightened, signaling with a nod.

Dr. Schickel's manner grew clinical. "Of course, we'll need to terminate her."

Robert raised an eyebrow. "I suppose we have no other option. When?"

The doctor didn't miss a beat. "No time like the present." He gestured to the tray. "Hand me the osteotome blade and mallet."

Robert complied, passing the tools with precise, almost reverent hands.

"Let's roll her over," the doctor instructed. Together, they turned the unconscious woman onto her stomach with the sheet pulled beneath her to keep her centered. As she rotated, her limp form settled onto the cold metal surface of the gurney.

The doctor wrapped the handle of the tool with a corner of the same sheet she had been lying on. Obtaining a firm grip, he positioned the blade against the nape of her neck and raised the mallet. His movements methodical and unhurried. With one heavy strike, the blade pierced the woman's brainstem. Her body shuddered once, then stilled.

He pressed two fingers to her wrist, waiting for the inevitable to come. After a pause, he withdrew his hand and nodded. "No pulse. Duck soup." The doctor's voice was detached.

Robert grimaced, pulling a slim notecard from his breast pocket. He marked off an item with a flick of his pen, his displeasure clear in the set of his jaw. "Such a waste."

Moving to the foot of the gurney, his attention seemed fixed on the instruments. But his hand drifted to the woman's right foot, gently separating two toes to reveal a faint diamond-shaped scar. His expression tightened for a brief moment before his composure returned.

"A pity," the doctor said softly.

The doctor reflected on how they were both dissatisfied with her fate, yet understood that their reasons for disappointment were vastly different—one rooted in the cold advancement of their work and the other in a lingering, unspoken desire for something more.

Chapter 4: Jason

Jason dropped Rufus off at his townhouse, having never heard the mysterious words or phrase. He then headed to the most prestigious neighborhood in McLean, Virginia: the Ballard Homestead. As anticipated, a gate blocked his entrance, so he punched in the code Gordon had given him. The double cast-iron doors slowly parted, revealing a winding, one-mile private road flanked by poplars, oaks, maples, and blooming white dogwoods.

The driveway led to the Dumas mansion, a grand estate that rivaled national landmarks in its opulence. Jason parked his truck between a sleek McLaren Elva and a Ferrari LaFerrari, noting with a frown how his vehicle didn't measure up among the luxury cars. He couldn't help but think of the Sesame Street song, "One of These Things (Is Not Like the Others)"—a sentiment that applied not only to his truck but to himself as well.

Jason approached the French chateau-style house, fully aware that he could never afford such a home—or even its upkeep. He had read about it: a stunning twenty-million-dollar, eight-bedroom residence. The property boasted a domed reception hall, a guest house, and a beautiful Mediterranean-style pool featuring a waterfall with an infinity view of the Potomac.

Jason rang the doorbell, and a chubby-cheeked teen answered. She was balancing a plate of cake in one hand while holding the knob in the other. She embodied the awkward age—lost between childhood and becoming a full-figured woman. She stared at him with wide eyes, biting her lower lip.

Jason sensed the young lady was nervous. "Hi. I'm here for the Newlife party. I'm with Gordon Formell." He expected her to invite him in, but instead she just stood gawking. She finally opened her mouth, but nothing came out. Jason could see her blue-stained tongue from the icing on her dessert.

He tried to put her at ease. "My name is Jason Fabrikant. I think your father, Sam, is expecting me."

She giggled, flashing her braces. "Grandpa." He noticed a smudge of icing on her cheek as well.

Gordon suddenly emerged from behind the young lady. He caught a glimpse of the girl and lifted her chin with a curled index finger. "Ashley, you might want to wipe your face."

She froze in place, then swiped with a napkin. After seeing the smear of blue, she spun around and stomped away. They could hear her departing dramatics, "Really? No one tells me anything. How embarrassing!"

Gordon smiled at Jason. "Smitten, in that boy-crazy phase. Watch yourself; you wield powers you've forgotten about. Come on in—you're a tad late."

He guided Jason through the foyer and into the kitchen, where a small celebration was taking place. Noise echoed from the partygoers, but the sound was partially absorbed in the cathedral ceilings.

On the way, Jason felt uneasy since he hadn't discussed the party with Gordon. "What do you need me to do?"

Gordon answered, smiling while putting his hand on Jason's shoulder, "Just be honest, my friend. Be you!"

Jason admired how effortlessly the CEO diffused tension in any situation. He quickly realized that part of this ability stemmed from Gordon Formell's calm formality. A distinguished man in his early sixties, Gordon stood nearly as tall as Jason, with fair skin and a clean-shaven face. His salt-and-pepper hair had just a shake of pepper, adding to his refined appearance. What truly set him apart, though, was his impeccable style—always wearing a suit that seemed to quietly command respect. Jason had been told it was a Fiori Di Lusso, though the name held little meaning for him.

Adding a layer of mystery to the CEO, Jason was well aware of Gordon's slight limp, perhaps because he had once limped himself. Gordon's impairment was the result of an injury from horseback riding in his youth, which had left him with a disability, causing one leg to grow shorter. To compensate, he wore a shoe with a three-inch heel. Strangely, the limp only seemed to add to his charisma, making the impeccably dressed man even more captivating.

He handed Jason a beverage from the Calacatta marble island and led him to a quiet corner. "You're tight. Relax."

Jason eyed Gordon. "Sorry. Since the operation, I have bouts of anxiety. Perhaps it would help to know what's about to happen."

Gordon's voice flowed smoothly, like warm honey. "Fair enough. We're here to ensure that Mr. Dumas is committed."

"How?"

"Let's just say that when you're selling something valuable, you want it backed with something tangible, like a down payment. Although your transformation was free, for them, a single ticket costs more than this house."

"And once he commits?"

"The science takes over."

Jason squinted, in thought. "You need DNA, right?"

"Right. We need to collect tissue samples."

Jason shrugged, "Why here?"

"It helps settle nerves. People prefer the comfort of their own home over the clinical setting of our lab. Making the event a catered celebration is even better. What more perfect way to usher in the promise of a youthful future than with Dom Perignon and Russian Volga caviar."

Jason nodded, "And my role?"

"That's for the psychological component, which is more complicated. As you know, the thought of transformation is daunting. You're here to ease their fears; after all, you're the test pilot. So, we do the marketing and the science and you simply answer questions."

Jason took a cleansing breath. "Okay, I can do that."

Gordon looked at his watch. "Pardon me, the show is about to begin." He left Jason alone and moved to the adjacent living room, choosing an empty spot as his stage on the natural stone floor. He spoke loudly, "Good folks, may I have your attention, please." Like a true veteran, he paused, allowing the noise to die down.

The small group of thirty people quieted and gathered around him, sipping their aperitifs, their presence filling the room with an air of luxury. Gordon exuded such comfort and familiarity with the surroundings that one could easily think it was his home. "As some of you know, I started FOY more than twenty years ago. It's been a long road to get here, but we've reached a significant milestone. It's so important, in fact, we'll be holding a press conference this Friday for a big reveal."

A voice rang out. "Let us in on it!"

"Funny you should mention that. Since the Dumas family has been kind enough to offer their home today, I wanted to give you just that—a sneak preview. It's a glimpse of the future." Gordon lifted his eyebrows, creasing his forehead in a polite yet stern fashion. "I trust you can all keep a secret?" Bobbing heads indicated his secret was safe with them.

"Good, don't make me take action."

There was an uneasy pause, then he continued, "To end the suspense, you lucky folks are about to witness history in the making. I'd like you to meet Jason Fabrikant, the seventy-year-old man pictured here." Gordon held up an eight by ten photo of Jason as an older man, showing a scarred and haggard figure, turning a full circle for all to see. "Although he might not look it in this picture, he's a trailblazer, the first person to undergo the patented FOY procedure. The good news is that you're about to meet him. In fact, he's in this room right now." Everyone looked around as if expecting an old man to pop out of the closet. They visually passed over Jason like he was a floor plant.

All eyes turned back to Gordon searching for a clue. Gordon grinned, "If we only had a drum roll." A few chuckles nervously escaped as the anticipation was building. "Jason, or as we call him, 'Client One', please come forward." Gordon, smiling like an elder statesman in a calming way, reached around the crowd to shake Jason's hand. As their grips met, he pulled him into the middle of the room, almost causing him to spill his drink. Jason found himself standing on Gordon's stage by his side. He could hear the gasps around him.

Gordon continued, "Just months ago, Jason stood before me as the man in the picture I just showed you. Now, as you notice, he has the physical body of a much younger man, aged twenty-five to be exact. His new body is a Xerox copy of his younger self." Gordon turned to Sam Dumas, raising a small champagne flute filled as a celebration mimosa. "To the Dumas family, I applaud your decision to join the limited ranks of those seeking an extended youth as did Jason." On cue, his small audience began to applaud. Gordon, having a natural panache for marketing, had command of the room.

Jason's role at the Newlife party was unmistakable: to charm the wealthy and put prospective customers at ease. As soon as the introductions ended, he found himself squarely in the bullseye of attention, a lone figure surrounded by tightening rings of eager onlookers. Questions flew at him like arrows, their rapid-fire intensity leaving little room to breathe. The first came sharp and direct, "How do you feel?"

In actuality, Jason felt suffocated, but he tried to overcome the sense of being closed in. The high ceiling somehow eased his claustrophobia, making the experience tolerable. "Before the surgery, I could barely walk a block. Now, I can run a marathon. Physically, I feel on top of the world!"

Multiple questions competed for his attention, but he tuned into one, "Are you experiencing any pain?"

"I never felt pain. In fact, you can hardly notice the scar." Jason offered a view of the back of his head. The crowd reached out to touch it, like the old films of women fighting over a scarf at an Elvis concert. Gordon interjected, "Let's settle down everyone, he's still a recovering patient." Gordon seemed to be masking his elation at the interaction.

The partygoers never took their eyes off Jason, "What do you remember about the surgery?"

Jason recalled, "I remember prepping for the operation, then I woke up feeling drowsy. They gave me a mirror and I saw a distant memory, forty-five years in the past, as the reflection."

One older man with a baseball cap asked in a confrontational tone, clearly out of place among the others. "I remember you and your sports injury when you played ball. You're the guy who got into that bar fight and had legal issues, right?"

Jason felt a wave of irritation at the curmudgeon's tone and the question, but he kept his emotions in check. "That's all behind me now."

The next question flowed in quickly. "Any regrets?"

Jason quipped, "Perhaps now, after that last question." The crowd laughed, but there was more than a thread of truth in his remark.

The interrogation continued. "How could you afford it?"

"I was never a wealthy man and could never have afforded this procedure. Since I was the first, I was offered the transformation for free, as a trial case."

The crowd was still starving. "Then how did you get selected?"

"You'll have to ask Mr. Formell." Jason looked around, but Gordon had disappeared from the crowd. He decided to speculate out loud. "We can ask him later, but ironically, the very athletic injury that ruined my career may have been the best thing that could've happened to me. I think the publicity of my injury gave me the edge. I don't think Mr. Formell could pass up a great promotional opportunity of restoring a professional athlete. The fact that I once limped like Gordon didn't hurt either." The crowd chuckled once again. Jason's instincts he had developed while dealing with the press were coming back to him.

"Would you recommend it?"

Jason grinned. "My God yes! There are emotional challenges, but in all, who wouldn't want to be young again?"

An older woman, who had long outlived her beauty, asked, "How can I be selected?" With this question, Jason noticed a shift in the tone of the interactions; the crowd was now turning to their own needs.

Jason grimaced, "I think the procedure requires a pretty hefty bank account. I'm sorry, perhaps that's not the answer you were looking for."

A man, looking like a businessman used to negotiations, probed further. "Do you have any influence over the pricing? Perhaps we can get a discount, given that this is still such a new technology?"

Jason didn't anticipate this line of questioning, nor did he feel he should field it. He simply ignored the man and waited for the next question. He continued to answer questions nonstop for fifteen minutes. The partygoers' appetites were insatiable, and the questions seemed insensitive and uncaring at times. He began to study the guests' faces, likening them to vultures, selfishly pecking at a carcass. Rather than meat, they were devouring information in hopes to extend their own longevity. They wanted to be young themselves, and he could see the lengths to which they would go to get it.

Thankfully, Gordon emerged with Sam from an adjacent room. Like a teacher entering an unsupervised classroom, the crowd regained its civility once they reappeared and stood next to Jason in the center of the room. Sam called his family over to join them, then put his arms around their shoulders and gave them a squeeze. He then addressed his guests. "I'd like to make an announcement. I've made an important life decision. I just placed a down payment on the FOY procedure for my wife, granddaughter, and myself."

Everyone clapped in excitement, except for Ashley, the granddaughter.

Gordon then spoke. "I want to thank the Dumas family for putting their trust in FOY. Now, if I could share another small treat." He glanced at Sam.

Sam seemed to catch the cue and turned to Ashley. "Go turn on the television."

Ashley's response was lackluster. "Huh … like, what for?"

"You're saying 'like' again, princess. We agreed you'd work on that."

Ashley rolled her eyes. "And you aren't supposed to call me princess. I don't even know the channel!"

Sam closed his eyes while speaking. "Please. Just put it on channel four." He then turned to Jason and whispered in his ear, "I try to be patient with her. She lost her parents in a car accident at a young age, and we've raised her ever since."

Soon, a wall-mounted high-definition screen flashed to life in the family room as Ashley turned up the surround sound. The screen caught everyone's attention, and they gathered around, making it the focal point of the room.

Gordon tapped Jason's arm and spoke softly in his ear. "It's our infomercial. I timed it to occur during the party so we could observe the reactions of those watching. I could use another pair of eyes."

Chapter 5: Jason

The fifteen-minute advertisement began with a commanding voiceover:

"Since 3,500 B.C., humanity has battled its ultimate foe—time. The Greeks imagined gods consuming ambrosia to preserve their immortality. Cleopatra, in 69 B.C., bathed in Dead Sea salt and milk, requiring the labor of 700 donkeys to sustain her indulgence. Centuries later, Wu Zetian, China's only female emperor, turned to motherwort 'fairy powder' in her quest to slow aging. From myth to modern science, the desire for eternal youth remains as powerful as ever."

Jason watched, mesmerized, as the narration unfolded over vivid imagery: Zeus atop Mount Olympus, Cleopatra submerged in silken milky waters, Wu Zetian delicately applying her mystical powder. References to Hollywood's fascination with immortality followed, with clips from *The Leech Woman* and *Death Becomes Her.*

"But despite movies shining the spotlight on humanity's enduring obsession," the narrator intoned, "time remains undefeated. Jeanne Calment of France, the longest-living verified human, reached 122 years before succumbing to aging's relentless march in 1997." A grainy photo of Calment appeared, her frail smile a poignant reminder of life's fragility.

The voice sharpened, taking on a clinical edge. "Modern science offers solutions, yet all fall short. Organ transplants rely on scarce donors, with the medical field resorting to cows and pigs at times. Emerging techniques like 3D bioprinting show promise but face steep barriers. And the root problem—the cumulative DNA damage caused by free radicals—remains unsolved."

Gordon elbowed Jason. "The free radical bit—too technical?"

Jason didn't respond right away, scanning the room instead. Every eye was glued to the screen. "You've held their attention."

The narrator's tone softened, adopting a note of hope. "At FOY, we've left outdated solutions behind. Why supplant a single organ, only to wait for the next to fail? Instead, we replace the entire body. By pairing the mind with a lab-grown body created from our client's own DNA, FOY offers what no one else can: the restoration of youth."

The tone of the narration shifted to a more clinical one. "Our patented process begins with advanced cloning technology, using DNA to create a new form, or 'shell.' Brain development is intentionally halted, leaving only the brainstem to maintain essential bodily functions. By administering a patented blend of hormones, we accelerate the aging process, allowing us to create an anatomy that mirrors that of a twenty-five-year-old in just ten years.

The program then displayed a time-lapse of a child rapidly maturing into an adult. "The result is a perfect replica of our client's youthful self, grown to adulthood in our state-of-the-art biotanks. Once fully developed, the client's neural tissue—the brain—is transferred into this new vessel. After the transplant, the outcome is extraordinary: a renewal."

Gordon leaned closer to Jason, his voice low. "We don't show the actual shells. Focus groups didn't respond well—it's too visceral."

The narration continued. "We utilize cutting-edge advancements in stem cell research to address the challenges posed by spinal cord injuries, offering innovative solutions for regeneration. Research shows the brain's aging process slows dramatically in a youthful body, even reversing the effects of free radicals."

Gordon whispered, "Watch this next part; it's a bit risky."

The camera cut to a grim nursing home hallway. Elderly residents, their vacant eyes and slack mouths bearing silent witness to time's relentless toll, sat motionless in wheelchairs. The few who were awake stared blankly at the featureless white wall before them, as if all meaning had been drained from their surroundings. . They existed at the fragile boundary between life and death, caught in a state of quiet limbo. Jason couldn't help but think that, unlike the grotesque caricatures in zombie movies, these were the real living dead.

Jason shifted uneasily, avoiding his task to observe others.

"This is the reality of aging," the narrator continued. "An inevitability we all face."

Gordon nodded knowingly. "Uncomfortable, right? It's supposed to make people squirm. Drives the point home."

The camera zoomed in on the wrinkles of an elderly woman's face. The image dissolved into canyons, morphing into a dry, cracked desert. From this barren expanse emerged a young woman, energetic and determined, scaling a cliff with fluid grace. Mozart's *The Marriage of Figaro* swelled as she neared the summit, still suspended, pulling an hourglass from her pack. With a triumphant smile, she kissed it and let it fall toward the ground below.

The hourglass tumbled in freefall, then shattered on impact. Now in slow motion, its jagged shards scattered and paused midair, sharp and angular, before seamlessly morphing into FOY's sleek logo.

"At FOY," the narrator declared, "we're shattering the myths of aging."

The screen brightened to show an elderly woman tethered to an oxygen tank. A beat later, she was replaced by her youthful self, sprinting along a sunlit beach. Laughter rang out as a muscular young man chased after her, their joy palpable and undeniable.

"Reclaim your youth. Discover FOY," the narrator urged.

The words '*FOY unveils a major breakthrough this Friday. Search FOY for details*,' scrolled across the screen in bold, captivating letters.

Jason exhaled slowly, letting the message sink in. The stark juxtaposition between the frail figures on-screen and his own flawless body felt unsettling.

Doubt seeped into his mind for the first time. This astonishing advancement—touted as a miracle—remained a complete mystery to him. He hadn't bothered to do his research to learn about the technology. And now, here he was, part of the team pushing it out to the world.

Chapter 6: Jason

In Jason's view, the advertisement had been a success—at least within the Dumas mansion. Applause rippled through the room, filling the space with electric excitement. The reception restored Jason's confidence in FOY's technology.

Gordon stood at the center of the room, effortlessly commanding attention as the applause grew around him. Yet he didn't indulge in the limelight. With an easy, fluid gesture, he shifted focus to a tall, willowy technician who had silently entered the room. She wheeled in a cart bearing an object that, at first glance, looked like a Disney figurine. Its glossy, contoured design was deceptively charming, concealing its true nature—a state-of-the-art medical device. Its silhouette evoked a bird in mid-flight, blending familiarity with a touch of intrigue.

Slipping to the side, Gordon moved with practiced ease, sidling up to Jason. He leaned in, his voice low and laced with certainty. "Timing, my boy, is everything. Watch the choreography—every move, rehearsed to perfection."

Jason was amused. "The only thing missing is a puff of Houdini's smoke."

Gordon chuckled, eyes twinkling. "Noted. Next time, we'll bring the smoke. Mirrors too, to remind our viewers that they're aging."

Jason's gaze shifted to the technician, taking in her presence with mild surprise. She wasn't the typical medical professional. Her long brunette curls spilled over her shoulders in a theatrical cascade. Her white lab coat, tailored into a form-fitting minidress, had a plunging neckline, showcasing her athletic figure. The shattered-glass FOY logo gleamed on her lapel, strategically placed near her ample cleavage—ensuring no one could miss it.

Jason raised an eyebrow, his voice low. "The magician's seductive assistant? Really?"

Gordon grinned, unbothered. "We're not just in the medical business, Jason. We're in the business of beauty and desire. This isn't only about extending life—it's about selling a vision of perfection. She's part of the allure. Watch closely."

Jason followed Gordon's gaze to Diane, Sam Dumas's wife. Her elegance was still apparent, though softened by the onset of age. Once striking, her features now bore the weight of time.

Gordon leaned closer. "On the subject of mirrors, we made sure to treat Diane to an expensive magnifying mirror—just the thing to showcase every line and wrinkle."

Jason frowned. "That's cruel."

"Not cruel. Business. Time and gravity are relentless foes unless you make them allies. We simply highlight the truth, as a favor, really. Her health improves, her confidence soars, and our bottom line thrives. Everybody wins."

"So, this is about money?"

"Money is simply a means to an end. Without it, we wouldn't be able to continue our research. We help mankind."

Jason's discomfort deepened, but he held his tongue.

Gordon took his place in the center of the room, clapping his hands for attention. "Ladies and gentlemen," he began, his voice commanding yet warm. "Allow me to introduce what we lovingly call *the Stork*." He gestured to the device, its beak-like probe gleaming under the lights. "This machine collects a small tissue sample containing your genetic code to be delivered to our labs in Maryland. There, our scientists begin crafting recombinant DNA to create a better you. The process is quick, painless, and transformative. Now, who will be our first volunteer?"

As Gordon predicted, Diane stepped forward without hesitation. Her cheeks were flushed with excitement, her childlike eagerness drawing amused chuckles and admiring smiles.

Gordon took her hand with practiced charm, as if inviting her to a ballroom dance. "Diane, allow me to guide you."

She settled gracefully into the chair placed at the center of the room, though her hands trembled slightly. The technician stepped forward, moving with precise efficiency as she guided Diane's finger into the Stork's orange beak. A soft stapler-like click echoed, sharp yet fleeting. Diane withdrew her hand, inspecting it with relief and pride as the technician applied a Band-Aid with a practiced smile.

Gordon held up the small vial containing Diane's sample. "And just like that, her journey begins."

The crowd erupted in applause as Diane stood, basking in the glow of their admiration. Jason watched her closely. It wasn't her appearance that had changed—that would take years—but her demeanor. She radiated newfound confidence.

The next volunteer was Ashley, Diane's pudgy and awkward granddaughter. The young girl hesitated, her uncertainty written all over her face. "Did it, like, hurt, Nana?"

"It was nothing," Diane reassured her, reaching out to brush a hand over Ashley's cheek. "A gift you'll appreciate more when you're older. We'll have your sample frozen, to be ready when the time is right."

Jason caught a subtle exchange of glances between Sam and Gordon—a flicker of tension quickly masked. He knew the backstory. Sam wanted Gordon to employ gene editing using

CRISPR, to alter his granddaughter's appearance, making her taller, thinner, prettier. Gordon would have no part in it, stating, "I'm no Nazi. I won't play into ideals, favoring one genetic trait over the other."

Ashley shuffled forward reluctantly, her procedure over in moments. She returned to her corner looking more self-conscious than triumphant. Sam followed shortly after, completing his part with little fanfare.

Soon after, Diane became the center of attention, reveling in the questions and interest from the other guests. "What will you do when you're young again? Ten years is a long time; how can you possibly stand the wait? Are you going to be the same age as your granddaughter? What if you get sick?"

Some of the questions left Jason wondering too; he listened from a distance.

A movement caught his eye, pulling his attention back to the cart. Near the equipment stood a woman he didn't recognize, her head wrapped in a silk scarf. Her back was to him, her motions quick and deliberate.

Jason blinked. Her hand darted out, touching one of the vials. Was it a switch? A theft? He couldn't be sure.

He instinctively turned to alert Gordon, but the FOY CEO was nowhere to be found. When Jason looked back, the woman had vanished as well.

Chapter 7: Bastien

The FOY infomercial had just ended, catching Bastien Landow off guard. Its slick promises—eternal youth, boundless vitality—landed like a punch to the gut. His fury boiled over before he could even process it. He grabbed the remote and hurled it across the room. The plastic clattered against the wall, leaving a prominent dent as the batteries ejected like shell casings, one rolling into a dusty corner.

A shared wall shook with quick, forceful thuds—his neighbor's way of showing disapproval. Rage surged through Bastien. He rushed over and slammed his fist into it, a deep dent forming on impact. Pain shot up his arm as he withdrew it, a streak of blood marking the paint. Ignoring the damage, he roared, "FUCK YOU!"

He waited to hear a retaliation, almost begging things to escalate, but the neighbor fell silent. Bastien's anger lingered, a hammer looking for a nail.

Breathing heavily, Bastien stared at the broken remote pieces scattered across the floor. The FOY commercial had done it—pushed him past his breaking point. "Great, let's just have everyone live longer," he muttered, pacing his cramped living room. "More people to suffocate the planet."

His therapist's voice crept into his mind, calm and detached: *Breathe deeply and focus on regaining control.* He scoffed at the memory. Nothing she taught him had worked. She was part of the problem, not worthy, her physical existence displacing valuable oxygen. The world was still broken, and he was still trapped in it.

His gaze shifted to one of the two phones on the table. The burner. He glared at it as if sheer willpower could make it ring. The Dish—his supposed FOY insider—had gone silent. Pacing again, he muttered, "Take your sweet time, princess. Afraid to own up to your lies?"

Desperate for distraction, he gathered duct tape, super glue, and rubber bands. He retrieved the remote's shattered pieces and clumsily pieced them together. When he finished, he held up the resurrected "Frankenmote" and pressed a button. Nothing.

Growling, he hurled it again—this time at the room's sole decoration: a framed mirror. The glass shattered, shards spraying across the carpet. Bastien stood there, staring at the fractured frame hanging crooked on the wall.

He approached, placing his hands on either side of the frame, and leaned in to examine his reflection in one of the only shards that remained intact. The man staring back looked much older than forty-two. Deep lines etched his pale, blotchy skin. His receding red hair hung stringy and unkempt, framing hollow cheeks and crooked, yellowing teeth.

"Orphaned," he muttered bitterly, though he knew it wasn't the whole truth. Genetics had its share of the blame for his looks, but it was easier to fault his adoptive parents. They'd never cared enough to notice him, never looked beyond their own indifference. As for his appearance, he'd stopped pretending to care long ago—no hygiene, no grooming, no smiles. What was the point?

A photo slipped from the cracked frame, fluttering to the floor. His aunt had only ever cared for her own, never for him. She was no mother. Bastien glared at the image, her eyes scratched out. *You never did see me.*

The shrill ring of his cell phone broke his concentration. Snatching it up, he barked, "Why the fuck are you calling me on this line?"

A hesitant female voice replied, "I'm sorry? I'm looking for Mr. Landow."

"That's me. What?"

"This is a courtesy call regarding your credit card balance. We—"

He hung up and slammed the phone down. Her words stabbed at his spiraling frustration—a sharp reminder of how far he'd fallen.

Instead of wandering aimlessly, he slumped onto the sofa, conserving his energy for what was to come. The rotted foam cushions collapsed under his weight. The couch, like most of his furniture, was a relic from Goodwill, its glory days long past. Stained, sagging, faintly reeking of mildew—it felt like a kindred spirit: worn down, overlooked, yet still holding on.

He reached into the wooden frame and fished out a LEGO brick—one of many forgotten relics from lives that had once brushed against its fabric. Coins, stale Cheetos, a pen, a bra, and countless orphaned socks had all emerged over time. To Bastien, the couch was more than just furniture—it was a time capsule, safeguarding fragments of histories he'd never know. Keeping it wasn't just practical; it was his quiet rebellion against a throwaway society, a defiant nod to things deemed obsolete—when perhaps it was the past owners who should be discarded.

Before he could retreat further into his thoughts, the burner phone finally rang. His pulse quickened. Snatching it up, he snarled, "Liar!"

"Bastien," the Dish's voice was calm, almost soothing. "I know you're upset, but—"

"Upset?" he interrupted. "Formell's plans are moving faster than you said they would! While you've been powdering your pretty little nose, he's been ramping up. Every second we wait, he gets closer to destroying everything. Indecision and delays are the parents of failure!" Having never seen her, he figured she was just another beautiful face at FOY, among the countless others, vainly calling herself the Dish.

The Dish remained level. "We're not ready. We need to rehearse the plan and—"

"Rehearse?" Bastien's laugh was sharp, humorless. "This isn't a play, Dish. This is the end of the human race!"

A beat of silence passed.

"Bastien, relax. You're worked up. We'll get there, but this takes time."

He raked a hand through his unkempt hair, standing up and pacing faster than before. "You contacted me, remember? You said we'd form a two-person cell, derail FOY's progress, expose their lies. And now? You're the one lying."

The Dish sighed. "We have the same goal, but your urgency could jeopardize everything. We need to execute with precision."

He stopped pacing, gripping the phone tighter. "Do you even read? The Doomsday Clock says sixty seconds to midnight. FOY's life-extending tech is gasoline on the fire. Ten billion people, Dish. The earth can't take it." His voice lowered, trembling with ire. "It's probably already too late."

"Bastien, you're spiraling," she said softly. "Take a breath."

"Don't patronize me!" he snapped, punching the wall again.

The Dish waited until his breathing steadied. "I chose you because you're brilliant. A man of action. But your intensity could be our downfall. You need to control yourself, or this won't work."

He clenched his jaw, refusing to acknowledge her point. "When are we moving? And don't say in a month."

There was another delay on the phone. "Okay, I give. How about next week."

"Tomorrow, or I'm out."

Her answer came after a long pause, this time longer. "Fine."

Relief coursed through him, happy that she couldn't see his grin. "About time."

"But Bastien," her voice grew firmer, "you have to pass as the technician getting off duty. No missteps. No outbursts. Can you do that?"

He smirked at his fractured reflection. "I've got it covered. The blond wig, the long white coat, the mannerisms—I've studied them all. I'll be in and out before they realize what hit them."

Her voice tightened. "Okay. I'll leave the vials at the new drop site tomorrow. Please don't get caught."

His laugh was cold, triumphant. "Don't worry. I'll be back home watching it all unfold from my couch, no traces."

The line went dead.

Bastien sat down, angular shapes of light from the cracked mirror projected against the barren walls, where only dents served as decoration. A quote from *The Matrix* echoed in his mind: *Human beings are a disease, a cancer of this planet. You're a plague, and we are the cure.*

For the first time in weeks, he smiled, baring his yellowed teeth. His plans stretched far beyond what the Dish had envisioned. *I am the cure.*

Chapter 8: Samantha

Samantha Morgan took a final bite of her Mediterranean salad, finishing her dinner with a small triangle of pita dipped in hummus. As a petite woman, her appetite was modest. After clearing the table, she sank into the overstuffed cushions of her sofa, brushing back her auburn hair.

She had already changed into her robe, slipped off her shoes, and—most importantly—freed herself from the discomfort of her bra. At twenty-six, she savored the quiet solitude of her Old Town Alexandria apartment. And things were about to get even better.

An open bottle of wine on the end table caught her eye. She had opened it just an hour earlier: a Cabernet Sauvignon from a local winery she hadn't yet tried. Treating it like a rare French blend, she let it breathe, allowing it to present its best self. She hadn't tasted it yet, but she could already feel the rejuvenating powers it promised. To Samantha, wine wasn't just a drink—it was an experience. The taste, the effect, but most of all, the tradition. She dimmed the lights and, with a soft voice, asked her smart speaker to play Adele, her favorite singer-songwriter.

Beside the bottle, a long-stemmed crystal wine glass stood, etched with a loving heart and an electrocardiogram pattern. It was a gift from her parents after her graduation from Johns Hopkins. Samantha picked up the bottle and glass, tilting them both gently as if sharing a delicate kiss. She poured, savoring the anticipation. With just a small amount in the glass, she could already smell the rich, peppercorn scent and admire the deep, dark cherry hue. She swirled the glass and observed the legs—the gravity-defying pivots, leaving delicate trails of wine behind. The movement reminded her of her profession: cardiology. The veins in the glass seemed to mirror the arteries she spent her days studying.

Just as she prepared to take her first sip, her cell phone blared, its ringtone dissonant with her smart speaker's relaxing music. The caller ID read *FOY*.

"Hello?"

A male voice responded, apologetic yet formal. "Sorry to bother you, Dr. Morgan. This is Dr. Schickel."

She recognized the name vaguely—an introduction from a past conference, though they had never collaborated professionally. A brief pang of concern fluttered in her chest; it wasn't typical for someone she barely knew to call her private number. She quickly ran through her list of patients in her mind, wondering if she had overlooked something in her care.

"Is everything okay?" she asked, uneasily.

"Yes, yes, absolutely. No emergency, sorry if I alarmed you. I just wanted to inform you of a new patient added to your caseload tomorrow. His name is Jason Fabrikant."

Samantha was momentarily puzzled. "New patients are added all the time. Does he require a special procedure?"

Dr. Schickel hesitated. "Well, it's just that you might notice some unusual patterns when you review his medical history."

Samantha's interest was piqued. "What patterns?"

He fumbled. "You'll see tomorrow. As his primary care physician, I'd appreciate it if you kept your findings to yourself."

Her eyebrows knitted together. "That's... unusual. You're asking for more restrictions than HIPAA requires. Our release forms already limit access to only necessary medical personnel."

"That's the concern," he replied, his tone awkward. "FOY management requested that you only share his records with me. There are sensitivities surrounding this patient."

Samantha's employer, FOY, was responsible for funding her research. But FOY shouldn't be dictating who collaborates on a patient's health. Something about the request felt wrong. "This doesn't seem to be in Mr. Fabrikant's best interest. I'm not comfortable with this."

Dr. Schickel chuckled lightly. "I was told you're passionate about patient rights... fiery, too. You have a reputation for being a pit bull, just in a chihuahua's body."

Samantha didn't appreciate the analogy. "I assure you, my size has no bearing on my capabilities as a doctor."

"Of course. Apologies," he mumbled. "I only meant to lighten the mood."

She ignored his comment. "Let's stick to the issue. I can't comply without understanding these 'sensitivities'."

"I'm not privy to the details myself," he said quickly. "But rest assured, there are no risks to the patient. If he needs medical attention, feel free to involve anyone you need. The CEO, Mr. Formell, just wants to restrict access to his records unless absolutely necessary."

Samantha's resolve hardened. "I'm sorry, Doctor, but unless you can give me more specific details, I need to ensure his medical records are properly reviewed by my competent staff."

"I see," he muttered, and the line went dead.

Samantha reclined on the sofa, the tension in her shoulders tightening. She steadied her wine glass on her knee, reflecting on the brief, strange conversation. The earlier FOY infomercial had only added to her unease, deepening her sense of disconnection from the company. After a year working for Mr. Gordon Formell, she had hoped for a chance to be involved in the groundbreaking genetic research the company was pioneering. But the infomercial, filled with promises of miracles and eternal youth, had left her feeling like an outsider in her own organization.

As she thought about her new patient, Jason Fabrikant, she opened her laptop to check her upcoming appointments. The electronic medical records system was separate from FOY's proprietary system, further isolating her from the company's inner workings.

Jason Fabrikant's file stood out immediately. A young man with a normal BMI; however, he had a history of cardiovascular disease, diabetes, hyperlipidemia, and hypertension. Interestingly, his latest bloodwork showed a remarkable improvement in all his labs, causing Samantha to immediately wonder if there was an error in the records. Rather than dive deeper into the inconsistencies, she redirected her focus. It was getting late, and she needed a mental break.

Her eyes fell on her glass. She took the smallest sip of wine, savoring the taste. It was full-bodied, complex, and dry—everything she had hoped for. But she needed to capture the experience with a word, defining its essence. After a delay, she smiled to herself. "Fruit-forward," she said to an empty room, pleased with herself.

As she closed her laptop, Adele's voice filled the room, and she sang along, knowing every word but rarely hitting the right note. It was a small comfort, but it was hers.

Just as she began to relax, her phone rang again. This time, the caller ID read *Gordon Formell.*

Chapter 9: Gordon

Gordon Formell stood outside the FOY building, his gaze fixed on a small food truck reversing into the loading dock. The night air was crisp, but the quiet was shattered by the truck's relentless back-up alarm. He scowled, irrationally. The noise was an unwanted disruption, threatening to draw attention to the covert activities taking place, even though the thirty-acre plot in Northern Virginia provided ample isolation. The truck came to rest, and the beeping stopped abruptly, leaving a sudden silence in its wake.

Gordon watched as the driver, Oliver Burton, emerged with purpose. Oliver's stride was brisk, his movements efficient, as he went to the back of the truck to release the tail lock and open the doors. A physical specimen, Oliver fit the FOY image to perfection: muscular, rugged, with short brown hair and a strong jawline that could have been carved from stone. Dressed in camouflage pants, a hoodie, and boots, he looked every bit the part of a military model. Oliver had served in the Marine Corps, and though his active-duty days were behind him, his loyalty to the Corps was still as strong as ever. "Semper Fi" wasn't just a motto—it was a lifelong code.

Inside the truck bed, Harper Faulton sat on a wooden crate, her distant gaze fixed on the floor. Gordon's voice cut through the silence. "Are you okay?"

Harper snapped out of her trance and stood quickly, offering a brief, wordless nod. She wheeled a hand truck to Oliver, who deftly positioned its nose plate between the crate and the pallet. With swift efficiency, Oliver lifted the load onto the hand truck, his silent movements speaking of urgency.

He glanced at Gordon, his expression asking a question without the need for words.

"Animal lab. We'll move it to the top floor later."

Oliver didn't need any more guidance. His drive was instinctive, woven into the very fabric of his being—something Gordon appreciated in a research company, where time seemed to drag on forever. Oliver's "get-it-done" mentality was rare, and Gordon had come to rely on him, confident that he could trust him with anything—even the darkest secrets. A single stroke of a pen was all it took to secure his unwavering loyalty. But it was his relentless attitude that earned him the rapid promotion to Chief of Facilities.

As Oliver disappeared into the lab, pushing the crate with ease and the sound of squeaking dolly wheels fading into the distance, Gordon turned his attention back to Harper.

"Where did you end up?" he asked, his gaze steady on her. Unlike Oliver, Harper's emotions were clear—she was upset, though doing her best to conceal it.

"Dupont Circle," she replied flatly, her usual eloquence gone. It wasn't lost on Gordon that these late-night trips were never her favorite part of the job.

Harper was dressed differently tonight—intentionally so. She wore a baseball cap, torn jeans, a black V-neck t-shirt, and white sneakers. The outfit was a deliberate attempt to mask her beauty. Even dressed down, though, it was impossible to ignore her striking looks: long brown hair with blonde highlights, sky-blue eyes, and a figure that commanded attention. Despite the undeniable attraction she exuded, Gordon knew there was no romantic tension between her and Oliver—both were too driven for that.

"Any issues?" Gordon probed, not so much for the answer, as an opportunity to gauge her state of mind.

"Smooth. No resistance," Harper responded, her voice empty of emotion.

Gordon pressed further. "The lure?"

"Just warm soup," she said, her words lifeless.

Her demeanor definitely felt off—like she wasn't fully present. He decided to let the conversation die there, watching her retreat to the truck. She just needed some time to unwind.

As Gordon watched her leave, his thoughts drifted back to the first time their paths had crossed. Harper had been an enigma—commanding, sharp, and undeniably ambitious. A Yale graduate with a degree in Economics, yet there was an edge to her, a rawness that spoke of a history she was determined to escape. Her mother had been part of the story too, even going so far as to try to seduce him at one point in a desperate bid to secure her daughter a job. But that was a game Gordon had no interest in playing. Even so, there was something about both Harper and her mother—something astute and resourceful—that he couldn't shake.

He took a risk and hired her. When she first joined FOY a decade ago, he began piecing together her story. Harper had fought her way out of a gritty past, determined to erase the stain it left behind.

He observed her, watched how she moved through the room with people. At first, he dismissed it as manipulation—something beneath the surface, and beneath him. But Harper delivered results. She knew how to wield her charm in the business world, whether with a glance, a flirt, or a well-timed gesture—tools far more effective than any formal pitch. She had a knack for getting people, especially men, to act on impulse—driven by a mix of desire, or for women, envy. Those impulses often translated into investments, and FOY's sudden growth was a testament to her uncanny ability.

He took another chance, promoting her within the company. His instincts proved right; her capacity to engage with investors, board members, and moguls was unmatched. Combined with her beauty, she was the perfect fit for FOY's medical-beauty venture. In fact, Harper had played a pivotal role in securing the initial capital that allowed FOY to expand its research, eventually earning her the title of Chief Financial Officer. It was her work that had made it possible to purchase the building, moving his business from a hidden sterile lab to an impressive modern edifice, with state-of-the-art biotanks lining the showroom.

Though he never confronted her directly about the methods she employed, Gordon understood them—whether or not he agreed. Who was he to judge? The line between right and wrong wasn't one he had the clarity to define. His request tonight had made that painfully clear.

As for this evening's task, even though she was upset, he knew she'd bounce back—she always did. She was resilient.

Part 2: Heart

Chapter 10: Jason

Thursday

Jason stumbled north along the dirt trail—more a loose path than an actual road—that ran parallel to a desolate highway stretching endlessly in both directions. He was stranded, desperate for a way back, each step a battle against exhaustion. His feet caught on scattered rocks, sending jolts of pain through his aching body. He managed to catch himself each time, but the effort drained him faster than he could recover. The sun blazed overhead, and thirst clawed at his throat, making every movement feel like an insurmountable challenge.

The land around him was barren—an endless, flat stretch of nothingness. Not a single hill or landmark broke the monotony of the horizon. There were no trees, no plants—just a lifeless, flat expanse that seemed to swallow all hope. The air pressed down on him, thick with an overwhelming emptiness, as if the world itself was holding its breath.

Trucks sped by on the highway, their engines roaring as they cut through the stillness of the desert. Every so often, the shriek of their air brakes cut through the silence like the sharp, jarring sound of gunshots, a brutal interruption that shattered the quiet and left an uneasy echo in the air. Jason glanced over to the road, his desperation mounting. He needed help. He could flag someone down, maybe even get a ride. But as he neared the edge of the highway, something caught him off guard. He stepped forward, and suddenly, the air in front of him seemed to solidify.

Without warning, his forehead slammed into an invisible wall: a sharp pain shot through him, splitting the skin above his eye. Blood trickled down his face, and he recoiled, instinctively wiping at the wound with a trembling hand. His eyes widened in shock as he realized a barrier was there, solid and unyielding, yet unseen.

He staggered back, staring at the empty space, still trying to make sense of what had just happened. No wall. No structure. But the surface was there—cold, firm, and invisible. His fingers brushed against it again, smooth to the touch. He walked a few paces, pushing forward, testing its limits, but the wall kept extending—seemingly endless, following him as he moved.

Panic crept up his spine, the weight of his helplessness starting to settle in. He tried to push through, walking along the barrier in search of an end. But the wall never stopped, never wavered. No matter how far he walked, it was there, an immovable line blocking his way, preventing him from reaching the highway.

He stopped, breathing heavily, trying to gather his thoughts. Then, with a desperate sense of dread, he turned around—hoping that perhaps there was a break in the wall from where he came. But the world had shifted. A perpendicular wall extended out, cutting him off from the path he'd just walked.

Jason's pulse quickened. He backed up, his steps frantic, and tried to retrace his steps again, only to find more walls emerging. Another wall appeared, and another, until he found himself in a glass box—trapped in a cage of invisible glass. He felt his breath catch in his throat as the air seemed to grow thinner, pressing in on him from all sides. He pounded on the surface in desperation, his fists weak with exhaustion, but the glass absorbed every blow, leaving no trace of his efforts.

Nearby, the highway stretched out, the traffic speeding by with no regard for his plight. The vehicles were all luxury—sleek Mercedes, polished Jaguars, glimmering Bentleys, and elegant Rolls-Royces. Each car glided past effortlessly, its occupants unfazed by the desolate landscape outside. Inside every vehicle, elderly faces peered out, their expressions cold and indifferent. They didn't flinch, didn't hesitate. It was as though they could see him, but chose not to. Their eyes locked on him for a moment before looking away, as if he was just another insignificant detail in the distance.

Jason's heart sank; he stood up, his arms flailing in a last-ditch effort to be seen. "Hey! Help! Please!" His voice cracked with desperation, hoarse and raw, but the cars on the highway didn't even slow. They just continued their march, apathetic to his cries. He shouted louder, his words lost in the emptiness, swallowed by the harsh dry air. "Why won't you stop?" he demanded, his voice breaking, but no one answered. No one cared.

And then it hit him: he was not only alone, but naked as well. Exposed. Displayed like a specimen in a glass aquarium, with no way to escape. He felt his skin flush with humiliation as he realized the truth: he wasn't just trapped in a box—he was part of the exhibit. A creature, exhibited in a tank to entertain those outside.

His mind began to spiral, a sense of profound helplessness suffocating him. And still, the world moved on, unempathetic to his plight. He flailed, mouth open, gasping—in the desert, a fish out of water.

Jason woke up, thrashing at an imaginary wall, his chest heaving and sweat soaking the sheets. Another nightmare.

Chapter 11: Jason

Jason glanced around, momentarily disoriented, before the familiar surroundings of his Reston townhouse came into focus. The nightmare—yet another one about being trapped—lingered in his mind. It wasn't just the intensity that unnerved him but their growing frequency. He had hoped they'd subside as his body adjusted, but being FOY's first client came with more baggage than he'd anticipated.

He swung his legs off the bed, trying to shake the unease. "Guinea pig number one," he muttered under his breath. No guidebooks, no testimonials—just a trail he was blazing on his own.

Pushing the thoughts aside, he grabbed his rejuvenation journal—a requirement of the FOY contract—and began his daily "inventory." Despite the nightmares, his body felt amazing, charged with youthful energy. His pen moved swiftly across the page as he recorded his progress: increased endurance, notable strength gains, and mental clarity that made him realize just how foggy he had been before—particularly when it came to his memory.

Time to test those limits.

Jason dropped to the floor and started his morning workout: push-ups, sit-ups, and pull-ups. He demolished his previous records, his body responding with a vitality that still felt surreal. Afterward, he grabbed his phone to tackle cognitive challenges: memory games, verbal puzzles, and spatial reasoning exercises. He aced every one, though the voice in the back of his head kept asking, *Was I losing my cognition, and not even realizing it?*

Bending to grab his slippers, Jason caught sight of his reflection in the full-length mirror. He straightened up, his eyes drawn to the flat plane of his stomach. No more bending awkwardly around a belly. He ran his fingers over his abs, grinning.

"Fat ass," a voice called from the living room.

Jason froze, then turned toward Rufus, the Amazon parrot perched smugly on his stand.

"Not anymore, my feathered friend," Jason replied, amused.

But the insult nagged at him. Were these the "mystery words" Emma had warned him about? Or had he somehow taught Rufus that himself? He shuddered, imagining his nephew Adam hearing it in front of his father, Greg, whose weight had been a sensitive subject for years.

Trying to pivot the conversation, Jason cooed, "Pretty bird."

"Fat ass," Rufus shot back.

Jason groaned, running a hand down his face. "Shit!"

The bird cocked his head, and Jason panicked. His fears became a reality.

"Shit," Rufus echoed, in a cartoonish voice.

Oh no. What have I done?

Worried, Jason grabbed his phone and called Emma. She answered immediately. "Hey, Jase! Just packing for Florida. What's up?"

Not admitting to the new word he'd inadvertently taught the bird, he said, "Rufus called me a fat ass."

Emma burst out laughing. "I was wondering when you'd call. Guess the mystery words revealed themselves!"

"That's a relief. I was afraid I taught him that!"

"Nope. Rufus came preloaded with insults," Emma explained, her giggles slipping through. "He's got a complicated past. We found out he's fifty years old and had a rough time with neglectful owners. His last owner taught him 'fat ass' during a bitter divorce. Apparently, the wife gained a lot of weight after cheating on her husband. So, to get back at her, the husband trained Rufus to say the insult whenever it was her turn to watch the bird—especially in front of her new boyfriend."

Jason stared at Rufus, who preened a patch of bald feathers. "A tool of revenge."

"Right? The wife sold him the moment the ink dried on the divorce papers. Rufus came to us scruffy, mean, and a little unhinged, but Adam's been working wonders with him."

Jason sighed. "Still, couldn't Adam have gotten a dog or something normal?"

"Dogs don't talk back, Jase. Where's the fun in that?" Emma's tone turned hurried as Greg's voice muttered in the background. She ended abruptly. "Gotta go, love ya!"

Jason hung up and turned to Rufus, who was now plucking furiously at his feathers. "Poor thing."

"Fat ass," Rufus replied without missing a beat.

Despite the affront, Jason was relieved Rufus had forgotten the new word. He made his way to the kitchen. After brewing coffee and taking a sip, he grimaced at its bitterness. His taste buds weren't what they used to be—or maybe they finally woke up, no longer dulled by his body's decay.

As he sipped, he wondered once again what he would do with his newfound youth. Enduring memories of his college days came flooding back. He thought of the time he and his friends set up a poker game in an elevator, smoking cigars, watching in delight as confused passengers opted for the stairs whenever the doors opened…smoke billowing out. The word "shenanigans" popped into his mind, an old relic of a term. Did anyone even use that anymore? Probably not.

His thoughts drifted deeper, to his roommate scraping pot across a shoebox lid to separate the seeds, and to the pungent smell of bong water and cheap beer that always lingered in their dorm room. Did people even call it *pot* anymore? Was it just *weed* now?

The nostalgia clashed with the realization that even his wildest memories felt outdated. Would this second youth be as exhilarating, or would it feel hollow, a cheap echo of what he'd already done?

Jason's gaze landed on his Rolex. Time felt different now—slippery and uncertain. He thought of his college friends, many of their faces blurred by time. They were two generations older now, their lives confined to routines he no longer shared.

Then came the pain—sharp and inescapable—accompanied by the thought of Anna, the only woman he had ever truly loved, his love for his mother and sister being different. He'd asked her not to drive to the game that night; the rain had made the roads slick. But deep down, he wanted her there. He wanted her to see him play. He could have and should have talked her out of it, but he didn't.

Had she lived, he would now be far too young for her. Oddly enough, he was once again the right age for when they first met. The realization left him hollow. There were no do-overs for the ones left behind. Was he still choosing selfishness, as he had with every decision since her death?

He felt unworthy. After all, he hadn't earned this second chance. Being chosen wasn't a result of any saintly actions on his part. The whole thing felt wrong—like a cosmic imbalance he couldn't escape.

His gaze drifted to Rufus, with his patchy feathers and wary eyes, nearing the end of his own timeline. "It's not all roses, Rufus. Life stinks sometimes," Jason murmured.

"Shit," Rufus echoed, the timing impeccable.

Jason chuckled at the irony, shaking his head. Maybe Rufus wasn't so bad after all.

Chapter 12: Jason

Jason's first cardiac evaluation with Dr. Samantha Morgan took him to a sleek medical complex south of National Harbor, Maryland. Though not part of FOY's main facility, the center lay just ten miles away as the crow flies. The drive, however, felt interminable as he navigated the notorious bottlenecks of the Woodrow Wilson Memorial Bridge and Alexandria's congested roads. Each minute stuck in traffic only deepened Jason's unease about his ties to FOY.

This was the bargain Jason had struck with Gordon Formell: he'd agreed to an exhausting regimen of examinations, granting FOY near-total control while he remained on their premises. Though the agreement promised him some freedom once he left, the invisible leash around his neck still felt as tight as ever. Today's tests promised to be invasive, with needles involved—just the thought made him grit his teeth.

After checking in, Jason was escorted to an exam room and left alone, the door clicking shut behind him. He stared at the closed door, feeling an unwelcome sense of confinement. Lately, doors seemed less like boundaries for privacy and more like cages. He felt a sudden bond with Rufus.

Sitting on the exam table, Jason swung his legs idly, trying to distract himself from the rising tide of anxiety. The room was standard-issue: medical equipment, disposable gloves, a counter lined with antiseptic bottles, and a variety of health posters—one titled *Anatomy of the Heart*.

The diagram caught his attention. Jason studied the intricate network of arteries and valves, marveling at how this organ, so functional and mechanical in appearance, had become a metaphor for love, courage, and even the soul. Phrases like "heart of gold" or "big-hearted" swirled in his mind. What did his new heart say about him? Crafted in a lab from his own genetic blueprint, it wasn't even the organ he was born with. Could it still hold his essence?

A knock interrupted his thoughts.

"Hello, Mr. Fabrikant. I'm Dr. Morgan."

Jason looked over as Samantha Morgan stepped in, tablet in hand. She was striking, with amber eyes framed by tendrils of curly hair that defied gravity. Her white coat hinted at a slender, athletic frame—the type he had always found attractive.

Months ago, he would have dismissed the idea of noticing someone so much younger. But now, with his new body, those constraints felt like relics of a distant past.

Samantha scanned his chart, her brow briefly lifting before she smoothed her expression.

"Is there a problem?" Jason asked.

"Not at all," she said, a little flustered. "It's just an unusual request. FOY wants a CT angio. Normally, I would start with just an echo, and go from there. Let's still do the Echo."

Jason nodded. "You're the boss."

She stepped closer. "You'll need to take off your shirt." Jason complied, revealing his toned torso. He noticed a brief crack in Samantha's initial steady professionalism, her eyes lingering just a moment longer than necessary. He wasn't blind to the changes—his abdomen now held eight distinct muscle segments, even surpassing the typical "six-pack" in both form and function. Dr. Morgan quickly regained her composure, applying gel and sweeping a wand across his chest before returning her focus to the screen. She began typing her observations.

"Am I going to live?" Jason asked, his voice light. She didn't respond right away.

"You're fine. Let's move on to the next test, the CT." She attached several electrodes to his chest and led him to another room with a large machine featuring a donut-shaped center.

Her tone was brisk. "Please lie down. I'll take several images— first without contrast and then with. When I inject the solution, you'll feel warmth—almost like you've wet yourself. Don't worry, it's just a sensation." Samantha numbed his wrist and inserted a catheter for the dye. Her hands were precise, and though her perfume was light, it still had a captivating effect on him. For the first time in weeks, even with half of his body enclosed in the machine, Jason felt his usual claustrophobia ease.

Samantha left the room, and the test began. The bed slid in and out of the donut, making odd sounds, causing Jason's anxiety to return. When it was over, she returned and instructed him to get dressed. As she studied the results, she muttered a word under her breath, something that caught his attention. Jason tilted his head. "Did you just say… 'unicorns'?"

She blinked, clearly startled. "Oh, sorry. It's just… these results are remarkable. Your coronary arteries are completely clear. No blockages, no abnormalities." Her brow furrowed. "This doesn't make sense. According to your records, you had an 80% obstruction. I'll double-check the equipment, but…" She looked up at him, her eyes meeting his with an intensity that made his heart race. "You're a miracle man."

Jason smiled knowingly but said nothing more.

"You keep yourself pretty fit, Mr. Fabrikant. Good for you."

"Please, call me Jason."

She hesitated, then nodded. "As for your health, it looks like you've earned yourself a glowing report."

Jason grinned. "Does that mean I'm cleared for a juicy steak?"

Dr. Morgan laughed, her clinical formality melting. "I'm a steak fan myself, but if I had free rein, I'd pick seafood. Lobster ravioli by the Potomac—nothing better."

"Throw in a glass of buttery Chardonnay, and I'm sold."

"Nice pairing," she said, raising an eyebrow. "But as your doctor, I should recommend oatmeal and raisins."

He chuckled. "Noted. But if we're confessing guilty pleasures, what's yours?"

Her lips curved into a smile. "Reese's Peanut Butter Cups. Don't tell anyone; it'll ruin my credibility."

The two fell into an easy rhythm of conversation, ranging from D.C. hotspots to favorite foods and literature. Jason, feeling a rare lightness, finally asked, "Dr. Morgan, do you know why I'm here?"

Her response was literal. "You mean for the cardiac assessment?"

"No, I mean—do you know *who* I am?"

Dr. Morgan met his gaze. "I only know that I'm to track your cardiovascular health under strict confidentiality. FOY's CEO, Gordon Formell, requested it. Beyond that, you're a mystery. I figure you're taking some type of experimental drug."

Jason leaned forward slightly. "Tomorrow, FOY will make an announcement, and I'm part of it. I can't say much, but I've been sequestered for some time…" He hesitated. "I'd like to feel human again. And it'd be nice to spend some time outside of a medical environment. Would you consider joining me for dinner tonight?"

Dr. Morgan looked away briefly before locking eyes with him. "You're a patient," she said, though her smile softened the reprimand. "But this business with FOY is intriguing, and I could use a break in my routine. I'd be interested in learning more about you, as elusive as your background is."

Jason felt the heat rise in his face. "I promise, no tricks. You'll understand everything after the press conference."

She hesitated, then smiled. "How about a meeting over a hot drink instead? Four o'clock, Sweet Tea Bakery?"

"Great." Jason smiled. "You're not tea...sing me, are you?"

Her laugh was both amused and admonishing. "A dad joke? Really? Let's hope you improve your material over coffee."

As she left, Jason watched her go, catching the reflection of a smile in the wall mirror. She glanced back, her smile lingering. "You can call me Samantha."

Jason felt fireworks he hadn't experienced in years. But the thought of his dad joke nagged at him. *Can I really fit in?* He turned to the anatomy poster once more, his thoughts circling his new heart. *Ironic,* he mused, *that the woman tasked with safeguarding my heart might be the one to break it.*

Chapter 13: Jason

Jason left his cardiology session and, with some time before his next appointment, swung by McDonald's to quell the hunger gnawing at him after fasting. He hadn't eaten fast food in years, usually feeling sick afterward, but today he told himself it might be just what he needed.

The fries, crisp and hot, were a familiar indulgence—but with each bite, a sense of discomfort crept over him. Was he already abusing the specimen FOY had created? They had gifted him the perfect, healthy body, but that effort now seemed at odds with his own behaviors. The contradiction pressed on him, making the fries feel heavier with each swallow. Still hungry, he resisted the urge to go back to the counter for a strawberry shake, guilt lingering, convincing him not to.

After finishing, he fought his way through traffic, maneuvering across the gridlocked Woodrow Wilson Memorial Bridge and weaving through the busy streets of Alexandria. By the time he arrived at FOY in the afternoon, memories of his time there made him tense. The facility, tucked away in the woods off a private road, always unsettled him. It had been both sanctuary and prison during his months-long recuperation.

The building itself stood stark against the natural surroundings, a sleek modern structure enveloped in greenery. Its glass windows stretched from floor to ceiling, allowing views of the lush woods outside, giving the illusion of openness, as if to say, "We have nothing to hide." Yet, the upper levels, shrouded by towering trees, remained obscured from view, leaving these levels as mysterious as the purpose of the facility itself.

Jason parked his truck and entered the lobby. Three guards stood behind a desk, their faces impassive, watching him with a cool detachment that made him feel like an outsider…an intruder in the very place of his own upbringing. He steeled himself for the security protocols ahead.

"Good morning, gentlemen," he said, his voice slightly more strained than intended.

The oldest of the guards, in his mid-forties, looked up, his expression unreadable. "Please pass through the metal detector and proceed to the access portal, Sir."

"Portal?" Jason asked, brow furrowing in confusion.

"Correct," came the clipped response. No further explanation followed.

Jason couldn't help but wonder why the guards always kept their distance. Were they trained to be so cold? Was the lack of conversation part of the protocol?

He realized what little he knew about the new security measures. Gordon had told him about an incident prior to Jason's recovery, when protestors—armed with crowbars, baseball bats, and mace—had overtaken the guards. They never reached the operations area, but their mission was clear: destroy the Glass Fountain, the beating heart of FOY's genetic operations. Since then, the facility had been on high alert, and the new security procedures, including this portal, were part of that response.

As Jason neared the portal, his stomach tightened. This would be the first time he was entering FOY since his transformation. He passed through the metal detector without incident, but the sight of the portal ahead made him anxious. It wasn't a revolving open barrier, as he had expected, but one that rose to the ceiling, made of cold, unyielding stainless-steel mesh.

Jason approached and pushed on the bar to enter the semi-circle, but as the door rotated, it clicked and locked, trapping him inside. Panic flared for a moment, and he instinctively pressed harder against the bar. The door held firm. His heart rate spiked.

"What the hell is this?"

"Please wait, sir," the guard's voice came through a small speaker, calm and monotonic. "A Q-tip will appear. Without using your hands, simply lick it."

Jason blinked. "What for?"

"It's a saliva check for DNA," the guard replied, the words matter-of-fact and rehearsed.

A robotic arm extended from a side compartment, offering a Q-tip. Jason hesitated, then reluctantly leaned in and licked the swab. The familiar tightness in his chest returned, but he tried to dismiss it. *Exposure therapy*, he thought. *They just want to show off their genetic advancements. This is nothing.*

He tried to crack a joke, to deflect the discomfort. "Tastes nasty—maybe use some flavoring, like Pralines and Cream from Baskin Robbins."

He got no response. Not even the hint of a grin. Annoyed, he muttered sarcastically to himself, "These guys are a blast. They would make great drinking buddies."

The older guard didn't budge, his face as stoic as ever. "Sir, we can hear you. Patience will expedite the process."

Jason felt the seconds stretch into eternity. The sound of the mechanical rattling as the system processed his DNA filled the small, enclosed space. His breath became shallow, sweat trickling down his neck and under his arms. The walls of the portal seemed to close in on him, though he knew it was just his mind. He pushed against the door again, frustration building, setting off a loud alarming noise.

"Sir," the guard's voice came again, sharper now, "do not push. Wait for the system to confirm your identity."

Jason clenched his fists, trying to breathe through the mounting panic. The seconds passed with agonizing slowness. Finally, a faint buzz signaled the release of the locks.

Relief washed over him as he swung the door open. He hurried out of the turnstile, stepping into the building. The air felt like freedom as it filled his lungs, a weight lifting from his chest. Taking a deep breath, he made his way to the nearest restroom.

In front of the mirror, he splashed cold water on his face, trying to shake the tension still coiling in his core. He caught his reflection—sweat circles under his arms, his shirt clinging to his back. His eyes rested on the hand dryer across the room, and he quickly removed his shirt to dry it. As he stood alone in the restroom, the full impact of his new life hit him.

The Glass Fountain. The secrecy. The guarded technology. Even he was a riddle. He found it ironic that they were preventing one of the biggest secrets from reentering the very building where it was grown—his body. Did they know and were just acting a part in an elaborate play? Or were they just as blind as everyone else?

Chapter 14: Gordon

Gordon Formell entered the conference room on the eighth floor with quiet authority, his presence immediately commanding attention. The team, already seated, shifted in their chairs with murmurs and the soft clink of coffee cups against polished wood. They straightened as he made his way to the head of the table. Each place setting was a study in order—laptops open, steaming cups of coffee at the ready, and neat stacks of documents topped with a solitary red pen. Along the wall, a side table offered an array of pastries and beverage urns, their warm, inviting aroma sharply contrasting the room's crisp formality.

"Good morning, everyone," Gordon began, the attention of those around him reflecting their respect. "Let's get started. Two new items to add to the agenda today: First, preparations for tomorrow's press conference; and second, the infomercial that aired yesterday."

His gaze swept over the group, briefly landing on Joan Bradley, his Marketing Director. Joan exuded competence, her notes were organized with precision. Her deep ebony skin, glowing with natural radiance, mirrored her vibrant energy. She was the embodiment of FOY's brand—intelligent, capable, and effortlessly elegant. Yet, he kept her outside the circle of those he trusted most.

He continued, "Before we dive into marketing, however, let's first discuss our operational metrics. Dr. Schickel?"

Dr. Schickel, FOY's Chief Medical Physician, grunted as he leaned forward and adjusted his laptop. His large frame strained against the edge of the table, and with a few quick taps, the screen at the far end of the room lit up with data and graphs. "As you can see, 149 out of 150 shells are performing as expected. The biotank environments are stable—no disruptions to electrical stimulation or nourishment functions. Also, our primary recycling system is now fully operational, thanks to Robert and his team."

Gordon shifted his gaze to Robert Gruber, the Chief Technology Officer, who beamed at the praise, rubbing the scar on his chin. Gruber's technical brilliance was undeniable, as were his ruggedly handsome looks. Gordon often mused that Gruber could have been the public face of FOY—if not for his eccentricities and unconventional personality.

In stark contrast, Dr. Schickel appeared flustered, dabbing at his rosacea-red nose and wiping his ample forehead with the same napkin. The sparse brown hair that remained, forming a horseshoe pattern around his head, was unkempt, as were his wild eyebrows. Gordon couldn't help but reflect on why he had labeled Schickel as an "internal"—a term for staff members rarely seen by new clients or investors.

Schickel's disheveled appearance was a sharp departure from FOY's meticulously polished public image. In fact, he might have fired him years ago—not just for his looks, but for his ethics. Yet Schickel remained the only one capable of performing a successful transformation.

"There was one anomaly," Schickel continued, his tone now laced with concern. "Shell #66. Hemoglobin A1C levels spiked unexpectedly, indicating the onset of diabetes. Following protocol, we flushed the biotank, and Robert and I initiated the disposal process. Fortunately, Harper secured the client's approval to restart the collection at no additional cost. Tanya, can you explain how the system caught the issue?"

Tanya Malbern, the only other "internal" at the table, was FOY's Chief Computer Architect. Gordon had made beauty a prerequisite for hiring, but with Tanya and Schickel, he made exceptions. While he valued Tanya's brilliance as a programmer, he often found himself distracted when he saw her. Her features— brown hair, brown eyes, a small nose, and full lips—should have been attractive; yet somehow, they never quite added up. It was as though she defied Aristotle's principle that the whole is greater than the sum of its parts.

Her voice broke his train of thought. "I adjusted the real-time telemetry thresholds to minimize false alarms. The only alert sent to our 24/7 operational staff was for shell #66. No longer desensitized by the usual flood of alerts, they responded immediately. The system is now performing as intended."

Joan leaned forward, her sharp gaze narrowing as she turned her attention to Schickel. "Who else knows about shell #66?"

Schickel hesitated, his eyes dropping to the table. "Other than the client, only those in this room and a few lab technicians are aware. Our NDAs ensure confidentiality. I recommend we keep this within the team."

Joan shook her head. "I disagree. The client may have shared this with others. Transparency is our best option."

Gordon nodded thoughtfully. "Agreed. We'll make it clear that no one's health was ever at risk and that we're investigating the tissue loss to prevent further issues. Does that work for you, Joan?"

Joan looked uncomfortable for the first time. "Well, I... yes, I suppose so."

"Great. Dr. Schickel, I'll need a root cause analysis on my desk as soon as possible."

Schickel's face flushed an even deeper red, but he nodded. Gordon turned his attention back to Joan. "Now, about tomorrow's press conference: What's the plan?"

Joan's focus returned, her posture straightening as she spoke. "We'll emphasize our commitment to safety and cutting-edge technology. If pressed on price, we'll highlight the extensive research costs and the quality of our product offering."

"And where will we be holding the event?"

"As for logistics—it will take place on our front steps. The press kits are ready, and your opening statement is in the handouts, along with a list of anticipated questions and responses."

Gordon scanned the materials. "Excellent. We need to ensure a clear, consistent message. Joan, continue."

Joan went on, "After your introduction, you'll handle most of the questions, redirecting to the appropriate experts when needed. Oliver will address facilities, Robert will cover technology, Harper will discuss financials, and I'll take questions on marketing. Jason Fabrikant has been prepped for select inquiries as well."

Gordon gave a subtle smile, pleased with Joan's thoroughness. "Thank you, Joan. You've planned this well. I'll practice my speech later, with you present. Now, what about the infomercial?"

Joan replied proudly, "Our online click-through rate has been very promising. We have the statistics and will share the analysis early next week. Additionally, the test audience responses were favorable. As for lessons learned, it's still too early to tell. We want to ensure that the depiction of the elderly in the video didn't offend anyone, but so far, I'm optimistic."

"Good," Gordon replied. "I think this is shaping up to be a successful day. Given the work we have in front of us, unless there's something urgent, I'd like to call the meeting adjourned."

After head nods from around the table, Gordon returned to his office, his eyes falling on a small acrylic block resting on his mahogany desk. The object—a shattered hourglass, its jagged glass fragments suspended inside—served as a three-dimensional rendering of FOY's logo. It symbolized the company's relentless drive to break through the barriers of life expectancy. The block caught the light, its transparency reflecting FOY's commitment to openness, much like the fountain in the center of the building, which stood as a reminder of their lofty ideals.

For a moment, Gordon allowed himself to reflect on his successes. Most notably, he was satisfied with his choice of Jason Fabrikant. Jason was everything they needed—articulate, likable, attractive, athletic—and had just the right amount of public intrigue. The accident that had nearly ruined him had only made his recovery more captivating.

The moment had finally come—the culmination of over twenty years of hard work. The team he'd assembled—a group of exceptional minds—had made FOY what it was today. Robert, the newest addition just a few years ago, had opened up new avenues, injecting fresh ideas and perspectives, changing the course, the solution. But each member was integral, and more importantly, each one had come under his control—every single one, except for Schickel. The one outlier in an otherwise carefully structured system.

Now, FOY was positioned to showcase the impossible—restoration of youth. He savored the pride of his accomplishments, a journey that had started with a personal tragedy—the death of his wife from kidney failure—and evolved into a company fueled by the promise of immortality. FOY had begun as a small bridge between organ supply and demand, but it had grown into a pioneer in bioprinting and cloning. Now, with their ambitious goal of immortality within reach, they were on the verge of something extraordinary.

Tomorrow, they would reveal a new chapter in the world of medicine. It would be marketing at its finest.

Success brought pride, but it also exposed vulnerabilities. He reclined in his chair, a sense of unease creeping over him. There had been compromises—shadowed choices that had steered him into murky waters. What would his wife have thought? Gordon pushed her out of his mind.

He knew that protecting FOY's methods was paramount. His hand hovered over the phone before dialing the number of his most trusted employee. Granting the man's mother a life-saving organ had earned him an unbreakable loyalty, one that would last a lifetime. The call was answered instantly.

"Oliver," Gordon said, his voice steady but edged with urgency. "Have you disposed of our problem?"

Chapter 15: Jason

Once through security, Jason proceeded to his appointment with Dr. Schickel on the seventh floor. The facility visually invited him into its spacious center. Impressive as it was, to Jason, the building seemed to lack continuity. The first floor showcased a biophilic architectural style designed to connect occupants with nature. Sunlight streamed through expansive picture windows, making the lobby feel even larger and creating the impression that the outside was an extension of the space.

Through these windows, he enjoyed a clear view of the outer gardens, witnessing the rebirth that only spring could offer. Deciduous wisteria and dogwood trees were on the verge of full bloom, while the warming weather infused life into their new, unblemished leaves. In a nearby plot, seedlings had germinated, stretching and curling to capture the sun's rays, poised to flourish into a lush garden. Surrounding the grounds, vibrant tulips in red, orange, yellow, green, blue, indigo, and violet bloomed in abundance. He couldn't help but admire the caretakers' skill, grinning at FOY's intentional message of its ability to nurture life.

Inside the building, flowering plants abounded, including birds-of-paradise. Jason learned these colorful flowers symbolized life on Earth, with their long stems representing spiritual ascension and enlightenment. He particularly appreciated the craftsmanship of the windows, etched to act as prisms, casting rainbow patterns on the white marble floor as if redirecting the tulip colors from outside.

The main level housed various long-term rehabilitation services, along with the security station, offices, a cafeteria, and an upscale restaurant.

The second through sixth floors were reserved for storage and they had an entirely different feel. These levels embodied the art of possible and the future of medical advancements. They contained cloned replicas of FOY's clients—bodies offering the ultimate promise of youth. This five-floor structure, referred to as the "Glass Fountain," was visible from a distance but accessible only to select cleared FOY personnel. Its name derived from its unique configuration and construction materials.

The fountain consisted of individual enclosures known as biotanks. Each biotank contained a single cloned body suspended in liquid and tethered to life support equipment. The biotanks, connected in succession, formed a large, circular enclosure enveloping the entire floor. From the first floor, the elevator passed through the center, offering a view from the inside of the technology at work. Each floor, from the second to the sixth, had identical glass enclosures. Altogether, the fountain resembled a huge cylinder, like a stack of five transparent donuts, with each layer representing a different level. The view from the elevator was designed to impress, with water cascading over every exposed surface of the glass, obscuring the details of the subjects housed inside. This flowing water aimed to protect the clients' identities while providing a refreshing auditory and visual experience.

While the biotanks met the biological needs of the shells growing within, the vast glass structure contributed to the building's aesthetics, demanding attention and awe. The combination of the young contained within and the flowing water on its surface made the structure a literal "Fountain of Youth," a physical manifestation of FOY's namesake. Jason stared at it with mixed feelings, knowing his own body had been on display, growing inside its enclosure.

Lost in thought, he nearly collided with a man pushing a bucket and mop.

Jason held up his hand. "I apologize. I wasn't looking where I was going."

"You look pale, sir. Can I help you?" The man wore white overalls, with the FOY logo on his baseball hat.

"I'm okay, just distracted. Thanks, though."

"You look familiar. Have we met?"

Jason shook his head, "I don't believe so."

The man squinted his eyes and moved on, leaving Jason wondering if he recognized him from the years when his shell had grown in the fountain.

Turning his attention back to his destination, he thought about the seventh floor, which was sterile and clinical. The ambiance resembled that of a hospital, favoring function over aesthetics. He knew this level well, having spent a few months preparing for his surgery and recuperating there. It contained operating and recovery rooms, as well as offices for medical staff, along with financial, marketing, and facility support services.

Above that was Gordon Formell's space, with his office and adjacent conference rooms spanning the entire eighth floor. Although accessible from the elevator, unlike the other floors, entry required a cipher or key. Jason had never been in Gordon's office, but it was described as masculine, maroon, and lavishly furnished.

He had also heard rumors of a ninth floor, but Jason remained skeptical. From the outside, there were no visible windows indicating another level existed, and the elevator did not offer an option above the eighth floor.

Beneath it all was a basement level, about which Jason knew the least. It served two primary functions. First, it housed the command-and-control operational center, monitoring the fountain and the life forms it contained. Second, it provided lab space for the research underpinning FOY's mission to extend the human lifespan.

As Jason approached the elevator, the fountain loomed above him, its cascade shimmering under the artificial light. A plain-faced man entered just before him, wearing jeans and a white shirt with the FOY logo. The man pressed the button for the seventh floor, correctly assuming that Jason was headed there too. Jason felt as though he were being escorted, always suspecting he was under a watchful eye at FOY. To him, FOY stood for 'Forever Observing You."

As the elevator ascended, Jason was mesmerized by the fountain. Hundreds of clones surrounded him, semi-curled and suspended in gel, growing as if in a petri dish. The shells were pale and naked. Though it was difficult to see details through the flowing water, each body seemed disconnected, their eyes vacant. As Jason stared, the bodies, in turn, also stared—mindlessly and in random directions, some even toward the passengers in the elevator. This collective staring amplified his discomfort at being watched. Despite benefiting from the rejuvenation process, he found the fountain deeply disconcerting.

As the elevator rose to the seventh floor, he became entranced by one young female form staring blankly in his direction. Water trickled in a manner that allowed him to catch clearer glimpses of her features. She appeared about ten years old, glowing with innocence. Struck by her childlike beauty, knowing she was just a shell available for transplant, he still empathized with her isolation. He resisted the irrational thought that she needed loving parents to embrace and care for her. Memories of his own childhood—or lack thereof—briefly surfaced, tugging at his conscience.

Then, unexpectedly, her eyes darted up, locking directly onto his. Jason froze, his breath catching in his throat. Although her head remained still, her brow furrowed as she peered at him intensely. He scanned the other clones and saw no other eye movements. Staring back at the young girl, he felt a chill run down his spine. Her head now tilted slightly, moving, tracking the elevator as it ascended, her expression darkening with unmistakable anger.

Flustered, Jason pointed at the girl to the other occupant. Unhearing and unseeing, the man was softly humming, deafened by his earbuds and oblivious to the entire situation. A ding rang out—a forewarning of their arrival on the seventh floor. Jason turned back to the girl, but the elevator's landing platform obscured his view. The doors opened.

Chapter 16: Old Man

The old man fought against the suffocating confines of the body bag, his struggle stretching through endless hours. He continued to gnaw at the plastic until he finally managed to rip a hole large enough for escape. A faint sliver of light crept in from beneath the door—left on by whoever had last visited—casting just enough illumination to guide his desperate work.

Finally, with great effort, he emerged fully from the bag and lay on the cold surface of the gurney, gasping for breath. His eyes darted around, taking in his surroundings. Rows of heavy metal shelves, twelve feet high and stacked with plastic bins and supplies, lined the walls. It was a storage room, sterile and cold. The sense of isolation pressed against him, but he knew one thing: he had to move quickly.

Summoning his remaining strength, he swung his legs over the edge of the gurney and attempted to stand. As his feet touched the floor, the gurney rolled out from under him, sending him crashing to the floor. Pain shot through his body as his backside struck the unforgiving surface. Dizzy and disoriented, he groaned and tried to push himself up, only to fall forward, splitting his lip and chipping a tooth.

He stayed motionless for a moment, fighting the urge to cry out. Screaming would accomplish nothing. He needed to stay calm.

"Survive," he whispered to himself.

With grim determination, he crawled on hands and knees toward a corner of the room. His bound wrists and ankles made every movement awkward, but he eventually propped himself against the wall and slowly, painstakingly, rose to his feet. The room spun, and tiny stars danced in his vision. He closed his eyes, breathing deeply, waiting for the dizziness to pass.

In the background, the hum of electronics was a constant presence, as though the building itself was alive, watching, reporting.

When the nausea subsided, he penguin-walked toward the nearest shelf, his bound feet limiting his stride. His eyes scanned the supplies until they landed on a scalpel. Relief surged through him.

With the blade, he carefully cut through his restraints, wincing as the tight bonds peeled away from his skin. Freed at last, he rummaged through the shelves, finding a set of scrubs that he quickly slipped on for warmth, doubling them up in layers to fight the chill in his bones.

At a nearby sink, he fumbled with the faucet until water sputtered out. Craning his neck under the stream, he gulped greedily, the cool liquid soothing his parched throat. But his stomach, unaccustomed to any nourishment, rebelled. A sharp cramp doubled him over, and he retched violently, the sound echoing through the room.

He steadied himself, trying to stop the dry heaving, his body trembling from the exertion. This time, he was more cautious. He allowed the water to trickle into his mouth, swallowing slowly, letting his system adjust. When he was done, he steadied himself and turned the faucet to warm, cupping his hands beneath the stream.

The heat seeped into his stiff, aching fingers, and he held them there, letting the warmth bleed into his frozen joints. Pain lanced through his hands—a cruel reminder of the numbness retreating—but with it came the faint tingling of circulation returning. It was agony, but it was also life.

Escape was his next thought. His eyes scanned the room once more. There, on another gurney, was a different body bag. He saw the name tag: "A. Grier, donor #30." He approached the bag, his heart heavy. Inside was a cadaver, an older man—likely Mr. Grier. He checked his own bag and confirmed his worst fear. His name was listed too. Whoever had left him here knew exactly who he was, and they had abandoned him, leaving him to die. *That solves the mistaken identity question.*

His mind, clouded with exhaustion, tried to piece together the events. The situation felt increasingly sinister, like a trap. Someone had planned this. He shuddered at the thought. He couldn't trust anyone. He had to stay hidden—out of sight, in the shadows. *Survive. Justice later.* Perhaps *revenge* was a better word.

His own plan began to form in his mind. He needed to cover his tracks. *I'm sorry, Mr. Grier,* he thought, guilt mounting. But survival came first. He swapped the name tags and began filling his own bag, now marked with Grier's name, with supplies he could use: gallon jugs of bleach, IV bags, and rolls of paper towels. He used surgical tape and self-adhering wraps to bind it all together, creating a semblance of a body. It took hours, and by the end, he was exhausted, trembling from the effort.

He lay on the floor for a moment, considering his next move. Then he heard voices approaching. Panic surged in his chest. He crawled behind a nearby cabinet, concealing himself in the shadows. The door opened with a loud clatter as a man in a white smock entered, pushing a rolling metal table ahead of him. The lights flicked on, the brightness stinging.

"Brr… I can't get used to this cold room. I can see my breath. We're looking for donor #29. The client cleared the assessment phase," the man in the smock grumbled.

A second man, wearing camouflage, followed him in and pointed to a gurney across the room. "It's over there. Let's grab it and go. Gordon wants this over with."

The man in the smock rolled the metal table over and glanced at the name tag. His brow furrowed. "Wait, this is #30. You're slipping, my friend." He scanned the room, his eyes landing on another gurney. "Check that one."

The second man inspected the other bag and grunted. "Yes, this is #29. That's odd. Someone moved things around." He surveyed the room, his eyes narrowing. "And look at this shelf— everything's out of place. It's not like Robert to leave such a mess."

The first man didn't seem concerned. "Maybe he was in a hurry," he muttered.

The man in camo didn't act convinced. He began to scan the room, his sharp eyes missing nothing. The old man's heart thudded in his chest. He couldn't be found. He held his breath, praying the camo-clad man wouldn't notice him.

Then, with a loud thud, the man in the white smock dropped the body bag. The camo man rushed over to help, and they both grumbled as they lifted the bag onto the rolling table.

"Damn, this bag's heavier than I thought," the smock-wearer muttered. Embarrassment turned to irritation. "I needed help transferring him. While you're playing Sherlock Holmes, I'm trying to get this done. It's freezing in here, let's get this guy to the chamber."

The two men rolled the table out as the man in the smock continued to complain.

"Did you try the lasagna in the cafeteria yesterday? I'm thinking they used some of the discarded protein from shell #66."

"Well, that would be one way to eliminate all evidence," the other man replied.

"Gross," the first man muttered. "Sometimes I think—" Their voices trailed off as they exited the room, the door closing behind them. The unsettling silence that followed was broken only by the building's creaks and groans, as if it too disapproved of what had just occurred.

Chapter 17: Jason

Jason rushed out of the elevator; an upsetting chill crawling up his spine. The man beside him was oblivious, lost in his music as the lift doors slid shut. Jason stood in the hallway, disoriented, trying to make sense of the strange movements of the girl in the tank. Was it his newfound surge of hormones playing tricks on him? Or perhaps the claustrophobia? He took several deep breaths, attempting to shake off the unease, and forced himself to focus on his next task: meeting Dr. Schickel.

The corridor stretched out before him, a radial spoke branching from the seventh-floor elevator. The lobby was the center, with a spiderweb design guiding him to his appointment. He soon found himself standing in front of a door etched with the name 'Dr. Henry H. Schickel' on frosted privacy glass. The door was ajar, and he knocked firmly, causing it to open slightly. Inside, a deep voice called, "Come in."

Unlike his past experiences with other medical practices, the FOY staff operated with remarkable punctuality—no waiting, no excuses. Given the exorbitant fees patients paid, he assumed such responsiveness was part of the service customers demanded.

He pushed the door fully open and stepped inside, immediately noticing that there was no desk in front of him. The office setup struck him as odd: the desk was tucked into a corner, hidden from view as Jason entered. Once inside, he saw the back of Dr. Schickel's balding head, the doctor standing and absorbed in X-ray images on the wall. When he finally spun around to greet Jason, he extended one hand for a firm handshake, a hot beverage in the other.

"Hello, Mr. Fabrikant. Please, have a seat."

Jason couldn't ignore the doctor's disheveled appearance. His smock hung open, revealing a partially untucked shirt and a crooked gig line—far from the professionalism Jason had come to expect at FOY. The strain of Dr. Schickel's belly against his shirt buttons was impossible to miss, and Jason found himself wondering if employees like him were offered the transformation as a perk. If so, this man seemed overdue.

The thought lingered as he noticed a trend: one by one, the FOY staff looked less polished, their imperfections more glaring. Jason wasn't surrounded by flawless faces anymore. He wasn't a new client being courted.

They both sat down as Dr. Schickel asked, "Mr. Fabrikant—"

"Please, call me Jason."

The doctor continued, "Perfect. Jason, then."

The soothing cadence of the doctor's voice didn't match his aura. Despite the deep baritone, there was something unsettling about the man—maybe it was the provocative art on his walls, suggestive of the feminine form. Jason couldn't put his finger on it.

The doctor set his cup down. "We've met before, but I imagine you don't remember."

"Where?"

Dr. Schickel grinned, flashing his coffee-stained teeth. "On the operating table. I was your surgeon. You were out with anesthesia."

Jason blinked, surprised. He had never been introduced to the man who operated on him. On the day of the transformation, he'd been heavily medicated and couldn't recall meeting anyone beyond the masked staff guiding him to the procedure.

"It's you I owe thanks to, then."

The doctor nodded. "It was a team effort, I assure you. How are you feeling?"

"Couldn't be better."

Dr. Schickel began to probe. "Have you had any side effects—nausea, dizziness, headaches?"

"Nothing." Then, recalling the odd sensation in the elevator, he added, "Maybe a little paranoia."

Dr. Schickel raised an eyebrow, intrigued. "Paranoia?"

Jason hesitated, then explained, "I could've sworn one of the clones looked at me as I was coming up. It almost seemed... cognizant."

The doctor's face softened as he closed his eyes for a long blink before speaking. "You're not paranoid. As you know, the shells are exercised with electronic stimulation multiple times a day to prevent atrophy. You probably just caught one of their exercise routines."

"I guess," Jason muttered, tension easing slightly as the explanation sank in. His gaze drifted to the doctor's desk, where an image of the fountain lay next to a pen. Two cells in the image were circled—both females.

Dr. Schickel seemed to catch his glance and quickly covered the picture by placing an open folder of Jason's medical file on top. He flipped through the pages with practiced efficiency, mumbling approval sounds. "It looks like you're recovering remarkably well. The X-rays show excellent healing of your skull." He rose and walked behind Jason, gently feeling the incision on his head. "You heal quickly. There'll be little scarring, and what does show will be hidden by your hair." He smirked. "Let's hope you don't go bald prematurely like me."

Jason wasn't sure whether to laugh at the self-deprecating humor, so he simply stayed quiet.

"I'm pleased with your progress, but let me look you over anyway," Dr. Schickel said.

The doctor proceeded with a routine check-up: measuring Jason's blood pressure, listening to his breathing, examining his pupils, and testing his reflexes. "Everything looks good," Dr. Schickel said, jotting notes. "Your vitals are normal, and your bloodwork came back without any outliers. Physically, you're in excellent shape—like a healthy twenty-five-year-old." He paused. "I was thinking of daily check-ups at first, but I believe we can scale that down to once a week."

Jason nodded. "What about my diet? The cardiologist said I could resume normal eating."

Dr. Schickel smiled. "I'd agree. No restrictions anymore. Now, psychologically, we anticipated some adjustment. I've heard about your claustrophobia since the transformation. This is a new symptom, correct?"

Jason nodded again. "Yeah. Those turnstiles at the security entrance are suffocating, and MRIs are a challenge as well. I've also been having nightmares—being trapped in a small space I can't escape."

Dr. Schickel paused, then handed him a card from his desk. "I'd like you to reach out to Dr. Lazarus. She's a top psychiatrist with a stellar reputation. She runs her own practice outside FOY, but she's excellent." The card read: 'Dr. Josephine Lazarus, Board Certified Psychiatrist.'

Placing a hand on Jason's shoulder, Dr. Schickel said, "You're recovering faster than we anticipated, Jason. You've been given a rare opportunity. You're blessed. Now, is there anything else I can do for you, my friend?"

Jason widened his eyes for exaggerated emphasis. "Actually, yes. Can you tell me how to get to the stairs?"

Dr. Schickel laughed. "That elevator really rattled you, huh? Understandable. Take a left out my door and keep walking. You'll see signs leading the way."

Jason grinned, relieved. "Thanks, Doc."

"No problem. Same time next week?"

"Yeah, sounds good." Jason shook the doctor's hand before heading for the door, grateful to avoid another encounter with the Glass Fountain.

Chapter 18: Bastien

Bastien slept late, knowing the night ahead would be long. He didn't bother with food or even brushing his teeth. Instead, he dressed quickly, grabbed the carry-on backpack he had pre-packed the night before, and made his way to Dulles Airport. Traffic was lighter than usual, which suited him. He parked in the economy lot, then took the Green Line bus to the main terminal. But he didn't go inside. Instead, he caught a ride on the Avis shuttle to the rental facility, then walked to Hertz, choosing a convoluted path to ensure no one could easily trace it back to his car, even with the security cameras.

At Hertz, he rented a small sedan using a fake driver's license and a matching credit card. From there, he drove directly to Arlington National Cemetery.

Considering the vast 639 acres of burial ground, it was surprisingly easy to find the gravesite the Dish had chosen. Bastien stood in front of the headstone that read: *Grace M. Hopper, RADM US Navy, World War II, Korea, Vietnam, Dec 9, 1906 – Jan 1, 1992.*

He smirked at the choice. Admiral Grace Hopper, a pioneer in computer technology and co-inventor of COBOL, had popularized phrases like, "It is easier to beg forgiveness than to ask for permission," and had coined the term "bug" to describe a problem with computer programs. Bastien couldn't help but think the Dish had chosen Hopper for her defiant spirit—a fitting parallel to their mission. Hopper wouldn't have asked for permission either, not with what they were about to do.

Near the tombstone, a small vase held a single flower—an aster. Bastien's mood soured immediately. The aster symbolized patience, and that irked him. Was the Dish sending a subtle message? Was she wavering?

"You better have come through," he muttered.

He crushed the flower in his fist and tossed it aside, tipping the vase to pour out its contents. Two small vials tumbled into his palm. He smiled. The samples were there, just as promised. Bastien inspected them quickly, ensuring everything was in order before heading to his next destination: FOY.

Bastien soon found himself back on the road. Within the hour, he was parked outside the FOY building, ready for his stakeout. His fingers tapped an uneven rhythm against the steering wheel, a telltale sign of his restlessness. Waiting had never been his strong suit, and today was no different. The minutes felt like hours, each one dragging on longer than the last. He caught himself checking the time every few moments, muttering curses under his breath. Patience was critical now, but it grated against every fiber of his being. The DNA samples from the Dish were secured, his plans meticulously arranged, and every contingency accounted for.

A change of clothes, including the white coat, sat within arm's reach, along with his "Men's Pocket Toilet"—a collapsible bottle for relieving himself. The thought of using it reminded him of the human condition and its toll on the environment, particularly the dependence on plastic.

The Semtex, however, was another story. That he was eager to use. Flexible and malleable, the red clay was more than just a bomb—it was a disguise. Molded against his torso, it transformed into a sagging belly, serving both as a costume and a deadly weapon. Two birds, one stone. The irony wasn't lost on him: the man who had invented it had met a fitting end in an explosion.

Bastien cracked open a Red Bull, his eyes scanning the steady flow of people. Medical staff, patients, contractors, and workers moved in and out of the building. None were the technician he was waiting for. A man limping toward the parking lot caught his attention. He lingered by a truck but didn't get in.

Suspicion flared. Was he FOY security in disguise? Bastien scrutinized him. Too old. Too obviously a patient.

His focus shifted to the building's surveillance cameras. He methodically counted them, memorizing their angles and blind spots. When he glanced back, the old man was gone. Bastien squinted, his eyes sweeping the lot. Where had he gone? The truck hadn't moved.

A flicker of doubt crept in. *Am I losing my edge?*

He downed another Red Bull, the liquid burning uncomfortably in his stomach and bladder. Reluctantly, he turned to the Men's Pocket Toilet to stay focused. Now, with the discomfort gone, he could dedicate his full attention to the task at hand.

He shifted his gaze back to the FOY entrance, continuing his stakeout. The minutes stretched out, his frustration mounting with each passing second. Bastien drummed his fingers harder, then stopped, annoyed at the sound. *Come on*, he thought, gritting his teeth. He shifted in his seat, glancing between the door and his watch, his leg bouncing uncontrollably.

Months of preparation hinged on this. He just needed his target to step through that door. The waiting game was always the hardest part, but it was one he intended to win. Time gnawed at him, every second feeding the simmering anger threatening to boil over. The Dish had checked the calendar; the technician's shift was over and should have left by now. *Dammit, is she toying with me?*

Chapter 19: Jason

Thinking of the young girl in the biotank, Jason left Dr. Schickel's office, relieved to avoid the elevator. Following the doctor's directions, he quickly found the staircase and began his descent, hopping downward and often skipping steps, enjoying his newfound agility. By the time he reached the bottom floor, he was still full of energy. He grinned, recalling how the physical exertion, just months ago, would have left him gasping for breath and moving at a fraction of the speed.

As Jason exited the stairwell, he expected to see familiar landmarks guiding him to the lobby. Instead, he found himself surrounded by white walls and dim corridors—a stark contrast to the bright, open-concept space he had anticipated. The motion-sensitive lights flickered on as he moved, revealing a maze of identical hallways. After only a few steps, he reached a T-intersection and hesitated. With no signs to guide him, he turned right and pressed on.

The deeper he went, the more his disorientation grew. He triggered more lights and took increasingly random turns, soon venturing beyond what he could confidently retrace. Jason was lost.

A wave of relief hit him when he noticed a fire escape map mounted on the wall. Studying the layout, he realized his mistake: he had overshot the main floor in his eagerness, landing him in the basement. Embarrassed, he memorized a path back to the staircase and turned to leave.

Faint noises suddenly stopped him. Curious, he focused, impressed by his newly heightened hearing, which allowed him to pinpoint the direction with ease. The FOY doctors had explained that his transformation restored not just his strength, but the intricate coordination between his ears and brain. He could now localize sounds as he had in his youth, with precision. What once had been a muddled sense now worked perfectly. A smile tugged at his lips as he marveled at the clarity—another affirmation of FOY's success.

The sound grew louder as he followed it, though its nature eluded him. It was a blend of whimpers, howls, and shrieks—inhuman yet unmistakably anguished. Subconsciously, Jason began to tiptoe. The eerie chorus guided him to a door marked "Animal Lab: No Unauthorized Entry."

Jason hesitated, his hand hovering over the doorknob. He tested it lightly, expecting it to be locked. It wasn't. The knob turned easily.

With the doorknob still turned in his hand, he pressed his ear to the door and listened. The sounds within were clearer now: whimpering, frantic shuffling, and occasional sharp cries. Jason's chest tightened. Despite his better judgment, he pushed the door open and stepped inside.

The smell hit him first: an overpowering blend of bleach, waste, and decay. He stifled a gag, his hand instinctively covering his nose. The source of the sounds became clear as he flicked on the light. Cages lined the walls, holding animals of various species and sizes. Larger enclosures housed pigs, goats, and chimpanzees, their cement floors stained and slick. Metal racks along the opposite wall contained medium-sized animals—dogs, cats, ferrets—stacked two cages high. Toward the back of the room, smaller cages were crammed into towering shelves, holding rabbits, guinea pigs, mice, and rats.

Jason's eyes moved from cage to cage. Many of the animals bore signs of cranial surgery: scars spiraling around their skulls or circular marks where bone had been removed and replaced. Some appeared comatose, their shallow breaths the only indication of life. Others, yet untouched by experimentation, were the ones making the most noise—as if they sensed their fate.

Compelled forward, Jason passed through an archway into a second room. This area was set up for procedures. Scrubs and lab coats hung on hooks, with gloves, hairnets, and booties neatly arranged on shelves. He moved through another opening into a third space, a small operating room. Two tables dominated the area, each equipped with restraints and medical instruments.

On one table lay a chimpanzee, restrained at the limbs and head. Its skull had been surgically modified, metal plates grafted to bone in a way that suggested preparation for additional procedures, and cranial space. Bloodstains marred the adjacent table, evidence of a recent operation.

Jason froze, his eyes locked on the chimpanzee. The animal's body was limp, but its eyes were wide open, filled with a haunting awareness. Its lips moved. Jason leaned closer, his pulse pounding. Was it mouthing a word?

"Help," Jason whispered, testing the thought aloud. "Are you saying 'help'?"

The chimp blinked slowly, then mouthed the word again.

A chill ran down Jason's spine. "Not possible," he muttered, shaking his head.

Before he could react further, the sound of the hallway door opening snapped him to attention. He darted behind a large crate, its faint acetone smell making him wince. Two men entered the first room, wheeling a hand truck. One was in a suit, the other in camo.

"Why the hell wasn't the door locked?" the man in camo barked, his tone sharp with irritation.

"Must have been Schickel, he's getting sloppy," the man in the suit replied, his voice equally annoyed.

"He also left the light on. Whatever, let's just get this crate upstairs and be done."

Jason's pulse quickened. If the men came near the crate, they'd see him instantly. He shifted carefully, his eyes darting to a supply closet just a few feet away. As the men maneuvered their hand truck around a corner, turning their backs, he slipped into the closet and eased the door shut, leaving it slightly ajar to get a view.

From his new hiding spot, Jason watched as the men approached the crate he had just abandoned. Neither seemed interested in using the sinks or protective gear.

He held his breath, silently praying they wouldn't notice him. The men secured the crate to the dolly and maneuvered it out of the room. As they left, they turned off the light and locked the door behind them.

Jason exhaled, his body trembling with adrenaline. He waited until the sound of their footsteps faded, then carefully slipped out, now in complete darkness. To move, he was forced to rely on his sense of touch. As he moved through the operating room, his fingers brushed against a cold metal table. Then, as he continued to the room with the animals, his finger slipped through a cage and made contact with something wet and furry. He felt a bite and recoiled. Heart racing, he proceeded, now careful to avoid using his hands.

The sounds of the animals grew louder as he approached the door leading to the hallway. Taking a steadying breath, he slipped into the corridor, quickly checking the bite mark on his hand. The animal hadn't drawn blood.

Happy to be out of the lab, he began retracing his path back to the staircase, careful and deliberate in the dim corridors. But as he neared the staircase, he caught a flicker of movement down a dimly-lit corridor. A man in a white smock stood at the far end, watching him, then he disappeared. Each time Jason turned his head to look, the figure darted around a corner, only to reappear moments later.

Unease prickled at Jason's skin. He hurried up the stairs, his heart pounding. When he finally emerged into the familiar lobby, he couldn't shake the feeling that eyes were still on him.

Approaching the security turnstile, Jason glanced at the guards, wondering if they had been alerted to his activities below. They showed no sign of suspicion. Relieved but shaken, he stepped into the mantrap and followed procedure, offering his saliva for swabbing. He waited for the locks to disengage, clearing him to pass.

But the locks didn't release. Instead, an alarm blared, trapping him in place.

Chapter 20: Harper

Harper Faulton, FOY's striking CFO, steered her yellow Corvette Stingray along the western bank of the Potomac, the D.C. skyline receding behind her. Crossing into Virginia, she arrived at a 16-acre estate once owned by George Washington. In full view of the river, the Graff family's opulent mansion sat like a crown jewel.

The Mount Vernon estate, valued at over $60 million, offered sweeping views of the Potomac, but it wasn't just the scenery that made it impressive. The main house—excluding the carriage and guest houses—boasted only seven bedrooms but twice as many bathrooms. This peculiar arrangement was necessary to accommodate the spa, gym, home theater, panic room, indoor pool, and steam room, all of which added to its decadence.

Harper's excitement simmered beneath her calm exterior. Today, she would finally meet Gerald Graff and his family. The international businessman was notoriously hard to pin down, always traveling. But when his plans changed unexpectedly, Harper had jumped at the chance to secure a meeting.

She had done her homework. Gerald, at just fifty-four, was unusually young for a self-made billionaire. He'd built his fortune by marrying GPS technology with business applications, selling his start-ups to larger corporations for a tidy profit. From there, he had expanded his wealth through savvy venture capital investments and the stock market, becoming one of the top 200 richest people in the world. Opportunistic by nature, Gerald was exactly the kind of investor Harper needed to propel FOY to new heights. Her ambition was to double the client base each year, filling the showroom, and, in the process, elevating her status beyond even more rich men.

Harper passed through the security gates and parked beneath the portico. Luxurious carriage lighting bathed the entrance, casting a glow so sharp it would expose even the smallest imperfection—yet there were none to be found on her pristine vehicle.

The Graff family chauffeur appeared, offering to park her car. Harper accepted with a smile, stepping out and surveying the grounds. A butler emerged from behind the grand African mahogany doors. "Miss Faulton?" the butler asked, his tone respectful yet expectant.

"Yes," Harper replied, her voice smooth.

"Please, follow me." He led her into the living room, where she was invited to sit. The room was a striking blend of modern and classic design—a Sputnik chandelier, a Jackson Pollock original, and a Hanako wood coffee table making bold statements against the traditional architecture and herringbone floors. Harper observed it all with a practiced eye, noting the perfect blend of counterpoint and balance.

Moments later, Gerald and his wife, Pamela, entered with glasses of wine in hand. Gerald was a handsome man, his brown hair peppered with gray at the temples, fit yet shorter than average. Pamela, once the epitome of beauty, had seen the years chip away at her looks. Harper suspected, even without heels, Pamela might be slightly taller than her husband. As they greeted her, Harper rose, even taller, a subtle statement of the power dynamics at play.

Pamela, ever the gracious hostess, broke the silence. "I see you have water. Would you prefer a glass of wine instead?"

"Water is perfect, thank you," Harper responded, her voice warm yet calculated. *Stay lucid.* "I'm so glad we could meet today."

Gerald nodded. "Yes, we were supposed to fly overseas, but plans changed."

Harper smiled. "A trip on your Bombardier BD-700 private jet, I imagine?"

Gerald grinned. "You know your aircraft?"

"I know my clients," Harper replied, maintaining eye contact. "And I also know where you like to spend your early spring— aboard your 300-foot superyacht."

"True," he admitted. "We were supposed to be in Monaco right now, but instead we're here, sorting out matters with our baseball team."

"You have a passion for professional sports," Harper observed, catching the brief glance he threw toward her chest.

"The thrill of competition," Gerald said, his eyes narrowing, a glint of something more than just business in his gaze. "Though, I'll admit, I could make more money elsewhere. There's something about the energy it brings into our lives."

"Energy," Harper echoed, her voice low, eyes flashing with an undercurrent of meaning. "And power."

Pamela, redirecting the conversation, interjected with practiced ease. "How was your drive, dear? Any traffic?"

"D.C. traffic is always a challenge," Harper replied sleekly. "But luckily, FOY's headquarters isn't far from here. If I were coming from Georgetown, it would've been a different story. I suppose owning a helicopter would be the only way to bypass the congestion."

Gerald chuckled, shaking his head. "Too risky. A twin-engine jet can handle a failure, but a helicopter's a different story."

"You like to calculate the odds?" Harper asked, her eyes never leaving his.

"Always," he replied, a touch of pride in his voice. "I don't take chances unless I know the odds are in my favor."

"Well, if you're worried about risks," Harper said, leaning in slightly, her gaze unwavering, "I think our services might be just what you're looking for."

Gerald's interest piqued. "I'm listening."

Harper felt the shift as she slid seamlessly into her pitch. "We're all born with just one heart," she said, her tone measured.

Gerald arched an eyebrow. "Interesting how most of our organs come in pairs, but not all."

"Exactly," Harper nodded. "And that's where FOY comes in. We offer medical technology that provides a backup, a safeguard against risks like heart attacks. Imagine a world where the dangers of life don't necessarily mean the end. We also offer something even more revolutionary: a cure for Father Time."

Pamela, who had been quiet until now, spoke up. "I saw the infomercial. Very impressive."

Gerald's mind seemed to be churning. "We both watched the commercial. As far as guarantees, though, what if we get sick and are unable to complete the operation?"

"If needed, we can use a temporary 'loaned' shell until your genetic clone is ready," Harper explained glibly. "Of course, a catastrophic event, such as a helicopter crash, can't be undone."

Pamela became lost in her thoughts. "Imagine… youth—not wasted on the young." She turned to her husband, a wistful look in her eyes. "You know, like when we were penniless."

Harper barely acknowledged Pamela's comment. Her focus remained squarely on Gerald. "Although they say that the best things in life are free," she said, her smile knowing.

Gerald produced a Cheshire grin. "That brings back memories."

Harper's laugh, louder than necessary, caught Pamela's attention. Pamela offered, "Why don't we all take a seat on the sofa and relax?"

Harper slid between them, positioning herself so that she had a clear view of Gerald, her back slightly to Pamela.

Gerald, in turn, seemed more engaged than ever. "So, what exactly are you looking for—customers, investors, advice?"

As she opened a binder on her lap, her knee brushed against his. She placed her hand on his thigh, making sure Pamela could see. "All of the above. Many of our investors try our services first. They're so impressed, they end up becoming partners. We're always looking for private equity, especially from successful individuals like you."

Gerald puffed up at the compliment, clearly enjoying the attention. Harper noticed the subtle tension radiating from Pamela, simmering beneath the surface.

Pamela, eager to be included, asked, "What's involved as a donor?"

Harper's eyes remained locked on Gerald as though he asked the question. "It's simple," she said. "We just need a tissue sample and a fifty percent deposit. Everything can even be done right here, in your home. If you're interested in investing, we can schedule a VIP tour of our facility. You'll be impressed, I'm sure."

Harper knew when to shift gears. She had Gerald's interest firmly in hand. Turning now to Pamela, she adjusted her posture so they faced each other. She needed to turn Pamela's jealousy into something more powerful—a desire to turn back time.

Harper widened her blue eyes and held Pamela's hands in hers. "You're such a beautiful woman," she said, her voice soft and persuasive. "It's no wonder you caught the attention of such a successful man. Time takes away beauty, but it no longer has to. Our doctors can restore your youth, unlock your full potential. It's a miracle. And you deserve it, Pamela. You've earned it."

Harper could see the struggle in Pamela's eyes—part anger at her flirtatious manner, part longing. Youth, as it always did, won out. Pamela's entire demeanor shifted, her desire for youth overriding her jealousy. "How much does it cost?"

Harper's smile curled into one of victory, but her voice remained steady. "Youth is priceless," she said. "But I'm sure we can come to a mutually agreeable figure. If you're interested, we can meet anywhere you like to discuss the details. It's well within your means."

Gerald cut in. "I'll be out near Warrenton next week. If that's more convenient, we can discuss things further."

Harper knew exactly what that meant—Gerald wanted to meet her alone. The deal was as good as done, and she had an irresistible recipe for closing it. It wouldn't be long before she had his John Hancock, securing another victory. Feeling confident and masterful, she imagined herself celebrating her success under the Pollock painting, her body moving in wild, frenetic rhythms—mimicking the artist's chaotic pour and splash technique. But unlike him, her offerings were far from abstract. They were clear, calculated, and if she was ever caught, they would have her dead to rights.

Chapter 21: Jason

Jason stood trapped in the small vestibule, the alarm blaring, each shrill note gnawing at his nerves. The sound was deafening, intensifying his fear of the enclosed space. He pressed harder against the turnstile's push bar, his palms slick with sweat, but it refused to budge. The sensation of being trapped tightened in his chest. Panic began to claw at him, growing stronger with every passing second. A chilling thought crept in, too real to ignore: *What if they can't get me out?*

Banging on the glass, Jason tried to catch a guard's attention. One was already on the phone, while the other walked over from behind the desk.

"Sir, please remain calm," the guard said, his voice steady but distant. "It's probably just a technical malfunction. My partner is calling management now. You'll be out soon."

Jason nodded, but didn't reply. The air felt suffocating, and the enclosure seemed to press in around him. He pushed harder against the turnstile, trying to force it open, but it stayed firm. His breath hitched. The space was too tight.

"Sir, we've talked about this already," the guard snapped, his patience thinning. "Stop fighting the turnstile! Relax. You're only making it worse."

Jason barely heard him. His heartbeat thundered in his ears, drowning out the guard's voice. He slammed his shoulder into the glass, desperate for the vestibule to give way. He felt cornered, trapped like an animal. "I need to get out!"

"Calm down!" the guard barked. "It's locked! Don't make this ugly."

Jason ignored him; the words barely reached him over the pounding in his chest. The alarm continued to blare as his mind raced, scattered and panicked. He could barely keep his thoughts straight.

Suddenly, Gordon Formell appeared, flanked by four others. He moved behind the desk to check the monitor. Without sparing Jason a glance, he walked to the turnstile and instructed a guard, "Step aside."

The guard returned to his position behind the desk.

"Jason," Gordon said coolly, his voice apologetic but measured. "I'm sorry for the inconvenience. It seems we've had a system fault."

Jason's frustration bubbled over. "Is this some kind of ploy?" he demanded, his voice sharper than he intended.

Gordon gave him a puzzled look. "What? No. Listen to me. Did the sampling arm take two swabs, one after the other?"

Jason exhaled slowly, trying to steady himself. "No," he muttered, barely audible.

"The system thinks you've already left," Gordon said, his eyes narrowing as he glanced toward the guard who had just sat down. "The database must be out of sync. That's never happened before." He instructed, "Press the override button."

The guard leaned down, and Jason heard a faint buzz as the locks retracted.

Jason stepped through the turnstile, the air thick in his lungs. Once free, he bent over, hands resting on his knees, trying to catch his breath.

Gordon placed a hand on his shoulder. "You alright?"

Jason straightened up, shaking his head. "Not a fan of your cages, but thanks for the help."

Gordon's gaze lingered, a hint of suspicion in his eyes. "Stay out of trouble, will you?"

Jason didn't respond, simply nodding before walking out of the facility. He didn't want to think about what had just happened— he just wanted to leave.

Out in the parking lot, he spotted his truck. As he approached, a small slip of paper tucked under the windshield wiper caught his attention. He unfolded it. We'll meet soon, 0226.

The number stopped him cold. It was his bank PIN, a number he'd kept secret—only he and his sister knew it, and she had never used it. A memory flickered of the psychological screenings he'd undergone, the questions about his childhood, about Chewie, his old dog. The note sent a chill down his spine. Someone from FOY had followed up, and the timing was too strange. Was it a warning or a scare tactic? Did this all have to do with what he'd found in the basement?

Jason slid into his truck, discomfort still clinging to him. He didn't want to return to FOY, but he knew he had no choice. His contract required it.

He started the engine, the roar of it grounding him for a moment. As the automatic locks clicked, he felt the familiar weight of being trapped again. With a deep breath, he manually unlocked the doors and rolled down the windows. A breeze carried away some of the tension, but not enough. His mind still churned.

The only thing that calmed him was the thought of Rufus. He vowed to himself that he would open the cage door the first chance he got.

Chapter 22: Jason

Jason left FOY, feeling a sense of relief as the building shrank in his rearview mirror. He thought of his upcoming date—no, meeting—with Samantha. As he maneuvered through the usual DMV congestion, he finally arrived at M Street. Jason parked his truck in an hourly lot and walked the short distance to the bakery where they'd agreed to meet.

Before heading inside, however, he decided on a detour. A flower shop caught his eye, and he stepped in to buy a single rose. A dozen might seem over-the-top, even desperate, so he opted for just one. It felt more personal. Then, across the street, he spotted a chocolatier—another deviation from the plan. There, he bought half a pound of peanut butter cups—though not the Reese's variety—and had them boxed with a ribbon. He couldn't resist sampling one first.

With his purchases in hand, Jason returned to the bakery, ordered a small coffee, committed to getting used to the taste again. He was limiting his caffeine intake to mornings only, hoping it would help him rid himself of the nightmares, but he allowed this small indulgence. He'd already broken the rules by eating the chocolate. Finding a semi-secluded table where he could watch the door, he settled in, sipping his hot drink, waiting for Samantha to arrive.

Fifteen minutes later, she walked in, and Jason's breath caught in his throat. Gone was the practical professionalism in her medical attire; in its place was a vision of understated elegance. Samantha wore jeans and a three-quarter sleeve sweater adorned with a soft pink floral pattern, the delicate design complementing her perfectly. Three-inch heels completed the look, adding a touch of sophistication to her casual ensemble. She looked like spring personified, effortlessly in sync with the cherry blossoms in full bloom outside. Her clothes fit her figure with tailored precision, and Jason found himself utterly captivated, unable to tear his gaze away from the quiet radiance of her presence.

He stood to greet her, his pulse quickening. "Wow, you look gorgeous. Thanks for meeting me here."

Samantha beamed, a dimple flashing on her right cheek. Her eyes flicked to the flower. "You're sweet. Is that for me?"

Jason, momentarily distracted, forgot he was still holding the rose. He grinned, awkwardly handing her the chocolates from the table—not the flower. "You look gorgeous," he repeated, feeling a warmth spread through him. His words echoed in his mind— he'd said the same thing just moments ago. He couldn't hide the internal fireworks he felt. These feelings, so intense and forgotten, seemed to come from a place he thought had long been sealed away in a previous life.

Samantha pulled off the ribbon and opened the box. "Peanut butter cups! You remembered. Thank you." She smiled at the flower. "And a peach-colored rose. So beautiful. You don't see those often."

Jason blinked, still holding the rose in his hand. He extended it to her sheepishly. "The color represents gratitude. Thank you for saying yes when I asked you to meet me."

"Well, this meeting feels a bit different than I expected. But the meaning behind the rose, that's so old-fashioned. Very classy. Very thoughtful." As she inhaled the rose's fragrance, Jason found it hard to focus. The attraction was undeniable. *Old-fashioned? Be careful.*

After ordering Samantha a cappuccino and a croissant, Jason decided to break the silence. "So, tell me a little about yourself."

Samantha sipped her drink before speaking. "Well, there's not much to say. I grew up in San Jose, California. My family struggled with my dad's health—he had a weak heart. I guess that's why I gravitated toward cardiology. After working hard to get into Johns Hopkins, I moved to Baltimore."

Jason gave her a teasing smile. "You seem like the summa cum laude type."

Samantha's lips tightened slightly. "I was very dedicated to my studies."

"And…" Jason prompted, a grin tugging at his lips.

She relented with a soft laugh. "Okay, yes, summa cum laude."

Jason chuckled and took a bite of his croissant. He could feel the layers of her story beginning to unfold.

"After med school, I was settled in Baltimore, but then I met Gordon Formell. He made me an offer I couldn't refuse," Samantha continued, her eyes betraying a hint of frustration.

Jason raised an eyebrow. "What, is he related to Brando?"

Samantha frowned. "I'm sorry?"

Jason froze, then laughed awkwardly. "Just an old movie reference. Before your— I mean, *our*—ti.. What then?"

Samantha smiled, easing the moment. "Anyway, I accepted because I'd heard FOY was cutting-edge in organ transplants. I was hoping for an office at their headquarters in Virginia, but that's still up in the air. Honestly, I'm starting to lose patience."

Jason smiled. "You haven't lost this patient."

Samantha shook her head, smiling back. "Another dad joke. I see I'm going to need to keep you in check."

Jason gave a shamefaced grin. *Oh God, a lifeline please.*

She continued, more seriously now. "My real passion is to help people, but after a few years, I realized I wasn't doing a good job at balancing work and life. Last New Year's Eve, while everyone was kissing their loved ones, I made a resolution to put more effort into meeting people. A few months in, though, I've made little progress. I rarely get asked out, and when I do, it's usually disappointing."

Jason narrowed his brow, confused. "Maybe it's because you call them meetings and not dates?"

Samantha explained, "I generally don't date my patients."

"Is there any wiggle room in my case?"

Samantha teased, "Perhaps. It's still early; the jury's out. But to your credit, I did bend the rule already."

Jason pressed his lips together. "One strike against me?"

Samantha giggled. "Maybe not. Let me hear your story. Fill in the blanks for me."

Jason hesitated. He needed to invoke his "representative." His representative was more measured, less opinionated, and far more guarded when it came to revealing intimate details. His contract prohibited him from disclosing his age, but he wasn't accustomed to lying, especially to someone like Samantha. Answering her question required finesse—balancing the truth with the need for discretion, all while keeping his carefully curated persona intact.

"I grew up in Northern Virginia," he started, mindfully crafting his response. "I was always into sports, baseball in particular. When an injury cut my career short, I became a bit reclusive. Then I was approached by Gordon. He said he could help me, but I'd need to be sequestered for a few months."

Samantha's eyes widened. "You fast-forwarded pretty quickly there. So that's how you got involved in the FOY procedure?"

Jason kept his answer brief. "Yes."

She leaned in. "I sense there is more here. You were in solitude for months?"

Jason nodded, not elaborating. "Yes."

Samantha frowned and leaned back. "That's it? One-word answers? I spill my guts, and you give me nothing?"

Jason could tell she was frustrated, and he didn't know what to say. "I admit I'm being vague. Unfortunately, my hands are tied. I've made a promise; I can explain more after the press conference tomorrow. I know I seem a bit secretive."

Samantha paused, then softened. "I give you credit for holding to your word, though. Mysterious, but admirable." She switched gears. "What about relationships? I'm sure Formell doesn't have control over you sharing that."

Jason squirmed. "I'm not in one right now. Haven't been for a while." He kept the truth buried—it had been forty-five years, after all. That was information he couldn't share. Besides, it was too soon to talk about Anna. Not mentioning that he had been in love and had purchased a ring felt like a disservice to her life, but he had no choice.

"I've never been married and have no kids. I would love to have a family someday." Once the words left his mouth, he realized that at twenty-five years of age, it might seem early to be talking about having a family.

Samantha's eyes remained gentle. "What do you want from a partner?"

Jason thought for a moment. "Just that, a partner. Not someone to dominate or be dominated by. I want someone who wants to be equally invested, with the flexibility and support to pursue their own passions."

Samantha smiled, taking another sip of her cappuccino. A dab of froth clung to the tip of her nose, unnoticed.

Jason, fully amused, leaned forward. "I know you're in the throes of a tough interview, but do you have a mirror?"

Samantha looked panicked, fumbling through her bag until she found a compact. When she saw the smudge on her nose, she gasped. "How long has that been there?"

Jason teased, "Since your first sip."

Samantha burst out laughing, dissolving the tension completely. "No way!" she said, wiping the froth off her lip and laughing so hard that she let out a slight snort. They both laughed even harder, her eyes sparkling with a mix of embarrassment and elation.

From that moment on, the conversation flowed naturally. They continued to connect over their shared love of art, music, food, and literature, though they disagreed wildly on television shows. After a couple of hours, Samantha glanced at her phone.

"I should probably head home," she said. "It's getting late."

Jason didn't want their time together to end. "Maybe we could try this again tomorrow? Something a bit more formal, like the Greek place on the corner?"

Samantha's face brightened. "I love Mediterranean food. How about 7:30? I'll meet you there."

Jason noted that she still wasn't ready for him to pick her up. "Maybe even call it a date?"

Samantha paused, then smiled. "That would be nice."

They both stood, and Jason, feeling bold, gave her a quick kiss on the lips as she left. The kiss was brief, but unmistakable. Jason felt the chemistry. He felt he'd passed the interview.

Chapter 23: Jason

Jason left the bakery and drove to a small bar in Southeast D.C. He wore sunglasses and a hoodie, pulling it tightly over his head as he walked in. It had been months since he'd been out in public—aside from his date with Samantha—and even then, he remained acutely aware of his surroundings.

His eyes darted around as he slipped into the pub, taking in the dark atmosphere and the familiar smell of old wood mixed with stale beer. The vintage charm of the bar was spoiled only by the large, modern screens mounted above, showcasing sports in 4K resolution. It was a sports bar, but a quiet one—just the kind of place where Jason could blend in without drawing attention.

Bottles of booze gleamed on floating shelves, each label screaming for attention, though Jason wouldn't fall into that trap again. His focus immediately went to the man sitting at the bar—his former coach, Herman Williams—hunched over a mug. He was staring into it like it was some kind of crystal ball, searching for answers in the amber liquid.

It had been years since they'd spoken, and this would be their first face-to-face meeting since leaving the team. Jason had called Herman that morning, and although he didn't explain why, Herman agreed to meet. Jason insisted on secrecy, knowing the last thing he needed was FOY catching wind of the meeting.

Even in his mid-seventies, Herman's presence remained formidable. A black man and ex-professional baseball player himself, his prominent, barrel-shaped stomach sat high on his abdomen. Unlike most older men whose bellies sagged and jiggled over their belt buckles, Herman's physique had defied the forces of gravity. The size of his forearms and legs still conveyed the strength of a man who had once been very powerful. His head was exceptionally large, earning him the nickname "Hoghead"—a moniker he accepted with good humor, often doling out nicknames of his own to players.

Jason approached silently, slipping behind Herman. His hand came down firmly on his old coach's shoulder. The man tensed, every muscle in his body coiling as his head snapped around, eyes widening in aggression—as if about to deliver a punch.

"Oh my God, what the hell?" Herman muttered, his voice half-laughing, half-shocked.

Jason held a finger to his lips. "Remember, secrecy."

Herman blinked, his mouth falling open as he studied Jason, disbelief deepening on his face. His voice dropped to a near whisper, filled with confusion. "You're not Stone." He started laughing, too loudly. "You're his grandson, right? Or a double he found on the internet."

Jason tried to take on a serious demeanor, but a smile kept breaking through. "Hoghead, it's me."

Herman's laughter faltered. His eyes searched Jason's face, and for a moment, it seemed like he was expecting the real Jason to jump out from behind the counter and reveal himself. But when the Jason he knew didn't appear, Herman's smile faded. "Look, kid, this isn't funny. I don't like being messed with."

Jason's smile faded too, his tone more solemn. "I promise, it's me."

The coach's gaze softened as he studied Jason with growing recognition. "If you really are who you say you are, then what did I tell you the first time we met?"

Jason sat beside him, the memory coming back easily. "You said I had to decide if I wanted to play ball or play doctor; baseball and carousing didn't mix. You knew about my reputation back then."

Herman leaned back, his brow furrowing as he searched Jason's face for something more. For a moment, Jason could feel the weight of his old coach's scrutiny, as if Herman was seeing traces of a past that had been erased. Then Herman's expression shifted, and he nodded slowly, as if seeing the man he once coached in Jason's eyes. "Shit... it is you. Did you win a ticket on a time machine? What the hell, Stone?"

Jason chuckled, trying to ease the tension. "I can explain more tomorrow, but for now, let's just say I've undergone... a procedure."

The mention of the procedure seemed to freeze Herman for a moment. "Remarkable," he muttered. "Why didn't you tell me sooner?"

Jason leaned in closer, his voice lowering. "I've been completely sequestered for months. They wouldn't let me communicate with anyone or even leave the hospital until yesterday. This is my first full day of freedom. Quite frankly, I'm breaking my contract just by meeting you here. They wouldn't be happy about it."

Herman's eyes narrowed. "Who are 'they'?"

Jason avoided the question, his gaze shifting for a moment as if checking the room. "I need to iron out some things before the press conference."

Herman blinked, clearly still struggling to comprehend what was happening. "Press conference?" His voice wavered as the words left his lips.

Jason nodded, his face grim. "Yes, tomorrow my transformation goes public. I need to figure some things out before the world knows about it."

The silence stretched between them, and Herman's disbelief melted into cautious skepticism. "What do you need to figure out?"

Jason sighed, dragging a hand through his hair, his frustration apparent in the set of his jaw. "I'm sure I'll be asked what I'm going to do with my life. Odd as it sounds, I hadn't even considered that until yesterday. I mean, what the hell do I do now?"

Herman, still trying to catch up, leaned forward, his massive forearms resting on the bar. "Are you thinking about coming back to baseball?"

Jason hesitated, his eyes flickering to the screen above the bar, where a game was in full swing. The crack of a bat hitting a ball echoed through the room, bringing a rush of nostalgia. Baseball had always been Jason's refuge, a space where he could feel alive when everything else seemed to unravel. It was one of the few areas where, as a man, he could safely and openly express emotion—whether through yelling in anger or jumping for joy. Emotions for men in most other settings, culturally, were frowned upon.

"I was thinking about it," Jason said, shrugging slightly.

Herman's eyes sharpened. "As a player or a coach?"

Jason let the question hang in the air, his eyes never leaving the screen. "I was thinking as a player."

Herman looked at him for a long moment, his gaze piercing. Then, his voice softened as he leaned back on his stool, folding his hands in front of him. "I remember Anna, Jason, and what that did to you. Then, soon after, you got hurt. You lost your purpose. I still can't get that image out of my head—your ankle twisted at an impossible angle. I was interviewed again and again. It was brutal. And after all those surgeries, the pins, the plates, and the screws—your ankle never fully healed, did it?"

Jason shook his head, the memory flooding back in vivid detail. It had been a brutal, unrelenting reminder—that life had betrayed him.

"And then the depression," Herman continued, his voice dropping a little. "The bar fights, the isolation—it was like watching you fade away, Stone. Baseball took everything from you, even those you loved. Why go back to it?"

Jason bristled slightly at the question, but he wasn't angry—just defensive. "Are you saying there's no place for me?"

Herman paused, considering his words carefully. "No. I'm saying *you* might not have a place for *baseball* anymore. Maybe it's time to move on. You've been given a second chance. A clean slate. Why go back to something that left you empty?"

Jason's jaw tightened as he absorbed the weight of his coach's words. The silence between them stretched again, but this time, it was less comfortable. The reality of what Herman had said hit hard.

"I'm not saying you're wrong," Jason finally said. "But I've been given this new lease on life. What the hell am I supposed to do with it?"

Herman shrugged, giving a quiet chuckle. "Enjoy it, man. You've got a chance to do anything, but this time with the knowledge of what's important. Don't waste it."

Jason couldn't deny the logic, but a part of him resisted. Baseball had been his whole life. To just walk away... it felt impossible.

In time, Jason guided the conversation to lighter topics, needing a mental break. But he kept his eyes moving, scanning the room. He worried that he might be spotted by someone.

Concern crept in when he noticed a man across the bar, leaning against the counter, partially obscured by the register. His heart rate quickened as the hours passed, the man not leaving. The only thing Jason could consistently see was his ear, always pointed toward him. There was something familiar about him. The rest of his face was hidden, but the sensation of that ear listening to him stirred a creeping paranoia, the weight of it pressing in.

Eventually, the conversation with Herman wound down, but his old coach had given him plenty to think about. Before heading home, Jason excused himself to go to the bathroom.

After he was done, he made his way to the exit, glancing toward where the stranger was sitting, anticipating that he would finally see him. But the man had vanished—gone. Instead of relief, a chill crawled up Jason's spine. He left feeling like someone had been on a reconnaissance mission, watching him. *One of Gordon's spies.*

Chapter 24: The Dish

A grilled shrimp salad sat untouched on the kitchen table. In the quiet corner of her high-rise luxury condominium, the Dish absentmindedly poked at it with her fork, her gaze fixed on the sprawling cityscape outside. For all its flaws, D.C. had always felt like the beating heart of America—a pulsing center of power, radiating far beyond the city's borders into Maryland, Virginia, and beyond. She had once reveled in the rhythm of it all: the city's constant hum, the endless flow of cars, planes, and trains carrying a currency far more valuable than gold—influence.

But today, her gaze pierced through the facade. The pulse of the city no longer felt full of life. It was suffocating.

From her vantage point, the metropolis appeared like an unstoppable machine, its gears clicking together to keep the world turning. Money flooded into the system through taxes, donations, and trade, while policies and laws churned out in return—a bloodline of power. Now, with the sunset casting a dim glow over the Potomac, all she could see was its fragility. The same fragility that had first drawn her to FOY—now corrupted beyond recognition. Even worse, she had been complicit in the deception.

Her fingers brushed the Phoenix pendant that dangled from her neck, a symbol of rebirth. Once a token of optimism, it had represented FOY's potential to change the world. The company had promised cutting-edge healthcare technology and the freedom to innovate. She had been young, idealistic, and exhilarated when she first met Mr. Formell. His vision of a revolution in medicine, of reshaping human potential, had seemed irresistible.

That excitement had curdled into betrayal as she unraveled the truth, layer by layer. At first, it had been small things—a line of code here, a discrepancy there. Then the pattern became undeniable. FOY wasn't about healing; it was about control, manipulation, and a terrifying agenda she could no longer ignore.

She closed her eyes, recalling her first encounter with Gordon. His charm had been disarming, his promises alluring. He had seen her potential immediately, pulling her into his secretive fold. But as she dug deeper into FOY's systems, the cracks in its facade began to show. Beneath its polished exterior were hidden machinations—abuses of power and technology that threatened far more lives than they could save. She had been horrified. Luckily, Gordon was still unaware that she knew the company's darkest secrets.

Her fingers tightened around the Phoenix pendant, as if trying to reclaim some semblance of hope. But that hope had long since shattered. Shattered, not as a promise, as the logo would indicate.

The decision to sabotage FOY's technology hadn't come easily. With shell #66, it had been a calculated risk: employing software to bypass key biomarkers, triggering side effects that would result in the patient's Type II diabetes. She hadn't anticipated the guilt. As her actions escalated, the person she had once believed herself to be became harder to recognize. The code she had written—dubbed "Grace" in homage to Grace Hopper and her "bugs"—had turned into a virus, infecting not just the system but her own soul.

Then, there was shell donor #29. The thought of that man—his life hanging by a thread—still haunted her. She substituted a lethal dose of potassium chloride with a non-lethal dose of Propofol. It had been a gamble. She hoped he had survived, but wasn't sure. The tension she had felt in that moment was unmistakable—a desperate bid to halt the project, to thwart Gordon.

Her attention snapped back to the present. The news of Mr. Grier's death had come just days ago. She had grown fond of him during their brief, illicit meetings. An older man, kind-hearted and unaware of the terrible fate orchestrated for him, he had been discarded like so many others by FOY's cold, calculating system. He had died alone after a promising series of treatments, meticulously designed to improve his biological metrics.

The thought of his death stung more than it should have.

She had considered going to the FBI, but doubt crept in. Gordon's reach was vast. He could erase anything—or anyone—who threatened his empire. She wasn't ready to become his next casualty. So she had stayed silent, watching as the system she once believed in continued its course, biding her time.

She pushed her chair back and stood, pacing the length of her condo. The weight of it all pressed on her chest. Sabotaging technology was one thing. Watching someone die because of it was another. Sleep had become harder to come by.

What could she do? How could she stop this? FOY was too large to dismantle alone, and Gordon's empire thrived on secrecy. She had seen firsthand how it corrupted everything it touched—every promise, every sacrifice, every truth twisted for the benefit of those in power.

Her thoughts turned dark as she remembered the colleagues she had once trusted. They, too, were complicit. She was no different.

The phone buzzed on the counter, jolting her from her thoughts. She glanced at the screen—her mother. She didn't answer. She couldn't. Not yet. Not when she was still tangled in this web of deceit. The glow from the screen illuminated her face, revealing the shadows beneath her eyes.

The woman who had entered FOY with dreams of changing the world no longer existed.

Little by little, she had to dismantle it all—before it consumed her entirely. At the Newlife party, she had switched the vials, her disguise almost superfluous as she lingered in the shadows. The act was done; the line had been crossed. There was no turning back now. A bitter smile tugged at her lips as she imagined their shock upon discovering they had cloned a chimpanzee.

Chapter 25: Jason

Jason steered his F-150 down the darkened streets toward home, his thoughts tangled with the conversation he'd had with Herman. Without baseball, his life felt unmoored, like a ship adrift without a compass. Baseball had been his anchor—a purpose, a sanctuary—and losing it had driven him into isolation. Now, the prospect of choosing a new path loomed before him, like standing at the edge of an empty field, uncertain whether to move forward or turn back into the unknown.

He tried to keep an open mind. Maybe going back to college was the answer. But what would he study? What career could replace the thrill of the diamond? The questions piled up like burdens on his chest. Gordon Formell always loved to say the world was his oyster, but now Jason realized finding the pearl was up to him. No one would hand one over.

Jason felt renewed empathy with high school seniors staring down the daunting decisions of adulthood. Back then, ignorance had been his armor, shielding him from the unknown unknowns. Now, experience weighed heavily on him. Ignorance really had been bliss.

Jason's first youth had left scars he couldn't ignore—both physical and emotional. It felt like madness to embark on a second one. Herman's words surfaced in his mind, a phrase the coach had once quoted after recruiting a young player over a more experienced one: "Young twigs bend in the wind, while old, hardened branches are inflexible." So, what was he? A twig or a brittle branch? Neither, he decided. He was something in between—a hybrid, pliable on the outside but rigid within. What he needed was balance. He had to find the fulcrum.

One thought brought him a shred of comfort: his small nest egg. Most college students didn't have the advantage of savings, and Jason could use his to soften his landing. It wasn't much. Many people mistakenly think that pros are paid a lot, and they are. But for most, their careers last only briefly, which must stretch over a lifetime.

On top of that, Gordon Formell had agreed to a two-year stipend to help him get back on his feet. Yet even that came with strings. The contract gave FOY leverage over him—a way to track and control his choices. Tonight, Jason had defied those terms. Meeting Herman had been a gamble—one that might cost him dearly. Regret clawed at him. He could have waited a day, faced the press alone, and avoided the risk.

As he pulled into his townhouse parking spot, his racing thoughts were interrupted by a faint rustling noise from the back of his truck. Jason froze, his hands gripping the steering wheel as his eyes darted to the rearview mirror.

A man emerged from under the black tonneau cover, moving with unsettling calm. He slid out of the truck bed and onto the ground, his movements deliberate, as if he had all the time in the world. The brim of a hat obstructed a view of his face, making him difficult to identify in the dim light. Jason's pulse quickened. Was this the same guy he had seen at the bar earlier?

The man didn't run. He simply faded into the woods bordering the townhouse complex, vanishing into the darkness without a glance back.

Jason considered chasing after him but thought better of it. *What if the guy is armed?* Once the man disappeared entirely, Jason stepped out of the cab and cautiously inspected the truck bed. Nothing seemed out of place—no damage, no left-behind items. Just an eerie sense of violation.

His mind raced, cycling through possibilities. Was this a random drifter looking for shelter? Perhaps, instead, FOY sent someone to keep tabs on him? Conspiracies began to take root, each more alarming than the last. What if they knew he'd met Herman? What if they were planning to cut off his stipend as punishment?

Jason entered his home, pacing the length of his small living room, his thoughts racing. He resented the grip FOY still had on his life—their policies, their sterile hospitals, their watchful eyes. But at least he was back in his townhouse now, away from the oppressive sterility of FOY's seventh floor. The memory of that place—with its humming machines and whitewashed walls— made his skin crawl.

Sleep wouldn't come easily tonight, but it was better than the sterile confines of FOY's hospital. Jason spent the hours turning over every possibility, every regret. One thing was certain: he wasn't going to tolerate the repressive oversight any longer.

Chapter 26: Dr. Schickel

It was late Thursday night, and Dr. Schickel's exhaustion was beginning to catch up with him. His eyes strained against the magnified view before him, but he forced himself to remain focused. Using the micromanipulator, he worked with meticulous precision—each macroscopic movement translating into microscopic adjustments. The equipment allowed him to perform feats no human hand could achieve unassisted.

So far, he had successfully transferred nuclei for two clients from the same family. Only one more remained.

"I can't believe they bought three, especially since one's a kid." Schickel muttered, his voice cutting through the quiet purr of the lab.

Across the room, Robert Gruber, FOY's Chief Technology Officer, fiddled with an electronic harness attached to a sleek, mobile workstation. Without looking up, he replied, "The Dumas family?"

"Who else?"

Robert shrugged, monotone. "I guess when you're swimming in money, why not throw millions at it? Spare no expense, right?"

Schickel smirked but kept his eyes fixed on the delicate operation in front of him. "When do we move on to the next project?"

"You mean shell #31?"

"Yep, our first female," Schickel spoke carefully, his fingers steady as he navigated the manipulator's controls.

Robert set down the harness and glanced over. "Any day now. Just depends on how 'Client Two' recovers. You know the policy—no more than two in-house recoveries at a time."

Schickel's voice took on a sly tone. "Well, Fabrikant has been released, and Grier seems to be doing fine. I'd say it won't be long before we move forward. She's a knockout, you know."

"Who?"

"The one we were just talking about. 31. That perfect cocktail of Asian and African-American genetics. Twenty-five years old and drop-dead gorgeous."

Robert frowned, his expression tightening. "Speaking of appearances, you might want to clean yourself up. Maybe then you'd find someone to take care of those... lustful tendencies. They're unbecoming, not to mention a moral failing."

"What?"

"Lust. Deadly sin. Ring a bell?"

Schickel sneered. "Not all of us can look like you. If I were tall, athletic, and blond, with those baby blues of yours, I'd never be alone. But you—wasting all that on work and self-righteousness? What a tragedy."

Robert didn't flinch. "See what I mean? You're obsessed. It's not just unhealthy—it's pathetic. Honestly, it's probably why you got booted from every medical practice you joined."

Schickel leaned back from his workstation, the nucleus transfers complete. He gave Robert a hard stare. "Oh, please. Don't act like you're a saint. Pride's a sin too, you know."

Robert folded his arms. "I'm not offended. I've never understood why pride made the list. It's not like gluttony, greed, or wrath. Feeling proud can push you forward, motivate you. It's not inherently bad." He paused, his voice softening. "Besides, it would've been nice growing up if I got a little recognition from my parents."

Schickel chuckled, a dark sound escaping his lips. "Ah, yes. So you built your own system of praise and rewards. I've heard it all before."

Robert ignored the jab. "If I hadn't, I wouldn't have accomplished half of what I did. Four advanced degrees don't earn themselves."

"Oh, here we go." Schickel rolled his eyes. "Molecular and cellular biology, biomedical engineering, biogerontology, and applied physics—blah, blah, blah."

"And who cracked the code to create youth for our clients?"

Schickel pointed a finger at him. "Exactly my point."

"What?"

"It's your blind spot. Yes, you're brilliant, but that pride of yours makes you easy to manipulate. You don't hear me bragging that I'm the only one that can successfully perform the very operation you invented. Throw a compliment your way, and you're putty. That's your Achilles' heel."

Robert's eyes narrowed. "No one's manipulating me."

"Formell already has. He stroked your ego to get you here. Remember when you had morals? You were going to break barriers for the good of humanity. Now look at what you've become."

Robert turned back to his workstation, his tone clipped. "We're advancing science. Groundbreaking discoveries require sacrifices. And don't forget—Formell recruited you too. Without him, you'd be on the streets."

"True," Schickel smirked. "But I've got leverage. I know all the dirty secrets. So, let's say I misbehaved—like with #31. What exactly could Gordon do?"

Robert stiffened, his expression hardening. "You're a pig."

"And you're a waste," Schickel shot back, venom in his voice.

The tension in the air thickened, the silence almost unbearable. Schickel turned inward, his thoughts spiraling away from the conversation. He began to fantasize about the many ways he could indulge himself in the offerings of FOY's shells. To him, they weren't just scientific marvels; they were opportunities, a smorgasbord of desires to be explored. Shell #31 was a perfect specimen, and Schickel knew that soon he'd have moments when they'd be alone, when the fantasies could become reality.

He and Robert were driven by completely different forces. But for all their differences, he knew there was one undeniable truth. They were both here, working late into the night, side by side, in the shadows of FOY's secretive ninth floor—a place where ambition, ethics, and desire blurred into something unrecognizable.

Even with their shared clandestine mission, Dr. Schickel alone concealed a bigger secret—one that would ensure Gordon needed him.

Part 3: Secrets

Chapter 27: Jason

Friday

Jason walked down a long, sterile passageway, the walls, floor, and ceiling all bleached white. The seamless transition between them made it impossible to tell where one ended and another began. The fluorescent lights buzzed overhead, casting a harsh, clinical glow. The air smelled of rubbing alcohol, and the faint scent of disinfectant lingered like an unseen specter. It was a place that rejected warmth, its atmosphere more mechanical than human.

Jason contrasted the cold, oppressive surroundings with the vibrant chaos of his mother's home. The two environments couldn't have been more different: the bright, sanitized corridors here felt as though they existed only for function, indifferent to human emotion, while his mother's house was filled with clutter, color, and life. The more he thought about it, the more the barrenness of this place gnawed at him.

The chill in the air crept up his spine, but Jason couldn't tell if it was from the cold or the soulless surroundings. He could see his breath in the air, thin wisps curling and evaporating, vanishing as quickly as they formed.

He walked on, lost in the maze of white. The people around him moved in sharp, efficient strides, their focus absolute, their eyes fixed on their destinations. They didn't notice him. Like commuters in a busy train station, they moved in and out of view without pause, absorbed in their tasks. There was no conversation, no acknowledgment of one another—just the relentless rhythm of motion. Their white smocks and pants made them blend into the environment, chameleon-like, with only their pale faces and hands betraying any hint of humanity.

As Jason moved forward, the corridor widened, and the flow of people increased. He spotted a raised platform in the center of a large room, and there, on a gurney, was a young girl. She was out of place—an anomaly. Her plaid school dress, red and green, was a stark contrast to the cold whiteness of her surroundings. Her black shoes and white lace collar were also at odds with the antiseptic quality of the room. She seemed frozen in time, a relic from another world.

Jason's heart skipped as he drew closer. Her eyes were wide open, yet they seemed empty—lifeless, as if her soul had already slipped away. Her cheeks were sunken, her skin pale, stretched tight over bone. She looked almost... vacant, only a shell.

The people walked past her without a glance, stepping around her like she was nothing more than another fixture in the room. Jason was the only one who noticed her, the only one who seemed to understand that something was wrong. He felt a growing urgency. Was she ill? Was she even alive?

His feet quickened, but as he tried to get closer, a stocky man bumped into him, throwing him off balance. He stumbled but regained his footing and pushed forward, only to be blocked again—this time by a tall, slender woman. His path was blocked once more by a burly young man. Each time, Jason was jostled, shoved aside, and the people didn't even acknowledge him. They moved with a singular purpose, oblivious to everything around them.

Frustration building, Jason yelled, "Do you need help?" His voice felt foreign in this hollow place, but there was no answer. He turned to the crowd, pleading, "Please! Can someone help her?" But no one stopped, no one responded.

His voice cracked. "Please, can't anyone see her?" His words seemed to echo in the sterile silence. He screamed again, this time forcefully: "LET ME THROUGH!"

For a moment, everyone stopped. Then, in unison, the crowd parted—suddenly, as though they had finally heard him. A path opened up directly to the girl, like an invitation, as if they had been waiting for him to command them.

Jason walked cautiously through the gap, his heart pounding in his chest as he drew closer. There was something eerily familiar about the girl. Her face, despite its hollow, vacant expression, was something he recognized—something unsettlingly familiar. The realization hit him like a cold slap: this was the same girl from the Glass Fountain. The connection hit him hard, and a chill ran through his body.

He reached the platform and studied her closely; her mouth slightly ajar, her lips frozen in eerie stillness. Her eyes were wide and dilated, as though caught between two states. She existed in limbo—neither fully alive nor truly gone.

He hovered his hand over her mouth, hoping to feel a breath, some sign of life. Her body was still—too still. He leaned in, inspecting her pupils. They didn't respond. There was no sign of life in her—nothing but emptiness.

Suddenly, a cold, clammy sensation brushed against his arm. Before he could react, the girl's fingers shot out, locking around his wrist. The touch was unnatural, chilling, and the sudden pressure made him tense up. Her fingers tightened against his skin, and Jason felt the painful scrape of her nails, digging into his arm.

Panic surged through him. He tried to jerk his arm away, but her grip only tightened, a strength that defied explanation. Her nails dug deeper into his flesh, drawing blood. His heart hammered in his chest, his pulse roaring in his ears as he struggled to break free. Then, he saw it—something in her lifeless, vacant eyes. Anger. Contempt. The intensity in those eyes was enough to freeze him in place, a silent warning that left him feeling captured—prey.

The girl's expression twisted into something even darker, as though she had just crawled her way out of the depths of hell. The air around them shifted, thickened, as if something foul was creeping into the room. The stench of rotting flesh assaulted his senses, making his stomach churn.

Jason yanked his hand back with more force, but the girl's grip was unyielding, his breath coming in short, ragged gasps. His heart hammered so violently in his chest that he thought it might explode. Desperation overtook him as he struggled to free himself from her deathlike grasp.

The pain, the pressure, the nausea—it all built until, with a violent jolt...

He woke up.

His body jerked in a cold sweat, the sound of his alarm clock ringing in his ears and syncing with the throb in his head. As his surroundings came back into focus, he heard Rufus squawking in the distance, "Fat ass," the words helping to ease yet another disconcerting nightmare.

Chapter 28: Jason

Jason got out of bed, trying to shake off the horrifying dream. He stumbled into his bathroom and began his morning ritual. It didn't matter how old he was; much of his routine stayed the same. First, he would remove things: his pajama bottoms, the stubble from his beard, plaque from his teeth, and the contents of his full bladder. After his shower, he would start to add things. This included deodorant, lotion for his hands, clothes for the day, and finally, food in his stomach.

With the last step in his routine to go, and still a bit groggy, he ambled his way to breakfast. He looked at his kitchen, thinking it was small and in need of a woman's touch. New questions continued to nag at him, distracting, cluttering.

Woman's touch—an outdated saying?

He snapped back, scanning the room. Whatever the term, the room was clean and functional but had almost no décor or unifying theme. The utensils were all different colors and brands, and the cookware was dated and scratched. The room simply provided a space to prepare food but offered no invitation for social interaction. It stood as a reminder that before the operation, he was reclusive. There were no guests to impress.

Jason needed to wake up and make a cup of hot, black Colombian coffee. Once brewed, he cautiously sipped his first mouthful. It felt as if the coffee bypassed his stomach and went directly into his bloodstream. It was almost like there were a mysterious organ in his esophagus that detected caffeine and channeled its contents into his cardiovascular system, perhaps dumping the drug into his aorta. Whatever was happening inside his body, it worked. Jason emerged from his morning fog, alert and appreciative of coffee once again.

While enjoying his piping hot elixir, he noticed that a kitchen drawer was slightly cracked open. Jason was meticulous—almost to an OCD level—and would never have left this particular drawer inviting attention. It was where he stored his valuables. He suddenly worried he had been robbed and quickly searched for his wallet and keys. Relieved, he saw that both were still there. He checked for his new ID, grateful that FOY had provided a driver's license with an updated picture. Satisfied everything was in order, he continued drinking his coffee and prepared four scrambled eggs, bacon, and buttered toast. His hunger now seemed limitless.

In no time, he had a cooked meal on his plate and left the kitchen. He turned on the television and sank into his weathered family room recliner, no longer grunting as he plopped down.

The morning news was airing a segment covering the upcoming Virginia State Pageant, scheduled for just a week away. Soon after, Maryland and D.C. would also select winners to represent their regions in the Miss USA competition in Las Vegas. Jason thought about the refocusing of the contest, shifting from surface-level attractiveness to inner beauty and skill. The change was most apparent when the swimsuit competition was eliminated, leaving the talent portion to gain additional importance.

He compared this evolution to the offerings at FOY, which seemed to be heading in the opposite direction. The company had started in the health business but now appeared to prioritize beauty. He wondered if the technology would be used more frequently than necessary, with clients simply wanting to maintain a youthful appearance rather than address actual ailments. For the wealthy, they could afford the procedure every decade, even if they were healthy. The result would extend well beyond a facelift, tightening every millimeter of their bodies.

The juxtaposition of the pageant and FOY's growing focus on beauty struck him. Jason knew the superficial allure, but as his thoughts turned to skepticism, he began to wonder: Had FOY lost its calling?

Jason shifted mentally to prepare for a busy and stressful day. He needed to face his mother, still living in his childhood home. It would be the first time he saw her since the transformation. Afterwards, he would head back to FOY for the press conference. Since the media promotion was to be conducted on the front steps of the facility, he hoped he wouldn't have to contend with the security turnstile.

Lost in his thoughts, he was interrupted by a call on his cellphone, which sat on the coffee table. Vibrating and rotating as if dancing to the ringtone, his phone flashed the name "Gary."

He answered, "Hello, Jason here."

"Jason, my friend, it's Gary, your old buddy from high school. How ya doing?"

Jason was confused. "Doing fine. Who's this?"

The voice on the phone remained undeterred. "You're funny. I know it's been too long—sorry about that. The phone does work both ways, though, just sayin'."

Jason rifled through his memory... "Look, I'm not trying to offend you, but I think you have the wrong number."

"Jason, quit kidding around! It's Gary Rayman. Your high school friend. Best friends! We shared biology and math class. We both crushed on that redhead, Nancy."

Jason's mind went blank. "I'm not sure who you're looking for, but I'm not him."

With his tone changing, Gary asked, "Jason Fabrikant, right?"

"That's correct!"

Gary sounded embarrassed. "Weird. Maybe there's another person with your name. Sorry for the wrong number." The line went dead.

As Jason put his phone back on the table, he noticed a sticky note nearby—he hadn't left it there. The hairs on his neck stiffened. The note read:

"Behind the Anne Frank book in the library, eighth floor at FOY, cipher 06121929. Don't throw this away."

The cryptic message meant nothing to him, except for the reference to FOY. His mind raced, but then he thought back to his wallet. Someone *had* been in his apartment. He jumped up and checked his wallet more thoroughly, and his suspicions were confirmed: his old driver's license was missing, along with one of his debit cards.

A sharp knot tightened in his stomach. He immediately called the bank, only to be told that someone had already used the card and withdrawn cash.

He felt exposed, vulnerable. Jason decided he needed to change the locks and walked to the door, his mind still spinning. The spare key he kept hidden outside, under a nearby rock, had always been his backup, but now that would need to be replaced as well. He stepped outside, walked to the hiding spot, and reached for the key. But when his fingers brushed the area underneath, he found only dirt. The key was gone.

Chapter 29: Harper

Harper Faulton lay awake in bed, her eyes tracing the faint patterns of sunlight that crept between the heavy drapes. The day before had been a whirlwind of calculated moves, each executed with precision. After her meeting with the Graffs, she checked into a suite at The Inn at Little Washington, a five-diamond oasis nestled in the eastern foothills of the Blue Ridge Mountains. The resort's romantic facade—a blend of French chateau elegance and English countryside charm—was the perfect setting for her ploy. To her target, it seemed like nothing more than a provocative dinner. To Harper, it was just another stage on which to perform, the illusion meticulously crafted to conceal her true motives.

The meal had been the highlight of her evening, not for the ambiance or the Michelin-starred menu, but for the game she had so skillfully orchestrated. At Gordon Formell's urging, she met with a prominent senator—one deeply entwined in organ donation legislation and the Health Resources and Services Administration. To win him over, she had called him "Puff," a nickname born from a heated exchange where he'd puffed out his chest and lashed out at Gordon for FOY's perceived opacity. The senator, as predicted, accepted the moniker with pride, as if it granted him a sense of distinction.

Harper played her role flawlessly, weaving charm and flirtation into her strategy. Over the course of a sumptuous meal, she lured the senator into a haze of indulgence. Each dish was paired with wine—a parade of artistry that dulled his senses with every sip. The pièce de résistance had been the oyster cocktails, delicately infused to mimic classic drinks like the Bloody Mary and Whiskey

Sour. As Puff savored each morsel, washing them down with wine, Harper sipped on Sprite disguised as a gin and tonic, her deception seamless. By the end of the evening, the senator was heavily intoxicated, a marionette whose strings she had expertly manipulated.

After dinner, she guided him to the bi-level suite she had reserved. Nothing had happened, of course, but appearances were everything. As she now lay beside him in the rumpled bed, her naked body beneath the sheets and his equally exposed form beside her, she watched his eyes flutter open.

"Good morning, handsome," she purred, her voice honeyed and warm. Her expression was practiced—a mask of adoration she wore with ease. In truth, the senator was anything but handsome. His balding head, bloated frame, and bulging eyes gave him a perpetually startled look, like a fish gasping for air. A pufferfish.

"Wait, wait, wait… I don't—this isn't—I don't understand. What happened? Did we…?" Puff stammered, his hands shaking as he tried to cover himself, eyes flicking nervously around the room.

Harper let the sheet slip just enough to reveal a single breast, ensuring his gaze landed where she intended. "We had dinner, drank a little too much, and then…" She trailed off, leaving the rest to his imagination. The truth was irrelevant—only his perception mattered.

The senator's face went pale. "If this gets out… my career…"

Sliding out of bed, Harper walked to the bathroom, unashamedly naked, before wrapping herself in a plush towel. "You've got nothin' to worry about, sweetie," she said casually, with Appalachian charm. "I'll make a quick call to Mr. Formell. He'll confirm you were at FOY for a late-night orientation. We'll say you got tired and stayed in one of the facility's guest suites. Your reputation will remain spotless."

The senator's shoulders sagged with relief. "You… you'd do that for me?"

Harper smiled, wrapping the towel tighter around her. "Of course, sugar. I'm not the type to exploit a situation like this."

He exhaled deeply, the weight of his panic lifting. "Thank you. I owe you."

Her mission was complete. Puff's gratitude was all she needed to secure his cooperation. The rest would fall into place; Gordon would ensure the senator delivered what FOY required. Harper found the ease of this particular operation almost disappointing. She preferred a challenge, something that required finesse beyond the predictable.

After Puff hurried through his shower and left the hotel, Harper lingered, savoring the rare quiet moment. She couldn't delay for long—the press conference was only hours away—but as she prepared for the day, a pang of melancholy settled over her. Today was her thirty-sixth birthday, a detail she kept to herself. Birthdays had always carried a quiet sting for two reasons.

First, they were a reminder of the life she had left behind, and the sacrifices that had shaped her. Harper's childhood in rural Appalachia had been defined by poverty and loss. Her father, a brakeman in a coal mine, had died in an accident before she ever knew him. Her mother, left to raise a young daughter on her own, had turned to the only resource she had: her beauty. Harper had inherited her mother's striking looks, but she had also inherited the lesson that beauty was a tool—one to be wielded for survival.

Watching her mother endure the leering attention of older, wealthier men had instilled in Harper a fierce determination. She vowed she would never allow herself to be subservient. Paradoxically, she learned that by pretending to be just that—subservient—she had harnessed the real power.

Even as a child, she had worked to shed the trappings of her upbringing. She studied the news, mimicked the polished accents of broadcasters, and erased every trace of her Appalachian drawl. Words like "winder" and "britches" became "window" and "pants." When necessary, she could still summon her roots with a strategic "How y'all doin'?" but only when it served her purpose.

Her mother's sacrifices had paid off when Harper earned a full-ride scholarship to Yale, becoming a source of pride for their struggling community. Yet, the bitterness of those early years never fully left her. Success had come at a cost, and birthdays were a reminder of what she had gained and what she had lost. As a child, she rarely received presents, but she had compensated for that a year ago by purchasing her dream car.

As she drove eastward in her yellow Stingray, the warmth of the rising sun washed over Harper's face. The spring landscape unfolded in vibrant shades of green, punctuated by blooming wildflowers. She glanced at the low-hanging clouds, their shapes shifting and curling. A childhood game surfaced in her mind, and she began identifying their forms: a dragon, a guitar, a shark. One cloud resembled a baby's bottle, and she felt a faint tug of regret. That was the second reason she disliked birthdays. Though she had no plans for children, the inevitability of aging—and the closing of that door—nagged at her.

Remaining young was an illusion Harper could only sustain for so long. FOY promised a kind of immortality, but to her, their transformation was no gift—it was a death sentence wrapped in the guise of salvation. She held no pity for the wealthy elites who signed up for FOY's services. It was their type that had cast her aside as a child, exploiting her mother without a second thought. Harper possessed something far more precious than looks: her cunning and an unshakable will to forge her own destiny. Accepting anything less would be nothing short of surrender.

Chapter 30: Jason

Jason sat at the kitchen table of his mother's home, his focus on an overly ripe apple. It rested inside a crystal bowl, its clear, polished surface still gleaming. But the apple, with discolored bruises and deep brown wrinkles, seemed to mock the bowl's intended elegance—an uncharacteristic display of decaying fruit, far removed from its purpose of being eaten. Jason couldn't help but think how people use the term 'rot' for apples, yet are far more polite when discussing the human condition of aging.

Rebecca Fabrikant, standing near the stove, prepared tea. She was in her mid-nineties, with thinning gray hair neatly arranged in a bun. Only over the past year had her appearance changed—her posture now stooped, and her skin marked with the signs of age, blotchy and speckled. Lines and folds had appeared around her mouth, creating small jowls. Always having been one step ahead of time, she finally looked her age. She was a marathoner, but even long races have a finish line. Jason was a sprinter.

"Can I get you some pie? I have strawberry glazed and apple," she offered, her voice warm but firm. The kitchen was her domain, and the social heart of the household. Not one for travel, she was happiest when serving guests in the safety and comfort of her own home.

"Where'd you purchase them?" Jason teased, looking up from the apple.

She glanced at him, feigning insult. "Watch those manners!" Her eyes twinkled with a mischievous spark. She never served a pie that wasn't her own, but the family loved to rib her, pretending otherwise. It had become a running joke with his sister.

She pressed, "So, which will it be?"

Thinking about the overly ripe apple on the table, Jason decided, "I'll have the strawberry glazed."

Pie was her answer to everything. As a child, if he skinned his knee, pie had the magical property of making tears disappear. It was hard to cry when something so mouthwatering was at hand. And not just any pie—her special homemade version, altered just slightly from recipes passed down by her fun-loving Aunt Rae. Jason knew the fruit she chose for her prized pies was crucial to their perfection. Maybe that's why the rotten apple still sat in the bowl—perhaps it didn't make the cut. Or maybe, Jason thought, it was a statement. A protest against the very procedure he'd undergone. She was clever that way.

As his mother served the dessert, Jason looked around the room. Having grown up here, it was home. The pantry doorjamb still carried the marks that tracked his growth as a child. From the kitchen, he could see the living room walls, alive with photographs documenting his past. The framed faces of family and friends smiled at visitors, keeping the house warm and inviting. Some were yellowed with age, including pictures of his father, long deceased. His mother would always say that he wasn't just smiling in the pictures, but from heaven as well.

"You know, Gordon, your boss, called yesterday—the second time this week," Rebecca said, setting the cup of tea in front of him, before sitting down.

Jason raised his eyebrows but returned to staring at the apple. "He's not my boss. What did he want?"

"What else? He wanted to ensure I'll keep your secret until after the announcement today. He also asked that I keep my opinions private. I reassured him that I would hold to my word, as any good

Christian would, though it's hard for me." She reached for her cross necklace and kissed the pendant, a gesture that felt like she was seeking something—maybe forgiveness, maybe strength. Even though her health was rapidly deteriorating, her ethical values remained sharp and unwavering. Under wrinkled lids, her hazel eyes still twinkled with life—the only windows to the vibrant woman she once was.

"Mom, I don't want to get into the same old ethical debate," Jason said, trying to steer the conversation away from the uncomfortable subject.

Unmoved, she continued, "Cloning opens doors that were meant to remain bolted shut," she clung to her principles like a robin protecting its nest. Like the bird, she couldn't physically fend off a threat, but she could make a great deal of noise. He was a product of that nest, and she was chirping loudly to protect him. "In my opinion, cloning is the devil's work, period."

Jason had passed her concerns on to Gordon during the candidate selection process. Gordon had briefly reconsidered choosing him, worried that her negative opinions would hurt FOY's public image. But Gordon had managed to convince her to keep her views private, for the sake of her son.

"Well, I'll admit you look great," she said, studying him with a mix of concern and pride.

"Mom, I truly feel wonderful."

She leaned in slightly, her gaze serious. "What about your friends, Jason? They're much older. Are you going to discard them like you did with your original body—the one I labored over?"

Guilt seeped in; she was good at that.

She drilled in. "Take Randy, for instance. What will you say to him at your next reunion?"

Jason frowned, trying to recall the name. "Randy?"

His mother's expression didn't soften. "Yes, Randy. Your roommate from college!"

Jason sat there, perplexed, was she confusing his friends with his father's? Had the signs of dementia begun to show? He tried to calm himself—it wasn't the first time she'd mixed up names. Growing up, he'd been called Andre countless times, after their French poodle. Still, he decided he would talk to his sister about their mother's mental state the next time they spoke.

His mom pressed on. "The problem, Jason, is that this newly created body you're piloting matches the young, but it doesn't belong to your time. Their experiences growing up are different from yours. Their language and culture are different. You're now an anachronism."

Jason was surprised at how precisely she chose her words. An "anachronism." He felt slightly better about her mental acuity. "Don't worry, I'll adapt. It won't take long to catch up. Look, I love you, and I don't want to argue anymore. Besides, the procedure is complete. I can't turn back now." Jason stood up, kissing her forehead gently. "We all know your baking prepared me in my first youth, and now it'll do so again." In truth, her homemade meals would barely satisfy his nutritional needs, as compared to the carefully curated diet of FOY's scientifically measured ingredients.

Rebecca smiled, the crow's feet around her eyes more pronounced, as if years of wisdom had gathered there, ready to be passed down. As he prepared to leave, Jason wondered if she was right. Was he promoting something morally wrong?

"I've got to go. Thanks for the delicious pie. Love ya, Ma!" He pressed a quick kiss to her forehead and hurried toward the door.

But as he left, he couldn't shake the nagging feeling that his mom's memory was slipping. She had always been sharp as a tack.

Chapter 31: Alfred

Like the industry he served, Alfred Grier felt fully charged after a peaceful night of sleep. His rest, no longer interrupted by the constant need to urinate every few hours, left him feeling unusually refreshed. The night before, he'd received the green light to shower, marking his first opportunity to bathe since the operation. It was a luxury he'd longed for, as sponge baths, no matter how attractive the FOY nurses, had never been his thing. The process of having someone wash his armpits and rear end felt humiliating.

He rose from his bed on the seventh floor of FOY, steady on his feet. The accommodations felt more like a luxury suite at the Four Seasons than a recovery room. Nothing about this experience was typical—then again, neither was the price tag. Fortunately, Alfred's shrewd investments in electrifying the nation had made him a rich man. For him, 'going green' had a double meaning: one related to reducing the carbon footprint, the other to raking in his favorite color—money.

Alfred knew he was 'Client Two', about one month behind the first. The identity of 'Client One' would be revealed at today's press conference, though Alfred didn't expect to meet that person. He felt a bit like Buzz Aldrin, the second man to step on the moon—forever in the shadow of the first. He wasn't destined to become a household name.

Still, he was pleased with his recovery. The transformation had left him feeling like a new man—and in truth, he *was* a new man. He stood two inches taller than he had a month ago, surpassing even his peak height in his twenties. A thick tuft of curly brown hair now crowned his head, replacing the patchy, sunken scalp that had once cried out for powder or a hat. Combing and parting his hair felt like something he could easily get back to—like riding a bicycle—both activities he hadn't done in years. Proudly, he discarded his loose-fitting sweatpants in favor of tight jeans, enjoying the sensation of having a firm rear end. These were all secondary benefits of his true motivation: to rid himself of stage 4 prostate cancer.

His daily routine had already improved. Grooming was now quicker and easier—no more dealing with nose hairs, overgrown eyebrows, or painful ingrown toenails. Cutting his nails, once a challenge, was now a breeze; his new body could bend and twist in ways that made it simple. He chuckled to himself: now, he was a lean, mean, nail-cutting machine. And best of all, he no longer had to swallow a dozen pills at every meal. Gone were the days of pill organizers—at least for the next few decades. The only downside? After his shower, he had to use a hairdryer. Before, a quick towel dry was enough, but now his thick hair needed more time.

Finished with his morning routine, Alfred felt a bit bored. He sprawled back onto his bed to watch a college baseball game. He longed for a cold beer but knew it wasn't permitted at FOY. Still, once he was free, he'd treat himself to a six-pack of a Belgian variety. They might be watching him now, but he wouldn't be under their thumb forever.

Most of all, Alfred craved freedom, a luxury he'd lost after years of cancer treatments. No more being watched and no more being doted on. After what he'd been through, he deserved a celebration—especially one with food. He imagined devouring a juicy bacon cheeseburger, loaded with pickles, ketchup, onions, pepper jack cheese, and a mound of crispy fries. It struck him as odd that he didn't crave anything exotic, like lobster risotto or chicken shawarma. He simply wanted the basics, and in large quantities. Jimmy Buffett had nailed it in a classic song—he wanted a 'Cheeseburger in Paradise,' and for Alfred, paradise meant anywhere but the lavish, stifling confines of FOY.

Just as the game reached an exciting moment, a light tap on his door broke his concentration. A man in blue scrubs entered, his presence almost ghostlike. He spoke in a monotone. "Morning. How do you feel?"

Alfred, lonely and eager for some conversation, smiled. "Great! Could use something to do. Mind you—I'm not complaining." The man didn't react, placing a few items on a nearby tray. Alfred's eyes narrowed as he studied the stranger. The man's appearance seemed off—he was middle-aged with blond hair, but his eyebrows were dark copper. His face looked gaunt, almost emaciated, and his crumpled scrubs were too small, only adding to the disjointed impression.

Alfred tried again. "I thought I knew all the staff, but I haven't seen you around."

The man, still focused on the items on the tray, remained silent.

Alfred pressed on. "So, what's the deal? Another pinprick for the guinea pig lying here?" He waited for a chuckle or even a grin, but the man didn't even smile.

"I'm just here to give you some key supplements to ease your recovery." The man handed Alfred two small plastic cups—one with pills, the other with water. "This will help you get home much sooner."

"So much for being done with pills," he muttered under his breath, then he swallowed the medicine with a gulp of water.

For the first time, the man engaged in small talk, though his voice lacked any real warmth. "Who's winning?" Alfred glanced at the TV. "It's tied in the fifth." He wasn't particularly interested in the conversation anymore—he suspected the man wasn't either. The man in scrubs fiddled with the bedding, adjusted the patient call button, then left the room without another word. Not the typical, cheerful FOY staff member.

Thirty minutes passed, and Alfred struggled to keep his eyes open. Even though it was a critical moment in the game, with the bases loaded, he felt a strange dizziness that made focusing nearly impossible. He chalked it up to the recent procedure, but it was odd since he'd slept soundly the night before. He tried hitting the call button but it was no longer functioning. When he turned his head, he saw the wire had been cut.

His head swam, and his vision blurred. Just then, the door opened, and the man in scrubs reappeared. Alfred tried to speak, his tongue heavy. "Hey, what did you give me? I feel really...?" His words slurred, his mouth struggling to form coherent sentences. The last thing he saw was yellow teeth, then everything went black.

Chapter 32: Bastien

Bastien felt a wave of relief as the wait ended. Despite his meticulous calculations, the sedative had taken longer than expected to take effect. Now, with the clone lying motionless before him, it was clear the drug had finally done its job. He refused to call it a person. The organic matter before him wasn't even a fragment of the original Alfred. The donor had already lived a full life. What lay before him now was nothing more than a biological construct, engineered for a singular, immoral purpose.

He looked down at the body, its once-alert eyes now dull and unresponsive. The imposter wouldn't offer resistance now. Without hesitation, Bastien leaned over, pulled the pillow from under its head, and pressed it firmly over its face. The act was swift, efficient—unflinching. There was no guilt. This wasn't murder. It was closer to swatting a Japanese beetle from a garden. But even a beetle was a creature with evolution on its side. This thing had nothing but artifice. It had started as nothing more than a virus in a petri dish.

At first, the clone twitched—jerky movements breaking the stillness—but soon its body relaxed. Moments later, the chest stopped heaving. The faint scent of urine rose from the remains of the fabricator, and Bastien, with a detached calmness, draped a blanket over the lower half to contain the odor. He checked for a pulse. Satisfied that the clone had no signs of life, he stood. Alfred Grier hadn't died twice. This tissue was a fake.

Bastien sat by the bedside, his expression one of quiet satisfaction. It felt almost ceremonial, as though he'd just earned a scouting badge. He wasn't a murderer. He was the answer to fraud.

The answer to a sick planet. He was the eliminator of ersatz humans, as alien as if they had arrived from a distant world.

So far, his plan had gone exactly as expected. The disguise had worked flawlessly. Entering the building in the white coat and blond wig, just as the Dish had advised, allowed him to blend in seamlessly as a technician. He planted the explosives with precision, every step calculated. But then he discovered something unexpected—something that forced him to improvise.

Adaptability was key, and Bastien was nothing if not adaptable. He'd quickly changed into a set of scrubs he'd found in a dirty laundry hamper. Wrinkled and ill-fitting, they served their purpose well enough. He could move undetected in them, like a chameleon.

The press conference would begin soon. As he sat watching, his attention fixed on the television, he felt a thrill rising in his chest. He waited for the right moment—the trigger words that would set everything in motion. His fingers fumbled for the remote device in his pocket, and when he found it, he held it poised, ready. A simple push of a button, and the detonators would activate. The explosions would create the perfect distraction.

In the ensuing chaos, he would slip away unnoticed, leaving the world to wonder if it was all a tragic accident—and perhaps learn something about FOY in the process. It would be hours before the FOY staff realized this fake Alfred Grier was dead, resting lifeless in his bed.

Bastien wasn't sure if the Dish would approve of the killing. But he didn't care. He had his own compass. "Just another pretty face working at FOY," he muttered to the empty room, his voice cold and indifferent. He paused, his thoughts shifting to the one figure that remained—Jason. He was the only real proof left that

FOY's transformation had worked. Jason was the final puzzle piece to eliminate.

Chapter 33: Gordon

Gordon Formell embraced the podium at the top of the concrete steps leading to the FOY entrance. Reporter microphones were strategically mounted on the lectern, displaying their logos and call letters.

"Good morning!" Gordon paused and adjusted his tie, waiting for the crowd of more than a hundred to focus on him. The beautiful FOY glass lobby, flanked by flower gardens, provided the perfect backdrop. "Thank you all for being here. This is a very exciting time at FOY, and we want to share our good fortunes with you. We believe that our successes will translate into a better life for everyone."

Gordon scanned the area outside the FOY entrance. Reporters and camera crews were scattered about, all listening, watching, and recording. He was pleased to see Harper, Oliver, and Joan supporting him. "As you know, our company was built with the single goal of improving the human condition. Our initial focus was on organ transplants. We understood that the supply of organs wasn't keeping up with the demand, so we pursued avenues to narrow that gap. We researched 3D printing techniques using stem cells, hoping to create complex structures to replace livers, kidneys, et cetera. However, what we found to be even more promising was cloning technology."

Gordon knew this was all a rehash, but he didn't care. He had earned it. "Through cloning, we could significantly reduce autoimmune rejection and further close the supply gap through natural biological tissue growth. Our research led us in a groundbreaking direction that prompted us to change our vision and our name. At FOY, we now believe that immortality is possible."

Gordon looked up, sensing the skepticism in the air. He had dreamed of this moment for years and was prepared to turn the doubters into advocates. He flipped a sheet of paper and continued reading.

"As you may have seen in our infomercials, we've promised an exciting announcement today. Well, brace yourselves." He paused again, giving the audience a moment to shift their attention. "For the first time in human history, our world-class staff of doctors, engineers, and computer specialists have successfully transformed an elderly person into a younger version of themselves. Let me repeat: we made someone young again." The crowd murmured, and a few nervous chuckles echoed, as if a punchline was coming.

"Yes, I hear the cynicism, and it's okay. To convince you that this is no myth and that I'm not here to promote a false panacea, I brought proof: a living, breathing example of our transformation. In a minute, I'll introduce you to 'Client One'." He had Jason wait in the lobby, hidden from view, until he signaled for the grand entrance.

Gordon continued, "He was a man who was 70 years old just months ago. He suffered from multiple health issues. Formerly blind in one eye, heavily scarred, with a heart condition and a limp, he is now fully restored. Better yet, physiologically, he has the body of a twenty-five-year-old. Remarkably, he's still the same person he was before. I continue to be amazed at his recovery and health. For any sports fan, you might even recognize him."

Gordon paused and smiled, taking in the sea of eager faces. If he could stop time, he would do it here, savoring the pinnacle of his career and his legacy. He cleared his throat. "Now, as Bette

Davis said years ago, 'Fasten your seat belts, it's going to be a bumpy ride.' You're about to witness the wonder of FOY."

After the buildup, he wanted to tease the crowd, almost theatrically. "Before I introduce the man and invite him to speak…" Laughter bubbled up from the audience at the delayed suspense. "I want to talk about something else we are also passionate about and that is safety. With each—"

Before Gordon could continue, a loud explosion erupted from within the FOY facility behind him. A few windows on the seventh floor shattered, and a plume of smoke billowed out. Glass cascaded to the ground, a safe distance away, but the sound was jarring. An acrid smell filled the air.

The crowd instinctively dropped to the ground. Shaken, Gordon turned to Oliver, his Chief of Facilities, and stepped away from the microphone. Oliver, equally confused, grabbed the mic. "Please remain calm while we figure out what just happened."

Gordon whispered off-mic in Oliver's ear, "Make sure to evacuate all non-essential personnel from the building and, for God's sake, lock down the ninth floor before the fire department gets here." Oliver, unshaken, ran into the building.

Chapter 34: Oliver

As Oliver ran into the building, he braced himself for the potential carnage inside. Years of military training kicked in, his thoughts snapping into a methodical rhythm: evacuate the occupants, secure the facility, neutralize the threat. There was no time to second-guess the situation or wallow in fear. Emotions were distractions he couldn't afford.

The fire alarm blared overhead, its shrill cadence blending with the distant shouts of evacuees. Oliver scanned the lobby, taking in every detail. Panic was contagious, but he remained calm. This wasn't the first crisis he'd handled, and it wouldn't be the last.

Ahead, the senior security guard, a former military man himself, stood at his post. His stiff posture masked nerves, betrayed by the sweat on his brow. "What are you doing with the evacuees?" Oliver asked, testing him, his voice clipped and steady.

"Opening gates, letting everyone leave unhindered," the guard replied, keeping his eyes trained forward.

"And?"

"No one is allowed back in."

"Right," Oliver said, his tone firm but approving. "What about the Fire Department?"

"We'll delay them as long as we can," the guard answered without hesitation.

"Good. What do we know about the blast?"

"It occurred on the seventh floor," the guard replied, meeting Oliver's gaze briefly before snapping back to attention.

"Don't leave your post," Oliver ordered.

Turning, he glanced at the Glass Fountain in the center of the lobby. Relief swept over him—it remained intact, its structure unharmed despite the chaos around it. With that reassurance, he made for the stairs.

He moved quickly, weaving through the crowd of people surging downward. Faces flashed past him—some streaked with tears, others pale with fear. Oliver noted them, not with empathy but with an instinctive calculation. Their reactions were data points, useful for understanding the scale of the panic.

On the seventh floor, the security team stood in a tight semicircle around a doorway that no longer had a door. The space where Joan Bradley's office door once hung was now an empty frame, the edges splintered and charred. Without waiting for a report, Oliver stepped forward, the guards parting to let him through. They knew better than to interrupt his process.

The office was a disaster zone. The desk and chair sat drenched, water pooling around a scorched hole in the carpet. Most of the glass from the shattered window had been blown outward, leaving only a few fragments scattered across the floor. Oliver moved to the window, inspecting the jagged edges. Outside, the FOY entrance was a hive of activity, the chaos below mirroring the scene in the stairwell.

"This looks contained, not catastrophic," Oliver said, more to himself than anyone else. His sharp assessment cut through the tension in the room. He turned to the senior guard. "Any additional damage?"

"None reported," the guard replied, his voice calm and professional. "The explosion had just enough force to break the windows and blow out the door. We extinguished a small flame. The lack of smoke kept the sprinklers from activating."

"Do we know what caused it?"

"No evidence of equipment malfunction so far," the guard replied.

Oliver nodded, his mind already moving ahead. "Thank the team for staying steady. Station two guards per floor to monitor the evacuation. I'll take care of the eighth floor. Alone."

The guard nodded, then barked orders to his team.

Oliver rode the elevator to the eighth floor, testing the facility's capabilities, his thoughts methodically reviewing potential scenarios. Sabotage? A defect? An accident? Nothing stood out to fit the evidence so far.

Once on the eighth floor, he made the rounds. Gordon's office was untouched, as were the other rooms he checked: the staff conference room, the war room, and the executive bathroom. He saved the private library for last.

Entering cautiously, he locked the door behind him. Everything appeared as it should: the center table sat undisturbed, the bookshelves immaculate. His fingers brushed over familiar spines until he reached *The Diary of Anne Frank*. Behind it, concealed on the top shelf, was a cipher keypad. He entered the code—06121929—and the lock clicked. A hidden spiral staircase revealed itself.

Unlike the families cowering in fear and innocence in Nazi-occupied Amsterdam, Gordon was guarding the most vital secrets of FOY. To some, the space might have seemed sinister. Whispers of a ninth floor had circulated for years, a rumor Gordon always vehemently denied. Only five individuals, the most trusted, were aware of its existence. Gordon would occasionally jest with Oliver about his Marine Corps background, referring to his team as the "Semper Five." Oliver, however, never found the joke amusing.

He ascended to the ninth floor, taking in each room with practiced efficiency. Everything was intact, including the crate he'd helped relocate the day before.

The stillness gave him a moment to think. His thoughts turned to the bigger picture, his mind racing over the question of physical access. Was this the work of someone within FOY? Joan's office had been the target, yet she was known to be at the press conference at the time. Then why her? A misdirection? She wasn't one of the five—certainly not trusted.

He thought about their past interactions. Joan wasn't privy to FOY's most sensitive operations. But if she was, her ethics could be a problem. She was honest… her weakness and the reason Gordon didn't bring her into the fold. Instead, Gordon kept her in the dark, deeming it safer that way, especially as she interacted with the press.

She was also good at her job but, in Oliver's estimation, like all marketers, too much talk and not enough substance. Low information density, words divided by content. Yet something nagged at him. Could she have stumbled upon something? Or had she been used as a pawn?

The possibilities spun in his mind, each one leading him to a single, undeniable conclusion—this was an inside job.

Chapter 35: The Dish

The Dish arrived home, exhausted yet gratified. Hours later, she found herself standing on the rooftop of the Watergate, a celebratory mojito in hand. The air was crisp, carrying the faint hum of city life below. She gazed out at the Lincoln Memorial, its columns reflecting a soft light. As her eyes traced the silhouette of the monument, she thought of the figure it enshrined—Abraham Lincoln, her favorite historical icon. His war-weathered face had always struck her as both weary and resolute, a man burdened by the weight of moral decisions.

One quote of his lingered in her mind: *"Those who deny freedom to others deserve it not for themselves."* The words fueled her as much now as they had when she first embarked on this journey. Lincoln had confronted corruption and inequality with unflinching resolve. Would he have approved of her methods? She couldn't say for sure. But standing atop the Watergate—a building symbolic of exposing injustice—felt poetic. Tonight, she'd taken a huge step toward exposing FOY.

Her plan had unfolded flawlessly. The explosion's timing had been impeccable, synced to Gordon Formell's self-congratulatory speech. The trigger word—"safety"—had set everything in motion, undermining the very message he was delivering. The irony wasn't lost on the press, who eagerly filmed the chaos as it unfolded. Her lips stretched into a satisfied smile. Gordon's reputation was in shambles, and FOY's illusion of control was cracking.

Never before had she felt so cunning, so clever—and most importantly, so empowered. For years, she'd been an outsider in this world of wealth and influence, but now she was playing chess with the powerful. Her opening gambit had landed perfectly, and Bastien had been her pawn.

Recruiting Bastien had been a calculated risk, one that still unsettled her. She didn't trust him—never had—but she'd recognized his potential as a tool. He'd first come to her attention during an anti-vaccination rally, his fiery rhetoric catching her ear. On closer inspection, his views were more extreme than she'd anticipated. His Facebook posts revealed a fervent belief in natural selection as a guiding principle, railing against anything that disrupted the planet's "delicate evolutionary balance." Humanity, in his view, had strayed too far, expanding unchecked and defying nature's limits. FOY's work—extending life artificially—was, to him, the ultimate sin.

He'd even written a manifesto, though calling it that was generous. It was more of a rambling tirade, often incoherent, but its core message was clear: humanity needed a reckoning. To her, that made him dangerous—but also useful. Convincing him to act hadn't been difficult.

She had been cautious, keeping her identity hidden throughout their correspondence. Those early exchanges had been clumsy, riddled with misunderstandings and missteps. But she had been persistent, presenting a shared objective while carefully omitting FOY's deeper secrets—knowing they would only provoke him further. Over time, she had molded him into a willing accomplice, though his unpredictable temperament remained a liability.

She grinned as she thought of her chosen alias—*Dish*. It wasn't a nod to her appearance but to her purpose: revenge. A lover of quotes, she had drawn inspiration from the French novelist Eugène Sue: 'Revenge is a dish best served cold." The name fit her perfectly. She had waited patiently, biding her time, striking when FOY least expected it. And tonight, the element of surprise had been hers.

But the next move would require more than patience. Bastien was volatile, a wild card in an otherwise carefully constructed plan. Keeping him in check would be her greatest challenge.

The mojito's cool tang lingered on her lips as she took another sip. Below her, the city glimmered, oblivious to the storm brewing within its walls. She wasn't done, not by a long shot. FOY hadn't been dealt a death blow yet, but the game was far from over. Each move would be calculated and deliberate; like the name she'd chosen, every strike would be an unexpected blow.

After all, the best revenge is slow and deliberate, served as cold as the ice in your veins.

Chapter 36: Jason

Citing safety concerns after the explosion, security quickly ushered all non-essential personnel off the FOY grounds, including Jason. He noticed that the media, in particular, were targeted and promptly escorted to their cars and vans, where they were monitored as they drove away. Security did not apply the same oversight to him, but the event left him feeling uneasy. At the same time, he felt oddly relieved that he didn't have to face the press.

He got into his truck and shifted his focus to his upcoming date with Samantha. As he drove along the George Washington Memorial Parkway, heading north to D.C., he realized it would take time to reach the Arlington Memorial Bridge into Georgetown. The drive gave him time to think about their last conversation.

Suddenly, nausea gripped him as he realized his predicament. With the press conference canceled, it was never revealed that he had undergone the transformation. Unfortunately, he was still not authorized to tell anyone he was 'Client One'. He had planned to tell Samantha everything tonight; even worse, he had actually promised her. Now, he'd have to break that promise. His mind churned, struggling to find the best way to handle the dilemma.

As he drove to D.C., debating what to say, he noticed a car behind him. He recognized it as a vehicle he had seen in the FOY parking lot. It stood out among the high-end brands that frequented FOY, like Lamborghinis and Mercedes. This car was a white Kia Rio with Colorado plates. It was an eyesore, a side mirror dangling and sporting a prominent dent on the passenger door. There was no question it was the same car.

Jason navigated the crowded lanes of K Street, weaving between cars in an effort to catch green lights and avoid parked vehicles. As he shifted lanes, the white Kia mirrored his movements, too synchronized to be coincidence. Glancing in his rearview, Jason couldn't make out the driver's features through the tinted windows, but he could see the short hair—definitely a man. His mind raced. Was this the same person who had hidden in his truck the night before? The one who had broken into his townhouse and left the cryptic note? It didn't feel random. Someone was watching him—again.

Eventually, Jason was certain he was being tailed. Reaching his destination, he turned into a parking garage, hoping the Kia would follow. Frustration boiled over. If this was Gordon's doing—spying on him in fear of a leak—Jason was ready to forgo his two-year incentive. He wanted to punch the Kia's driver in the nose, a bloody message to send back to Gordon.

As he pulled in and prepared for the worst, the white sedan drove past. His pent-up frustration deflated, and he took a cleansing breath. The driver was just another commuter, taking the same route. It had been a coincidence. He had let his emotions get the better of him. *Testosterone.*

After parking, Jason walked to the Mediterranean restaurant, where he was greeted by a thirty-something hostess in a sleek blue dress. The upscale, Michelin-rated venue stood apart from the usual chain diners, not hiring teens as a customer's first welcome.

Jason had eaten here before, intrigued by the unique dining experience. No menus—just a few questions about allergies, followed by small plates of whatever the executive chef had prepared that day. There were usually twelve to fifteen exotic dishes, each offering contrasting flavors that provoked lively conversation. By the end of the meal, Jason was always satisfied, though his waistline had expanded, and his wallet had thinned.

The hostess greeted him, "Welcome. Do you have a reservation?"

"Yes, I'm a bit early. 7:30."

"Name?"

Jason felt a pang of reluctance. He had promised to remain sequestered until after the press conference. He had no choice. "Fabrikant."

The hostess scrolled on her display. "Perfect, I see a table for two. We can take you now if you'd like."

Jason looked around, not seeing Samantha. "Unfortunately, my date isn't here yet."

"Well, you're welcome to sit at the bar and wait."

"That'll be fine. Do you mind sending her my way when she arrives?"

"Certainly. What does she look like?"

Jason began to stammer. "W… Well, she's got auburn hair. She's petite. Uhh… Beautiful."

The hostess smiled. "I'm sure she's stunning. How about you just tell me her name?"

"Yes, of course. Samantha."

"Thank you." She then motioned towards the bar.

Jason hoped his date with Samantha wouldn't be as awkward. He headed to the bar for a drink to calm his nerves, scanning for a chair with lumbar support but finding none. Then he remembered: his back no longer needed pampering. Instead, he comfortably settled on a backless stool, resting his elbows on the counter and interlacing his fingers—an unspoken plea for a drink. His gaze drifted to a glowing message board on the wall, where fluorescent colors displayed the day's specialty drinks, each letter an expression of the bartender's artistic flair with neon dry-erase pens.

After a quick scan, nothing caught his eye, so he opted for his usual. Without a word, the bartender approached, polishing a wine glass and turning his ear toward Jason. Taking the cue, Jason ordered, "Straight bourbon."

"You got it!" the bartender replied, and the drink arrived promptly in a Glencairn whiskey glass, set carefully on a napkin. In no hurry, Jason took small, reflective sips and thought about Samantha. He hoped she was looking forward to the date. He spent the following moments agonizing over what to tell her and finally arrived at an answer: Gordon wasn't going to like it. But what troubled Jason more than Gordon was the date itself—he hadn't had a romantic outing in over three decades. FOY was the least of his worries.

Finishing his drink, Jason considered another when the hostess appeared, escorting Samantha in. She was radiant. Her auburn hair, styled in lively spirals, cascaded past her shoulders. She wore a little black dress with an off-the-shoulder cut and a hem that flirted just above her knees. A silver belt glittered with sequins, matching her pointed metallic pumps. She was sparkly, sexy—and most of all, hypnotically beautiful.

Jason rose to greet her, but words seemed to fail him. She, however, made the first move, pulling him into a warm hug.

"I'm so glad you're safe. It was hard to get the full story from the news. I don't think anyone was hurt, right?"

Jason tried to recover from the fireworks. "Well, I think Gordon Formell's pride was hurt; he seemed shaken. I've never seen him speechless."

She looked at him, straining her eyes. "What do you think happened?"

With limited inside knowledge, Jason speculated, "The blast occurred on the seventh level, a floor with a lot of medical equipment. It's either a malfunction of a device, a flaw in the building, or someone has a real problem with FOY. I'm sure we'll learn more about the cause over time."

He couldn't let the moment pass any longer. Looking her over—from top to bottom—his confidence and swagger returned. "By the way, you look gorgeous."

She never stopped staring into his eyes, watching him watch her, smiling. "Well, thank you. You look handsome yourself."

Jason pulled out a chair, and Samantha sat at the bar with him. He quickly realized he needed to tend to his manners. "What would you like to drink, or would you rather start at our table with dinner?"

Samantha smiled. "Wine would be lovely." She seemed in her element, energizing the entire bar. She looked over the wine list. "How about the Marlborough Sauvignon Blanc."

For Jason, it was time to face the music. He took a swig of air from his empty glass. He wasn't going to break his promise, so he planned to come clean, especially before their relationship progressed any further. "Samantha, I have something to tell you. I hope you won't feel I've misled you in any way."

Samantha narrowed her eyes, seeming guarded, but tilted her head in curiosity. "So, the mystery is about to be unveiled." Her demeanor didn't mask her discomfort.

Jason began, "You teased me about not sharing my soft underbelly, so I'd like to share now. Have you seen the FOY infomercials?"

Samantha squinted more. "Of course. Why do I feel like you're going to say something that's a dealbreaker?"

Jason ignored her question. "Well, today FOY was going to introduce me as the first person to have gone through the transformation." He placed his hands over hers. "Samantha, I'm much older than I appear." He cleared his throat. "Let me restate that. While my body is the equivalent of twenty-five, I have memories that date back much further. I'm seventy."

Samantha instinctively drew back. Her eyebrows furrowed as she glared at him, shaking her head. "I'm sorry. What?"

Jason looked down at his drink, unable to explain his history and digest her reaction at the same time. "I've gone through a transformation that has taken forty-five years off my age. I've been reborn, in essence. I'm really sorry if this is too much to process. I just want to be honest with you."

She looked him over, fidgeting in her chair. "How many drinks have you had?"

"Samantha, I'm not drunk. You're looking at me like I'm a psycho, but I'm serious. Think about it—my medical records, for one. You saw it yourself; I've made a miraculous recovery from poor cardiac health."

She studied him. "There is something I sensed that's displaced about you. Your manners, maturity, beyond your physical years. Quotes and references from the past, before we, or… I was even born."

"Don't forget FOY spoke about a big reveal of restored youth. They were talking about me… my transformation."

Samantha tightened her lips. "If this is true, then you purposely duped me. You misrepresented yourself, a man pretending to be from my era."

"I never lied to you."

"You lied by omission; it's the same thing." She placed her hands on either side of her head. "This feels overwhelming. I need things to slow down."

"Take your time. If you want to leave, I'll understand."

She paused for a long time, then took a breath. "Give me a moment to adjust. I have to admit, if this is true, it must be hard on you. Why you? How did you get selected?"

Jason took a deep breath and focused on transparency, hoping to regain her trust. "I used to be a professional baseball player, like I mentioned on our first date. Early on, I suffered a loss."

Samantha seemed reengaged, "You mean the injury you mentioned?"

"It actually started with a girl—I had the ring and a speech prepared. Then I was told about the car crash. The ring ended up in the ocean. Things quickly fell apart after that."

"What happened?"

"Lack of focus, and a career-ending injury. Secretly, I think I welcomed it. My recovery didn't go well, and I knew my future in baseball was over. I no longer had the heart. Fans sensed it I think, as did my coach. I became depressed and angry."

Samantha's look softened. "That's sad."

"It gets worse. One night, drunk and looking for trouble, I found myself in a bar. A guy next to me figured out who I was and started trashing me. At my breaking point, I swung at him but missed... several times. Strike one, two, and three. The next thing I remember, I woke up in a hospital bed with lacerations on my face and a detached retina."

Samantha's shoulders melted.

Jason continued. "I was a mess, and I withdrew from everything. It ultimately led to Gordon finding me—my fame, my isolation, it was a perfect PR opportunity for FOY. But after the explosion, that plan seems to have fallen apart."

Samantha tightened her lips, "I'm so sorry you went through all of that."

Jason needed to know where she stood. "Now that you know my background...." He didn't finish the sentence.

There was a long silence. "This *is* a bit strange." She swirled her wine glass. He could see she was reaching a critical junction and needed to choose a direction.

Finally, she answered, "Well, I've dated guys from my era, and they haven't panned out. I'm not sure how I'll feel tomorrow, but I'd still like to continue with our date, if that's okay with you."

Jason simply said, "That means a lot to me. Thank you."

Samantha tried to lighten things up. "So, given your newfound youth, what are you going to do when you grow up?"

Chuckling, breaking the tension, Jason replied, "Oh, the Places You'll Go!"

Samantha got the reference. "Ah, finally, something I recognize, Dr. Seuss."

"Timeless."

They both laughed.

Jason struggled with the answer. "Actually, for now, I was thinking of 'going' on travel, getting away for a bit. Listening to your wine choice, maybe New Zealand."

Samantha probed more. "What about a career, a purpose?"

Jason frowned. "That's a tough one. It's the exact question I was trying to prepare myself for before the press conference. I'm thinking it won't be baseball again. I met with my old coach yesterday. He seemed to think I ought to try a different profession, something new."

Samantha remained quiet as he sorted out his feelings.

Jason continued, "The bottom line is, I just don't know what I'm going to do. I'm honestly wondering if I'll fit in anywhere. It's a bit scary."

She then offered, "If you'd like to talk about it, I'd be happy to listen. I'm a good sounding board."

Jason looked at Samantha. "Well, I was actually hoping that we..."

His cell interrupted the moment by blaring music.

Samantha asked, "Is that your ringtone?"

"It's an old Kenny Rogers song. I apologize, but I need to get this. It's FOY. I normally wouldn't take a call while on a date, but it's probably about the explosion."

Samantha nodded. "It's okay, please."

Jason picked up the phone. A familiar voice came through. "Jason, it's Oliver Burton, Chief of Facilities at FOY." His tone was both authoritative and tense. Jason recalled him from the facility orientation, his no-nonsense, militaristic demeanor. "You need to come back to headquarters immediately. We'll explain everything when you get here."

Jason sighed. "This is a really inconvenient time, Oliver."

In a non-negotiable tone, Oliver said, "You need to come in ASAP."

"Right. Okay." After hanging up, he turned to Samantha. "I need to return to FOY right now. Please, forgive me."

She seemed genuinely disappointed and simply said, "Of course. If you can help in some way with their investigation, I think that's important."

"By the way, it's titled 'The Greatest'."

"I'm sorry?"

"The Kenny Rogers song, you should listen to it."

Jason got up, gave her a hug, and settled the bar tab. "I'd like to pay for her dinner."

Samantha interjected, "That's sweet, but not necessary."

He left the building, wondering if she would ever date him again. He also wondered if he'd been caught speaking about his transformation and was about to be reprimanded. Oliver could be intimidating.

Chapter 37: Joan

Joan Bradley, the marketing director, was one of the few employees asked to stay on the compound after the explosion. She tried to relax in her BMW in the near-empty FOY parking lot, jotting down notes on a pad in anticipation of a media release. She still didn't know the cause of the explosion but figured she could fill in the blanks later. After an anxious wait, the building was eventually cleared, and she received the call to make her way back through security to her office.

Once on the seventh floor, she witnessed the destruction firsthand. Only her office appeared to have been affected. The scene was chaotic: remnants from the fire-retardant foam clung to the carpet and furniture, leaving everything stained with its chemical residue. The air was thick with the sharp stench of burned fabric. Most pictures had been blown off the walls, with torn canvases and shattered frames scattered across the floor. A cold breeze swept through, stirring scorched papers. Some sheets adhered to the surface as though glued in place with water. Her desk and file cabinets, though intact, also showed marks and burns—evidence of the turmoil.

Inside, Oliver was seated in her chair, his boots propped up on her charred desk, casually flipping through a folder labeled '*Alfred Grier*'. Most of her locked drawers were now open, their contents spilled out.

Joan stepped into the wreckage, her heart pounding with a mix of anger and apprehension. "What are you doing?" she demanded.

Without looking up, Oliver replied, "Looking for clues." His voice was calm, almost dismissive, as if her presence were incidental.

Feeling violated, Joan crossed her arms. "I don't think you'll find answers in my personal files."

Oliver finally met her eyes, his expression unreadable. "I would presume you have nothing to hide. Can you think of any reason the explosion happened in your office—and only *your* office?"

Joan stiffened, refusing to let him see her discomfort. "No idea. Do you mind putting my private paperwork back where it belongs?"

With deliberate slowness, Oliver closed the folder and tossed it onto her desk. He stood and walked close, towering over her, his presence oppressive. "As you know, Ms. Bradley, everything within the walls of this facility is FOY's property. You acknowledged that when you signed your employment agreement." His breath carried the acidic tang of coffee, and his tone carried the weight of authority.

He continued, "We've quarantined everything in this office until further notice. Not to worry—we've assigned you a new workspace. Once we're done reviewing your files, you'll be permitted to retrieve them. Your logon credentials have been locked as well. IT will provide you with a temporary account and laptop to resume your work."

Joan's frustration boiled over. "Without my computer or physical files, I won't be able to make much progress."

Oliver's lips tightened into a faint, condescending smile. "Whatever it is that you do, I'm sure you'll manage."

She turned to leave, but his hand shot out, gripping her arm firmly. His voice dropped to a menacing whisper. "I would be careful if I were you. We wouldn't want you to make any mistakes you might regret. I hope, for your sake, you haven't already done so."

Joan yanked her arm free and walked out, masking her unease. He had rattled her, and she hated that he knew it.

Her new office was a far cry from her former space. Located in an isolated area of the building, it felt more like a storage room than an executive suite. The walls were bare, and the only furniture was a desk and a single chair. There were no windows, no file cabinets, and no space for visitors. A ceiling-mounted camera stared down at her desk like an unblinking eye.

An IT technician was setting up a docking station as she entered. "Sorry if I'm in your way, Ms. Bradley. I'll come back later," he said, backing toward the door. "It'll take an hour to finish setting up your hardware, printer, and software. Once you're up and running, I can update your system remotely." Without waiting for a reply, he slipped out, closing the door and leaving her alone.

Joan sat in the chair, staring at the sterile room. It felt like a punishment. The lack of windows made the space oppressive, and the silence was deafening. She glanced at the camera, wondering if it was live and how many others might be watching.

The phone rang, jolting her. She picked it up hesitantly. Gordon's voice came through, brisk and authoritative. "We need to meet to discuss how we're going to handle the press."

Joan swallowed her irritation. "Right. I started drafting something in the parking lot. It would help to know what happened."

"I'm hoping to get that soon," Gordon replied. "I'm meeting with Harper and Oliver after our war room session. I'll call you afterward." He hung up without a goodbye.

As Joan tried to focus, the overhead light began to flicker. A loud pop echoed through the room, plunging her into total darkness. The pitch black was disorienting, the absence of windows making it impossible to find her bearings. She fumbled her way to the door, her fingers exploring until they found the cold surface of the knob. She twisted it—nothing. She tried again, this time using both hands, but it wouldn't budge. *Locked.*

Panic began to creep in. She pounded on the door, shouting for help, then listened. The building was eerily silent. Her breathing grew shallow as she tried to think. Feeling along the wall back to her desk, she located the phone and picked it up. Before she could dial, Oliver's voice came through the receiver.

"Is there a problem?" he asked, his tone calm, almost mocking.

"I didn't dial you," Joan snapped.

"So, you don't need me?"

Her jaw tightened. "Yes, I seem to be locked in this office."

"The building seems to have control over you. I wonder who controls the building?" Oliver said, his amusement evident.

Joan gritted her teeth. "Are you going to help me, or just gloat?"

"Why would I ever do that?" he replied smoothly. "I'll send someone." The line went dead.

For fifteen excruciating minutes, Joan sat in the dark, her senses heightened. She became acutely aware of distant sounds: the hum of machinery, the faint gurgle of water, and the occasional creak of the building's infrastructure. Her thoughts turned to the Glass Fountain and the bodies suspended in their biotanks, their unnerving stillness haunting her.

Finally, the IT technician returned, unlocking the door. "Sorry about that, Ms. Bradley. I didn't realize it locked from the outside. Weird."

Joan fixed him with a hard stare. "Did he tell you to lock me in?"

The technician blinked, confused. "Who?"

"Never mind," she muttered, brushing past him. For the first time since joining FOY, Joan felt truly afraid. And for the first time, she didn't trust anyone.

Chapter 38: Samantha

Samantha hated being at a bar alone, but she wasn't about to waste her glass of wine. Jason had left, and she certainly wasn't going to take him up on his offer to eat dinner alone at a romantic restaurant. As she thought about him, she struggled with the complexity of his transformation. Having a past was one thing; she understood that baggage accumulated over time. But with his psychological age, she wondered if he carried more emotional baggage than she could manage. Facing multiple lifetimes' worth of issues felt daunting—maybe even insurmountable. Dating him, therefore, seemed like a gamble. Of course, being risk-averse and waiting for Mr. Perfect's shining armor hadn't worked out for her either.

Samantha decided to clear her mind, as if cleansing her palate between wine tastings. She turned her attention to the restaurant's bustle, needing something else to focus on. People-watching always helped, but she had to be careful not to make eye contact with someone who might misinterpret her intentions.

Scanning the dining room, conveniently positioned over the counter, she looked for something interesting. An elderly couple immediately caught her eye. They sat lost in their own thoughts, not interacting. Both were in their mid-eighties and had probably been married for many years. He wore a sports jacket, and she wore a white blouse and skirt, complemented by a pearl necklace. Her attire matched their hair color.

As Samantha watched, she noticed they didn't communicate. It was as if they were at separate tables, blankly staring over each other's shoulders. Neither seemed happy or sad; they simply existed, sharing space while remaining oblivious to one another. Samantha wondered if couples ran out of things to say after years of marriage. Why they'd gotten dressed up was a mystery. To her, they seemed to have run the course of their lives and were waiting for the next phase—like someone bored, waiting for a train to take them elsewhere.

She guessed they were old souls. Samantha's father had been an old soul. Her mother had always said old souls had lived before, perhaps at the peak of Greek power or during Caesar's reign. In this life, they were born into their current bodies, possessing more wisdom and experience. As a result, old souls were grounded and less excitable—after all, they'd seen it all before.

In contrast, her mother would describe herself and Samantha as new souls. For them, this truly was their first trip. They were born with wonder, observing the world with fresh eyes. They had fun, but that also meant they made more mistakes—prone to taking their energy in the wrong direction, but still enjoying the journey.

Continuing to scan the room, Samantha noticed a younger couple in their twenties. Their eyes lit up every time they looked at each other. They were obviously in love, sharing a liveliness in their conversation that the older couple lacked. Samantha guessed they were new souls—not because of their age, but because of their energy. She began to think about Jason and wondered what type of soul he embodied. Of course, the only way to know was to keep dating him.

Her people-watching diversion had provided the clarity she needed. She was in a rut and needed to make some changes in her life. It was time to follow her own New Year's resolution—focusing more on her happiness and less on her career. She would follow her predisposition and pivot to 'new.' *New experiences for a new soul.* A healthy work-life balance always seemed elusive, and Jason just might be part of the answer. She'd let the relationship grow and face her vulnerability with courage. There was physical attraction, but now she needed to see if they were emotionally and intellectually compatible. That would take time.

Feeling relieved by her decision, she realized Jason left without asking for her phone number. Optimistically, she hoped he'd reach her through the clinic. If they dated again, she wanted to wear something that would grab his attention. It was time to update her wardrobe.

As she prepared to leave, her attention shifted to a man sitting alone at a corner table in the bar. His newspaper blocked his face. She guessed he was an older gentleman, since younger people used electronic devices to stay current. He wore a white dress shirt with dark slacks and seemed to be struggling to get comfortable in his chair. Something about him was striking, but she couldn't pinpoint whether it was his posture or mannerisms. Without enough information to make a judgment—new or old soul—she lost interest and turned her attention back to her mission. She left the restaurant for some retail therapy.

Soon, she was walking down M Street, popping in and out of stores, accumulating bags. While shopping, she caught glimpses of the man with the newspaper, still never seeing his face. Convincing herself he was too old to matter, she decided to visit a tea shop. In line with her new mantra, she wanted something fresh. She found a black tea labeled "Golden Monkey," and the name made her smile. Without sampling it, she took a leap of faith and bought eight ounces purely on instinct. The tea came in a tin, and as she left the store, she felt a sense of satisfaction. She was finally putting herself first.

After a few more stops, she made her way to her car with her arms full. As she entered the parking garage, she glanced around but didn't see the man with the newspaper. She took the elevator down to the third basement level, where her Lexus was parked. Opening the door, she tossed her purchases into the passenger seat and settled into the driver's seat, feeling a little tired. It had been a long day, and she was certain a glass of wine awaited her at home.

Samantha started her car but noticed a musty smell. The windows were slightly steamed up. Fear prickled her skin as she glanced into the rearview mirror and saw a dark figure sitting in the back seat. Panic gripped her as she tried to scream, but a hand shot out to cover her mouth before any sound could escape. She squirmed, but it was futile. The hand pressed down firmly, and she couldn't break free. In those moments, she thought about her short life and the loving parents she'd leave behind.

Chapter 39: Gordon

Gordon sat at the head of the war room conference table on the eighth floor, its wooden surface cold beneath the fluorescent lights. The room, long reserved for problem-solving, had never felt as urgent as it did now. Just before the meeting, the fire department had cleared the building, and the senior staff had been summoned to respond to the day's unsettling events. Gordon faced the whiteboards mounted along the walls, stacked eight deep, sliding in and out like oversized cards in a sinister deck.

One board already bore a title in harsh, unyielding handwriting: "Alfred Grier's Death – Observables." Below it, the beginnings of a list:

- Deceased with covers over his head.
- Nurse call button cut

The other boards—"Actions," "Candidate Causes," and "Timeline"—remained empty, waiting for answers no one had. Gordon let his gaze sweep the table, meeting the tense, expectant faces of his team. The silence hung in the air. *Good. Let them feel it.*

"Who found him?" Gordon finally asked, his irritation deliberate, sharpening the atmosphere like a whetstone.

Oliver, Chief of Facilities, spoke first. "A guard doing a sweep. He was missed during the initial evacuation. They thought he'd already exited the building—he was covered up."

Dr. Schickel, seated halfway down the table, added briskly, "When I examined him, he'd been dead at least an hour, maybe two, based on body temperature."

"And the cause of death?" Gordon pressed.

Schickel's tone softened, as if the details deserved some level of decorum. "Petechiae in the eyes suggests asphyxia. No obvious blockage—no food bolus, no injuries. The pathologist is running a full autopsy as we speak. Until then, we're ruling nothing out. Could be self-inflicted, or a homicide... If it was smothering, it was done cleanly. No bruising on the throat."

Gordon absorbed this before turning back to Oliver, disappointment edging his words. "Was Grier targeted? What about Jason Fabrikant? Is he in danger?"

Oliver's voice lacked its usual certainty. "It's possible, sir. Someone might be targeting us—our reputation, even. We've already reached out to Jason. He's on his way back to the facility, and once he arrives, we'll place him under our protection."

"Protection?" Gordon repeated, the word bitter in his mouth. He gritted his teeth. "Where was security during the press conference? I'm starting to lose faith in the systems we've put in place."

Oliver's voice cracked, just slightly. "Sir, we're reviewing the logs and combing through surveillance. So far, nothing unusual has surfaced. We might be dealing with an inside threat."

Inside threat. The words sank in like stones, heavy and chilling.

Gordon let the silence stretch, then spoke again. "Well, that's a terrifying thought." He glared at Oliver. "What do you propose?"

Oliver stood and slid out another whiteboard, this one labeled Indicators. Beneath it, an unsettling list:

- Financial difficulties
- Sudden wealth
- Unexplained absences
- Behavioral shifts
- Odd remarks made

"We need to reassess every staff member," Oliver said. "Surface anything suspicious—financial strain, loyalty shifts, outlier behaviors. Until we find the leak, we consider everyone a potential risk."

Gordon's eyes swept the room. Robert. Harper. Dr. Schickel. Joan. Tanya. And Oliver himself. The team—their trust now a fragile thing—returned his look, each silently assessing each other.

"Are you suggesting sabotage for hire?" Gordon asked, narrowing his eyes.

"Whether for hire or out of a vendetta, I'm saying we can't rule it out." Oliver's voice remained steady, though his posture stiffened. "Nor can we rule out anyone sitting at this table."

The air grew colder. Joan shifted, visibly irritated. Gordon noted the change—Joan, normally so vocal, now silent. *Interesting.*

"All right," Gordon said, breaking the tension. "What are we doing about security?"

Oliver was ready with an answer. "Until tomorrow morning, only essentials are allowed in the building. We've also implemented 100% bag checks in and out of the lobby."

"Good." Gordon exhaled through his nose, his jaw loosening slightly. "What about the explosion in Joan's office?"

Oliver moved to another board, diagrams sketched hastily in red. "We know the device was triggered remotely—an electronic detonator. It could've been activated miles away, but someone had to plant it, meaning direct access to her office. The timeline suggests the perpetrator was still nearby when it detonated."

Gordon looked at Joan. "You were in there thirty minutes before. Did you see anything unusual? Maintenance? IT?"

Joan shook her head. "Nothing."

Her tone was sharp, her face pale—a woman used to commanding now oddly subdued.

Oliver added, "Given the timing and the small blast radius, I think we can agree it was just a message… A loud one."

"Tell that to Grier," Joan said bitterly.

The room fell silent again. Gordon turned to Tanya, the MIT-educated Chief Computer Architect. "What about our command-and-control center? Any anomalies?"

"No, sir," Tanya replied immediately. "I checked all alarms prior to this meeting. Everything's nominal."

"Of course it is," Gordon muttered, mostly to himself. He could feel the exhaustion settling in, the collective strain weighing on the team like iron shackles.

He softened his tone. "Listen. I need all of you here tonight. I know it's an imposition, but we can't afford gaps—not until we understand what we're up against. You can sleep on the seventh floor. There are rooms, showers. No one outside this room can know. Understood?"

Around the table, there were nods. No objections. They wouldn't dare.

"We reconvene tomorrow morning," Gordon said, rising slowly. "Until then, nobody talks about this. Not to spouses. Not to friends. Any leaks will violate your contract, and I will enforce severe consequences. We control the message. Is that clear?"

"Yes, sir," the team murmured.

"Good. Harper, Oliver—with me. The rest of you, dismissed."

Chairs scraped against the floor as the team dispersed. Gordon noticed that Joan remained seated, staring blankly at the whiteboard. She was lost in thought.

She's hiding something, he thought. He'd find out what it was soon enough.

Chapter 40: Tanya

Tanya Malbern, Chief Computer Architect, shut the door to her office and leaned against it, exhaling sharply. The sterile hum of her computer monitor filled the room, but her mind replayed the war room meeting, the words echoing like a fever dream. *Inside threat.* The phrase clung to her chest, suffocating.

She pushed herself off the door and sank into her chair, her fingers hovering over the keyboard, trembling. *Focus. Think.* But instead, her gaze drifted to the FOY Award on her desk—a sleek glass trophy gleaming under the cold fluorescent lights. Her lips turned downward in disgust as she picked it up, testing its weight. Once, she'd felt pride when she'd earned it. Now, it felt like a mockery. She slammed it back down, the thud ringing out in the empty office.

Tanya pressed her palms to her face, steadying herself. What had started as a small diversion—just a controlled explosion to draw attention to FOY's flaws—had spiraled into a nightmare. A murder. Alfred Grier was dead, and she had played an unintentional role in it. *What have I done?*

The thought left her breathless, her carefully constructed world feeling like it was falling apart around her.

Involving Bastien had been a mistake—colossal, reckless. He was unpredictable, dangerous, and everything about him unsettled her. She had reached out to him as a last resort, hoping he could cause a controlled disruption. But control had been nothing but an illusion. Alfred's death was never part of the plan.

She took small comfort in the fact that Bastien didn't know her name. To him, she was just "the Dish"—a code name, an anonymous voice, a ghost. That anonymity had once been power; now, it felt like a shield she prayed would hold. She had never told him about Jason—FOY's prized proof of concept. But how had Bastien known about Alfred? Had someone else leaked the information? If Bastien had pieced that together, could Jason be next?

The most chilling part of the war room replayed in her mind: Oliver speculating about an insider threat. Tanya had kept her expression neutral during the discussion, but inwardly, her stomach churned. She wouldn't be flagged for the behaviors listed on the board. But breadcrumbs existed—her code, her access logs. Trails that could be traced back to her if anyone bothered to look.

And FOY always looked hard.

She exhaled shakily; it would take time for them to find her fingerprints on this mess, but time was running out. She needed to act—and fast. Unfortunately, Gordon had locked them all inside the building, a wrinkle she hadn't expected. Escape was impossible.

Tanya clenched her fists, forcing herself to focus. Her first instinct was to reach for the Xanax in her drawer, but she resisted. She needed clarity, not a haze.

Instead, she grabbed the FOY-issued landline on her desk. Personal cell phones were forbidden inside the facility—a paranoid FOY protocol Tanya had once dismissed as overkill. Now, it felt like a prison. She dialed the only number that felt safe: her mother's.

"Hello?"

Hearing Betsy Malbern's voice was like stepping into the sun after days of storm. Tanya's throat tightened, but she forced lightness into her tone. "Hi, Mom. Just wanted to see how you guys were doing."

"Hi, honey! Oh, we're fine. Your dad's out golfing—it's perfect weather, as always."

Tanya usually dismissed her mother's hints to move back home to San Diego; but today, it almost broke her. She blinked back tears. *Stay steady.* "What are you up to?"

"Oh, you know me. Tea, shortbread, and my soaps. You don't usually call this early. Is everything okay?"

"Everything's fine," Tanya lied, her voice wavering on the last word. "I just had a window to chat. I'll be out late tonight, so I wanted to call now."

"Out?" Betsy's voice brightened with hope. "A date?"

Tanya stiffened. She had always been too afraid to tell her mother she was gay. After years of reflection, she had intended to have the conversation, but the moment never felt right. That had been five years ago. Now, there were no romantic interests in her life. No need to address it yet.

"No date, Mom. Just... a friend." She took a shaky breath. "I just wanted to tell you I love you."

There was a pause on the other end, and then her mother spoke softly. "We love you too, sweetheart. Are you sure everything's okay?"

The words almost shattered Tanya's composure. For a fleeting moment, she wanted her childhood back, safe behind a picket fence, cocooned in her parents' unwavering love. But there was no safety now. FOY certainly couldn't rewind time.

"I'm fine, Mom," Tanya choked out. "I've got to go. Give Dad my love, okay?"

"Of course. Take care of yourself, honey."

Tanya hung up quickly, her hand shaking as she set the receiver down. She swallowed against the lump in her throat, forcing herself to think clearly.

What if Bastien finds out about Jason? She needed to warn him—FOY wouldn't, Gordon wouldn't. The man was a master of illusion, always hiding the real dangers behind layers of smoke and mirrors. Jason might be walking into a trap, and he wouldn't even know it.

Her gaze fell on the FOY award again, its base porcelain and hollow, with a small vent hole at the bottom. Perfect. She grabbed a pen and paper, her hand steadier as she wrote a letter to her parents.

I hope with all my heart that this letter never reaches you...

She finished the letter, curling it into a tight roll and slipping it into the hollow base of the award. If FOY found the note, it would be incriminating. But if they didn't, and something happened to her, at least her parents would know the truth.

Tanya leaned back, staring at the award—a jagged shard of glass trapped within a block of clear acrylic. Escape was impossible, every flaw laid bare. The fractured hourglass, its sand frozen mid-fall, mirrored her own state—trapped, vulnerable, and watched. But she refused to let that paralyze her. She had to find a way to set things right.

Chapter 41: Jason

Once Jason arrived at FOY, a senior security guard greeted him with a rare cordiality. "Good evening, Mr. Fabrikant. We've been expecting you. Please follow me."

It was the first time anyone in security had spoken to him so nicely. Jason managed a faint smile but said nothing, not up for small talk.

The guard paused before the security turnstile. "I heard you're uncomfortable with confinement. We can check your DNA manually instead, then I'll pat you down."

Jason's relief was palpable. "Much better. Thanks."

The "ad hoc procedure" was swift, surprisingly considerate. "You'll need to leave your phone here," the guard added, holding out his hand. "We've got phones you can use inside."

Jason hesitated for a moment before handing it over. The exchange felt like a silent surrender. He hadn't realized how much he depended on his phone, how much it kept him connected to everything outside FOY. Now it was gone—his lifeline severed.

In the lobby, Jason paused for a moment before the Glass Fountain. The figures inside their biotanks—zombie-like, suspended, unaware—were untouched by the recent explosion. No cracks, no signs of damage. He found his eyes searching for the young girl again, the one whose face haunted him. His stomach turned.

"Elevator's ready," the guard said, keying in a passcode and selecting the eighth floor.

Jason closed his eyes during the ascent, unwilling to see the fountain again. It felt like they were descending deeper into something hidden, not moving up. The elevator's soft chirp between floors was the only noise, a counterpoint to the muted sound of water cascading from the fountain. The sound felt like a warning.

When the doors opened, the contrast startled him. It was like stepping into another world: luxury and grandeur that felt entirely out of place. Gordon was waiting in the vestibule, smiling broadly as he extended a hand.

"Jason, good to see you." Gordon's handshake was warm, almost too familiar. "I'm sorry to pull you in like this. I'll explain soon. How are you holding up?"

"I'm fine. You? Dealing with the explosion?"

"We're still looking into it. But before we chat about that— how about a tour? I don't believe you've been on this floor before."

Jason shrugged. "Sure."

Gordon led him into the vestibule, pulling away with a sweep of his arm. "Take a look. The marble flooring beneath us, vaulted ceilings above—those frescoes are outlined with gold leaf. And these Corinthian columns, enriched with acanthus leaves, stretch from floor to ceiling." He grinned, clearly enjoying himself. "I hope I'm not boring you. Architecture's a side passion of mine."

Jason thought of his own home—plain, white clapboard—then shook his head. "No, go on."

"The walnut tables along the walls feature marquetry patterns—maroon, cinnamon—perfectly restored. Busts and sculptures punctuate this space, each piece intentional. Opulence, symmetry, and sophistication." Gordon's smile sharpened. "The theme?"

Jason blinked, clueless.

"The Renaissance," Gordon said. "A revival of the past—timeless, beautiful, and aligned with FOY's vision."

Jason nodded, though unease prickled at him. FOY was all about beauty and perfection, but beneath the veneer was something else, something…fake.

Gordon led him down a long, marble-floored hallway. Jason trailed a couple of steps behind, while the guard followed, halting at the entrance to Gordon's office. Jason glanced over his shoulder; the guard's stiff, watchful posture reminded him of a Buckingham Palace soldier—unwavering and vigilant, just without the red coat. The realization hit him like a cold draft: he was being controlled more than escorted.

Inside Gordon's office, Jason recognized Oliver, FOY's Chief of Facilities, seated on a couch. Beside him sat a woman he didn't know—a striking brunette with blonde highlights, who looked sharp enough to cut glass.

"Jason, you've met Oliver," Gordon said as they rose. Oliver's handshake was predictably overbearing. "And this is Harper, Chief of Finance." Her handshake was more delicate but no less calculated.

"Before you arrived," Gordon continued, "we were discussing our financial stakeholders. Naturally, they're… concerned." He gestured for everyone to sit.

Jason sank into the deep cushions, feeling small, surrounded, and suddenly out of his depth.

Gordon's tone remained gracious. "First, I'm glad you made it here safely. Safeguarding you was Oliver's idea, and we believe it's for the best. Until things calm down, we'd like you to remain here, at least a couple of nights. We'll make sure you're comfortable, and we'll send a team to pick up anything you need from your home."

Jason frowned. "Safeguarding? From who?"

Gordon smiled, too smooth. "Anyone who doesn't have FOY's best interests at heart."

Jason's shoulders tensed. He'd assumed he was being sequestered from the media, but Gordon's word choice stuck with him—safeguarding. "I've got a parrot at home, watching him for my nephew. I need to feed him, clean the cage..."

Gordon waved it off. "We'll take care of all that. Just leave us your house key. You can write down everything you need from home or the store, along with any tasks or chores you had planned." He didn't look like he was in a compromising mood, so Jason let thoughts of freedom slide, for now.

The CEO continued, "As for dinner, you'll find a menu in the room, so feel free to order anything you like. The meals you've had in the past were from our cafeteria, but you'll order from our restaurant tonight. You'll find the courses are a step above, quite exceptional."

Gordon's expression shifted to a serious demeanor. "Jason, we ask that you stay in your room. Our security team is still scouring some remaining areas of the building, and we want to ensure your safety." Jason knew FOY held tight control over communications, which was part of the contract he signed. He wouldn't have access to his cellphone for the duration of his stay. But now, he couldn't even leave his room.

Gordon continued, "One last thing: don't tell anyone you're here in this facility."

"Why?"

Gordon skirted the question. "Another precaution that we can discuss later. Thank you, Jason, for working with us." He then turned to Harper. "Now, about the Dumas case..." He stopped and looked at Jason, as if surprised he wasn't leaving. "You're free to settle in. The guard will show you the way."

Jason left the office feeling abruptly dismissed. The guard led him to the seventh floor and to a patient room. To Jason, the room looked more like a hotel suite, complete with a robe and slippers. The view was beautiful, overlooking the wooded grounds behind FOY. The suite included four rooms: a master bedroom, a bathroom, a kitchenette, and a sitting area.

Left alone, Jason collapsed into a desk chair, eyeing the menu left on the table. Italian, French, Japanese—FOY's restaurant offered everything. He thought of Samantha—her amber eyes, her laugh, and the little black dress that complimented her so well. He should've been with her, not stuck here like a pampered prisoner.

The desk phone rang as if on cue.

"Good evening, Mr. Fabrikant. What can we bring you for dinner?" The voice was polite, familiar with his name. Too familiar.

Jason hesitated. "Small pepperoni and mushroom pizza, Caesar salad, Coke." He knew that alcohol was not on the menu.

"Of course. It'll be thirty to forty minutes."

Jason hung up and stared at the notepad beside the phone, blank and waiting for his list of chores, and his house key. His jaw tightened. Rufus would have to survive in a dirty cage for now. Gordon's team wasn't stepping foot in his house. Then again, maybe they already had.

He walked into the bathroom, where fresh towels and toiletries waited. He undressed and turned on the shower, steam quickly filling the room, blurring his reflection in the mirror. Stepping into the stall, he hoped the hot water would ease his unease. It didn't.

Despite FOY's luxury, despite its polished surfaces and pristine design, he felt like he was trapped in a prison in disguise.

Chapter 42: Samantha

Samantha woke in an unfamiliar bed, her mind heavy with the fog of sleep. But then, the memory of the assault hit her like a punch, sharp and terrifying, snapping her into full awareness. Adrenaline flooded her body. She had been certain she was going to die, but now—now she was alive. The realization felt overwhelming, almost impossible to process.

Instinctively, she checked herself over. Her clothes were still on, and there was no soreness where there shouldn't be. He hadn't assaulted her—not physically, at least. He hadn't tied her up either, which meant she could move. But why had he left her this way? Her purse rested innocently on the nightstand, an odd detail. It made no sense. If he was after money, why hadn't he taken it?

Her eyes swept over the room, taking in the stark, impersonal space. A bare bed, a nightstand, a closet, white walls—nothing that would offer any clue as to who brought her here or why. She glanced at the door leading into the kitchen. A figure stood at the stove, his back to her. He was focused on what he was doing, oblivious to her waking up. This was her chance.

Her mind raced. There had to be something she could use. Blankets, pillows, a baseball bat. Her heart stuttered in her chest as her eyes landed on the bat, propped against the corner. The bat would work; she had to make it work.

Moving quietly, she slipped out of bed, careful not to let the frame creak. She grabbed the bat and tiptoed toward the door, her nerves on edge. There was no way to leave without being seen. Her grip on the bat tightened, caught between fight and flight. The only option was aggression.

Taking a deep breath, she raised her voice, aiming for confidence and authority. "BACK OFF! I'll swing if I have to. I'm leaving!"

The man in the kitchen paused, then his head slowly turned toward her. On seeing him, her breath caught in her throat. She lowered the bat in disbelief, her heart stalling in her chest.

"It's you. It can't be."

The man who approached her was much older, his face disfigured with deep scars, a pronounced limp slowing his movements. He didn't seem threatening, though. He moved carefully, as if in no rush. He reached out, taking the bat from her hands with a steady, almost apologetic air, and placed it on the floor.

"I'm sorry I had to detain you," he said, his voice rough and strained, laden with something that almost sounded like regret.

"'Detain'?" she repeated, unable to keep the disbelief out of her voice. "I think 'abduction' is a little more accurate."

The older man frowned as if the weight of her words had struck him harder than expected. "Yes, you're right. I didn't want to hurt you. I thought... I thought you might scream, attract attention." He sighed, shoulders sagging. "I couldn't risk it."

Her anger flared, sharp and uncontrollable. "Well, congratulations, you've got my full attention now. Where the hell am I?"

He gestured vaguely toward the room. "You're in my apartment. I've tried to make you comfortable."

Comfortable. The word felt like a cruel joke. Samantha's mind spun. A bird squawked from somewhere in the background, its shrill voice calling out, "Fat ass."

She stared at the older man. "How are you here? I know you—well, a younger version of you. Is this some kind of trick? Makeup? A stunt double?"

"No trick," he said, his eyes distant, a haunted expression on his face.

Samantha's brow furrowed. "How can you both exist?"

"I'm trying to figure that out myself. The man you dated... he's my younger clone. I escaped FOY because I was in danger, and now he's in danger too."

"Okay, let's say I believe that. How'd you escape FOY? Their security is tighter than Fort Knox."

A bitter smile tugged at his lips. "It wasn't that hard. I saw my younger self enter the building. We share the same DNA. When he went through security, they logged him as being present. That made it easy for me to leave. Exiting isn't as scrutinized. I just passed the DNA test and walked out. But I'm guessing when my younger clone tried to leave, the system alarmed. Of course, I didn't stick around to find out."

Samantha's disbelief felt justified, but something in his voice rang true. "So, what do you want from me?"

The older Jason rubbed his chin thoughtfully, his fingers brushing the stubble. "You create an avenue. I need to talk to my younger clone. I have questions—questions that only he can answer. Together, we might be able to figure out what's going on. I've left him clues. But... I'm not in the best condition. My vision's poor, I can barely walk. You were... an obvious choice. You have access to him and FOY."

Samantha shook her head. "Convenient for you, I'm sure. Not so much for me."

He looked worn, the weight of his situation heavy in his eyes. "I know I'm asking a lot."

Her eyes narrowed as she processed his words. "Why do you think FOY wants Jason...I mean your clone back?"

The older Jason's expression darkened. "At first, I thought he was part of it, something evil. But now I think he's a victim too. They want him back to control the evidence. He is part of the evidence. So am I. Under their model, we both can't exist at the same time. I'm worried they'll try to eliminate one of us—or worse, both of us. They have the means."

Her pulse quickened. "What are you saying, 'they have the means'?"

The old man's voice dropped, his tone grim. "Two days ago, I woke up in a body bag on the ninth floor. I was left for dead. There's a cremation chamber in that building."

A cold shiver ran down Samantha's spine. "Why would FOY need that?"

"Exactly my question. Maybe for defective clones, maybe for other purposes," he said, his voice hollow. "I don't know. I managed to escape down a hidden staircase. I got to a library, then to the main floor. When I saw my younger self enter the building, I took a chance and fled."

Samantha hesitated, piecing everything together. "Why not just call him?"

"I missed my chance. I didn't trust him. Now, I can't reach him. They probably took his phone when he was called back. Landlines are too risky. FOY monitors everything. I can't visit him without setting off alarms, either. My DNA's still in their system as being inside. But you... you have a reason to see him. You're his cardiologist. His health needs to be monitored, documented."

Samantha's thoughts raced. "His test results are the healthiest I've seen in years, but I was still asked to track his progress. I guess I could help. It's hard to turn a blind eye to what FOY is doing."

The old man's lips twitched into a wry smile. "I know all about blind eyes." He placed a finger high on his right cheek, just below his eye with the detached retina.

Samantha winced. "I'm sorry. I didn't mean to—"

"Don't worry about it," he said, cutting her off. "It's a reminder of a past mistake. It was my own fault."

She weighed the decision. This was all so unexpected, but something in her wouldn't let her walk away. "Okay. I'll do it. I'll contact Dr. Schickel tomorrow, arrange a meeting with him at FOY. I'll say we need to discuss Jason's medication."

The older Jason frowned, accentuating some of his scars. "I'm Jason. I'm not sure who he is."

Samantha didn't know how to respond, and remained silent.

He cut the tension. "Let me order Chinese food for tonight, and you can sleep here. I'll take the sofa."

Samantha agreed.

He added, "Thank you, Samantha." She looked into his eyes and could see the familiar younger man trapped within.

Trying to comprehend everything that had happened, Samantha realized that she wasn't only in this older man's apartment but in young Jason's as well. She looked around to gain a little more insight into her date. Everything made sense to her, except the bird.

Chapter 43: Robert

Robert Gruber, Chief Technology Officer, started every day the same way—with a meticulously crafted checklist. Each item was preceded by an empty box, ready to be marked off once completed. He had begun this ritual in middle school, refining it over the years into a system that he credited with his scholastic and scientific success. For Robert, the act of checking off a task wasn't just satisfying; it was tangible proof of his efficiency—his greatest obsession. Waste, in all its forms—time, effort, or even human tissue—was abhorrent to him.

This obsession, however, made Robert rigid. His relentless need for structure left little room for spontaneity, earning him the label of an extreme 'J' on the Myers-Briggs Type Indicator—a Judging type through and through. Dr. Schickel often mocked him with juvenile quips about his "tiny 'P'-ness," a jab at Robert's lack of Perceptiveness, with 'P' being the opposing side of the scale. While the joke annoyed him, it also reaffirmed his disdain for Schickel, whose chaotic impulses constantly clashed with Robert's well-organized plans.

After the explosion, Robert had little to contribute to the war room meeting led by Gordon, but Oliver's warning of an insider threat disturbed him. It was a distraction that wasted precious time, forcing him to revise his schedule. More importantly, it raised concerns about the integrity of the ninth floor, where his valuable documents were stored. Though Oliver mentioned some disarray, Robert couldn't trust the military man to keep track of all his supplies and procedures. He had to see for himself.

The ninth-floor cold room greeted him with signs of disorder. Shelves were out of place, and a quick scan revealed missing items—nothing incriminating, but enough to irritate him. He muttered under his breath, cursing Dr. Schickel's sloppiness. As he moved toward the operations room to check his binders, a wave of nervousness crept over him. These weren't just any records; his "rainbow series"—binders color-coded by topic—documented every discovery, procedure, and trial he had conducted. They were his life's work.

At the back of the room, the binders appeared untouched. Robert let out a quiet sigh of relief and marked the task as completed on his checklist. Even now, the sight of those multi-colored binders filled him with pride. They held the results of countless experiments, including intricate standard operating procedures for testing on live subjects. Today, he planned to practice for an upcoming procedure using one of three cadavers: a crate from the animal lab, a body bag labeled "client donor #30, Alfred Grier," and the remains of shell #66. He chose the crate.

Robert backtracked to the supply room to retrieve the body. He loaded the crate onto a hand truck and grabbed a pry bar before navigating the hallways back to the operating room, careful not to bump into walls. Once there, he pried open the container, releasing a pungent wave of decay that even a bowl of vinegar in the corner couldn't mask. The corpse inside—a middle-aged man, shaved and emaciated—was clearly the product of a hard life. His decayed teeth, track marks, and distended stomach painted the picture of a man who had known poverty and addiction. Robert noted the man's unkempt appearance, even in death, with clinical detachment.

He transferred the body to the operating table and began preparing his equipment. His latest procedure involved testing electronic interfaces with the hippocampus, a delicate and demanding task. He was perplexed that only Schickel had success on live subjects, but pushed the thought out of his mind. As he worked, the methodical rhythm of sawing through bone allowed his mind to wander.

Robert's thoughts turned to his childhood, a bitter reservoir of memories. His parents were distant at best and destructive at worst. His father, a high-powered lawyer, found time only to critique him, calling him a disappointment. His mother, harsh and impatient, dismissed his achievements as meaningless efforts. Their constant bickering left Robert starved for stability. Science became his refuge. Numbers didn't lie; their logic provided an unshakable foundation. In science fairs, he found fleeting moments of recognition—moments his parents never cared about.

He recalled one project in particular: a four-stroke engine model crafted from coat hangers and toilet paper tubes. It had earned him a blue ribbon and the admiration of his teachers, but not his parents. His father had criticized the lack of polish, while his mother scoffed at its impracticality. In frustration, Robert had smashed the model on a table, but it bounced off, leaving a scar on his chin—a lasting reminder of their rejection.

These memories fueled his drive. His work was his legacy, his means of proving his worth to a world that had doubted him. He wouldn't just succeed—he would excel, carving his name into the annals of scientific history.

Lost in thought, Robert barely registered the moment the procedure was complete. The cadaver had served its purpose, its brain yielding valuable insights for his next innovation. With precision, he returned the remains to the body bag and crate before wheeling them back to the cold room. Later, he would fire up the crematorium to eliminate any trace of his work. For now, he marked the task off his list with a sense of quiet satisfaction— pleased to have reclaimed the day and turned it into something productive.

Chapter 44: Bastien

Bastien paced the length of his Fairfax home, simmering with resentment. He had risked everything to execute the mission flawlessly, yet once again, there was no call from the Dish to acknowledge his efforts. The silence felt suffocating, and the longer he stared at his phone, the more his frustration festered. He had followed their plan to the letter—at least, until the moment inspiration struck.

He replayed the mission in his mind, each detail reaffirming his belief that he deserved recognition. Getting into the FOY building had been child's play. Dressed in a long white coat, he blended effortlessly into the flow of employees. No one spared him a second glance as he glided past security. He would hide out until making his way to the seventh floor. Joan Bradley's office was exactly where the Dish said it would be. Planting the explosives had been a simple, practiced task. In and out without a hitch, every step executed with surgical precision.

The plan called for the explosives to detonate remotely during the press conference to ensure zero casualties. Bastien had adhered to that, but what the Dish didn't know was how much more he'd accomplished.

Walking into the building, Bastien had been struck by the audacity of FOY's display: the Glass Fountain, an obscene monument to their excess, glinting with cloned tissue harvested for the rich and vain. He had seen photos, but standing before it was something else entirely. The fountain wasn't just grotesque— it was a testament to everything wrong with humanity. Its very existence churned his stomach, a carbon-emitting shrine to greed.

To destroy it wouldn't just be an act of defiance; it would be a moral imperative.

It was easy enough to divert some of the Semtex for the fountain, but the real revelation came in Joan Bradley's office. As he planted the charges, his eyes caught a stack of notes on her desk. There, in plain sight, were references to two successful transformations: Alfred Grier and Jason Fabrikant. The Dish had never mentioned either name.

With curiosity piqued, Bastien took a moment to investigate. Alfred Grier was conveniently located on the seventh floor, and Bastien dealt with him swiftly. Killing the clone felt like erasing a stain from the planet—one less resource-hogging fraud breathing precious air. Jason Fabrikant, however, was another story. Bastien couldn't locate him in the building, but he made a mental note: Jason's time would come.

Now, as he sat in his home, Bastien seethed at the Dish's lack of gratitude. If she disapproved of his methods, then she was no better than the liars in D.C. He was doing what needed to be done—what she had failed to do. The Mall would be better off as a swamp than a playground for politicians and policymakers spinning empty promises while the planet burned. He was justified. The Dish's silence only fueled his resolve.

What stung most was the media blackout. Not a single report on the clone, the so-called 'Alfred,' and his demise. Was FOY powerful enough to bury the story entirely? If so, the Dish wasn't just ungrateful—she was incompetent. Still, Bastien was not one to give up easily. If necessary, he would continue alone. By morning, he would execute his backup plan, infiltrating FOY again with or without the Dish's approval.

He still had one of the two DNA samples from the technician, a detail that reassured him. Entry would be easy enough. The technician had Saturdays off, making the facility more vulnerable. This time, Bastien would ensure his actions couldn't be ignored.

It was getting late on a Friday night, and Bastien let the Dish play her silent games—he had his own plan. Nothing—not indifference, not incompetence, not even FOY's shadowy influence—would stop him. Bastien gathered a water bottle, syringe, needle, chloroform, and a glue gun. He needed to prepare his backpack for his next mission. By tomorrow, the world would finally see FOY for what it truly was.

Chapter 45: Dr. Schickel

Dr. Henry Schickel stood alone in the glass elevator, the smooth hum of a fan the only sound as it hovered silently on the fourth floor. He hadn't pressed a button, allowing it to remain still. The fountain below had stopped cycling for the night, conserving energy and leaving the biotanks on full display. The water's cessation cleared the view, presenting the shells in their full, undisturbed form. With the building closed to visitors, there was no need for secrecy; the hosts' identities could remain visible.

Schickel gazed at the biotanks with the focused intensity of a foodie studying a menu. His eyes lingered, moving over each shell as though weighing a choice, considering his mood for the night. He wanted something new, something different—a shift from the usual. Perhaps something with an ethnic or religious twist. Like a child pressing his nose against a candy shop window, he finally settled on shell #221, an equivalent 18-year-old female. Her donor—a beautiful woman in her late fifties, Jewish—was a memory that still loitered in Schickel's mind. He could see the return of that donor's elegance blossoming in the young form before him.

At first, Schickel stared, but his vision became unfocused as his mind turned inward, reflecting on the journey that had brought him here. Unlike Robert or Harper, who had grown up in broken homes or harsh environments, Schickel had been raised in wealth and privilege. His early years had been filled with a nurturing, loving family. But even then, he knew that something was off. As a child, he'd been captivated by death, dissecting frogs and chipmunks with a clinical curiosity. One day, he had choked the family cat with a rope, just to watch it struggle for air. He hadn't been a sadist; he was merely fascinated by the fragility of life. His parents, ever concerned about his tendency to lie and disregard the sanctity of life, caught him at times—but their worry was never enough to recognize the true danger within him.

Young Henry, clever as ever, had learned to mimic the right emotions, fooling them into thinking he felt guilty, that he was remorseful. But his real genius lay in covering his tracks. No one had ever suspected that he had killed the neighbor's dog or inspected the carcass of a dead deer in the nearby woods. His mother's doting affection kept her blind to the monster he had become—a perfectly tended garden can still yield poisonous fruit when nurtured unrecognized.

Then puberty arrived, and his desires shifted. What had once been a fascination with death had evolved into a need for control, for power over life itself.

Dr. Schickel snapped back to the present, his choice made. He pushed the elevator button for the basement and proceeded to the control room.

Spotting the lead technician, he instructed, "I need to perform routine maintenance on shells #221 and #58."

The technician responded with some hesitancy, "Now? Both the male and the female at the same time?"

"Yes, disconnect them and deliver them to my seventh-floor office for evaluation."

It was a familiar request, but the technician was new and didn't know the routine. Schickel made similar requests at least twice a week.

Once the clones were delivered, he would move the male aside and roll him into the closet, the door shutting quietly behind him.

To avoid suspicion, he often ordered pairs—one male, one female—ensuring that the technicians saw nothing amiss. The real treat, as always, would be with the female.

He locked the office door behind him, the sound of the bolt clicking into place like a signal that the outside world no longer existed. This space was his own, his desk always pushed to the side—a place where he could indulge his darker inclinations.

After satisfying his needs, he covered the body back up except for one foot. He took a scalpel from the tray beside him, his hands steady as he made a small incision between the two largest toes of the young woman. The cut was deliberate and precise, forming a small diamond-shaped scar. To Schickel, it was a mark of conquest—a trophy. Much like the Koh-I-Noor diamond, it was a symbol of victory over time. This scar was the price the donors paid in their desperate race to cheat death, and he relished the power it gave him. He would see that mark again on the transformed body, and he would know exactly what he had done. He would revel in it.

He then made a call.

A voice answered. "Control room."

"Hello, this is Schickel. Have the shells returned to their respective biotanks."

"Yes, sir, we'll leave immediately."

As he placed the receiver back down, a thought crossed his mind: What if Gordon was listening in and knew? But Schickel wasn't concerned. He was untouchable. Gordon, for all his power, was too focused on the bigger picture to notice the small details. And Robert had far too many notes to ever see the subtle change he made in his procedures, altering the voltage just enough to ensure a live operation would never work. Robert would never have success alone. Schickel was in control here.

Satisfied with another successful interlude, Dr. Schickel began mentally preparing for the tasks ahead. There would be logistics to consider, bodies to dispose of. The work never stopped. As he retired for the night, he felt a quiet satisfaction—knowing that tomorrow, as always, the world would remain blissfully unaware of what had been done in the quiet corners of FOY.

Part 4: Deception

Chapter 46: Jason

Saturday

Jason tried to open his eyes, but couldn't. Everything was pink, a soft, enveloping hue. It felt as though he was lying on a sunlit beach, peering through his eyelids on a bright day. Shadows hinted at a form, but nothing came into focus—only an endless expanse of pink.

He felt weightless, as though suspended in liquid, yet he could still breathe. The temperature was just right, neither too hot nor too cold—Goldilocks perfect. He floated in a fetal position, deeply relaxed, overcome by a sense of comfort. No spa could compare to this level of serenity.

Muffled sounds reached him, distant voices, but his ears felt submerged. The rhythmic bubbles of breathing drifted around him. His senses were present but seemed distant, as if he were untethered from them.

He tried to move—lift an arm, wiggle a toe, even blink—but his body wouldn't respond. No matter how hard he tried, movement was beyond his abilities. Slowly, the awful realization sank in: he was paralyzed. His mind was awake, alert, but his muscles remained completely still. He was trapped in an unresponsive body—not able even to thrash about in panic. There was no escape, no way to change his situation. He was a prisoner in his own body—to others, likely appearing in a persistent vegetative state. Alone, helpless, and at the mercy of whoever might be tending to his physical form, hoping they kept him alive.

Suddenly, Jason jolted awake in his FOY suite, shouting with a mix of terror and confusion. Cold sweat coated his skin, followed by a wave of embarrassment. He hoped his cry hadn't disturbed anyone on the floor. Grateful it had only been a dream—or more accurately, a nightmare—he exhaled in relief. He could scream. He could move his toes. Thank God for that. His dreams had been growing more frequent and vivid, unsettling in their intensity. It was clear he needed to see Dr. Lazarus, the psychologist FOY had suggested.

Jason lay back in bed, too exhausted to move. The paralysis still clung to him, but it stirred more thoughts of his dreams—and the human brain. He reflected on how humanity always looked outward when confronted with the unknown, fixating on the stars. For centuries, the vast cosmos had driven mankind's curiosity, inspiring astronomers like Kepler to study the heavens. Jason thought of the Hubble and Webb telescopes, marvels that allowed us to peer into the farthest reaches of space. The universe—its stars and dark matter—holds mysteries beyond comprehension, with distances so vast that light from Andromeda, the closest galaxy, takes 2.5 million years to reach Earth.

But in an ironic twist, Jason realized the greatest mystery was much closer, resting on his own shoulders. Before the operation, FOY had briefed him on the brain, explaining that it generates just 23 watts of power—barely enough to light a small bulb. It is made up of 75% water and weighs only about three pounds. Unlike the grand stars, the brain is small and unassuming.

Yet to Jason, this tiny organ was the most intricate and miraculous thing in existence. It was the ultimate enigma. The origins of his thoughts, memories, and emotions seemed as vast and unknowable as the cosmos itself. Unraveling its secrets felt daunting, but at least he had been granted time to explore them.

Chapter 47: Harper

First thing Saturday morning, Harper Faulton sat at her desk, reviewing a list of people to contact. As one of the 'trusted five', she shouldered the responsibility of steering the company through uncertain times. After the explosion, the waters were uncharted, but she had a compass. Her primary mission: safeguard FOY's investment base. The next person on her list was Sam Dumas, the wealthy entrepreneur with a wife and young granddaughter. He wasn't just a client—he was a crucial financial stakeholder.

She dialed his number. "Hi Sam, this is Harper from FOY. How are you?"

"I'm fine," he replied. "I've been expecting your call. The news has been a bit vague. Are you okay? Is anyone hurt?"

"Yes, we're all fine. No one was hurt." Lying was not foreign to her. "I wanted to reassure you that everything is back on track. There was minimal damage at our facility, and none of the clones were affected. Your family's DNA collection is completely safe. I didn't want you to worry."

"That's a relief. What happened?" Sam asked.

Harper recited the scripted explanation, the words feeling detached from her. Crafted by Gordon, the statement was designed to calm stakeholders and offer closure. If rumors of a more sinister cause spread, it could take weeks to investigate, destabilizing the portfolio and revealing FOY's most guarded secrets.

She tried her best to sound like she wasn't reading: "We traced the explosion to a faulty portable oxygen tank. We've inventoried all remaining tanks and found no others that are defective. We identified the lot number and proactively removed all similar units from our facility. It was just an unfortunate incident. I'm sorry if the explosion caused you any concern." She worried it sounded too rehearsed.

Sam's tone brightened. "Well, I'm not worried now. That's great news! I appreciate the call. I know FOY is looking out for me, my family, and my portfolio. Thanks for everything."

The plan was working. Harper would continue calling investors while Joan handled the press. The difference was Joan didn't know the explanation was completely fabricated—she wasn't one of the 'trusted five.' As for Alfred, Gordon convinced Joan not to mention the death for now. The truth was, he would ensure the disappearance would never be linked to FOY.

Sam's voice grew more casual. "By the way, would you like to meet for a drink sometime? We could discuss the portfolio in more depth. I recently sold some real estate and I'm looking to reinvest—we're talking 8 or 9 figures."

Harper knew exactly what Sam wanted—and she would deliver. "That sounds great. How about next week, maybe at the Marriott bar in Chantilly?" She chose that location for a reason; it offered rooms to rent.

"Perfect. Thanks again for the call and for clearing things up about what happened at FOY," Sam replied.

Harper hung up, satisfied with the flow of the call. How *easily* lying had become. She wondered when she had stopped noticing the small shifts that led her away from her moral compass—the delineation between right and wrong. She checked Sam off her list, then made the next call pondering how many men she would need to sleep with. It didn't bother her. In securing the right investors, she had become FOY's judge, jury, and '*sexecutioner.*'

Chapter 48: Samantha

Samantha woke in a cold sweat, her body tense. The events of the previous day churned in her mind, sharp and unsettling, refusing to fade. She longed for the comfort of her own bed, where at least the familiarity might offer some relief. But this space was foreign and uncertain, leaving her uneasy. Through the bedroom door, she spotted the older Jason in the kitchen, moving quietly as he prepared breakfast.

Catching her gaze, he approached, carrying a tray with scrambled eggs, buttered toast, a tea infuser, sugar, and silverware. The gesture surprised her. "Good morning," he said, his voice calm despite the weight of the day ahead.

Samantha, still in yesterday's clothes, wrapped her hands around the warm tea. Not until the heat seeped through her fingers, easing some of the strain, did she realize how tightly wound she was. The first sip soothed her dry throat. "Thank you," she said quietly.

Jason hesitated, watching her closely. "I didn't have any tea of my own, so I used the Golden Monkey you bought. Hope that's okay."

Samantha gave a faint smile, the tea's flavor grounding her. "It's perfect."

But the calm didn't last. "We've got a lot to do. I need to call Dr. Schickel and set up a meeting. Then we have to stop by my apartment—I need a shower and clean clothes."

The older Jason nodded. "I figured as much."

Samantha studied his face, scarred from a life of hardship. Beneath it, though, she saw the man she spent time with just yesterday—a younger, more familiar version. A wave of sadness hit her. How much had he been through? Would the younger Jason age like this? Or would he even get the chance?

After breakfast, Samantha called Dr. Schickel. The doctor agreed to meet, even though it was his day off, mentioning he was already at the facility. Once the call ended, she and Jason headed for her apartment in Alexandria. Jason explained he'd left his car in a Georgetown garage. It was better that way—her Lexus would blend in at FOY, while his dented Kia Rio, its side mirror hanging off, would stand out.

At home, Samantha quickly showered and changed, feeling more focused. When she emerged, her expression was firm. "I have an idea," she said. "But we need to stop at a cosmetics store on the way."

Jason raised an eyebrow. "For what?"

"A disguise," she said, grabbing her bag. "I'll explain in the car. Let's go."

The stop at the beauty supply store was quick. Samantha grabbed a few items, her mind already racing ahead. The drive back to FOY was thick with silence, each of them lost in their own thoughts.

When they reached the FOY parking lot, Jason broke the quiet. "This is too risky. I can't let you go," he said, voice heavy with concern.

Samantha turned to him, her expression firm. "First of all, only I have a say as to what I do and don't do," she paused, realizing her tone was harsh. "Though, I'm open-minded; do you have a better idea?"

He shook his head and sighed, pulling into a spot out of view from the security cameras. "It's just that I feel I'm repeating past mistakes. I wish I could get past the DNA test," he said quietly, "but waiting here, not knowing if you're okay... it'll drive me crazy. I didn't stop someone I cared about in the past, and I don't want to make the same mistake."

Samantha's resolve softened for a moment, but she stuck to her plan. She dug into her purse, pulled out her phone, and handed it to him. "They won't let me in with this anyway. Hold onto it. If I run into trouble, I'll call this number. If I say the words 'Golden Monkey,' you call the police—no hesitation."

A faint smile crossed Jason's face. "Smart girl. I'll call them if I don't hear from you in a couple of hours, too."

She shook her head. "Give me four hours."

Jason hesitated, then nodded. "Fine. But before you go in, there's something you need to know." He reached for her hand. She instinctively started to pull away, but then let him guide her fingers to the back of his head. His expression turned flat—serious.

He asked, "Do you feel that?"

Samantha frowned. "Barely."

"Exactly," he said. "They were supposed to operate on me, remove part of my skull, but they didn't. Just two tiny incisions, each smaller than a penny. Whatever they're doing, it's not what they say. I have questions—too many to ignore. Who is this younger Jason? How does he know so much about me? Is he an imposter, or does he really think he's me?"

His words hit her hard. The younger Jason had seemed real, familiar, but now doubt crept in. *Was he part of FOY's lies?* She had suspected the organization was hiding something, but this raised the stakes. Still, she was too invested to turn back. She had to see it through.

"I'm glad you didn't tell me this earlier," she said, her voice shaky. "I might have backed out. But now, I've come this far. I'm going in."

Jason's gaze was steady, his tone both firm and caring. "Just be careful, Samantha. Please."

She nodded, her heart pounding as she stepped out of the car. Every step toward the building felt heavier than the last, as if the weight of her decisions was turning the pavement to quicksand. At the door, she turned back to see Jason, but the car was out of her line of sight. Taking a deep breath, she straightened her shoulders and walked into the unknown.

Chapter 49: Bastien

The sharp buzz of Bastien's alarm startled him. He'd been lying awake, staring at the ceiling, but the noise still felt jarring. Insomnia had become a constant companion, especially when he felt anxious. Despite the long list of tasks awaiting him today, he wasn't ready to move—not yet.

To steady himself, Bastien let his thoughts drift to his childhood. Growing up in New Orleans, his family had been his anchor. He could still hear his father's encouraging voice as they played catch in the backyard, and he could almost taste the powdered sugar from his mother's homemade beignets. A faint smile broke through as he remembered tormenting his older sister with rubber spiders, expertly planted near her pillow.

Then, Katrina changed everything.

The hurricane hit in 2005, and life as he knew it vanished. His aunt and uncle had taken him in as a precaution before the storm, their home being inland and safer. But after the floodwaters receded, the news came: his parents, his sister, and his childhood home were gone. What was meant to be a short stay with his relatives became permanent. They tried to provide for him, but grief had hollowed him out. He was just a kid, and the weight of loss was too much to bear. Most nights, he cried himself to sleep.

As he grew older, he searched for purpose in the chaos. Working for his uncle's shrimping business gave him a sense of routine—until the Deepwater Horizon spill in 2010. The Gulf was poisoned, and no one wanted contaminated shrimp. Financial ruin hit his new family hard, and their focus shifted entirely to survival. Bastien became invisible in their struggle. At fifteen, bitterness overtook him, and he ran away. He lived wherever he could—abandoned houses, street corners, or shelters—carrying nothing but anger and the faint memory of what he'd lost.

It was during those desperate years that Bastien's worldview began to take shape. To him, humanity had become a plague on the Earth. Gas-guzzling cars, carbon footprints, and reckless consumption were fueling global warming. Hurricanes like Katrina were growing stronger, more frequent, and more destructive. He saw offshore drilling rigs and oil tankers like the Exxon Valdez as symbols of human greed, choking the planet for profit.

Bastien became obsessed with what no one else seemed to talk about: overpopulation. People were living longer than ever, thanks to companies like FOY, with their advanced medical technologies. To him, this wasn't progress; it was a death sentence for the planet. More people meant more mouths to feed, more resources to consume, and accelerating the destruction. The Earth was crying for help, but no one was listening.

The thought made his jaw clench. Bastien threw off the covers and sat up, his purpose snapping into focus. Killing Alfred had shaken him—he couldn't deny that. But through the lens of consequentialism, the end justified the means. A better world required sacrifice. He'd long admired Machiavelli's cold pragmatism. Now, more than ever, it felt necessary.

Not hearing from the Dish had been a disappointment, but Bastien realized it might be a blessing in disguise. Without her interference, he could act on his own timeline. There was no room for hesitation or compromise. He alone would take the next step.

Today, he would cut off the head of the snake.

Chapter 50: Young Jason

Jason was famished as he glanced over the breakfast menu. He ordered eggs benedict with hash browns and a large black coffee. Since the meals were complimentary, he decided to add biscuits with gravy and a fruit bowl as well. Within minutes, his order arrived. He devoured everything in record time, realizing he hadn't eaten that quickly—or that much—in years. It felt good to have such a hearty appetite, especially knowing he'd burn off the calories without gaining a pound. Still, as he thought about his new metabolism, he regretted not ordering the blueberry scone instead of the fruit.

His simple thoughts of food were interrupted by a faint knock. He opened his room door to find a woman wearing a headscarf and sunglasses. She placed her index finger against her lips in a shushing motion. He complied and stood silently.

"May I come in?" she whispered.

Jason didn't know her but saw no reason to refuse in the secure environment of FOY. Without saying a word, he motioned her inside and closed the door. He then guided her to the settee.

Still standing, she took off her sunglasses and spoke at a normal volume. "I'm sorry if that seemed rude, but I have to be careful. We don't have much time. Jason, my name is Tanya Malbern. I work for Gordon Formell as his Chief Computer Architect." He wouldn't have guessed she worked for FOY. She looked rather plain compared to the beautiful people he was used to seeing among the staff. Dressed in a business suit instead of medical attire, she wore no makeup. The only striking feature was her necklace, a beautiful tri-gold Phoenix pendant.

"Nice to meet you," Jason said, politely. "It seems you already know who I am. I hope the events of yesterday didn't disrupt your work too much."

Tanya's eyes darted around the room. "Actually, that's why I'm here. I believe your life is in danger. It's not publicly known yet, but a FOY client was killed yesterday. He was murdered on this very floor. His name was Alfred Grier. He underwent the procedure one month after you. He was FOY's second successful transformation and their first paying customer."

Jason felt alarmed by the news of a murder, but he couldn't understand why she was discussing this with him. Searching for a suitable response, he awkwardly said, "I'm so sorry to hear that."

Tanya continued, "I'm worried that someone has issues with FOY's medical advancements and is trying to eliminate any proof of success. After Alfred's death, you're the only remaining real-life example that FOY's technique works. I fear you might be targeted next."

Caught completely off guard, Jason tried to piece together what she was saying.

After a pause, she elaborated, "The person who killed Alfred is also likely responsible for the explosion yesterday. They had access to the building. You must remain vigilant and be prepared to…"

"Whoa!" Jason held up his hand, trying to keep up. "I hadn't heard the cause of the explosion yet. Are you saying someone planted a bomb?"

Tanya squinted; her brows knitted. "Yes, someone with access to the building planted explosives, killed Alfred, and they may be trying to kill you. I'm sorry to dump all this on you at once. I've come at great risk, especially if they knew I was here."

"Who are 'they'? Have you told FOY? Let's call them now, together," Jason suggested.

Tanya's eyes widened as she waved her hands. "You'll find that FOY has its own motivations. I wouldn't involve them. That's all I can say for now."

"Wow, I think I'll need some time to process what you're telling me. How do you know all this?"

"That's not important," she replied, glancing toward the door. Then she locked eyes with him. "You have to believe me and prepare for the worst. The murderer could be in the building right now. As for FOY, don't trust them. Gordon has his own secrets, hidden away on the eighth floor."

"Well, I don't have access to it anyway."

"That's easy. I can give you the code for the elevator. It's a four-digit cipher: 1474, the year Ponce de León was born. But there are cameras almost everywhere, except inside the suites and the common bathrooms. The eighth floor doesn't have cameras either, but there's no way to get there without being seen. Just be aware—the building is watching, don't do anything that would arouse suspicion."

"How can I reach you if I have questions?"

She shook her head. "You can't. I need to go. Please stay safe."

With that, Tanya put on her sunglasses, headed for the door, and left without another word.

Chapter 51: Oliver

Oliver was making his rounds in the basement of FOY headquarters, satisfied that all seemed quiet. The only sound was the familiar buzz of the fluorescent lights. Suddenly, his two-way radio shattered the silence. This was unexpected since he had just left security fifteen minutes earlier.

It was the guard in the lobby. "Sir, you asked to be informed if Jason Fabrikant had any visitors."

"That's right," Oliver replied, his attention now piqued.

The guard continued, "A woman just left his room."

Oliver stopped mid-stride. "How do you know?"

"We picked it up on the hallway surveillance camera outside his room. I'm looking at the replay."

A tight knot formed in Oliver's stomach. "Can you see who it is?"

The guard hesitated. "She's wearing a scarf and sunglasses, but I think I can still tell. If I'm not mistaken, it's Tanya Malbern. I wasn't sure if it mattered since she's… well, a senior and all."

Oliver was disbelieving. "Tanya? Are you sure?"

There was a brief pause before the guard spoke again. "I'm looking at the video now. Pretty sure it's her. You can come up and see for yourself."

Oliver turned off the radio without another word, his pulse quickening. He dashed up the stairs, taking them two at a time, his feet pounding against the concrete floor. In minutes, he was in the security control room, joining the guard behind the counter. The two exchanged no words; they simply stood side by side, their eyes fixed on the screen.

The guard hit play.

Oliver leaned in, watching closely as the woman entered Jason's room. After a few moments, the guard fast-forwarded, and Oliver saw the same woman leave. His jaw clenched.

He slammed his fist on the table. "DAMMIT! What was the elapsed time?"

"Maybe five minutes," the guard replied, voice soft, as if intimidated.

Oliver grabbed the security log, flipping through the pages, his eyes scanning the entries. "Just to confirm—she wasn't added to the list of approved visitors, right?"

The guard hesitated again. "No, she wasn't. But, being Tanya and all—"

"Did Mr. Formell say anything? Or Schickel?"

"No one."

Oliver didn't waste another moment. He turned on his heel and headed straight for the elevators. Minutes later, he stood in Gordon's office, interrupting a meeting with Harper, Dr. Schickel, and Robert. The 'trusted five' were all present.

Oliver was slightly out of breath as he spoke, his urgency apparent. "Tanya was just spotted visiting Jason."

The corners of Gordon's mouth dipped slightly. "Well, we may have just found our insider threat. Any recommendations?"

Robert spoke up. "We should bring her in for questioning. She might have a plausible reason for the visit."

Oliver's voice grew tense. "I can't imagine what that reason could be. As you know, FOY interactions with its clients are strictly controlled. She wasn't authorized to make contact with Jason."

All eyes turned to Gordon. He rubbed his chin thoughtfully. "We'll need to find out her intentions, let's bring her in. But Dr. Schickel, we may need to use the precautions we've discussed."

Dr. Schickel's lips stretched into a smirk. "Understood."

Gordon's voice sharpened. "It's nothing to be happy about." He turned to the others. "I assume she'll be here for the staff meeting. Let's ask her to stay afterward. I want all of you there. We'll start with soft questions, but we may need to get confrontational. Her responses will guide our next move. Be prepared for a tough interrogation if it comes to that."

The executives dispersed to their individual tasks, but Oliver stayed behind. He would never challenge authority in front of others, but, alone with Gordon, he was ready to voice his concerns. He was convinced that more stringent controls were needed for the building—and he had strong opinions about how to handle Tanya.

Chapter 52: Samantha

The first thing Samantha noticed as she entered FOY headquarters was the small table manned by two guards. Their presence was new, and the sight sent a jolt of nerves through her already anxious body. She considered turning back, but her legs carried her forward as if on autopilot.

One of the guards greeted her. "Good morning, ma'am. What's the purpose of your visit?"

Samantha forced her voice to sound calm. "I'm here to see Dr. Schickel. I'm scheduled to meet him in his office."

The guard rifled through a clipboard. "Name?"

"Samantha Morgan." She gestured toward the lobby desk. "Usually, you're stationed over there. Is this a new protocol?"

"That's correct," the guard replied, marking something on his list. "You're clear to proceed. Please enter the security portal."

Without another word, she moved on, relieved to end the interaction. Once locked within the turnstile and sampled, the DNA scanner emitted a soft beep, and the latch released. Samantha stepped through without issue. She headed to the seventh floor, glancing at her watch. She was early.

She quickly found Dr. Schickel's office, but the door was closed, and the frosted glass revealed no sign of movement inside. After knocking and receiving no answer, she decided to explore.

The FOY headquarters was a labyrinth of corridors she had never bothered to navigate. As she wandered through, she noticed how busy the offices were, even on a Saturday. *Perhaps they were catching up on work delayed by the explosion,* she thought.

Retracing her steps to the elevator lobby, she noticed the building's spiderweb-like design, with hallways radiating outward. She picked one at random and followed it to a corner of the building. Here, the layout shifted, revealing what she guessed was the executive wing. The spacing between doors suggested that these offices were larger than the others.

Most doors were marked by engraved plaques and privacy glass. Light shone through two of them. The first read: Harper Faulton, Chief Financial Officer—her office appeared to be the largest. The second belonged to Oliver Burton, Chief of Facilities. Both doors were firmly closed.

Further down, Samantha spotted an open door and slowed her pace, glancing inside. Two men were mid-conversation: one in a white coat, the other in a suit behind a desk. Their tone was clipped, tense.

"What do you mean it's missing?" the man behind the desk demanded. He caught sight of Samantha and sprang to his feet, slamming the door shut. The plaque read: Robert Gruber, Chief Technology Officer.

Feeling unwelcome, Samantha turned back. On her way, she passed a smaller office with its door ajar. The engraving read: Tanya Malbern, Chief Computer Architect. The lights were off, but faint rustling came from within—papers shuffling, cabinets opening. Someone was working in the dark.

Uneasy, Samantha made her way back to the elevator and descended to the ground floor. She tried to distract herself by watching the biotanks within the fountain, but the sight, once awe-inspiring, now felt sinister. She shifted her focus to the opaque elevator floor instead.

Stepping into the lobby, she immediately felt eyes on her. The guards were watching her movements closely. This wasn't the usual gawking she sometimes attracted. Their stares felt probing, suspicious. Were they on edge because of the explosion? Or had she somehow drawn attention to herself?

Shaking off the discomfort, she headed to the cafeteria. In short order, she purchased a cold bottle of brewed tea and made her way back to the lobby. To pass the time, she stood by a window, her eyes drawn to the vibrant tulips outside. Their bright colors offered a moment of solace, but the sense of calm was fleeting.

A hand landed on her shoulder.

Electricity shot through her, and she froze, her thoughts spiraling. Had she been caught? Was her plan already exposed? Running was pointless; she was trapped in this building.

She turned, heart pounding. It was the man she saw moments ago in the heated discussion, wearing a white smock. His nametag read Dr. Schickel.

"Dr. Morgan, my apologies for startling you," he said, smiling oddly. "You're early—I was just grabbing some food."

Samantha exhaled, forcing a smile. "How did you know who...?" She paused, then added, "I guess I'm a bit on edge after the explosion. Are you free to meet now?"

Dr. Schickel nodded. "Of course. Let me grab a snack, and we'll head up to my office."

As he walked away, Samantha's hand drifted to a pill container in her purse. Her fingers closed around it tightly, and she whispered a silent prayer: *Please let this work.*

Chapter 53: Bastien

Bastien left his townhouse in the same rental car he had driven the day before. He arrived at FOY, following his new plan. As he parked, he was surprised to see more cars than he expected, especially for a weekend. Scanning the lot for situational awareness, he noticed an occupied Lexus. Given the explosion yesterday, he worried there might be heightened security and that the person inside could be a plainclothes guard. However, after closer inspection, he saw that it was an older man and not a likely candidate for enforcing security. Bastien guessed he was a patient.

He turned his attention to getting through the security process in the lobby. With the small vial of DNA that Tanya provided, and the same disguise, he felt confident. After all, it had worked perfectly the day before—what could go wrong? He also carried a backpack filled with items to help him execute his mission. Most importantly, he had a plastic 3D-printed Glock tucked into the back of his pants. Being plastic meant the weapon could pass through metal detectors unnoticed. The gun would fire only once, but that was all he needed. Bastien grabbed his backpack and entered the building, projecting an air of calm confidence.

Once inside, he approached the entry portal, but two guards were blocking his path, standing behind a table. A sign read, "100% Mandatory Bag Inspections."

One of the guards gestured toward him. "Sir, please place your backpack on the table." Seeing no alternative, Bastien complied. The guard pulled out a bottle of water and ensured it was sealed. Then he removed duct tape, a phone, and a spool of nylon rope.

Raising an eyebrow, the guard asked, "Sir, can you tell me what you plan on doing with this rope?"

Thinking quickly, Bastien replied, "I just moved to a new apartment and needed it to secure furniture in my truck. Honestly, I forgot it was in there."

The guard studied him for a moment before nodding. "You can have your water, but we'll keep the other items here in your backpack if you don't mind. You can pick everything up when you leave. Just so you know, we don't allow phones past the security entry point either."

Bastien nodded, indifferently. "Understood." He started to walk away.

The guard called out, stopping him. "What's the purpose of your visit?"

Bastien paused but had his story ready. "I work here. I'm a technician. I just wanted to stop by to grab a book I forgot to take with me."

"What's your name?" the guard asked.

"Smith," Bastien replied, elated that the name of the technician he was imitating was also a character in *The Matrix*. The guard wrote the name down.

"So, no appointment?"

"Right."

One guard glanced at the other. "Explains why he's not on the list."

"Very well. Proceed to the turnstile."

Imbeciles. Bastien marveled at how easy it was to sneak in the gun and explosives, let alone the water bottle. The night before, he had punctured the plastic and drained the contents. Then, using a syringe, he injected chloroform, sealing the small hole with a dab of transparent glue. He didn't care about the rope; he wouldn't need it. As for the phone, he could use one of FOY's landlines if necessary. Outsmarting these guards wasn't just easy; it was almost embarrassing.

As he approached the security turnstile, he slipped the small DNA vial into his mouth and stepped forward. Locked in position with no ability to leave until cleared, he followed the swabbing instructions, aligning the vial with his tongue. He then slyly provided the technician's DNA. Confidently, he waited for the familiar buzz of the disarming locks.

Instead, he heard nothing.

He froze, waiting for release, but the turnstile remained silent. Suddenly, an alarm blared in the distance. Bastien wondered if there was a power disruption or mechanical malfunction. Trapped and visible like a goldfish in a bowl, he watched as guards took positions at the entry and exit points of the turnstile.

"What's the problem? What's happening?" he demanded, his voice crackling for the first time.

There was no response. After an excruciating couple of minutes, he heard the locks disarm, and the guards pulled him out forcibly. Weapons drawn, one of them directed him firmly into the building. "Sir, you'll need to come with us."

Confused but trying to maintain his composure, Bastien protested, "I haven't done anything. What's going on?"

"We'll find out." The guard offered no further explanation. He took Bastien by the arm and led him to a small, windowless holding room, locking him inside—alone.

Chapter 54: Gordon

Gordon slammed his fist on the desk, his voice rising higher than usual. "What do you mean you can't find Alfred? Oliver and Schickel told me he was dead in his bed just a couple of hours after the explosion! HOW COULD YOU LOSE A DEAD BODY?" He stared at Robert, his CTO, who sat slumped in his chair, his usual confidence shattered. Gordon had never yelled at him before. "Maybe if you weren't so focused on your records, you'd actually see the bigger picture."

Robert, now more animated and no longer shrinking under the pressure, snapped back. "No, I'm talking about the original Alfred, not the clone! The Alfred you're referring to—the one who was murdered—is the young clone, shell #30. The real Alfred, the client, is missing. We found the dead clone and went to transfer it to the cold room, only to discover his donor's body was gone."

Gordon's anger simmered, but a flicker of understanding crept in. He took a deep breath, trying to steady himself. "Let me get this straight. You've got the dead clone, but not the client? You told me the client's body was on the ninth floor. We need it back in his house, planted there like he died in his sleep." He rubbed his chin. "So, the body bag was missing?" His tone was sharp.

Robert shook his head again. "No, the bag was there. But inside, instead of the old man's body, we found a mock figure. It was made from surgical tape, cleaning fluid, toilet paper... all sorts of supplies. We don't know where the real body is."

Gordon took a moment, his mind working through the possibilities. "That confirms it. We're dealing with an insider threat. If the younger Alfred kept quiet about the procedure before his death, then we're still in the clear. As for the original Alfred, we'll have to treat him as a missing person. The police won't suspect FOY, as long as the insider is caught. I'm still hopeful we can avoid media fallout—provided we handle this correctly."

Robert clenched his fist and rubbed his knuckles. "Agreed. I'm beginning to think Oliver was right. Tanya is the key."

Gordon frowned, his thoughts racing. "Well, someone breached the ninth floor. That's a real concern."

Just then, Gordon's phone rang. It was Oliver. "Gordon, someone just tried to enter the building using one of our technician's DNA."

Gordon's frown deepened. "And?"

"The technician's already on duty, called in for overtime."

"So, we have an impostor?"

"Exactly. We've got him detained on the ground floor in one of our isolation rooms. I thought you'd want to come down and question him yourself."

Gordon wasn't sure whether to feel relieved or more worried. "Interesting. What's his name?"

Oliver hesitated. "At first, he said he was Agent Smith, which is obviously a lie. Now, he won't say anything unless he talks to you. I have ways to make him talk."

Gordon's tone was flat. "No rough stuff. Get him some coffee, maybe a snack if he wants it. Make him comfortable. I'll come down after the staff meeting and our chat with Tanya. You'll be there for both, I assume?"

Oliver replied, "I might be a little late to the staff meeting, but I'll definitely be there for Tanya."

They both hung up. Gordon's mind raced, his thoughts tangled with everything that had just unfolded.

Chapter 55: Dr. Schickel

Dr. Schickel cared little that his office was often described as disheveled. After all, they said the same about him. To him, the clutter was offset by the antiseptic smell, a clear sign that germs were held at bay. In fact, for once, nothing was stacked on the visitor's chair, and he gestured for Samantha to sit.

Before the meeting, even before calling her days earlier, Dr. Schickel had done his homework. He knew that Samantha had been stationed at a remote location for a reason. She was still under observation to determine her commitment level and moral flexibility, and therefore wasn't privy to FOY's more sensitive information. Her evaluation had taken much longer than most, due to her strong will, demonstrated during a couple of medical disagreements and paperwork entanglements.

It had been decided that she would be 'read in' to Jason's pedigree only after the press conference. But the explosion had halted all communication. Until now, distracted by multiple unfolding issues, everyone had simply forgotten about her. That is, until she called for an appointment.

Looking for updated guidance, Dr. Schickel had spoken with Gordon. The conversation was rushed, and Gordon's decision swift. He made it clear that Jason's delicate transplant procedure was still not to be disclosed; thus, the meeting would require finesse. Gordon also requested a follow-up call to discuss how the meeting went and to hear Samantha's assessment of Jason's health.

Dr. Schickel glanced at Samantha, trying not to focus on her shapely figure. Despite finding her attractive, he was determined to keep their interaction professional and brief. She was seated with her legs crossed, fidgeting with her purse strap. Their eyes met briefly across his cluttered desk. Dr. Schickel decided to start with small talk.

"It seems we both share responsibility for Jason's health."

She nodded. "I don't believe we've ever been assigned the same patient until now."

"I think you're right. I remember seeing you at one of our symposiums."

"So many people, it's hard to remember." Samantha's attention briefly drifted to the calendar on the wall. "How long have you been assigned to Jason Fabrikant?"

Dr. Schickel carefully chose his words, twisting the truth. "My first scheduled visit was just two days ago."

Samantha nodded. "So was mine. I guess we both met him on the same day. What's your view of his health?"

Dr. Schickel felt the question veering into dangerous territory. He quickly deflected. "Since he's a new patient for me, I still need to dive deeper into his medical records. I haven't had the chance yet."

Samantha raised an eyebrow but said nothing. She shifted in her seat. "Per the instructions I was given, I performed some tests on Jason when he visited my office. You should know that his blood pressure was slightly elevated."

Dr. Schickel blinked. Her voice trembled slightly, a hint of nervousness that caught him off guard. Strangely, he felt a trace of unease himself.

"That's interesting," he remarked. "But not surprising given his background." He realized he had just demonstrated more knowledge about Jason than he had feigned seconds ago, and quickly tried to recover. "What do you recommend?"

Samantha hesitated. "It's not serious, but we may want to control it medically for now, while we investigate further."

Dr. Schickel was skeptical; he couldn't imagine Jason having any systemic health issues. His body had been meticulously maintained and monitored. Then his mind darted to shell #66, and a cold jolt ran up his spine. There was no reason to doubt Samantha's diagnosis—he had no grounds to question her judgment. *Sabotage again?* The disposal of this clone was too late. "Of course. I'll put in the order with our pharmacy downstairs."

Samantha reached into her purse, pulled out a small pill bottle, and placed it on the desk. "No need. I brought Amlodipine. It's a small dosage."

He stared at the bottle, surprised by her initiative. "Thank you, Dr. Morgan. I'll see that he gets this. Is there anything else you recommend?"

She gave a slight shake of her head. "No, but we'll stay in touch. Thank you, Dr. Schickel."

With that, she left the office, brisk and efficient. Dr. Schickel watched her go, letting his eyes rest on her bottom as she walked out. Once gone, his shoulders relaxed as the tension drained from him. Surprised that she left so easily, he was thankful the meeting had been brief.

As soon as she was out the door, he picked up the phone to make the follow-up call.

"Hello, Gordon. Dr. Samantha Morgan just left my office. She still doesn't know anything about Jason's transformation. Oddly, though, she found his blood pressure slightly elevated, which still confuses me. I'll need to follow up on that. In the meantime, I'll have someone deliver the medication to him. Just wanted you to know."

The response was clipped and professional. "Thank you for maintaining confidentiality. Please let security know since all visitors to Jason's room are being monitored."

Chapter 56: Tanya

Tanya nervously sat at the conference table during the FOY executive staff meeting. Dr. Schickel was droning on about a graphic projected on the screen for everyone to view, but her mind was far from the topic. Gordon had asked her to stay afterward for a tag-up, and her thoughts raced with all the possible reasons why.

She hadn't heard Dr. Schickel's question until he repeated it, his voice cutting through her thoughts. "Tanya, it's your turn to report. Anything unusual?"

Suddenly alert, Tanya quickly answered, "All systems were nominal." The meeting continued with others reporting their areas of responsibility. No one mentioned Alfred's death or the explosion. Tanya guessed Gordon no longer knew who to trust, so he kept certain topics off the table. After a short time, everyone was dismissed except for her and the Semper-Five seniors. They relocated to Gordon's office.

Gordon wasted no time with pleasantries. "Tanya, I want to be frank with you. As we've discussed, we have concerns about an insider threat at FOY. Given this, we've had to start monitoring our own employees, which includes you. Our security team flagged that you visited Jason Fabrikant a couple of hours ago. You know that this kind of unauthorized interaction is strictly prohibited. Can you explain?"

Tanya wasn't prepared for this question. She knew there were security cameras mounted throughout the building, but never thought the company would monitor its own people in this manner. She ad-libbed. "After it was announced that shell #66 was defective, I was concerned there might be a software bug in our nutrients supply algorithm. I was afraid other shells might experience the same medical problem."

Gordon's expression hardened. "Jason's transformation was some time ago. Why see him now?"

Tanya kept her voice even. "I wanted to ask how he felt when he first woke from the procedure. I was looking for clues to help narrow down the subroutines I needed to evaluate. As you know, we maintain millions of lines of code. Even the smallest hint would save me hours of work."

Gordon pressed on, "Why didn't you follow procedure and call security?"

She lowered her eyes, forcing a frown that seemed sincere. "I simply forgot. I got caught up in troubleshooting."

Gordon leaned back in his chair, his eyes narrowing as he studied her. The silence stretched, and then he turned to his team. "Thoughts?"

Dr. Schickel spoke first. "Dr. Morgan made me aware that Jason has slightly elevated blood pressure. Tanya's concern for his health seems reasonable."

Robert added, "Isolating problems with the code can be tough, especially without any clues. Her explanation makes sense to me."

Tanya felt a moment of relief. She had given an answer that, on the surface, sounded plausible. If they bought it, she might be in the clear. But she couldn't relax just yet. Oliver had yet to speak.

When he finally did, his tone was different—tight, with a barely restrained edge. "She's been briefed on our security protocols, and she chose to ignore them."

Gordon didn't hesitate. "What would you have us do, Oliver?"

Oliver's expression remained tense, his words clipped. "Thinking about the intruder in the isolation room on the ground floor, I have an idea that I'd like to discuss in private."

They escorted Tanya out of the room, leaving her alone in the hallway, the door closing as she left. If they gave her the chance to leave the building, she would run—maybe even flee the country.

Chapter 57: Young Jason

Jason was worried about the potential threat to his life. He also considered the possibility that Tanya was just some crazy lady who had escaped the psych ward. Maybe she was merely a demented patient wandering the halls and scaring people. He had never met the company's Chief Computer Architect, nor had he heard of Tanya Malbern. Nonetheless, considering her demeanor and the conversation, he chose to take her warning seriously.

If there truly was a threat, Jason now faced three choices. Unfortunately, they were all bad. One option was to hunker down in the room, where he would be a sitting duck for a killer. He would need to devise a way to defend himself.

Alternatively, he could try to go home, but that would go against Gordon's wishes. Even if he attempted to sneak out, he would likely be stopped by security and ushered back to his suite.

Finally, he could share his concerns with FOY, but Tanya had suggested that they couldn't be trusted.

Jason felt trapped.

Churning over his options, his concentration was broken by another knock on the door. At first, he thought it was Tanya, perhaps returning to retract her warning or further explain the danger. Then he became worried; the knock might be a prelude to the very threat she had warned him about.

Looking at the door, he noticed there was no peephole to offer a clue about who was outside. To make matters worse, he realized there was no keyed lock. The rapping continued, and he tried to ignore the sound, but the person was persistent. Finally, he spoke loudly through the door: "Yeah, what is it?"

The response came in an equally elevated volume: "Sir, Dr. Schickel asked that I deliver some medication. He mentioned that the dosages are included in the bag, and he'll discuss the reason at your next session."

Jason wasn't going to let him in. "Please leave it by the door. I'm not properly dressed."

The man incoherently mumbled, and then Jason heard his footsteps fade, gradually blending into the normal buzz of the building. Still cautious, Jason looked for a chain on the door and became frustrated that there was no security of any kind. The facility, typical of most hospital settings, had no such protections for the patients.

Instead, Jason planted his foot a few inches back to block the door in case someone tried to force their way in. Cracking it slowly open, just enough for his hand to pass through, he noticed a small white bag on the floor. He reached through the doorjamb and grabbed it, then quickly closed the door. Mimicking what he'd seen in various movies, he tilted the desk chair against the doorknob, unsure it would provide any added protection.

Jason turned his attention to the bag and fished out its contents. True to the visitor's word, inside was a bottle of pills along with instructions. Looking over the paperwork, he saw that he was prescribed thirty pills to be taken each morning for a month. He toyed with the idea that someone was trying to poison him, but he also realized he might be overreacting. Tanya's warning had left him anxious. Better safe than s... dead.

Then, the older persona from his past emerged, wondering if the pills might be too large—hard to swallow. He shook the small container, hearing no sound of pills rattling within. Curious, he twisted the cap, only to find the annoying cotton ball that controls moisture. Pulling it out, he still saw no pills. Instead, he found a small, folded note.

The note read: "You're in danger. Go to the bathroom on the seventh floor, farthest from the elevator. You'll find supplies and instructions in a black bag hidden in the trash receptacle. Please be careful." It was signed: "The girl with the rose."

At first, a smile crept onto his face: Samantha… Then, the message sank in. This was Jason's second warning about being in danger. Now fully distressed, he realized he had no secretive way to access the public bathroom, but he had to slip out somehow. With security cameras mounted in all the common areas, trying to be stealthy would be a challenge. He looked around the suite and thought about escaping through the windows, but they were fixed, not designed to be opened. They were also made of tempered glass, difficult to break. Even if he managed a way out of the window, he was seven stories above the garden, with no balcony or ledge to climb onto. As much as he had enjoyed comic books as a kid, he wasn't Spiderman, nor was he going to tie sheets together and plunge to his death.

Suddenly, his eyes rested on a potential solution.

Chapter 58: Bastien

Bastien sat alone in the quiet, windowless isolation room. The door was locked, and guards stood outside to ensure he wasn't going anywhere. He was pleased he hadn't carried identification with him, keeping his identity a mystery. To FOY, he was a complete unknown. As leverage, he had promised to divulge his name if he could meet the FOY CEO, Mr. Gordon Formell.

Bastien mentally replayed the sequence of events since entering the facility, guessing that the technician he was disguised as *had* been working today. The Dish had shared his schedule, so he was puzzled why this had happened. If the technician was already in the building, the security system should have alerted them about the double-entry attempt. He cursed himself for not checking the lot for his car. Though it was unfortunate, Bastien took comfort in knowing he had a viable backup plan. His actions were still in play.

Despite his circumstances, Bastien had to admit he was being treated well. He was offered restroom breaks, which had so far been unnecessary. He had been given a sandwich, an apple, and a cup of coffee, which he accepted and consumed. The wait and lack of freedom, however, were grating. He sat in silence, simmering with frustration.

The silence was broken by the sound of approaching footsteps. He speculated that he was finally about to meet Gordon face-to-face. Bastien considered his options as the moment drew closer. His bag had been confiscated, but he still had the chloroform. Better yet, since he wasn't frisked or even cuffed, he could reach behind to his lower back. The plastic weapon was still there, tucked into his pants, resting against his upper buttocks. He calculated that he could get through the metal detector as long as only one bullet was in the chamber, no magazine necessary. Grinning, he felt the handle, mentally visualizing the moment when he would squeeze the trigger.

The door unlocked, and two imposing guards entered the room. One was well over six feet; the other was a stocky five-foot-eight. Bastien quickly inventoried their gear. He saw multiple pouches on their Kevlar vests, one holding a two-way radio and others that likely contained supplies—batteries, gloves, pens, paper—who knows what else. Secured to their duty belts, with belt keepers attaching them to their inner belts, were a flashlight, baton, handcuffs, keys hanging from a carabiner, a taser, and most notably, a Glock 22. They were fully equipped, like cops, and would serve as his mobile supply depot.

The taller guard spoke firmly, "Sir, you'll need to follow us."

Bastien, feeling optimistic, asked, "To see the CEO?"

The guard ignored his question, taking him by the arm and leading him to the elevator on the first floor. Bastien had been there once before and cast a quick, disdainful glance at the fountain. The shorter guard entered a code and pushed the eighth-floor button for access.

Within a minute, the familiar ding of the elevator announced their arrival. Upon exiting, Bastien saw the decadence of the floor and felt confident that he was about to meet the CEO. He was also pleased he wasn't handcuffed, giving him the freedom to act with one fatal motion if necessary. They led him to a closed door, and a guard rapped lightly to announce their arrival.

A voice from inside responded, "Come in."

Bastien entered, counting four people already inside. Two men were standing. One was athletic, dressed in camo attire, and seemed to be directing the activities. The other was a blond-haired, handsome man in a suit—an executive. Bastien had seen pictures and video of Gordon Formell, and neither of these men resembled him.

A woman sat in a specialized chair, hooked up to a polygraph. He could see the cuff on her bicep measuring her blood pressure, as well as the connections to each of her hands. One hand had an electrodermal sensor to measure perspiration, while the other measured her pulse. Around her chest and abdomen were straps to detect any variation in her breathing. A polygrapher sat nearby, fiddling with electronic equipment.

Bastien looked at the woman but didn't recognize her. She was plain, uncomfortable, and certainly didn't fit the profile of someone he'd expect to be under such scrutiny. He was told to observe her for a moment before being asked if he knew her. Bastien remained silent, refusing to cooperate. They repeated the question to the woman. She hesitated but complied, answering that she didn't know him. After a brief glance, Bastien was escorted out of the room. He wondered who she was and why she was being questioned. He briefly considered that she could be the Dish but quickly dismissed it. This woman was unattractive, and would never have referred to herself as such. Moreover, the Dish was assertive, while this woman seemed resigned, almost defeated.

Bastien was led to the ground floor by the same two guards and brought back to the isolation room.. Frustrated, he wondered if he would ever get his opportunity. Convinced that Gordon was in the building, he made a bold decision. As the guards turned their backs to leave, Bastien reached for his plastic Glock.

Chapter 59: Young Jason

Jason stared at a wall vent and decided to remove the grill. The HVAC intake was sized for commercial purposes, large enough for his body to fit through. With no other options, he climbed in and blindly followed the ductwork wherever it led. It sloped downward.

The passageway narrowed as he descended, and the fear of being boxed in once again took hold of him. Slowly lowering himself further into the unknown, he realized he was trapped in a small, enclosed space. Panic set in as he couldn't believe he'd forgotten his new phobia and had voluntarily put himself in this position. Desperate to escape, he began to flail, feeling the air grow scarce.

He kicked repeatedly at a joint, managing to dislodge it, and crawled through the side of the ductwork. He dropped to the cement floor, gasping for breath in relief.

Looking up, the space where he landed was unfamiliar—an open area only five feet high. Jason was forced to stoop to avoid banging his head on the ceiling. He stood in an area wedged between the sixth and seventh floors, a level hidden from the view of security cameras. Surrounding him were an array of HVAC ductwork, extensive plumbing, and electrical wiring. Concrete trusses stretched across, likely providing structural support and reducing the need for additional columns.

Jason crouched to explore, his foot sinking into something soft and mushy. Animal droppings, each pellet the size of an olive, littered the floor. His senses heightened, and he heard the distant scattering of tiny feet. He shuddered, fearing mice—or worse, rats—and hoped there was another exit besides the ductwork. The thought of being trapped again, with a rodent dropping from above and slithering down his shirt, was enough to make him shudder.

Refocusing, Jason reminded himself that his mission was to find the bathroom mentioned in Samantha's note. Searching the space to gain his bearings, he spotted the elevator shaft in the center of the floor. The elevator didn't stop on this level, but when it paused on the sixth floor, he could access its ceiling panel. Jason knew the lift had a security camera trained on the passengers inside, so he decided to disable it, anticipating he might need to change floors unnoticed later.

While waiting for the elevator to stop on the floor below, he noticed a sign labeled "Interstitial Level." It made sense—this level allowed the hospital and the labs above to be reconfigured without costly staging. It also provided access to support cables and plumbing for the Glass Fountain below. This floor minimized disturbances to the electrical and mechanical systems, ensuring that operations above remained unaffected by any work done below.

The elevator finally arrived on the sixth floor. Jason spotted the camera and its cable grommet, then reached through an access panel and yanked to disable it. He was hopeful it would take hours—if not days—for security to restore their visuals. He could now travel up or down by climbing on top and entering through the ceiling panel, unseen. Unfortunately, he couldn't exit the car without triggering hallway surveillance cameras to flag him. So, he withdrew from the shaft area and stayed on the interstitial floor, continuing his search for another way to access the bathroom.

As he moved through the space, Jason followed more ductwork to an area he guessed led up to the public bathroom. He had no other choice and inhaled deeply. He kicked at another vent to dislodge it and reluctantly climbed in, fearing rats as he ascended. Climbing was much harder than descending, requiring him to wedge his body upward, inch by inch. Mentally bracing himself, he controlled his breathing, determined not to panic. Just as he began to relax, something brushed against the back of his neck.

He yelled, "RATS!" His voice cracked higher than he intended, far too loud for someone trying to remain unheard. He was convinced he'd felt a slimy rodent tail slithering along his neck and swatted at it with one hand. It turned out to be nothing more than loose wiring, harmlessly dangling above him. Embarrassment gave way to fear, and he hoped his scream hadn't alerted anyone. Trying to calm himself, he found a bit of humor in the situation: *Great. Like, you're a 13-year-old girl at a boy-band concert...like.*

Shaking off the panic, Jason continued upward through the vent shaft. He reached a side grate, and through its slits, he could see a woman in the bathroom. He immediately felt like a peeping Tom, but reassured himself when he saw she was just washing her hands, having already finished in the stall. The sound of the faucet drowned out most of the noise he made while climbing, so he remained hidden in the shadows—and, so far, undetected. He waited in darkness, trying to ignore the growing sense of unease as he wondered what might crawl up his leg. Spiders, he thought, and shuddered.

The woman seemed to take forever, slowly reapplying her lipstick. Then, as if the gods were testing his patience, she pulled out her eyeliner and then extended his torment by primping her hair. Finally, after making clothing adjustments and posing for one last look at her rear end, she left. Jason quickly popped the grill off the vent and awkwardly fell out, landing on his hands and knees on the bathroom tile. It was a crash landing, but he was free, and he was relieved. He immediately closed the door and locked it.

Knowing there were no cameras inside the bathroom, Jason took a moment to regain his composure. Following Samantha's instructions, he reached into the trash bin. Sure enough, there was a black bag tucked under paper towels, just as she had said. He smiled to himself, elated to have found the right bathroom on his first try. Opening the bag, he began to inspect its contents, his grin widening.

Chapter 60: Samantha

Samantha sat in a lounge chair tucked behind a large potted plant. There was no turning back now. She prayed she wouldn't get caught. She had positioned herself deliberately so that Jason wouldn't see her as he entered the unisex bathroom. She wasn't sure if she could trust him. As a test, she watched carefully, waiting to see if he appeared with FOY security. If he showed up with the guards, she'd have to assume he was privy to FOY's secrets. In that case, she'd find a phone, cry "Golden Monkey" to her lifeline—the elder Jason waiting in the parking lot—and sequester herself until help arrived. If, however, the younger Jason arrived alone, she'd assume he was a victim, just like his donor.

The verdict would come any moment now. Samantha tried to remain calm, but anxiety gnawed at her like a pending biopsy result. She hoped the younger Jason was innocent. She liked him. Replaying their limited time together, she recalled how guarded he'd been when they met for coffee. His explanation at dinner the following night had seemed logical—his reluctance to share his background made sense, given that his identity as 'Client One' wasn't public knowledge. She thought of his classy demeanor, his sharp wit, and his penetrating green eyes. But whether he was truthful or not, it was too late to turn back. She only hoped not to become ensnared in FOY's web as she sat along one of the building's spider-like radial corridors.

Samantha considered her next steps. If Jason was innocent, there were two possible courses of action. First, she could inform him about the elder Jason. Then, she would leave the building alone to get help, knowing Jason likely wouldn't be allowed to leave. Once the police arrived, they could share their observations and try to piece together FOY's operation. But what could they actually prove? If they came up short, they might have to leave the DMV, adopting new identities under witness protection.

Her second option was to collect evidence, which meant reaching the executive floor. Even accessing the eighth floor would be a challenge without the cipher. If they made it there, they might find something incriminating. What that might be? She had no idea. If she did uncover evidence, she'd call the elder Jason, who would alert the police.

As these thoughts cycled through her mind, Samantha kept her eyes on the corridor traffic. Finally, a woman exited the restroom, leaving the door slightly ajar, signaling the single occupancy room was empty.

Seeing the door open, Samantha started to doubt her plan. What if Jason didn't see the note she'd left? He might never show up. If so, the cleaning crew could eventually find the suspicious bag she'd hidden in the trash. It wasn't too late. *I can still retrieve the bag and leave.* She stood, ready to abandon her flawed plan.

Suddenly, loud noises erupted from the bathroom. The door swung shut and latched. Samantha froze. She hadn't seen anyone go in. A chill ran through her. Could it be the cleaning crew? Should she flee the building immediately? Her instincts told her to wait, though fear clawed at her resolve.

Minutes passed; whoever was inside stayed for a long time. Samantha impatiently tracked the second hand of the nearby wall clock. Finally, the door opened, and a man emerged. He wore a white lab coat, glasses, and an N95 mask. His curly brown hair looked unfamiliar, yet Samantha recognized him instantly—Jason. She'd provided the disguise. He was alone. Relieved, she discreetly motioned for him to enter the elevator. Neither acknowledged the other—just as she'd instructed in the note.

Her original plan had been to head to the cafeteria. There, they'd sit at separate tables, grab snacks, and exchange notes. She'd let him know the elder Jason was waiting in the car. But as the elevator doors slid shut, Jason pressed the button for the eighth floor. He typed in a code, and the elevator ascended. *How does he know the code?* A fresh wave of doubt choked her. Her stomach sank.

When they arrived, Jason took her hand and led her to an unoccupied conference room. They slipped inside without turning on the lights.

Jason leaned in and gave her a quick, unexpected kiss on the lips. "Thank you for the message. I'm so happy you're safe," he whispered.

Samantha stiffened, still on guard. "How did you get into the bathroom without using the door? I was sitting right outside, watching. And how do you know the code for this floor?"

Jason kept his voice low as he explained. "Earlier today, a woman came to my room and warned me that I might be in danger. She gave me the code to Gordon's floor and said I might find answers in his office. When I got your note, I figured my movements were being monitored. The only way out was through the ductworks. I popped out through the bathroom grate. I found the bag, followed your instructions, and dyed my hair. It took longer than I wanted, but it worked. I owe you so much more than just the dinner I promised."

Samantha, softening, asked, "Jason, please tell me you're not part of FOY's hidden agenda."

Jason looked pained. "I swear, I have no idea what they're up to."

She studied his face, searching his green eyes for deceit but found none. Her shoulders relaxed slightly. "Jason," she said, hesitating. "There's something I need to tell you. You're not going to like it."

"What is it?" he asked, his brow furrowing.

"There's a man in the parking lot waiting for us. He's older, with scars on his face and a terrible limp. He says his name is Jason Fabrikant. He's claiming to be you. I believe him."

Chapter 61: Oliver

Oliver received a distressing call from housekeeping and abruptly left Tanya's polygraph session while it was still in progress. Within minutes, he arrived in Jason's room. A young woman with an Eastern European accent sat in a chair, wildly gesturing as she spoke, while a guard stood nearby, taking notes.

The guard noticed Oliver and raised a hand to calm the situation. "There's no need to get defensive, ma'am. No one's blaming you. Take a deep breath and relax. Please, start from the beginning and tell us exactly what happened."

The housekeeper shifted her gaze to Oliver and spoke, her tone more composed, Eastern European accent thick. "As I say, I am told to bring lunch menu for Mister Fabrikant from food services. Also, I need to restock toiletry items and bring fresh towels. I knock on door, but there is no answer. When this happen, we are trained to enter slowly and announce, yes? So, I try. But when I push door, something is blocking it. I push harder, and then I hear loud thud! A chair fall to floor—it was wedged under knob."

Oliver listened carefully while scanning the room for clues. Out of the corner of his eye, he spotted a small screw on the floor beneath a vent grate. He walked over and noticed that all the screws were missing, leaving the grate loosely attached only by friction.

Grimacing, Oliver grabbed the phone in the room and called the first-floor guard. "It looks like Jason escaped through a vent. Expand the search immediately—he could be anywhere. Also, check the database to confirm he's still in the building."

After hanging up, Oliver dialed Dr. Schickel.

The doctor answered promptly. "Hello."

"This is Oliver," he began briskly. "You mentioned something about Fabrikant's blood pressure. Can you tell me more about your interaction with him today?"

Dr. Schickel replied, "Well, to clarify, I haven't seen Jason since Thursday. My only involvement today was to prescribe medication—actually, Dr. Samantha Morgan, his cardiologist, prescribed it earlier this morning. I just facilitated the pharmacy delivering it to his room."

"I know we were told about the delivery. Do you know if Jason was in his room at the time?" Oliver asked.

"Yes, the pharmacist confirmed that he had talked to him."

Oliver's tone sharpened. "How long ago was your meeting with Samantha?"

"About two hours ago," the doctor replied.

"Did anything seem suspicious?"

Dr. Schickel hesitated, his voice faltering. "N-no, not exactly. Other than my surprise at Jason's health indicators. I didn't expect those results. I'm worried someone is tampering with something, and he has health issues similar to shell #66."

Oliver pressed further. "I'm just trying to figure out a timeline. Would you say the meds were delivered about an hour ago?"

"Yes, that's roughly correct."

Oliver ended the call without another word and immediately redialed security. "I have a task. Find out if Samantha Morgan is still in the building. If she is, don't let her leave. Also, locate her car's make and model. If it's here, send a team out to keep an eye on it. Report anything unusual."

Chapter 62: Tanya

Tanya replayed her polygraph session in her mind. At first, the questions had been simple, requiring nothing more than a simple yes or no. "Is your name Tanya Malbern?" and "Do you work for FOY, Inc.?"

Then they held up a blue fabric patch and asked if it was red. They instructed her to lie. Following their directions, she answered, "Yes," knowing it was wrong, and heard the needle jump in response.

"The sound of those needles, Ms. Malbern, means we've established a baseline. We have you calibrated."

It was clear—they knew when she was being deceitful. Their physiological objective had been met.

Then, the real interrogation began.

"Did you kill Alfred Grier? Did you plant the explosives?"

Since she hadn't done either, she thought she was doing okay. But then, they brought Bastien into the room. Though she'd never met him in person, she knew his background, his politics, and most unfortunately, his face. All her defenses crumbled the moment they asked, "Do you know this person?" Her heart skipped. She lied, but her body betrayed her—and her world shook, needles scribing as if a magnitude seven earthquake had just hit. It was her first time taking a polygraph, and she failed miserably.

After the test, they led her back to Gordon's office. He was sitting there with his senior staff, all except Oliver, who had been called away earlier.

Gordon wasted no time. "Tanya, I hired you directly from MIT, correct?"

Tanya's throat tightened, and she could barely force the words out. "Yes, sir."

He continued, "If I recall, you wanted to be at the forefront of medical advancements. We offered you a chance to be part of something groundbreaking. Now, it seems you're trying to sabotage everything we've worked for. Let's not play games, dear. Why?"

The impact of his words sank in; there was no use denying it. Hoping against hope, she blurted the truth—her words tumbling out in a desperate rush. "I found out about FOY's methods through the computer code. When I saw what was happening with the clones, it felt wrong, unethical. I should've come to you right away about my concerns. My mistake was not speaking up from the start. I'm sorry."

Gordon's eyes narrowed, as if reading her every movement. He changed tactics. "Who's the man we brought in during your polygraph, and how do you know him?"

Tanya's stomach clenched. She took a deep breath before speaking. "His name is Bastien Landow. I recruited him. I found him on social media and used him during the press conference, hoping to start an investigation. It backfired. It was a huge mistake. I never intended for anyone to get hurt." She fidgeted with her Phoenix pendant, the implications of her actions bearing down on her.

"Who else knows? Did you ever involve the police or the FBI?"

"Just Bastien and me, I swear."

Gordon flashed a smile, one that didn't reach his eyes. "Relax. Don't be nervous."

She pleaded with him, her voice shaky. "Please, give me another chance."

In a calm, almost soothing voice, Gordon responded, "We're not going to harm you. I'm sure we can work something out. Of course, we'll need to detain you for a couple of days while we assess the damage you've caused."

Gordon turned to Robert and Dr. Schickel. "Gentlemen, please take her upstairs and make her comfortable."

She didn't believe him; she'd seen this manipulation before. But she was confused about the reference to upstairs. What did he mean?

At gunpoint, Tanya was escorted through the building, her legs feeling heavier with each step, as if the weight of her fate was pulling her down. She feared she was being led to her death. No one knew she was at FOY—she would simply disappear, a nameless casualty of their secrecy. The only solace she had was that she told her mother she loved her in their last conversation. With limp legs, the two men nearly had to carry her to the library.

Her shock deepened when they revealed a cipher and opened a hidden stairwell behind a bookcase.

"What's this?"

Dr. Schickel's expression remained neutral. "A stairwell to the ninth floor, pet."

Her legs were completely useless now, and they supported her weight entirely as they ascended, step by step.

Dr. Schickel's voice was unnervingly calm. "Don't worry, sweetheart. As Mr. Formell said, we aren't going to hurt you. Just relax. We need to keep you out of sight for a few days until we finish our investigation. After that, you'll be free. We have a few rooms upstairs where you can relax. You'll find them much more comfortable than the recovery rooms on the seventh floor. We'll even let you choose which one you like."

Tanya wanted to believe him. Perhaps the meeting in Gordon's office hadn't gone as terribly as she thought. Maybe there was still a chance.

Robert had holstered his gun, no longer holding it, and said nothing. They guided her to a room that looked more like a storage closet than a place for a guest. No bed. No bathroom. Just shelves stocked with supplies. It was colder than the other rooms.

She glanced around, her breath caught in her throat. "I don't understand. Where...?"

Before she could finish, a sharp pain struck her neck. She turned and saw Dr. Schickel pulling a syringe away from her skin. The world blurred as dizziness swept over her. She tried to fight it, but her body wouldn't respond. She collapsed, her head spinning, and Robert caught her before she hit the ground. Everything went blurry. Her eyelids fluttered. She felt herself drifting, as though she were floating above her own body.

From her dreamlike state, she watched the men move her onto a gurney. Her mind flashed to memories of her father, smiling, holding her small hands as they played with ladybugs. But the warmth faded. The last thing she felt was an overwhelming coldness. Then, all went black.

Chapter 63: Old Jason

It was getting warm in the car, so the older Jason pulled up his sleeves. In doing so, he noticed a pale band of skin on his left wrist. For a moment, panic set in—his Rolex watch was gone. Then he remembered: his younger clone now owned the sentimental timepiece. Not only had his identity been stripped away, but his possessions were gone too. He took a deep breath, trying to adjust to his new normal.

The wait in Samantha's car would be long. The seats were stiff, making it difficult to relax. He decided to close his eyes, hoping his thoughts would distract him from the discomfort. Soon, he began to drift back to his days as a baseball player.

The best memories weren't about the games themselves but about the camaraderie of the team. He recalled the pranks they played on the long bus rides. Though the average baseball player's age hovered around twenty-nine, they acted much younger when together.

Jason smiled, remembering how they'd write on the faces of teammates who'd fallen into a deep sleep. The laughter bubbled up as he pictured the silly messages: "Pobody's nerfect," surrounded by hearts and daisies, or "I Love You, Man." Keeping a straight face while talking to the unknowing victim afterward was always the hardest part.

Another prank involved sticking notes on a player's back before interviews. What began as innocent "Kick Me" signs evolved into absurd confessions like "I pee in swimming pools." The media found it hilarious and played along with the jokes, especially at the rookies' expense.

But the funniest moment, in Jason's mind, was at a post-travel strategy meeting. Coach Hoghead, ever the disciplinarian, insisted on reviewing game film despite their exhaustion. Mid-meeting, Campy, the ill-tempered shortstop, fell asleep in his chair, snoring. The team seized the chance, plunging the room into pitch darkness and pretending to continue the session.

When Campy woke, he could hear the discussion— their voices calm and serious— but saw nothing but blackness. Rubbing his eyes frantically, he shouted, "I'M BLIND! I'M BLIND!" Laughter erupted, shaking the walls and carrying far beyond the room. His ensuing anger only made things funnier.

Jason missed the baseball fields—the smell, manicured and rich with memories, and the roar of the crowds. The laughter of his teammates felt like a distant echo, some of them now gone.

Not all memories involved baseball, although another one would also include a diamond. Anna was always there in his mind—a ring purchased, never offered on one knee. It wasn't just because she was beautiful, although she was; it was because he truly loved her. *God, if only I could undo one thing.* The regret gnawed at him, forcing him to redirect his thoughts.

Jason reflected on his past and the ups and downs of his scorecard. Considering his failing health, his longevity and contributions had run their natural course. Hopes of reshaping his youth and making better decisions on his second go-around faded away. Instead, he would have to be satisfied with his single opportunity, just like every other person who had ever walked the earth.

He had to accept that he'd never be young again. Since escaping FOY, he had been consumed by uncovering the company's secrets. Gordon had promised a second chance, but it was a lie.

The reality of his fate hit him harder with every passing day. He had already mourned the loss of his youth once; now, he would mourn again.

A loud rap on the window snapped him out of his daydream. FOY security stood outside, tapping a baton against the glass. Jason considered driving off, but two Range Rovers had boxed him in.

Reluctantly, he rolled the window down. "What's your business here, sir?"

"I'm waiting for a friend," Jason replied, keeping his tone respectful.

"You need to follow us. Step out of the car." The guard's tone was clipped, leaving no room for negotiation. Without waiting, the guard opened the door, while two others flanked him.

Jason was escorted into the building. He knew better than to ask any questions, so they walked in silence. After a brisk pat-down and confiscation of his phone, the guards led him toward the elevator, bypassing the turnstiles. Jason's age and disability made it hard to keep up, but the guards' pace was unrelenting.

Soon, he found himself in an executive office, standing before a massive mahogany desk. Behind it sat the man Jason had once trusted with his life: Gordon Formell, FOY's CEO.

Chapter 64: Young Jason

Samantha and Jason remained hidden, finding a safe spot outside on the eighth floor. They positioned themselves behind a cabinet in an unoccupied conference room, with a view of the elevator lobby and a long hallway. They had just witnessed Gordon's office door swing open, and watched in silence as three people exited. The trio disappeared into another room lined with bookshelves.

After they were gone, Jason whispered to Samantha, his voice tight with disbelief, "That was the lady! The one who warned me about FOY, Tanya Malbern. She claimed to be the Chief Computer Architect. She looked awful—gaunt and listless. Something bad is happening. The man in the white smock was my doctor, Schickel."

Samantha nodded. "Yeah, I met him earlier today, and the man in the suit— I saw those same two men arguing in one of the executive offices. As for her…" She squinted. "I agree, she was petrified. Do you see how those men were gripping her?"

Jason nodded. "She looked like death. Her feet are barely touching the ground. They were carrying her, as if she was too weak to walk… or to resist."

Jason blurted, almost too loudly, "Wait a minute. That's the room!"

"What room?"

Jason pulled out his wallet and retrieved a note, showing Samantha what was written: "Behind the Anne Frank book in the library, eighth floor at FOY, cipher 06121929."

Samantha took an uneven breath. "Jason, I'm scared."

He didn't say a word. Instead, he ran his palm gently over the back of her hand. He hoped the three would reemerge so they could explore the area.

Samantha spoke quietly. "If we make it upstairs and find something…incriminating, I'll need to find a phone. I can use FOY's landline to call my partner—that is, the older you. We established a code word for help, so even if FOY is monitoring the call, they'll never suspect anything…"

An elevator chime interrupted them. They both looked to the lobby and saw an older man briskly ushered from the lift into Gordon's office. They could only see the back of his head, but his limp was unmistakable. Samantha whispered, "Speak of the devil." She stopped, frowned, and rubbed Jason's shoulder. "I'm sorry, he's certainly no devil—just the opposite, in fact. This must be hard for you."

Jason's emotions exploded as he saw his donor for the first time—anger, betrayal, depression—leaving him speechless.

Samantha grimaced. "What are they going to do to him?" After a delay, her mouth suddenly fell open. "Oh my God, our lifeline. Jason, we have nobody to call. We're on our own!"

Jason felt more vulnerable than ever, compounded by guilt for getting Samantha into his mess.

As the older Jason was led into Gordon's office, the door was left ajar. From outside the room, they tried to catch snippets of conversation. Gordon's voice was distinctive. "Jason, I'm sorry for the ordeal you've endured."

As Gordon spoke, the two men who had escorted Tanya emerged from the library, but she wasn't with them. Jason shifted his focus to what they were saying. The suited man asked, "What'd you give her, anyway?"

Dr. Schickel replied flatly, "Propofol—lethal dose."

"You've become pretty skillful at deceit. That made it easier—efficient."

The doctor nodded. "A lifetime of practice. We need to think about the backlog. With this fourth body, we'll need to fire up the chamber later. And if my instincts serve me correctly, I'm thinking we'll soon have another one."

The suited man asked, "What does Gordon want to do with the intruder downstairs?"

Dr. Schickel replied, "Gordon will try for a full confession to see if there are any other players. Depending on how things go, he might just send him down to the basement lab. I could use a live subject."

They both fell silent as they entered Gordon's office and closed the door, cutting off any further conversation.

Samantha looked at Jason, her mouth quivering. "Something evil is going on here. That man we just saw, the older you, told me there's a ninth floor."

Jason held out his hand. "We need to find out. Let's go check the library."

She took his hand as he led her out of the shadows.

Chapter 65: Bastien

Bastien sat in the isolation room, watching as the guards turned to leave. Once their backs were facing him, he drew his plastic Glock and aimed the nozzle at the taller man's head. "Not so fast, Sasquatch! You too, Butt-Plug—arms up!" They spun around at the command, eyes locking on the weapon.

The shorter guard was the first to comply, despite the gun being aimed at his partner. The taller guard made a subtle move toward his firearm.

Bastien reacted immediately. "Do the math, genius. You'll be shot before you even get your hand on it."

With clenched jaws and lips pressed tight, the larger man slowly raised his hands to the ceiling.

Bastien focused on the bigger threat, giving his instructions. "Okay, Sasquatch, listen carefully, or I'll shoot you in the crotch—with your left hand, undo your belt and drop it to the floor." He aimed the weapon at the large man's genitals, squinting as though taking aim. Once the belt fell, he shifted his attention to the shorter man. "Your turn, Butt-Plug." His belt clattered to the floor.

Bastien felt in control. "Now, kick them lightly over here." Reluctantly, both guards complied, sliding their belts within a foot of where Bastien stood. Using his heel, he dragged the belts closer and retrieved the handcuffs. "So far, so good. I might let you live, despite being traitors to Mother Earth. Next, take off your vests and then your clothes—very slowly. Let's start with you." He pointed the gun at the shorter man.

As instructed, one after the other, the guards undressed until they stood before him, wearing only their underwear.

Bastien grinned. "Let's not stop there—drop those panties."

Reluctantly, both men removed their underwear.

Bastien laughed, mocking the taller man. "Guess you're not the bigger man after all. Or is it just cold in here?"

With a pile of clothing and gear on the floor, Bastien barked, "Okay, Sasquatch, lie down on the floor, stomach down, with your hands behind your back." He turned to the shorter man. "You, put these on him." He tossed a pair of handcuffs at the guard, hitting him in the stomach. The guard gasped but caught the restraints and secured his partner.

Bastien commanded, "Show me that they're secure."

The shorter guard demonstrated with a tug.

"Good. Now, lie down on your stomach, right next to your buddy, shoulder to shoulder."

Soon, the shorter guard was restrained as well. Both men were now naked, lying with their bare chests against the cold floor, wrists bound behind their backs.

Bastien smiled, feeling a rush of power, retrieving their weapons from the ground, and tucking them in his belt. He then reached for a baton and smacked it against his palm. "Now, unless you want me to get creative with this stick, you'll tell me where you stashed my bag. You know, the one you confiscated." He let the baton's end brush against the shorter guard's inner thigh as he stood over them. The man quickly spilled the location.

Bastien grabbed one of the T-shirts on the floor, drenched it in chloroform from his water bottle, and held it as a rag over each of their faces, starting with the larger man. Within seconds, both guards were unconscious. He then set out to retrieve his backpack, containing his phone, duct tape, and nylon rope. The two guards remained motionless.

When Bastien returned with his supplies, he tore more loose clothing into strips, forming a ball to shove in their mouths. He secured the rags as gags by wrapping duct tape fully around their heads, leaving their nostrils clear for breathing.

He then positioned the guards' limp bodies facing away from each other. Bastien used rope and more tape to bind them together. He positioned them embarrassingly, conjoined at the buttocks. Naked and bound, Bastien figured that when they woke up, they'd be desperate to regain some dignity by freeing themselves before calling for help—delaying any alarms.

Donning the larger man's security uniform, Bastien struggled slightly with the size, but it would suffice. He loaded the belt with the guards' weapons, keeping his 3D-printed gun tucked behind his back. He had developed a bond with the plastic weapon, which had made this entire operation possible. He'd even given it a name—The Cure—to honor it. As he left, fully armed, he focused on the mission ahead: Gordon Formell.

Chapter 66: Young Jason

With Gordon's door closed, Jason and Samantha stepped into the library, their eyes sweeping over the rich walnut bookcases lining two opposing walls. The shelves stretched floor to ceiling, brimming with hundreds of books—many requiring a sliding ladder to access. The room exuded a quiet grandeur, its diverse selection spanning literary fiction, historical nonfiction, mystery, science fiction, and more, all curated to reflect the floor's Renaissance theme.

Jason clutched his note, his expression taut with worry as he surveyed the sheer volume of books they'd have to search. He spoke quietly, his shoulders slumped. "We'll never find it."

Samantha's eyes darted along the shelves, her determination unshaken. "Yes, we will. They're organized by category. The far wall looks like medical science and computer technology—all nonfiction. The near wall has a mix, sorted by genre. We'll start there. Do you remember the book's size or color?"

Jason frowned. "You're kidding, right? I haven't read that book since middle school—almost sixty years ago!"

Ignoring his frustration, Samantha began scanning the shelves, while Jason absently browsed the classics, spotting familiar names like Hemingway, Steinbeck, and Dumas.

Samantha's voice broke his focus. "Got it! The Diary of Anne Frank." She slid the book out from the shelf.

Jason blinked in disbelief.

She shrugged. "It was easy. I just looked in the section about WWII."

Jason shook his head. "I'm inviting you to my house to find my pills."

"I'm guessing you don't need them anymore." Samantha stretched her neck to peer in the gap she had created. Through the empty slot where the book had been, they saw a cipher keypad. Jason pulled out the surrounding books and keyed in the code. With a soft click, the bookcase unlatched and swung partially open. Behind it was a spiral staircase leading upward into darkness.

Jason took Samantha by the arms, meeting her gaze. "So, the rumors were true, there is a ninth floor. If we weren't trespassing before, we certainly are now." He paused for a moment, replacing the books so nothing was out of place. "Listen, I don't know what they'll do if they catch us. Maybe you should stay here."

Samantha shook her head firmly, though her nervousness was evident. Jason kissed her hand before they both stepped through the hidden door, carefully closing it behind them.

With the door shut, they were enveloped in pitch blackness. They crept up the staircase, each footfall deliberate, their nerves attuned to every creak beneath them. Fingers skimmed the railing, tracing its cold surface as if reading its texture like braille for guidance.

At the top, a dim light revealed their surroundings. A passageway led to a curved hallway forming a circular path around the floor, with the staircase at its center. To proceed, they had only two options: left or right. Jason chose left, moving counterclockwise.

Samantha's voice was barely a whisper. "Do you smell that? Sickening."

Jason said nothing but quickened his pace.

After a few steps, they reached a closed door. Swallowing his apprehension, he turned the knob. A flood of relief hit him when it opened to reveal a bathroom. He quickly searched the cabinets and storage spaces, finding only standard supplies: sterile pads, toilet paper rolls, rubbing alcohol, and paper towels. Nothing unusual.

They returned to the corridor and continued to the next door. A rush of cold air greeted them as they stepped inside.

"It's a storage room," Jason observed. "Shelves full of IVs, syringes, saline solution, and surgical instruments."

Samantha examined a different section. "And here's the larger equipment: defibrillators, anesthesia machines, EKG/ECG monitors, gurneys. All medical."

A stack in the corner caught Jason's attention. "Are those body bags?"

Samantha's expression turned uneasy. "They seem occupied. That's... disturbing. Forgive me if I don't open one up." She moved further into the room, pointing. "This isn't just a supply room. Look."

Jason joined her and saw racks of computer equipment on a raised floor. The humming of fans provided ample white noise.

"No wonder it's cold in here. This is a data center. Servers, routers, storage systems."

"Why would they need this kind of computing power?" Samantha asked.

Jason shook his head. "I don't know, but the flickering lights indicate it's active and online. Whatever they're doing, it requires massive calculations."

They left the room, relieved to escape the chill, and continued down the hallway. The next room featured double doors. A slight pressure change greeted them as they stepped inside.

Samantha stated, "This room has positive air pressure. It's an operating room, but the table setup is unusual."

Jason followed. "Side-by-side surgical tables. I saw the same configuration in the basement."

Samantha frowned. "I'm not sure why it's arranged this way, but otherwise, it's standard—lights, tables…utility columns."

Jason approached a bookcase at the back of the room, where colorful binders were neatly arranged. One was open on the counter. "Can you make sense of this?"

Samantha joined him, flipping through the notebook. "It's detailed documentation of medical procedures. Extremely meticulous, but I'd need more time to understand its purpose. Let's finish exploring and come back later to see if anything in these binders point to what they're up to."

They returned to the hallway. Just before completing the circuit, they encountered the final door.

Trying to break the tension, Jason quipped, "Let me guess: Wayne Brady holding a goat?"

Samantha gave him a blank stare.

He sighed. "You know, *Let's Make a Deal?*"

Her expression didn't change.

Jason winced. If they survived this, he'd stop making outdated references. "Thank god I didn't say Monty Hall, or you'd have been really lost."

They opened the door and were met with a faint, sweet smell—nauseating and oddly reminiscent of tanned leather. The room was small but dominated by a large metal structure. Gauges were mounted on its surface, one showing a temperature of 1,750 degrees Fahrenheit. Another was a digital timer, counting down: 1 hour and 45 minutes remaining.

Jason's stomach twisted. Samantha's voice wavered. "What is it?"

He hesitated but spoke honestly. "A crematory. And it's running."

Nearby, a small table held a box. Jason looked inside and froze. His breath caught in his throat as he realized the horror. He knew instantly who was in the oven.

Chapter 67: Oliver

Oliver sat on the bed in Jason's abandoned recovery room on the seventh floor, alone and seething. He had lost control. Mentally, he reviewed his growing list of failures.

The young Jason Fabrikant was missing, somewhere at large in the building. Dr. Samantha Morgan, Jason's cardiologist and a FOY employee, had also vanished. To make matters worse, his security team discovered that the older Jason—the original donor who was supposed to be dead—was alive and sitting in Dr. Morgan's car in the parking lot. On top of that, there was an intruder who had attempted to breach security, likely with help from Tanya Malbern, yet another rogue FOY employee. Tanya's subsequent death only complicated matters, creating a mess that would need to be explained or, more likely, covered up.

Failure was never an option for Oliver, but this was chaos. He closed his eyes, breathing deeply to steady himself. To be effective, he knew he needed absolute control over his body, mind, and spirit. A mantra repeated by leaders throughout history came to mind: "There's only one way to eat an elephant: one bite at a time." Though the saying wasn't about the literal consumption of a magnificent animal, it reminded him to break down overwhelming challenges into manageable pieces.

Refocusing, he reminded himself of the positives. Tanya Malbern was eliminated, removing at least one insider threat. The older Jason Fabrikant had been apprehended and would soon be dealt with. The new intruder was locked in the isolation room and would likely end up as another subject for Robert or Dr. Schickel's surgical experiments. Capturing the intruder had also saved them a trip to D.C., where they'd planned to nab another test subject. The immediate concern was the two individuals still unaccounted for: young Jason and Dr. Morgan. Fortunately, both were contained within the building.

Feeling steadier, Oliver turned his focus to the facts. Security footage confirmed that Jason and Dr. Morgan were together. Both had entered an elevator on the seventh floor, with Jason donning a disguise. Clearly, they were avoiding detection, marking them as a direct threat. Oliver reasoned that Dr. Morgan must have been tipped off by the original donor, who was now aiding young Jason. With this, he officially labeled both Morgan and young Jason as adversaries.

A troubling detail lingered in his mind. The elevator camera was mysteriously inoperative, and none of the lobby footage showed them getting off. The only possibility was the eighth floor—a restricted area with no cameras that required a code. Tanya must have given it to them, but it was too late to confirm that now.

Oliver's jaw tightened as he devised a plan. He would concentrate his efforts on the upper floors and work his way down. Since the older Jason had escaped from the ninth floor, it was plausible the young couple knew about it. That floor housed Robert's incriminating records, which had no additional safeguards. While nothing appeared missing during his last check, the risk of discovery was too high. If the couple found those records, they could pass them to the local law enforcement—or worse, the FBI.

Taking no chances, Oliver called the lobby guard. "Disable all outgoing calls from the building."

"But, sir, th…"

Oliver interrupted. "NOW!"

He hung up and exited Jason's suite, his resolve hardening. With each step, he ascended toward the top of the FOY building, ready to reclaim control.

Chapter 68: Bastien

Bastien stormed through the lobby, his steps echoing sharply on the polished tiles. His target was clear: Gordon Formell, the snake who had caused him so much trouble. Reaching the elevator, he jabbed the button for the eighth floor. Nothing happened. He pressed harder, frustration bubbling as the unresponsive button mocked him. Then it hit him—the elevator required a code.

With a furious growl, Bastien slammed his fist against the elevator door, the sharp sound reverberating through the empty space. His plans unraveled, but only for a moment. Exiting the lift, he pivoted toward the security area, his mind already formulating a new strategy.

A single guard sat at the desk in the front lobby, monitoring personnel traffic. He looked young, his wide eyes betraying his inexperience, and his nervous fidgeting with a pencil only confirmed Bastien's suspicions. Normally, FOY had two guards posted at the entrance, but Bastien guessed the reduced staff had something to do with the two guards he had duct-taped in the isolation room.

Bastien approached the kid with his weapon raised and barked, "Okay, Dove Eyes, hands up!" The Glock 22, seized from one of the more seasoned guards, glinted in the artificial light. "Take me to the eighth floor—Gordon Formell's office."

The guard dropped his pencil, raising trembling hands. "I—I don't have access," he stammered, his voice cracking.

Bastien's lip twitched in disdain. "Maybe you didn't hear me," he said, his tone low and menacing. "Take me to the CEO."

The guard swallowed hard, his Adam's apple bobbing visibly. "I'm sorry, sir. They haven't given me access to the eighth floor. This is my first week."

Bastien's eyes darkened, scanning the desk for options. A pair of scissors gleamed beside a neatly stacked pile of brochures. "You're not processing what I'm asking," he growled, gesturing with the Glock. "Let me help clarify. Give me those scissors."

The guard froze, his face as pale as a sheet. Bastien took a step closer, the barrel of the gun hovering near the young man's forehead. The unspoken threat shattered the guard's hesitation, and with shaking hands, he passed the scissors across the desk.

Bastien's attention shifted to the brochures, their glossy pages extolling FOY as a beacon of medical innovation. The corporate propaganda felt like an insult. "Put your right hand on these," he commanded, slamming the stack onto the desk. "Like you're swearing on a Bible."

The guard obeyed, his hand trembling as it rested on the slick paper.

"Last chance, Dove Eyes," Bastien hissed, leaning in. "Prove your mother made the right choice not aborting you. The cipher. NOW."

Tears streamed down the guard's face as he shook his head frantically. "I—I swear, I don't know it. Please, don't kill me!"

Bastien's patience snapped. With a cold, deliberate motion, he drove the scissors through the guard's hand, knifing through to the desk. The metallic crunch of steel breaking bone was accompanied by the guard's guttural scream, raw and unrestrained, echoing through the empty lobby.

"Maybe now you'll think harder," Bastien snarled, his voice like ice. "Tell me the code, or I'll start on the other hand. After that…"

He leaned closer, his voice dripping venom. "We'll see what other appendages you don't value."

The guard gasped, his chest heaving as blood seeped onto the desk, pooling around the blood-soaked brochures. His voice was barely audible. "I—I have Mr. Formell's phone number."

Bastien's lips twisted into a cruel smile. "See? You're helpful after all. Too bad about the hand, though. You could've saved yourself some trouble."

He yanked the scissors free, the sound wet and sickening, and hurled the stained brochures to the floor. Grabbing the desk phone, he glared at the guard. "The number. Now."

Chapter 69: Old Jason

The older Jason stood before Gordon's desk, his eyes fixed on the man who had promised him youth. The room, steeped in Renaissance grandeur, loomed around them—dark wood, intricate carvings, and heavy tapestries exuding masculine power. Gordon's expression remained unnervingly calm, his posture relaxed.

"Jason, I'm sorry for the ordeal you've endured," Gordon said, his voice smooth but carrying an undercurrent of something darker. "None of this was meant to make you suffer. But at least one mystery is solved—we now know our security system worked. You must have left the facility before your clone, causing our system to flag him. That gave you a window to escape, very clever of you."

He straightened in his chair, and his voice grew sharper. "You've been… naughty. Sneaking around where you don't belong. But let me be clear: you were never meant to be here at this point."

The older Jason's pulse quickened, the words hitting him like a hammer. "You were supposed to restore my youth!"

"And we did," Gordon replied smoothly. "But before I explain, let's take a step back. You were chosen for a reason, Jason. Your troubled past, your isolation from family and friends, a heart eternally broken—that made you the perfect candidate. Others were selected for similar reasons. People who had no one to notice if they disappeared."

He leaned forward. "And let us not forget, you signed a contract. You knew that old, tired body of yours was going to be discarded."

Jason's frustration flared. "I know what I signed up for—and it wasn't this. What I don't know is why I'm standing here, in my old, tired body, while someone else is walking around pretending to be me!"

Gordon gestured toward a figure in the shadows. "Dr. Schickel, perhaps you can clarify."

Dr. Schickel stepped from a corner of the room, his demeanor clinical and detached. "In the beginning, the company attempted direct brain transplants into cloned bodies, as we advertised. But the process proved... problematic. The human brain's twelve cranial nerves, which control senses like vision, hearing, and touch, failed to integrate with the new nerve connections."

Gordon interrupted with a hint of disappointment: "Even with advancements in stem cell therapy, we couldn't establish a reliable functional link."

Dr. Schickel continued. "The result? The transplanted brain remained isolated—trapped in a body it couldn't sense or control."

Jason stared at the doctor, his hands curling into fists. The words sounded cold, as if they weren't dealing with human lives. "You're talking as if you're dissecting a frog in biology class."

Schickel didn't flinch. "I assure you, our subjects felt no pain. As for our progress, their brain stems maintained vital functions—heartbeat, breathing—but without sensory input or motor control, they were effectively locked in a nonresponsive body. Eventually, life support was withdrawn."

Jason's stomach churned. "What you really mean is murder—you killed them. You're no better than Josef Mengele, Hitler's Angel of Death!"

Dr. Schickel remained unfazed.

Jason turned to Gordon, his anger boiling over. "You pulled the plug on people who trusted you—who believed your lies!"

"The homeless mainly. Not paying clients."

He paced, his voice trembling with rage. Then confusion hit. "But I've seen him. The younger me. You must have accomplished something."

Gordon raised a hand to calm him. "Yes, Jason, we did triumph. After years of failure, it was your DNA that gave us our first success. Your clone isn't just a replica—he's proof of concept. We finally created something we can show the world. Your clone, Jason, after so many past failures. The first to reconnect with family. The first to be celebrated. You should be proud—you're part of something revolutionary."

Jason's voice cut through Gordon's monologue. "Proud? There are two of me, Gordon. Did you figure out how to restore youth or not?"

Gordon hesitated, his confident facade cracking. "Well... yes and no."

Before Jason could press him further, a shrill ringtone sliced through the tense conversation. Gordon glanced at the phone on his desk, his expression darkening as he read the screen. "Excuse me," he said, his tone ominous.

He picked up the receiver, his voice low but firm. "This better be important."

Chapter 70: Young Jason

Jason was now certain that he and Samantha were in trouble. The small box just outside the crematory chamber was haunting. Inside, he could clearly see Tanya's golden charm—the Phoenix.

He felt dizzy, staring down at the delicate pendant as the room seemed to spin. His stomach churned, the realization of what he was smelling—Tanya's remains—almost too much to bear. Finally, he looked at Samantha and explained, "This was Tanya's necklace. That sweet, putrid odor you talked about earlier? That's her body burning in this furnace. I think she lost her life trying to warn me."

Samantha's eyes welled with tears. "It's not your fault. You've done nothing wrong."

Jason wiped the moisture from her cheek with the back of his index finger. "Perhaps not, but I can't say the same if something happens to you. I should've talked you out of coming up here with me. I'm repeating old mistakes." He looked away, swallowing hard.

Samantha looked at him inquisitively. "The older you said something very similar in the car."

"I'm really sorry that I got you into this mess."

Samantha's voice was firm. "I got myself into this; you didn't force me. I'm scared, but I brought myself here, not you."

Jason admired her bravery, but his past was still tearing at him. He realized how much he cared for her. They shared an extended gaze.

Changing the subject, he said, "Now we know what they're capable of. I've seen enough. We need to get out of here. Our best chance is to get back downstairs and figure out how to escape this building—maybe call for help without raising any suspicions."

He grabbed the pendant carefully, wrapping it in a tissue to avoid leaving fingerprints. "This might be the evidence we were looking for," he muttered, tucking it into his shirt pocket, near his heart, and giving it a soft pat to secure it.

As they made their way back into the corridor, he paused. Before he could think of their next move, the sound of footsteps in the stairwell shattered the fragile calm. Alarmed, Jason grabbed Samantha's hand and pulled her toward the cold supply room, closing the door quietly behind them. It seemed like the best place to hide—with its shelves, cabinets, and equipment. They searched frantically for something to duck behind. Nothing seemed to work.

Then Jason's eyes locked on three body bags in the corner—clearly occupied, each one lying on a gurney.

They exchanged a look, their decision unspoken: it was life or death. They each picked a bag to unzip, revealing cold, naked bodies. Mutilated corpses—skulls sawed open, brains exposed. They climbed into the bags and lay down. Jason fought back the bile rising in his throat.

He whispered, "Tuck yourself under the cadaver."

"That's disgusting. Why?"

"As a precaution. And don't forget to zip up."

Jason followed his own advice, positioning himself beneath the corpse. Lying on his back, with the cold, clammy body on top of him, he reached around and zipped himself in as best he could. In the tight space, cold trickles of blood dripped down onto him. One drop landed on his lips, and he silently gagged, the dead man's hair brushing against his mouth.

Initially, the stench was faint, but once sealed inside the bag, the air turned stale, amplifying the odor. His claustrophobia immediately surged, making it almost unbearable. Jason fought the panic as best he could, distracting himself by silently counting to two hundred, hoping to stave off the dread that threatened to overwhelm him.

In the distance, doors opened and closed, the noise getting closer. Then, the supply room door squeaked, signaling someone had entered. Footsteps. Movement.

The steps stopped near him, and Jason felt the corpse resting on him being punched. The dead body absorbed the blows. Seconds later, he could hear something similar happen to the other bags, with Samantha being in one of them. Like him, she didn't make a sound.

A man muttered, "Where the hell are they?" The voice unmistakably belonged to Oliver.

Jason held his breath, listening intently. There were no other voices. He hoped Oliver was just talking to himself.

Finally, the door squeaked again, and the footsteps faded. Relief flooded Jason, but he stayed perfectly still.

After a few tense minutes, he felt safe enough to emerge. Samantha had already freed herself, sitting upright, her gaze meeting his.

She spoke first, her voice shaky and arms held out in disgust. "We're covered in blood."

"Yeah, and other unidentifiable fluids." Jason glanced at the bag he had been in, then pointed. "I thought he was just punching us. But those are puncture marks. He was stabbing with a knife."

Samantha's face drained of color, but she didn't say anything. They both knew the danger they were in.

Chapter 71: Oliver

Oliver positioned the chair in the library on the eighth floor, just outside the bookcase that concealed the passage to the ninth. The secret door was closed, and he sat at a distance, ensuring nothing would obstruct its swing. He knew Dr. Morgan and young Jason were hiding above, and sooner or later, they would need to descend. It pleased him to know that their efforts to unravel FOY would ultimately lead to their undoing. They were now his enemies.

He felt calm. There was no need to chase them down—like a fisherman with a baited hook, his prey would come to him. "The two most powerful warriors are patience and time"—he knew *War and Peace*, Leo Tolstoy, inside and out.

With his newfound sense of control, Oliver began planning for the evening. By nightfall, everything would be resolved. The crematorium would burn into the late hours, erasing any trace of evidence. The intruder in the isolation room posed no threat, since only security knew of his presence in the facility. He could dispose of the body in the chamber, ensuring there was no link back to FOY. The same fate awaited the older Jason once Gordon was finished with him. His family believed him to be a young man now, and so the older donor would be disposable and unmissed.

Young Jason and Dr. Morgan posed a greater challenge. He would need to stage their deaths outside the facility, making it look like they perished together. Perhaps he could set fire to Jason's apartment with both of them inside. Careful not to leave forensic evidence—no bullet fragments—he considered a lethal injection.

The fire would be the perfect cover, provided he used enough accelerant to obliterate any trace of chemicals in their bodies.

Tanya's disappearance, however, would be the most difficult to manage. He'd need to alter the security records to show that she had simply left work. She would vanish, and he could plant evidence in her home to suggest an abduction. He ran through possible scenarios, weighing each one.

As he calculated the work ahead, he began counting how many bodies he would need to dispose of in the incinerator. He ticked them off in his mind:

- The homeless man
- Shell #66
- Old Jason, the donor
- Albert's clone, shell #30
- Maybe Bastien, depending on what Gordon wanted to do with him.

The couple on the ninth floor wouldn't be included—they would die elsewhere. That made five bodies, not counting Tanya, who was already meeting her fate. It would take more than a day to process them all. Perhaps he could dispose of two at once; he'd have to ask Robert if that was feasible. One thing was certain: the crematorium would be running like a pizza oven on a Friday night.

A noise interrupted his thoughts. A door creaked open and shut. Moments later, Robert entered the library with an update. "I just came from Gordon's office. He's still with the donor, Jason. We should prepare upstairs for a new arrival."

Oliver snorted. "I've already mentally added him to the list. But right now, I need to remain here so the others don't slip by."

"What others?" Robert asked, clearly confused.

Oliver realized he hadn't shared the latest developments. "I'm pretty sure Jason's clone and his partner are hiding up there."

Robert looked puzzled. "What partner? What the hell are you talking about?"

Oliver's irritation flared—he wasn't used to elaborating. He preferred issuing orders, not explaining them. "I checked the security footage. Young Jason was last seen in disguise, entering an elevator with his cardiologist, Dr. Samantha Morgan."

"So what?"

"They never exited the lift. The only floor not under surveillance is the eighth. With that in mind, I inspected this floor, then the ninth—something didn't add up."

Robert looked alarmed. "What didn't add up? Did they touch my work? My binders?"

"Not sure," Oliver replied sharply. "It was Tanya's pendant. It's gone. You told me you placed it in the box."

Robert still seemed uneasy. "I *did* put it in the box. More importantly, did you check my documents? Years of research, not to mention specialized equipment. You know I don't back up files on a disk. Firewalls fail, and information can get stolen."

"Calm down."

"This is the foundation of our operation we're talking about, and my legacy! Are you telling me they're running free, untracked? Why aren't you hunting them down?"

Oliver, the bigger man, leaned in. "Gruber, if I'd searched every room, they might've slipped past me and gone downstairs. Don't tell me how to do my job." He forced himself to lower his volume—Robert wasn't one of his guards. "Listen, this is the only way out. When they come down, they'll have to pass through that bookcase door, right into my sights."

Robert began pacing, then stopped abruptly. "I'm going up. They shouldn't have been left alone."

Oliver frowned. "Suit yourself." He pulled his Glock from its holster and pointed it sideways. "If you go, take my weapon. I've got another. I'll stay here to make sure they don't escape."

Robert grabbed the weapon and headed toward the secret passage.

Chapter 72: Young Jason

Sickened by the thought of hiding under corpses, Jason and Samantha grabbed fresh scrubs from a supply shelf and headed for the operating room. Their clothes still reeked of dead flesh, so they quickly stripped down to their underwear and discarded their bloody garments on the floor. Half-naked, they spotted a drop-in sink against the rear countertop. Using paper towels, they scrubbed off the blood and odor as best as they could. Still, Jason couldn't shake the offensive smell, unsure whether it was real or just lingering in his mind.

Once visibly clean, Samantha approached the bookcase with the large collection of neatly arranged binders. The binders were color-coded and organized like a rainbow, with titles printed in large font on their spines. Jason followed her and grabbed one. "I'm not medical, but I'm guessing these could tell us what FOY is up to. Maybe you can make sense of them."

Samantha scanned the titles. "'Preoperative Testing Checklist,' 'Cognitive Testing,' 'Electrode Stimulation Placement…' Interesting." She pulled out a binder and flipped it open. "They're all related to neurosurgery, not my specialty, but still worth a look."

She pulled out more binders, spreading them across the back counter. To make room, she pushed aside medical supplies— rubber gloves, cotton swabs, and various fluids, including one labeled 'hydrochloric acid.'

"This one's about deep brain stimulation," Samantha said. "The person who took these notes was thorough, recording the time, facts about the subject, equipment used, placement, and duration of stimulation…" Her eyes widened. "This looks like human experimentation."

They both leaned over, engrossed in the material. Stooped, with their backs to the door, trying to make sense of the notes, Jason suddenly felt cold metal press against the nape of his neck. His muscles tensed.

"I'll ask that you stop touching those binders," a voice said. "Put them down and slowly lift your arms. Don't make me ask twice."

Both complied. Jason cursed himself for not hearing the man approach—he'd made a potentially fatal mistake.

The man stepped back. "You can turn around." As they did, Jason recognized him as one of the men who had escorted Tanya upstairs. Now, he wore an open white smock over the same business suit.

Jason asked, "Who are you?" They were both still in their underwear.

The man with blue eyes spoke flatly. "At this point, I guess it doesn't matter if you know. My name's Robert Gruber. I'm the Chief Technology Officer at FOY. You're Jason Fabrikant. It was my research that enabled your transformation. I was in this very operating room with you a couple of months ago. Had you not been so nosy, you'd be living the good life. It's a shame—you had such a promising future."

"What transformation? There was never a transplant. The original Jason Fabrikant is still alive. I saw him with my own eyes."

Robert ignored the comment and turned his attention to Samantha. "I'm guessing you're the cardiologist, Dr. Morgan. You've chosen… interesting attire."

Her voice quivered. "Yes, I'm Samantha."

"First-name basis, huh? So personal. Nice try." Robert glanced at the back counter, shaking his head. "Looks like you've been rummaging through my personal records. I doubt either of you have the intellect to understand the groundbreaking discoveries documented in those binders. Ironically, though, you'll both be contributing to their content today." He paused, then waved his gun toward a nearby table. "Jason, I suggest you lie down. Samantha, strap him in on the operating table. Use the leather restraints for each limb."

Jason tested him. "And if she refuses?"

Robert grinned. "Then I'll shoot Samantha in the femoral artery, and we'll both watch her slowly bleed out. Fitting for someone who works with the cardiovascular system, don't you think?"

Jason climbed onto the table, hoping to think of another way out. Samantha began strapping him down, working as slowly as possible. Robert watched, ensuring each strap was tightened properly. "Tighter, please."

Samantha's eyes flicked to the medical tray within reach. She saw an opportunity and, with her head tilted toward the far side of the room, asked, "What should I do with the dirty clothes over there?"

Robert glanced at the clothes just long enough for Samantha to grab a scalpel and slip it into Jason's restrained hand. He tucked it under his arm.

Robert turned back, squinting. "Let's see your hands."

Samantha complied, showing that her palms were empty.

Robert pursed his lips. "You two have made a mess of this room." He gave Samantha a menacing look, his teeth bared. "Get on the other table." As Samantha obeyed, he walked to the medical tray and handled something out of Jason's view. At first, Jason worried Robert had spotted the missing scalpel, but then he feared Robert was working on something far worse. Robert turned to Samantha. "Quit looking and sit upright, with your back turned to me."

She complied, her legs dangling off the far side of the table, leaving her blind to what was happening.

Robert finished his task and approached her from behind. Calmly, he said, "Be still."

He swiftly hooked his arm around her neck, holding a cloth over her face. Samantha struggled, but it was futile; within seconds, she was unconscious.

Jason, panic rising as he watched, yelled, "What the hell are you doing?" Robert didn't answer. He approached Jason, holding the same cloth. Jason's last view was Robert pressing it against his nose and mouth until he couldn't hold his breath any longer.

Chapter 73: Young Jason

Jason's mind returned slowly, dragging itself through thick water. His eyelids fluttered, heavy and reluctant to open, struggling with the bright light. His limbs felt numb, unresponsive, as the restraints dug into his skin. A cold, metallic clamp held his head still. Pain throbbed in his skull, each heartbeat making it worse. The air was sharp with antiseptic and something metallic.

Out of the corner of his eye, Jason saw Robert Gruber standing by a tray, picking up instruments with careful precision. A bone saw caught the light, its jagged teeth gleaming. Jason's stomach churned—these weren't surgical tools; they were weapons.

His eyes dropped to Robert's waist. A gun rested inside his belt, yet another threat to contend with. Robert moved like he was in control, his every motion calm and deliberate.

Robert turned and met Jason's eyes. A slow, detached smile spread across his face. "Ah, good. You're awake. It's mandatory that you're lucid for this procedure—for the mapping... I need the interaction. We're just waiting on your friend now. She'll be joining us soon."

Jason's throat tightened. "What are you going to do to us?"

Robert unwound a length of wire, his movements slow and deliberate. "Testing neural interfaces. Revolutionary stuff. Quite a privilege, really." His voice was casual, but his eyes were sharp. "A little bone removal, some hardware installation. Don't worry—I'll numb your scalp. The brain itself has no pain receptors." He smirked. "I'm not a sadist... unless I need to be."

Jason's breath came faster. "You don't have to do this. Please."

Robert's face turned cold. "If you'd stayed out of this, we wouldn't be here. But no, you had to mess with things you didn't understand. Don't worry—your body will still be useful. It took ten years to grow it, accelerating your age with hormones. We can't let all that effort go to waste." His voice was clinical, as if talking about a benign experiment.

Jason's pulse quickened as Robert pulled a notepad from his pocket, scribbling something down before eyeing the double doors.

"I'll be back in a minute," Robert said, almost routinely. "Just need a few more tools. Oh, and don't bother shouting. This room's soundproof. All you'll do is hurt your throat. And trust me..." He leaned in close, his breath whisking by Jason's ear. "You don't want to make that head clamp your enemy."

The door clicked shut, leaving Jason in silence. His mind raced, searching for a way out. A soft groan broke the quiet.

"Samantha! Wake up!" Jason whispered, his voice shaking. "We're in trouble."

She stirred, her voice slow. "Jason...? What's happening?"

"We're strapped down. Gruber—he's planning something. Are you okay?"

"I think so. I can't move my head."

"Me too." He didn't want to tell her it was a head clamp.

"Do you still have the scalpel?" she asked. "It should be near your right hand."

Of course, the scalpel. Jason's fingers fumbled across the table. His heart raced when he made contact with cold metal. He gripped it tightly, but his trembling hands caused him to nick his thumb. He bit back a curse.

"Got it," he muttered through gritted teeth.

He began sawing at the leather strap binding his wrist. Each stroke of the blade felt agonizingly slow. Sweat beaded on his forehead, dripping into his eyes, but he didn't stop. The scalpel slipped once, nearly falling to the floor. His chest tightened, but he caught it and pressed on.

His left hand finally slipped free. He wasted no time, attacking the restraint on his right wrist with his other hand. His muscles burned from the awkward position, but in moments, he was free. He unscrewed the clamp from his head, biting back a wince as it scraped his scalp.

Jason sat up, his eyes scanning the room. Samantha lay bound on the table next to him, her auburn hair splayed out like a fan. Her wide, terrified eyes locked onto the ceiling.

"I'll get you out," he whispered. But the sound of approaching footsteps and squeaky wheels froze him.

Jason laid flat onto the table, hiding the scalpel under his thigh. He set his wrists back into the leather, feigning restraint just as the door creaked open. Robert entered, pushing a gurney piled with tools that sparkled ominously with their reflections. He paused at the doorway.

"Fantastic!" Robert exclaimed, his tone unnervingly cheerful. "Both of you are awake. Perfect timing. Lemonade from lemons."

"Let us go!" Samantha's voice cracked with desperation.

Robert's smile remained fixed. "Oh, I'm afraid that's not an option. You've seen far too much. And, I need to warn you..." He rummaged through the tools on the gurney. "That thick, beautiful hair of yours will have to go. Such a pity."

Jason's fists clenched on the gurney. His heart raced as he calculated his next move. He figured the gun was still tucked into Robert's waistband. It would be a gamble, but he had no choice.

Jason made his move and clutched the scalpel. He sat up abruptly, immediately slashing through the restraint on his right ankle. The sudden movement caught Robert's attention.

"What the—?" Robert's hand darted to his gun, but Jason was quicker, cutting through the final strap. He tumbled off the table just as Robert pulled the trigger.

Instead of striking Jason, the bullet tore through a jug of hydrochloric acid perched on the counter behind him. The corrosive liquid splashed out, hissing as it spilled over Robert's prized binders.

"No!" Robert roared, his face twisting with panic. "My life's work! That's my only copy!"

He bolted to the back of the room—to the counter—frantically trying to salvage the soaked records. In his haste, his hands swept through the pooling acid. A guttural scream escaped his lips as his skin began to blister and peel, the chemicals eating away at his flesh. He staggered back, staring in horror at his ruined hands as his precious research dissolved before his eyes.

"You bastard!" he snarled, turning to look down at Jason, who was still sprawled on the floor. Robert's nostrils flared, his face a mask of rage. "Do you even comprehend what you've done? Those records contained breakthroughs—years of effort—gone in seconds! All because you couldn't leave well enough alone! Don't you get it? These procedures are the reason you're alive! You wouldn't even exist without them!"

His voice cracked, and his fury crumbled into despair. Looking down at his disfigured hands and the disintegrating binders, his shoulders slumped. Tears welled in his eyes. "My legacy... It was supposed to prove them wrong. My parents, everyone who doubted me..." His voice broke as sobs wracked his body.

Without thinking, he wiped at the tears forming in his eyes, but his hands were coated with acid. The chemicals bit into his corneas with merciless speed. He shrieked, clawing at his face.

Blinded and enraged, Robert staggered forward, his outstretched hands grasping for Jason. "I'll kill you!" he roared, lunging blindly, clumsily.

Jason rolled out of the way, adrenaline propelling his movements. Seeing no other choice, he tightened his grip on the scalpel still clenched in his hand and thrust it into Robert's neck.

Robert went limp mid-lunge, crumpling to the ground. He lay motionless, his breathing shallow.

Jason pushed himself to his feet, his breaths ragged. He turned to Samantha, who stared with wide, fearful eyes. Her tension melted.

"Oh, thank God it's you, and you're okay," she whispered, her voice trembling. "I couldn't see what happened. Please, get me out of this… this thing."

Jason quickly freed her from the clamps and leather straps. As soon as she was released, she collapsed into his arms, her body trembling with silent sobs of relief and exhaustion.

Then, she knelt beside Robert, assessing his physical state, studying his wound.

Robert's chest rose and fell with quick breaths.

"I believe he's paralyzed; I think the scalpel severed his spinal cord. He's alive but helpless," she said, her voice steady. She leaned closer, meeting his blank, unseeing stare. His face was badly burned. "You're cruel. You deserve whatever comes next."

Jason leaned down and looped his hand under her arm, gently lifting her to her feet. "We're not safe yet. The only way out is through the eighth floor."

Chapter 74: Young Jason

Jason was looking down at Robert when the double doors burst open, causing Samantha to let out a startled scream. Oliver was semi-crouched, steadying his weapon with both hands, aiming directly at him. They both instinctively raised their arms in the air, hoping not to get shot. Robert remained unmoving on the floor, crumpled with his weapon beside him. Jason thought of reaching for it, but he knew it would be fatal to try.

Oliver barked in a commanding tone, "Stand back, away from that man." Jason and Samantha complied, making room for Oliver to approach.

Oliver kept his muzzle trained on Jason but directed his voice at his coworker. "Robert, what's wrong? Get up."

Samantha spoke up. "He's not going anywhere; he's injured."

Oliver crouched to inspect Robert. "Why are his arms like that, bent so awkwardly? What did you do to him?"

Jason answered, "We defended ourselves. He threatened to shoot us."

"What the hell? Why is his skin blistered? And what's that?" He pointed with his free hand at Robert's neck. "Is that a scalpel?"

Jason didn't offer any further explanation.

Oliver lifted Robert's arm, letting it drop. "Robert, can you move?"

Robert strained to breathe, but didn't answer.

Oliver pinched one of Robert's legs and got no response. "Can you feel anything?"

Robert remained silent. "Hold tight. I'll get Dr. Schickel," Oliver said, his eyes narrowing in a controlled rage. He stood up, fire in his eyes. "Where are your clothes?"

Samantha pointed at a bloody pile on the floor a few feet away.

Oliver glanced in the direction, then snarled, "So you hid in the body bags…clever. Grab the scrubs and start walking down to Mr. Formell's office."

Under gunpoint, both Samantha and Jason were led down the spiral staircase, through the library, and entered the CEO's office. Inside, Gordon was sitting at his desk with Harper and Dr. Schickel standing behind him, looking over his shoulder. The original Jason stood in the room, facing Gordon with his back to the door.

Oliver guided Samantha and Jason to stand next to the older Jason, then joined the others.

The CEO asked, "Where's Robert?"

Oliver shook his head. "It's not good; he's lying on the floor upstairs. Looks like a spinal cord injury. He needs medical help, but it might be too late."

The CEO frowned. "Dr. Schickel and Harper, go attend to him. It seems the rest of us have our hands full down here." The two hurried out to find Robert.

Gordon turned his attention to Samantha and Jason, looking disappointed. "Underwear, really? Please put on the scrubs you're holding; this isn't a bachelor party." They complied without explaining.

For the first time since the transformation, young Jason stood closely to his donor, still confused. His older counterpart looked equally bewildered. Gordon observed the two exchanging glances. "I suppose introductions are unnecessary, though I'm sorry you two have met. This means things have gone terribly wrong. I had hoped never to be in this position."

Jason eyed his older donor, "It was you following me, right? You were the person stowed in my truck?"

His donor looked tired. "Well, okay, technically it's my truck, but yes. I was trying to piece everything together."

"Why didn't you just talk to me?"

"At first, I didn't understand how or why you existed. It took me a while to realize that you were a victim, just like me. I'm still unclear how we're both here, alive at the same time."

Gordon jumped in, "Well, I can explain." He shifted his gaze to Samantha. "But first, hello Dr. Morgan."

Still under gunpoint, Samantha replied, "I'm surprised you recognize me, since we've only talked on the phone."

Gordon frowned. "How could I forget. Johns Hopkins University, cardiovascular. My instincts were right to keep you from joining us here at headquarters. I think your ethics would have gotten in the way; I was trying to protect you from yourself. You and your partner have been a bit mischievous—two intrepid explorers. For your sake, dear, I wish you hadn't discovered the ninth floor. I'm afraid there'll be consequences."

Gordon turned back to the younger Jason. "Dr. Schickel was just explaining our operation to your donor; I see no reason why you can't hear it as well. You deserve to know the contributions you've made to science before we decide on the best course of action. Since the doctor is gone, let me pick up where he left off."

He shifted in his chair, alternating eye contact with the three unwitting individuals standing in front of his desk. "As previously mentioned, our initial attempts at transplanting the brain were unsuccessful. We had to try other methods to keep our investors happy. Some of our clients date back more than ten years. Although their pockets are deep, I assure you, their patience is not."

Gordon loosened his tie and continued, "When Robert came on board a few years ago, new avenues opened up. With his mastery in cellular biology and computer science, we were able to explore alternative techniques. We started to study how the brain stores and retrieves memories. As is commonly known, the brain retrieves information much the same way it stores it—just in reverse.

"Well, I think your research has come to an end. He's not in good shape."

"Tragic, yes. But as for FOY, I'm not worried, we have his documents."

Neither the young Jason nor Samantha said a word, thankful that Oliver hadn't noticed the ruined binders.

Gordon continued, "We initially focused on the hippocampus, learning how episodic memories are formed and indexed for later access. Our breakthrough came when we discovered how to intercept these signals as we stimulated different parts of the brain. We learned to retrieve information from our donor and transfer it into the clone as stored memories. The scar you have in the back of your head is not from a transplant, it was needed for access, connecting the clone to our equipment.

Samantha had the look of disdain. "You copied him."

"Yes, a neural replication from one brain to another."

The older Jason shook his head, "Transfer to what? I thought you developed the shells with only their brain stems? You advertise that you arrested the growth of the remaining portions of the brain."

Gordon answered, "Well, that was a necessary diversionary tactic."

Both old and young Jason spat back in unison, "Gobbledygook. You mean you lied." They looked at each other, noting their exact same timing.

Gordon extended his palms upward, shrugging. "Call it what you wish, my friends; I won't argue. The shells actually have fully functional brains. They're not just shells—they're perfect copies, well, almost perfect. We simply keep them in a comatose state while they're developing for ten years, until they reach an appropriate age for the transformation—the equivalent of twenty-five, with the help of hormones."

Young Jason asked, "What do you mean, 'almost perfect'?"

"We can't transfer all the memories; it would take too much time."

The cloned Jason pressed his lips together. "Well, that explains it then."

His older version glanced at him. "What?"

The wheels turned in the younger Jason's mind. "Do you know a Gary?"

"Sure, he's a high school friend."

"There's also something my m... err, your mom said. She mentioned Randy."

"Yeah, he was my roommate in college. You saw my mother?"

"Yes. I thought she was showing early signs of dementia. Figures! Turns out, I'm the one with the problem."

The older Jason frowned. "I have to admit, I'm struggling with you visiting her, presenting yourself as her son."

"You miss her."

The old man bowed his head. "Of course."

The young Jason's heart sank, a hollow ache spreading inside him. "I guess I can say I know how you feel… how I felt when I saw her, and Em earlier in the week."

"Em? I'm the only to call her that." He paused for a moment, processing what he was being told. "I guess you, of anybody, would know how it feels—the loneliness of not seeing them."

The younger Jason's spirits sank along with his donor. "And I'm trying to resolve her not being my mom. I guess I don't even have a mother, really. I'm not even an orphan…not sure what I am."

The old man frowned. "I'm very sorry. It was my choices that got you into this. I must know, how did my mom react to you?"

"Now that I think about it, not well. She sensed something was wrong. And, like always, she was right. I've stolen a life… your life. But you… your hopes have been shattered as well. Youth was just a broken promise."

"I'm coming to terms with that. Honestly, I never deserved it to begin with. The hardest part… I must confess… was watching you take my place…like I no longer existed."

Gordon cut in. "Not to interrupt this reunion, but time is not on my side. There's one more unfortunate consequence of the process that requires my attention."

The younger Jason looked up, irritated. "All right, I'll bite. What's next?"

Gordon opened a drawer and pulled out a revolver. "There's a technicality that you should each understand. With computers, there's an important difference between copying and moving information. We didn't want to copy memories; we wanted to move them. A brain transplant, in essence, is a 'move' operation.

The young Jason didn't understand the relevance. "Either way, you're transferring memories."

"The problem is, with Robert's solution, we performed a 'copy', subtlety different. So, once the neural transfer was complete, we needed to simulate a move."

The elder Jason nodded. "The problem is having two versions."

Gordon shook his head. "Exactly, so we need to get rid of the original."

At this point, Gordon raised the revolver at the older Jason. "I'm sorry, my dear old friend, but you are the original." He pulled the trigger calmly, and the old man fell to the ground, dead from a single gunshot to the temple.

The younger Jason was horrified. It felt as though he'd just witnessed his own death. It was surreal. He could hear Samantha screaming in disbelief beside him, but he knew emotion wouldn't help their chances for survival.

Gordon remained unmoved, staring at the body. "Consider the original deleted."

He turned to Jason. "You are now the one and only, uniquely Jason Fabrikant. I would've preferred to eliminate you instead, but we made the mistake of sharing your success publicly much too early. Your family and others now know about the transformation and therefore expect you to exist in your youth. You can see that my only option was to eliminate your donor. After all, we can't have two versions of you existing at the same time. As you just witnessed, I have corrected this discrepancy."

Jason tried to compose himself, his mind racing. "You're deceiving your clients. People are paying you money only to have themselves copied and then deleted."

"Yes, to be clear, people are unknowingly paying me to murder them. A result of their own selfishness."

"If anyone actually knew what you were doing, no one would buy your services. No wonder you haven't undergone the procedure yourself. You don't want to die."

Gordon rubbed his chin. "You figured that out pretty quickly. Impressive. Your brain seems to be functioning well. Of course, everything you say is true. As I said, we have no alternative. Our investors have poured a lot of money into this, and we feel enormous pressure. It's their greed that led us down this path."

Cutting the tension, Gordon's phone rang. He answered it, and Jason could only hear his side of the conversation:

"A skirmish? I'll be right down." He hung up and turned to Oliver. "We need to go down to the lobby. Go get Dr. Schickel; we may need him too. It appears the man in the isolation cell has escaped and is making demands. We need to be armed. Let's also bring these two troublemakers, we'll lock them in the isolation room." Gordon pointed his weapon at Jason and Samantha. "Let's go on a little field trip, shall we?"

Chapter 75: Dr. Schickel

Dr. Schickel entered the operating room with Harper and immediately felt his lungs burn from the toxic fumes. He saw Robert on the floor, the scalpel deeply embedded in his neck. He didn't dare remove it. A pool of deadly chemicals was slowly expanding, fed by the dripping counter above. The chemical had already reached Robert's listless body, touching him and blistering his nose and forehead. His eyes were open, cognizant but unable to escape its path, burning in silent agony.

Coughing from the gases, Dr. Schickel knew he needed to act fast. He explained to Harper, "Normally, we wouldn't move a patient with a spinal injury, but unfortunately, we have no choice. Hook your forearm under his left armpit, and I'll take his right. Let's drag him out of here. Watch that you don't get any chemicals on your hands or clothes."

Harper nodded, trying to drag Robert in her heels. Dr. Schickel could feel his lungs burn and did his best to minimize breathing, or even talking.

They pulled Robert facedown across the slick tile floor, through the double doors, and into the hallway. He could see Harper tearing from the fumes. She offered a suggestion, "The operating room has positive pressure, so the vapor is seeping into the hallway. The crematorium has a sealed door; let's take him there."

Dr. Schickel nodded. "Smart girl."

They continued into the chambered room, pulling Robert's limp body onto the wooden floor until he was clear of the swinging door. They slammed it shut and both gasped for fresh air.

Dr. Schickel assessed Robert's worsening condition. As he studied his coworker's body, he saw that Robert's hands, forehead, nose, and eyes were severely burned, blistered, and discolored. Most concerning was Robert's struggle to breathe and the fact that he couldn't move his limbs. Panic gripped Schickel, not out of a desire to save Robert for any noble reason, but because of the invaluable knowledge Robert held.

In Schickel's mind, Robert's physical ability was irrelevant. What mattered was access to the information Robert possessed— the ones needed to replicate the process Robert had invented for transferring memories. It would take a lifetime to duplicate those techniques on his own, if he even could.

Robert, in turn, thought that Schickel also possessed unique skills. But, in fact, it was all trickery. Schickel selectively altered the instructions in Robert's books, introducing purposeful mistakes. He understood that these errors resulted in failures—clones that had to be destroyed. In fact, the many failures were his doing. Yet, the deception served a specific purpose: to convince Robert that only Schickel himself possessed the ability to perform the delicate operations. All it required was a simple reversal of the very errors he planted when Robert wasn't looking.

He turned to Harper. "He's struggling to breathe on his own; we'll need to intubate him. I'll be right back with the proper equipment." Dr. Schickel raced over to the supply room, grabbing a gurney on the way. He loaded the rolling bed with everything he thought he needed, including a portable mechanical ventilator, oxygen tank, laryngoscope, and a host of other equipment. He struggled to think of what else was required, but nothing came to mind. Satisfied, he rolled the gurney with all the items back to Robert.

Harper gently patted Robert's leg, avoiding the acid, but offering words of encouragement. "You'll be okay; Dr. Schickel is a genius. He'll fix you up good as new."

They laid out blankets alongside Robert and gently rolled him onto them. He was now lying face up but still on the floor. Dr. Schickel elevated his head to align his airway but accidentally touched the acid on Robert's forehead. "Ouch, dammit. Fucking gloves! That's what I forgot!" His hands were stinging, and there was no sink in the room. "I'll be right back." He scurried out once again to wash his hands. He reemerged coughing, but now donning surgical gloves. He looked at Harper. "We're going to do this without anesthesia. You're going to be my RT."

Her eyebrows drew together. "What does that mean?"

"It means you hand me shit when I ask for it!"

He performed the makeshift intubation procedure, starting with the laryngoscope. He walked through the entire process, ending with an adjustment to the vent level settings and a check of Robert's pulse oximeter. Soon after, the patient's breathing stabilized.

Dr. Schickel looked at Harper. "The hard floor of a crematorium isn't an optimal place for complex medical procedures. But for now, I'm happy that he's stable." He knew there was much more that needed to be done, but that would take time, the right sterile environment, and proper equipment.

Oliver suddenly appeared and looked directly at Dr. Schickel. "Smart that you moved; the operating room reeks! What's his status?"

Dr. Schickel replied, "We had to intubate him, but he's okay for now. We need to get him downstairs on a stretcher. It'll take two of us to lift him."

Oliver countered, "We have larger problems right now. Gordon wants you to come down to the lobby. You can come back up afterward."

Harper reassured the doctor. "I'll watch over Robert. I'll get more blankets from the supply room." The two men left, as she pulled off his shoes, then lay down parallel to him, staring at him.

Chapter 76: Bastien

Bastien stood on the ground floor, a short distance from the elevator lobby, waiting for Gordon Formell. This was his opportunity to meet the enemy face-to-face. As he looked up, his gaze fell on the expansive fountain—a grotesque display of bodies. Each time he glanced at it, a surge of anger welled within him.

His backpack was slung over his left shoulder, and he gripped his 3D-printed weapon in his right hand. Pressing the gun firmly against the injured guard's back, he would use the young man as a human shield. They both faced the elevator, watching the lights above change as the car descended from the eighth floor. Bastien found it hard to concentrate as the guard moaned in pain. Bastien snapped at him, "I stabbed your hand, not your throat! Stop whimpering, or I'll shoot you in the spine. They don't hire guards in wheelchairs."

Finally, the elevator chimed. The doors slid open, and five people stepped out—far more than Bastien had anticipated. He recognized one immediately: Gordon Formell. The CEO stood strategically behind the others, well shielded from Bastien's gun. In front of Gordon was the man in camouflage, pointing a gun back at him. Bastien had expected to be a target, but he trusted his human shield would protect him. A heavyset man in a white coat also had a gun, strangely aimed at the remaining two members of the group, who were also acting as shields.

Gordon, unarmed and calm, appeared personable despite being protected by his entourage. "What can we do for you, Bastien?" he asked.

Bastien raised an eyebrow in surprise. "So, you know my name." He glanced at Samantha. "I'm guessing you told him, pretty face. You're the Dish, right?" In his mind, she fit the bill perfectly. He assumed she must have been caught and was now under gunpoint. *Serves the bitch right!*

Samantha remained silent, looking confused."

Gordon interjected, "No, Bastien. You saw the Dish being polygraphed. She's been dealt with. You're obviously outnumbered. To avoid further loss of life, please hand over your weapon."

Bastien felt a surge of confidence. "Well, I'm prepared to die today. Are you? I only need to fire one shot, and it'll be aimed right at your head. Then I'll have completed my mission."

Gordon remained level-headed. "And what mission is that?"

"To cull the herd, you despicable scum." Bastien had envisioned this moment countless times. For him, admonishing Gordon Formell, the CEO of the vile FOY empire, would be even more satisfying than the act of taking his life itself.

Gordon narrowed his eyes. "I don't understand."

Bastien responded, adopting a patronizing tone. "Oh, I'm sure you do. It literally means removing inferiors from a population."

Gordon shot back, "You consider me inferior?"

Bastien responded indirectly. "Let's consider the wildebeest of the Serengeti. They're hunted by mongoose, lions, and cheetahs; even pythons prey on them. The hunters don't typically catch the strongest of the herd. No, they take the sick, the weak, the old— the frail. This is the natural order. It's how Mother Earth—or Pachamama, as the Peruvians say—maintains balance. You and your immoral minions have upset this delicate equilibrium."

Gordon countered, "Bastien, we're restoring youth; we're making people strong again."

Bastien's anger flared. "NO! You're offering an extension of life—not through Darwin's natural selection, but through the almighty dollar. You provide your services only to those who can afford it. The rich! In essence, they get to live multiple lives while others barely eke out a single existence. Your technology selectively increases the population, not based on genetic merit, but on inheritance. You're weakening the human genome."

Gordon retorted, "If the demand weren't there, FOY wouldn't exist. You're trying to suppress human nature. If you knock us down, like whack-a-mole, the technology will just pop up somewhere else. People desperately crave our services. They're starving to regain their youth. One could argue that the demand for youth has enabled our technology. In actuality, one can't exist without the other. It's a chicken-and-egg scenario."

Bastien scoffed. "You obviously know nothing about evolution. The chicken-and-egg scenario you speak of is a common misnomer. The egg came first. Look it up, old poop. A mutation in the DNA caused an egg to hatch, which contained the first embryonic chicken. In your fountain above us, on sickening display, exists the result of your mutant eggs. But unlike the chicken, they weren't created naturally, under God's hand. They were fabricated."

With his free hand, Bastien pulled a burner phone from the outside pocket of his backpack. "I have a confession: I don't intend on shooting you. As for the imposter clone, Albert, I had no qualms about disposing of him. He wasn't real—just a monster, a Frankenstein poured into a Hollywood body. On the day I took him out, I had the chance to explore your facility. In the moments

leading up to the explosion in Ms. Joan Bradley's office, I devised
a critical plan. Hidden above us, in various nooks and crannies of
your glass fountain, I planted Semtex. The clay is wired to a
detonator, which I can trigger with this phone. I suggest you look
upward and witness the collapse of your business model."

Oliver, who was still aiming his muzzle at Bastien, reacted
decisively. With one swift pull of his index finger, the military man
discharged his weapon. Bastien was hit in the jaw, forcing him off
balance. He fired back in return, using his 3D-printed weapon.
Oliver was hit in the forehead and died before collapsing to the
floor. The unreliable plastic gun, monikered 'The Cure,' served its
mission. Unfortunately, it also blew up in Bastien's hand, slicing
off his forefinger and thumb. Injured but undeterred, Bastien lost
his grip on the guard, who fell at his feet. Bloody but resolute, he
pressed a button on his phone with his working hand.

Within seconds, everyone instinctively crouched as a series of
small explosions rumbled from above. In the excitement, Bastien
had forgotten about the second gunman but caught a glimpse of
the doctor taking aim. He was hit in the throat and snapped
backward, struggling for breath. Bastien fell, then lay helplessly,
watching as the entire fountain began to crack. He had served his
purpose, a happy martyr protecting the planet. He relaxed his body
and proudly accepted his fate.

Chapter 77: Jason

The glass structure gave way and began spilling out its contents from the upper floors. Shattered glass, water, and bodies tumbled downward. In the confusion, Jason seized the opportunity to wrestle the weapon away from Dr. Schickel; there was little resistance. Oliver and Bastien both lay dead on the floor.

Gordon watched as his life's work unraveled from above. He ran out, ignoring the falling debris, almost as if he could catch and save the dropping human bodies. Instead, he was showered with broken glass, lacerating his body. Shards sliced into his skin, leaving dozens of deep cuts, one of them severing his jugular. He fell to the ground, bleeding heavily.

After the fountain collapsed, Dr. Schickel walked up to his boss and stood over him. Gordon grimaced in pain and mouthed the words, "Help me." The doctor stared at him, ignoring the Hippocratic Oath, and unemotionally watched him bleed out. In the end, Gordon Formell, the FOY CEO, lay dead among piles of broken glass, much different from the shattered hourglass logo.

In the aftermath of the fountain's destruction, Dr. Schickel was unarmed and compliant. Jason walked among the ruins with Samantha, keeping his weapon trained on the doctor. The stark, naked remains of the cloned bodies were clearly visible for the first time, no longer obscured by the running water over their respective biotanks. Now lifeless, the clones wouldn't deliver the promise of youth for their donors. Among them, Jason spotted the small, motionless body of the young girl he had seen in the elevator. She was created alone and died alone, her entire life defined by solitude. A lump developed in his throat, knowing that this was just a poor child who had never been given the chance at her own life. She was born to take on the personality of another. In essence, her life was created and stolen; she was grown to be harvested.

Jason continued to walk among the dead. Suddenly stunned, he came across a body that looked exactly like his own.

In anger directed at Dr. Schickel, he snapped, "There were more versions of me?"

Dr. Schickel's expression was flat. "You were our first successful patient undergoing a memory transfer, but there were failures before you. Although you were advertised as 'Client One', you're actually shell number 29. You will find this number tattooed behind the antihelix of your left ear. These other shells were available as backups in case your transformation failed. They have their own unique numbers. After your procedure was a success, these duplicates were scheduled to be relocated to the basement lab for experimentation and then cremated. Beyond research, we had little need for them any longer."

Jason, trying to comprehend, asked, "If I was number 29, does that mean there were twenty-eight unsuccessful attempts to create me?"

Dr. Schickel nodded. "There were twenty-eight shells before you, but not all were created using your donor's DNA. Also, we had many more failures than that. In the beginning, we attempted the actual organ transplant method as we advertised. Since the clones themselves take many years to grow, we didn't want to waste them on unproven techniques. We found other subjects to experiment on. There was always a complication that developed, and we had to destroy the results."

Samantha's face reddened as she glared at him. "How can you be so heartless? You mean you killed the people you experimented on?"

Dr. Schickel's countenance remained expressionless, logical. "We lost some of our clones as well as real-life subjects. We used the chamber to dispose of our failures."

Samantha shook her head slightly. "You monster! How is it that you weren't caught? People went missing, and no one noticed?"

Dr. Schickel coldly explained, "D.C. has an abundance of forgotten homeless people, perfect for our research. We lured them with the promise of a warm meal and a clean bed, using a food truck and offering sedative-laced drinks and sandwiches. Once they were out, we crated them and brought them here, alive. This gave us the chance to practice severing and reconnecting brain vessels and nerves, along with animal experiments in the basement lab. We never achieved 100% success. After Robert developed the memory transfer technique, it took several failed attempts before we succeeded. Some of those failures, Jason, were grown using your donor's DNA. Without us, you wouldn't exist in your current form."

Jason's fist flew toward Dr. Schickel with all the fury he had been holding back. The punch landed squarely on his mouth, snapping his head back and sending him crashing to the floor. He lay there, dazed and gasping, wedged between two lifeless bodies—his eyes wide with shock, staring up at the ceiling.

The full impact of Dr. Schickel's cold and disconnected explanation hit Jason hard. He realized that he was never born; rather, he was grown in the likeness of another. The memories he could recall were not from his own personal experiences. His life was as fraudulent as the company that created him. For the first time, Jason began to weep.

Chapter 78: Harper

On the ninth floor, Harper heard the fountain crashing on the lower levels. Leaving Robert's side, she ran to the spiral staircase and descended quickly. As she reached the elevator, she looked down through its glass walls. The fountain was destroyed. Dead bodies and piles of broken glass were scattered across the ground level. FOY's secret would soon be exposed to the public; the company would cease to exist. Her career was over, and more importantly, she faced a lifetime of incarceration, if not capital punishment.

Weighing her options, Harper made her decision and picked up the phone.

A guard answered, "Security."

She took a steadying breath, ensuring her voice was authoritative, not anxious. "This is Harper Faulton. I need you to disable the sprinkler system."

"Ma'am, the fountain sustained massive damage. I'm concerned that we have frayed wiring that could jeopardize the building."

Lying came easily. "We have a delicate operation ongoing upstairs. The sprinklers must be off. Do as I say."

"Yes, ma'am."

She hung up, her arms limp, feeling like a "dead man walking." She reentered the secret stairway and ascended back to the ninth floor. In the crematorium, Robert lay motionless where she had left him—still conscious, still breathing. She spoke softly to him. "We'll take our final journey together."

She turned to the crematory chamber and opened the oven door. The sickening smell of Tanya Malbern's remains filled the air. She saw the glowing embers and grabbed the chamber shovel. Scooping up the red-hot remains, she spread them onto the wooden floor, creating a large circle around Robert. When she was satisfied, she knelt beside him, watching the glow turn to flames, and spread.

Harper thought about her life, the decisions she had made, and remembered the boiled frog syndrome. As a child, she was told that if you throw a frog into hot water, it will jump out to avoid being scalded. But if you place the frog in tepid water and slowly raise the temperature to a boil, it wouldn't recognize the danger in time and would die. Harper later learned the story was a fable, but the lesson stuck.

Reflecting now, she realized the metaphor applied to her. She started the company wanting to leave her past behind. But slowly, little by little, she compromised her principles, rationalizing getting back at those who mistreated her and her mother. Inch by inch, she followed a path of manipulation and deceit. She wondered when she lost her true north. Maybe it was when she overlooked the murder of the innocent, the homeless. Now, surrounded by flames, about to burn like the proverbial frog, she realized the danger too late.

The heat of the fire felt warm against her skin. She tried to imagine soothing shapes in the flames, like she did with clouds, but instead, each teardrop-shaped flare resembled devil horns rising from hell. She coughed, soon uncontrollably, struggling for air.

As the heat rose, she dropped to the floor, seeking fresh air. She looked at Robert—still alive. She had always admired his intellect. He wasn't like the others. Most men in her life were driven by sex, which she used to her advantage. Robert was different, destined for greatness, like Edison or Tesla. But pride would be his downfall. Both of their legacies would be marked by evil, their contributions to the world tainted by a lack of compassion.

Harper watched as the fire spread outward and inward, closing in on her. Within minutes, she felt her flesh beginning to burn. Tanya's face emerged from the flames. In that moment, Harper realized that it was Tanya's ashes that sparked the end of FOY's fraudulent practices. Tanya had lived a life true to her pendant—a phoenix, rising from the ashes.

Part 5: Visions

Chapter 79: Jason

Two Weeks Later

Jason reclined in a plush chair, surrounded by comfort objects: fidget toys, stuffed animals, and a real-life French poodle named Pickles. The room was a sanctuary of soft colors and soothing textures, designed to create a judgment-free space where patients could open up about their deepest struggles. This was the office of Dr. Josephine Lazarus, a board-certified psychiatrist recommended by Dr. Schickel. Importantly, Dr. Lazarus had no ties to FOY, Inc. She was simply a compassionate professional, well-equipped to help Jason navigate his unprecedented circumstances.

It was their second session. In their first meeting, Jason had revealed more than his infamous backstory—he'd shared the surreal details of his life that no news outlet could capture.

Dr. Lazarus, seated upright in her recliner, greeted him with a warm smile. "Jason, you look well. How are you feeling today?"

Jason ran his fingers through Pickles' soft fur, a familiar gesture of comfort. He took a deep breath, steadying himself. "Overwhelmed, honestly. I've been consumed by thoughts of the early years of my life—if I can even call it a life. I was suspended in the Glass Fountain, a spectacle for the world to see, just like the girl I saw in the elevator. I was nurtured physically, but emotionally? Nothing. It's hard to accept that I'm not the person I was supposed to be. My memories aren't even my own. I'm someone different—but who? It feels like my life is a blank canvas, painted over with someone else's brushstrokes."

Dr. Lazarus nodded with understanding. "That's completely understandable. If it helps, the memories you've created since your transformation are uniquely yours. You're building your life now, piece by piece. But I can see how much there is to process." She glanced at her notes. "Last session, you mentioned having dreams. Sometimes, sharing them can bring clarity. Would you like to talk about them?"

Jason shifted in his seat, scratching behind Pickles's ears as if seeking reassurance. "They're not just dreams—they're recurring nightmares. Three themes, all equally disturbing."

"Let's start with the first one," she suggested.

He nodded, unease creeping into his voice. "In the most recent one, I'm walking along a remote highway, trying to find my way home. Suddenly, I'm encased in glass, like I'm in an aquarium. I'm screaming for help, but everyone just stares at me, like I'm some kind of exhibit."

Dr. Lazarus's expression softened. "That's a powerful image, and an insight into your claustrophobia. In reality, you were on display in the biotank—trapped in a literal aquarium. It's no wonder this memory is surfacing in your dreams. Even if you don't consciously remember it, some part of you was aware."

Jason's lips pressed into a thin line. "I see that now. I've always assumed I was oblivious to my surroundings, but maybe I wasn't."

"And the next nightmare?" she prompted.

Jason hesitated, his hand still on Pickles' fur. "It's always in a white, clinical setting. There's a little girl—helpless, alone, neglected. She's so sad, and no one helps her. I know it's connected to the girl I saw in the fountain. Thinking about her still upsets me." His voice cracked, and his eyes shimmered with unshed tears.

Dr. Lazarus leaned forward, her tone soothing. "It's entirely natural to feel this way. That girl's image left a strong impression on you, and your empathy is a testament to your humanity. We'll work on ways to address this in time. What about the third nightmare?"

Jason's shoulders tensed. "The last one is the worst. I'm trapped in my own body, unable to move or respond. I'm fully aware but completely paralyzed. It's torture—being conscious but cut off from everything, including my own body."

Dr. Lazarus's expression grew thoughtful. "That aligns with what you've described before—a loss of control. It's likely that during your time in the fountain, some level of awareness persisted, even if it didn't register as memories. That would explain why these fears and sensations are so deeply embedded. The fact that your donor's memories include scuba diving, something that now triggers anxiety for you, highlights the conflict between his experiences and your own trauma."

Jason's voice grew heavier. "I feel like I've lost more than a third of my life. What did I gain from those years in the fountain? Nothing but phobias and unanswered questions. I'm a living blueprint of who I'm supposed to be, but I've never truly lived."

Dr. Lazarus set her pen and folder aside, her gaze steady and kind. "Jason, you're right—there's no precedent for what you're going through. But that makes your journey all the more unique. Recovery will take time, but with patience, I believe you'll uncover the person you were always meant to be. Your experiences may be complicated, but they're yours now. Embrace them as you move forward."

Jason's lips stretched into a faint, grateful smile. "Thank you, Dr. Lazarus. I needed to hear that."

As he left the office, leaving the doctor and Pickles behind, Jason felt a glimmer of hope amidst the daunting uncertainty. The path ahead was uncharted, but for the first time, it felt like his to navigate.

Part 6: Aftermath

Chapter 80: Dr. Schickel

Two Months Later

On this night, Dr. Schickel once again found himself suffering from insomnia. His overweight cellmate's incessant snoring rattled the cell, amplifying his frustration. Carefully, he climbed down from the top bunk, making sure not to disturb the man. Waking him would only invite trouble.

He settled on the cold cement floor, sitting on his pillow and stared at the trickling stainless-steel toilet. It had been leaking for a week and still hadn't been fixed. His eyes lingered on the brown stains beneath the rim, hoping they were from rust and minerals, not the biological remnants of the large man lying just a few feet away. Either way, the toilet emanated a foul odor from which he couldn't escape.

It had been two months since the fire at FOY, and Dr. Schickel felt as though he was no longer truly living. Awaiting trial, he had been remanded to a high-security federal prison. His days now consisted of tasteless meals, cold surroundings, and, most appallingly, physical and sexual abuse.

Confined to a space less than fifty square feet, he reflected on the time since his arrest. Upon his arrival, he hadn't understood prison life and had made four critical mistakes. The first occurred when he failed to properly address his new cellmate. Instead of offering a neutral introduction like, "My name is Henry; they told me to bunk here," he arrogantly said, "I'm Dr. Schickel. I have bad knees, so I'll require the bottom bunk." His cellmate wasn't impressed by his title nor pleased with his request.

Later that evening, when things escalated, ending with his cellmate punching him in the stomach, Dr. Schickel committed his second mistake: he complained to a guard. He identified his assailant by name, quickly earning the label of "snitch," a reputation that spread throughout the prison.

The third mistake was his greatest failure. The exploits of FOY were all over the news, dominating social media and fueling rumors across the country. The public's insatiable curiosity about the scandal led to an unspoken fascination with the company's only surviving senior member, besides Joan.

What wasn't widely known was that Dr. Schickel was a sex offender. Naively, trying to win over some convicts, he bragged about his exploits while eating in the chow hall. The inmates quickly branded him as "checked-in." The Shot Caller, the prison's gang leader, got word and immediately ostracized him, leaving Dr. Schickel without any protection. He learned that being either a sex offender or a snitch was a bad thing in prison. Being both was a death sentence. He quickly became the target of constant physical and sexual abuse, with the guards feigning ignorance.

Dr. Schickel's fourth and final mistake followed: he had requested protective custody. He soon learned that it was like being in a jail within a jail. His days were spent in solitary confinement, with only one hour for recreation. On weekends, he remained in his cell for the entire day, deprived of sunlight. He was not allowed to join others in the chow hall, the rec yard, classes, or even church services. Open visitation was also disallowed, though no one would have visited him anyway, except for the press and documentarians.

Although a psychopath, Dr. Schickel still craved social interaction. Within a few weeks, he requested to be reinstated with the others, figuring it would lead to his demise, ending his hell. He welcomed it, but he needed to figure out how to end his life painlessly.

To avoid daily beatings, his cellmate demanded oral submission each morning and night, occasionally sodomizing him, and even selling him to other inmates for cigarettes. Many took pleasure in his agony as they gratified themselves at the doctor's expense. Dr. Schickel had learned not to complain but simply comply. Physically incapable of defending himself, he had no choice but to endure. After two months in prison, he had reached his breaking point and needed to act. He never did play by the rules.

On this particular night, out of the corner of his eye, he noticed an ant making its way across the floor. He had always admired ants, living organisms with one of the largest brains relative to their body size. With a quarter million neurons, each ant's behavior combined with the social structure of the colony created impressive collective intelligence.

Unaware of any danger, the ant continued its journey toward Dr. Schickel. The doctor knew the shortest distance between two points was a straight line, but the ant seemed to defy this rule. It moved quickly but often veered off course in seemingly random directions. Yet, despite its erratic path, the species arrived at its destination, thriving.

The small black insect and Dr. Schickel shared a common function: they were both service creatures—one serving its queen, the other serving time. In Dr. Schickel's mind, the ant's effort seemed the more valuable commodity. He watched it move, driven by its genetic need to serve. Without a second thought, Dr.

Schickel crushed the bug with his thumb, disfiguring it. He left it to suffer, knowing it would take hours to die.

The ant's plight sparked the solution he'd been looking for, and his attention turned to his cellmate.

Dr. Schickel's strength lay in his understanding of anatomy. He stood up and studied his cellmate, observing the man's pendulous, hairy belly jiggle with each deep breath. The man lay on his back, head turned to the side, lost in deep sleep. The doctor quietly grabbed a pencil while eyeing his target. Knowing the bone around the temples was thin, Dr. Schickel aimed for the middle meningeal artery, hoping for a brain bleed.

With precision, he thrust downward, hitting his mark. After delivering the strike, he placed a pillow over his victim's head to muffle the sounds, then waited patiently for the man to fall unconscious. He left him in a vegetative state, where, like the ant, he would die slowly.

Feeling that he was now effectively alone, Dr. Schickel dampened a sheet in the sink. It would better serve its purpose wet. He tied it to the top railing of the bunk and tugged it tight to ensure it held, then wrapped the other end around his own neck. With one final, deliberate motion, he simply sat down, his weight pulling the sheet into a noose. The constriction quickly cut off his airflow and blood circulation. The irony of taking his own life for the same reasons he had inflicted on others went unnoticed by him. He was just happy to end it all. Then, just before he lost consciousness, he saw a guard rush to his aid.

Chapter 81: Joan

It was dusk, and Joan Bradley bent down to look at a young seedling, stretching upward, curling in search of its first sunlight. She stepped on it, twisting her foot to ensure it didn't survive. The thought of any life sprouting here gave her the creeps. This wasn't sacred ground—it was a mass burial site.

She stood on the rubble that once was the FOY complex, thinking it should be replaced with cement, ensuring nothing ever grew there again. Alternatively, perhaps it could be the perfect location for a nuclear power plant. Joan was still angry over FOY's deception and those she had trusted. Her role as Marketing Director and spokesperson for Gordon and his senior team of deceivers was infuriating. Her only satisfaction was that they had all gotten what they deserved, with only Dr. Schickel surviving. *Let him rot in prison.*

Joan panned the landscape. In the aftermath of the fire, police officers, crime scene investigators, and forensic photographers had all taken turns at the property. Most of the evidence was now in the hands of lab specialists, including the bones of the deceased. The courtroom proceedings would follow, drawing significant public interest, along with FOY's wealthy clients.

As for the property, it was decided to bulldoze what little remained of the structure. Soon, a series of backhoes and crawler loaders would fill dump trucks and take the non-biodegradable chunks of debris to the nearest landfill. The decision was made to rezone the area as a park, not only out of respect for those lost but also in consideration of a real estate market that would never be able to sell land with such a horrific past. It would have been easier to list acreage that once held a repurposed cemetery. Instead, the land was being cleared for trails and joggers. Joan still would have preferred cement.

As she viewed the surroundings, she felt a burden settle over her, as if an albatross hung around her neck. Her career had come to a screeching halt as she faced skeptical hiring managers, all unwilling to take a chance on her. She understood—who could blame them? The deception had occurred right under her nose. They suspected she was either wicked herself or completely ignorant, neither of which made her desirable for employment.

Her future felt dismal. Worse than anything was the struggle to forgive herself. Joan had hoped that returning to the crime scene would bring closure, but it was her third visit, and each time she left feeling more depressed than before. Despite her therapist's recommendation, she knew this would be her last trip.

She walked along piles of smashed concrete, bent rebar, scorched furniture, and twisted metal. Even wearing a hard hat, construction gloves, and hiking boots, she had to be mindful of rusty nails piercing her soles and snakes hiding in the recesses of the rubble. The area seemed to attract snakes in particular, both past and present.

While picking through the wreckage, something caught her eye, shimmering in the fading light. She climbed over the debris to reach the object and was disappointed to discover it was merely aluminum flashing used for ductwork. She didn't know what she was looking for anyway, other than spiritual guidance. It was unlikely to emerge miraculously from a pile of rubble. Then she saw another reflective object nearby, mostly buried under rocks and dirt, barely visible.

Joan dug with her gloved hands and retrieved an acrylic block mounted on a porcelain base. She recognized the figure as one of FOY's award statues and read the engraving: "Tanya Malbern—in recognition of sustained excellent performance." It seemed surprisingly intact, except for a corner of the porcelain base that was chipped off. She could see inside the hollowed-out compartment and noticed a piece of paper curled within it. Joan fished it out. It was a note, dated one day prior to the fire. She read it.

Dear Mom and Dad,

*I hope with all my heart that this letter never reaches you. But if it does, please know that I am still with you, always, in spirit. My love for you has never wavered, and it never will. I want to thank you*for being the most incredible parents a daughter could ever ask for. From the moment I was born, I felt your love and your unwavering support, every step of the way. You were my safe haven, my biggest supporters, always there cheering me on, even when I didn't always deserve it. Through every high and every low, you guided me with so much patience and understanding.*

You've always taught me to be honest, to live with integrity—and that's a lesson I hold close. But there's something I've carried with me for so long that I never had the courage to share, something that's made my heart heavy. I'm gay. I know I've never spoken about it, and I can imagine the pain it might bring you to hear this, especially you, Mom, because I know how badly you wanted grandchildren.

I'm so sorry I couldn't say it to you sooner. Please understand that it's something I've known about myself for a long time, and for the most part, I've lived happily and authentically. But I've also struggled with the fear of disappointing you, even though I know, deep down, that you would have accepted me without question. I hope you can forgive me for hiding this part of myself from you.

There's more, though, something I need you to understand. I've found myself in an impossible position, a battle between my values and the world I've been a part of. I've learned that FOY has been committing unforgivable wrongs— practices that not only defy the law, but destroy lives. In the face of that truth, I could not stay silent. I've become a whistleblower, following the values you instilled in me, even when it meant putting myself in danger.

FOY has done things that are so terrible, so cruel, that I cannot stand by and let it continue. I've tried to expose them, but I wasn't able to finish what I started. And now, I'm asking for your help. I need you to finish this for me. Please take this letter to the authorities so they can find the evidence and shut FOY down. There's a man named Alfred Grier—a wonderful soul I had the honor of knowing. His death wasn't an accident. The truth of his passing could unravel the dark secrets of this company. Please, help them find the truth, for him, for me, and for everyone they've hurt.

No matter what happens, know that I love you both with all my heart, and I always will. You've given me everything—unconditional love, a sense of right and wrong, and the strength to face anything. I am so proud to be your daughter.

Always and forever,

Tanya

Joan's heart pounded in her chest. She knew Tanya well and regretted not understanding her coworker more. She decided she would pass the note on not only to her parents but also to the FBI.

Part 7: Identity

Chapter 82: Jason

One Year Later

It was just a matter of seconds before the Lockheed C-130 Hercules, a four-engine transport aircraft, reached an altitude of 1,250 feet. Jason, along with fifteen others, was seated shoulder to shoulder in the main cargo area, forming one long human column that stretched from the front to the back of the aircraft. He was near the rear cargo door. Three other columns stretched in parallel, with more than sixty passengers in total. He felt like he was in an unopened tin of human sardines.

Each person was equipped with a main parachute, as well as a reserve system. Jason quickly realized this wasn't a military operation. Instead, it was preparation for a deployment of a different kind. All the passengers were young. In fact, Jason guessed that he was the oldest person on board. Oddly, they all wore thin white bodysuits that fit tightly. Even more peculiar— and embarrassing—was that everyone's outfit was wet, and one could clearly see through their clothes. It was as if they were competing in a wet T-shirt contest, though it wasn't limited to their upper bodies. Jason was shocked to discover that he wore the same outfit and attempted to modestly cover up.

He looked at his traveling companions. They stared in odd directions, seemingly unaware of their surroundings. Each person was hooked to the aircraft via their static lines, their only physical attachment to the plane. Otherwise, they sat snugly, hugging their knees, with only their bottoms and feet on the metal floor. The static line itself wasn't the typical cord used by paratroopers, but was instead a tube that seemed to be filled with fluid. Small air bubbles revealed that something was flowing within.

Without warning, an explosion occurred near the cockpit, releasing a deafening wave of pressure and a flash of heat that singed his hair. The Herk's nose violently pitched upward. At the same time, the rear ramp opened, exposing the terrain thousands of feet below. With the aircraft pointed toward the noon sun, the passengers began sliding out like beans from an opened can—or, in this case, not beans but 'beings.' They all fell through the opening and out of the plane. Instead of screaming in panic, they descended expressionlessly and stoically, unconcerned of their peril. Jason wanted to scream but was unable to utter a sound.

Finding himself falling, he remembered that he was wearing a parachute and wondered why the ripcord didn't work. He tugged at the handle, but nothing happened. Releasing his main chute, he tried his reserve, punching the bag to deploy it. The bag was empty. He was free-falling with no ability to slow his descent. Looking around, he saw that all the other passengers were in free fall as well; not a single chute had opened. The ground approached quickly, and he watched in terror as the ant-like cars rapidly grew in size. Closing his eyes and knowing the inevitable, he braced for the end.

Jason woke up in a sweat from yet another nightmare. As his mental fog lifted, he recognized that these nightmares were becoming his reality. They would likely continue for the rest of his life, and he would just have to learn to live with them. His psychiatrist had given him tools to cope, and he was doing his best. One tool was to try to understand them, to determine their source.

He did enjoy interpreting their meaning, although this new one seemed fairly straightforward. Just before the fire at FOY, he had witnessed the horrifying event of bodies falling from the fountain. In this nightmare, he was one of those falling bodies. The 'ripcords' represented the umbilical tubes exchanging fluids used to provide nutrients to the clones and remove waste. Their transparent clothing was a substitute for their glass enclosures, symbolizing their complete vulnerability.

Unlike the unfortunate fountain clones, Jason had been able to wake up and enjoy his new life. He felt lucky and blessed. His mood was positive as he thought about his day. He was nervous, though, since he was going to meet Samantha in D.C.

Chapter 83: Jason

Hours after his dream, Jason walked alongside his favorite person, Samantha. They held hands as they strolled among the elegant cherry trees near the tidal basin, inhaling the sweet aroma of the blossoms. It was early spring, and the weather felt crisp and revitalizing.

They marveled at their surroundings. The trees had accomplished something that had long eluded man, as well as FOY; they were more than 150 years old. Jason knew that there were even older trees, like a Bristlecone Pine, almost 5,000 years old, located in California, northeast of Fresno.

As for the present, Jason was still adjusting to his new life. One year had passed since the devastating fire. Afterward, he felt lost and depressed. In his heart, he knew that his donor, the original Jason Fabrikant, had achieved many things, some great, and some not so great. His donor was a famous baseball player, still loved by family despite his choices. In the end, his donor gave up his life in the pursuit of truth and justice, an admirable quality.

Samantha interrupted his reflections. "A penny for your thoughts—isn't that the old saying?"

"Ha, funny girl."

Samantha made small talk, but it wasn't small to Jason. "Where's your Rolex?"

He suddenly felt weak. "The Fabrikant family asked me to return it."

She frowned, brows furled. "Oh no, I'm so sorry."

"It's a fair request. I'm mad I didn't think of it myself. It's now earmarked for Adam when he comes of age, to be given to him in memory of his grandfather."

She bent her neck to make eye contact. "How'd that make you feel?"

Jason fought his emotions. "Like an orphan." She squeezed his hand, which helped. He loved her kindness. "Emma offered to stay in touch, but she never initiates a call. Rebecca, the mother, is distant as well. To her, I'm the result of an ungodly act. I realize now that I'm not family—not really. At best, I'm a human time capsule, storing their brother and son's memories, like music is stored on vinyl."

Samantha said warmly, "Well, we can both take solace that FOY had been dismantled, its leaders gone."

"Only Schickel lives, trapped in solitary confinement—sweet justice, to be trapped in the state's version of a biotank. You know, Gordon took pride in surrounding himself with a diverse team but failed to recognize one common missing component."

"What's that?"

"Empathy. That is the trait that was their collective blind spot and ultimate downfall."

Samantha smiled. "At least we know this won't happen to anyone else."

"Don't be too quick to judge. With all the advances in AI, who knows? Perhaps people's memories will be copied and loaded into computers—or worse, into humanoid robots.

Samantha turned to him. "Let's not go down that path. Besides, I'm proud of you."

Jason raised a single eyebrow in surprise. "Yeah? Why?"

Samantha looked at Jason in admiration. "You've found a purpose, a place in this world."

Generally guarded, Jason felt comfortable with her, sharing his deepest thoughts. "You pointed out that I need to live in the moment and let go of the past. Funny, though."

"What?"

Jason shook his head. "Most of it is not my past anyway." He kissed her on the lips.

She smiled as he pulled away. Jason knew that the memories he was creating were now his own and not borrowed. He could also make his own choices and build his own future. In the process, he had already made two important decisions and was about to make a third. His first decision was made out of respect for the original Jason Fabrikant. He felt it wasn't appropriate to share the same full name with his donor, so he legally changed his surname.

His second decision had to do with his career choice. He decided not to pursue baseball or coaching but instead chose to go back to college and earn a medical degree. He also developed a passion for helping people, and volunteered to write grants for underprivileged children. He wanted all young people to have the opportunity to aspire, and feel a sense of belonging and support. These opportunities were never available to the young girl behind the glass. This nameless girl would inspire him in many ways.

Jason watched a red cardinal dance and sing as it leaped and flew among the branches of the cherry trees. It was free and full of life, unlike poor Rufus and his caged existence. At least the scrawny bird had a companion now, Emma's son, who was providing the attention needed, and not be treated like a novelty. Even so, the cage still bothered him.

Jason stopped Samantha at one particularly inviting cherry tree, still holding her hand. The white marble structure of the Jefferson Memorial and its reflection on the water provided the perfect backdrop. Jason decided it was time to act on his third decision. He turned to Samantha and bent down on one knee. He pulled out a small box from his jacket pocket and looked into the eyes of a potential future. "Samantha, I love many things about you. I love your kindness, your courage, your intelligence, and your beauty. Most of all, I love us together. You're the partner I want for my lifetime. Will you marry me?"

Samantha was instantly tearful. She knelt down to embrace him, as if to make the point that they were equals, not one above the other. Although her answer was already given with the hug, she said in a quavering voice, "Yes, I'd be proud to be Mrs. Samantha Phoenix." The two stood up and enjoyed a long kiss, then beamed as he put the ring on her finger. "It's perfect; I love it." After admiring how it looked on her hand, they resumed walking arm in arm, smiling like two new souls.

Jason placed his hand on his chest, thankful to an unsung hero. Under his shirt, on a thick gold chain, Tanya's Phoenix pendant hung close to his heart.

/

Did you love The Glass Fountain?

Try *Deadly Equations,* coming soon*!*

When reserved speech pathologist Luna is unexpectedly left holding an infant during a morning stroll, she faces a heart-wrenching choice: report the child, ensuring its death, or protect it and become a fugitive. Her decision sets off a chain of events that will reshape her life.

In a near-future ravaged by climate change, Luna's quest for safety leads her from a migrant camp to Felicity, a city hailed as a beacon of hope. But beneath its promising facade lies a dark truth.

As Luna uncovers the harsh realities of scarcity and the city's true nature, she emerges as a leader among the oppressed, grappling to save others in a world in crisis.

Perfect for fans of biotech thrillers, speculative fiction, and suspenseful mysteries.

About the Author

Jeffrey Rosoff grew up in central California, moving through cities that serendipitously start with 'S'—Sacramento, Salinas, San Jose, San Carlos, and Stockton—all close to Silicon Valley and the settings of Steinbeck's stories. Influenced by classic sci-fi series like *The Twilight Zone* and *The Outer Limits*, Jeffrey continues to be drawn to reruns and finds inspiration in their timeless intrigue.

He holds degrees in computer science and business administration from the University of the Pacific and San Jose State University. His career at Lockheed Martin spanned over thirty years, culminating in a director role where he managed major defense-related projects in Washington, D.C.

Though writing is a beloved pursuit, Jeffrey's greatest joy is his family—his wife, children, and four grandchildren. When not writing, he delights in world travel, gardening, lively discussions, and discovering unique restaurants.

The Glass Fountain was the first novel Jeffrey wrote, while *Chipped* was the first to be published. His upcoming title, *Deadly Equations*, is scheduled for release soon. If you've enjoyed his work, please consider leaving a review on Amazon, Goodreads, or your favorite retailer—it makes a tremendous difference. You can reach him at JeffreyRosoffBooks@gmail.com. Follow him on:

- instagram.com/jeffreyrosoffbooks/
- facebook.com/JeffreyRosoffAuthor
- goodreads.com/Jeffrey_Rosoff
- amazon.com/Jeffrey_Rosoff

Acknowledgements

This is the first book I ever wrote, inspired by a plot I had ruminated on for more than twenty years. Once I took pen to paper (or fingertips to keyboard), it took time to develop each character's depth and motivations. After several iterations and failed attempts, I finally learned the nuances of creative writing. Had it not been for the perseverance of those around me, I would never have completed this novel. Their encouragement kept me motivated to press forward. For these reasons, I must thank…

Julia Rosoff – For providing the inspiration to write a novel to begin with. Your optimism is motivating.

Frani Rosoff – For your support, never complaining as I stowed away in my office for hours at a time. You're so much more than my best friend (and a great proofreader).

Marilyn Rayman – For your encouragement, especially when I felt I had reached a dead end.

Steven Rosoff and Niki Snyder – For helping me with character development and meticulous proofreading, respectively. I'm so very proud of both of you.

Madelyn & Max Snyder, Lucas & Calvin Rosoff – For giving me a reason to leave something lasting. You are the future, make it count!

John Breidenstine, Jorge Camacho, Beverly Feldman, Thomas Fonner, Greg Foster, Kent Matlick, Melissa Meyers, Joyana Peters, Robert Romano, Mike Rozzi, Burt Schatz, Ken Smith, Bryce Snyder, and Kelly Sunday – For reading my early drafts along the way and giving me invaluable feedback.

www.ingramcontent.com/pod-product-compliance
Lightning Source LLC
Chambersburg PA
CBHW020551120726
47903CB00001B/220

* 9 7 9 8 9 9 2 0 4 9 6 3 3 *